# THE HIGH ADVENTURE

## *THE WORKS OF JEFFERY FARNOL*

THE BROAD HIGHWAY
THE MONEY MOON
THE AMATEUR GENTLEMAN
CHRONICLES OF THE IMP
THE HONOURABLE MR. TAWNISH
BELTANE THE SMITH
THE DEFINITE OBJECT
THE GESTE OF DUKE JOCELYN
OUR ADMIRABLE BETTY
BLACK BARTLEMY'S TREASURE
MARTIN CONISBY'S VENGEANCE
PEREGRINE'S PROGRESS
SIR JOHN DERING
THE LORING MYSTERY
THE HIGH ADVENTURE
THE QUEST OF YOUTH
GYFFORD OF WEARE
THE SHADOW
EPICS OF THE FANCY
ANOTHER DAY
OVER THE HILLS
THE JADE OF DESTINY
CHARMIAN, LADY VIBART
THE WAY BEYOND
WINDS OF FORTUNE
JOHN O' THE GREEN
A PAGEANT OF VICTORY
THE CROOKED FURROW
A BOOK FOR JANE
THE LONELY ROAD
THE HAPPY HARVEST
A NEW BOOK FOR JANE
A MATTER OF BUSINESS
ADAM PENFEATHER, BUCCANEER
MURDER BY NAIL
THE KING LIVETH
THE "PIPING TIMES"
HERITAGE PERILOUS
MY LORD OF WRYBOURNE
THE FOOL BELOVED
THE NINTH EARL

# The High Adventure

by

# Jeffery Farnol

This reprinted edition published by

DIPLOMA PRESS LTD.

40 Broadway, London, SW1.

Published in this edition 1974
& reproduced from the impression of 1951
published by SAMPSON LOW



MADE AND PRINTED IN GREAT BRITAIN BY
WILLMER BROTHERS LIMITED, BIRKENHEAD.

TO

"BILL"

JOHN WILLIAM STERT MILNES

HIS AFFECTIONATE FATHER-IN-LAW

DEDICATES THIS BOOK.

AS A MARK OF

FRIENDSHIP,

LOVE AND

ESTEEM,

IN THE SURE HOPE THAT COMING YEARS

MAY DRAW

EACH TO EACH

EVER THE NEARER

*Sunnyside*, 1925

# CONTENTS

# CONTENTS

# THE HIGH ADVENTURE

## CHAPTER I

### AND CONSEQUENTLY BEGINS THIS HISTORY

SIR JAMES TREVOR glanced up from the defunct beetle he had just impaled, and frowned slightly as a discreet knuckle rapped softly and the door opened to discover his soft-voiced, soft-treading valet.

"What now, Nixon?" he sighed.

"Mr. Jeremy, sir, if you please."

"Ay, to be sure, it usually is Mr. Jeremy—heavens, man, what's come to your cravat? And your hair all on end!"

"'Twas Mr. Jeremy, sir."

"Ah—indeed?"

"Mr. Jeremy nigh strangulated me, sir—swallowing I find painful, Sir James! And all on account o' poor Mr. Arthur——"

"Nixon, pray be explicit."

"Why, Sir James, it seems Mr. Arthur and—Mr. Jeremy had words again, and I ventured to interfere—alas, vainly, Sir James, for Mr. Jeremy blacked poor Mr. Arthur's eye, split poor Mr. Arthur's lip, and knocked the unfort'nate young gentleman into the pond, Sir James—extremely brutal, sir!"

"Dear me!" murmured Sir James, carefully pinning his beetle to the setting board and regarding it beneath gently puckered brows, "Extremely distressing! We must see Mr. Jeremy! Bid him hither to——"

But at this juncture was a flutter of voluminous petticoats and a large, elderly woman appeared, red-faced and rustling indignation:

"Oh, Sir James, sir——"

"Mrs. Garrett!" exclaimed Sir James in shocked amaze, and fixing her with his passionless, chilling stare, "God bless my soul, mam—I believe this is my study——"

Here the housekeeper curtseyed and burst forth anew:

"Oh, Sir James, begging your parding, but Oh, Sir James, sir, goodness, gracious me—begging your parding again most 'umble, but that wicked Mr. Jeremy do ha' treated pore Mr. Arthur that shocking and outrageous! His pore nose a-bleeding and him in the pond——"

Sir James raised a slender yet imperious hand.

"Thank you, Mrs. Garrett, you may retire—and Nixon, do you bring Mr. Jeremy to us."

"Bring him, sir?" repeated Nixon dubiously. "I will so endeavour, Sir James, though begging to remind you as he knocked down Sims, the groom, last week——"

"Enough, Nixon! Say we command his presence here—immediately!" His valet having bowed himself out and closed the door, Sir James unpinned his beetle and began to examine it by the aid of a large magnifying glass, turning the insect this way and that, humming softly the while.

A sharp rap, the door opened and in strode Mr. Jeremy, a shortish, broad-shouldered and just now, a most unlovely figure, his sandy hair tangled, his square chin aggressive, his deep-set eyes sullen beneath their thick brows.

"Well, Uncle?" he demanded, and stood with powerful arms folded across a chest that seemed bursting from the tight-fitting, silver-buttoned, green coat, "Well, sir?"

"Ill, Nephew!" retorted Sir James, still peering at his beetle. "Ill—as usual. Your blackguardism offends us and is a menace to all and sundry!"

"If you refer to Arthur, sir, he deserved all he got."

"As to which, Jeremy, we do not enquire; suffice it your conduct is and was offensive to us. Only recently you knocked down the groom Sims, I think?"

"Man's a scoundrel!" growled Jeremy.

"Pray how old are you, Nephew?"

"Twenty-four, sir—as you well know."

"Twenty-four years," sighed Sir James, "which you have very diligently employed in rendering yourself and other people uncomfortable. Indeed your career is, in its way, remarkable. You were expelled from school, I believe?"

"Unjustly, sir!" muttered Jeremy, scowling.

"Concerning which we do not trouble ourselves, Nephew—though to be sure, the guilty regard all punishments as unjust, I believe. Again, if I remember correctly, you left the University under a cloud."

"Because I would n't blab——"

"Blab is an objectionable word, Jeremy—on the whole—yes, having regard to your career so far, Jeremy, it is perhaps as well that your parents died so very young——"

"How—why—why so, sir?"

"The answer is sufficiently obvious, surely! As for you, Jeremy, we remember you a sullen, solitary child, shunned by your kind and with never a playmate. To-day you are the same with none you may call 'friend'—and why, do you suppose?"

Jeremy knit his heavy brows and seemed to ponder the question.

"I suppose," he answered at last, "'t is because folk don't take to my sort—howbeit I prefer animals!"

"And therein, Nephew, we commend your judgment, for, being endowed of lesser reason, animals know less of sin than humans. The companionship of animals should be a powerful deterrent to sinful man. We thus purpose removing you to a region where animals abound in a noble freedom, Nephew. For your body's future welfare and soul's salvation, we intend transporting you overseas, Jeremy."

"You mean—abroad?"

"To the Brazils, Jeremy."

"Indeed, sir?"

"And in very truth, Nephew."

"Pray when, sir?"

"Four days hence. You will go aboard ship in charge of one Captain Johnson, a somewhat stern yet admirable mariner."

"The ruffianly looking fellow was here to see you a week ago?"

"You are prejudiced against him, 't would seem."

"And suppose I refuse to go?"

"Force or artifice shall constrain you, Jeremy." Here Sir James took up his beetle while his nephew scowled at him beneath sullen brows.

"Why then, sir," said Jeremy at last, grim-lipped, "I do refuse to go."

"Gad so!" murmured Sir James, cocking an eyebrow. "And yet we venture to prophesy that five or six days hence you will be—heaving upon the bounding billow——"

"I say no, sir!" retorted Jeremy, his voice harsher even than usual. "I'll not be got rid of thus—understand, sir, that I am a man——"

"And I," murmured Sir James but with a fierce arresting gesture, "I, to my sorrow, am your guardian! By the terms of your father's will I remain the arbiter of your destiny until you attain the ripe age of twenty-five, when I shall very thankfully yield up to you this your heritage—this estate of Veryan I have held in trust and nursed so carefully for you all these years."

"If I'm alive!" added Jeremy.

Sir James, in the act of once more examining his beetle, fumbled the magnifying glass so awkwardly that he nearly dropped it; so he set it by and leaning back in his chair, glanced up at Jeremy beneath raised brows.

"What might you mean, Nephew?" he enquired.

"Accidents!" answered Jeremy, frowning into the unwinking eyes that stared into his.

"You allude to the accidental discharge of Mr. O'Leary's gun yesterday, I presume?"

"That among other incidents, sir—but my life has been a chapter of accidents, and they have grown more frequent o' late."

"Quite so!" nodded Sir James, serenely. "How often have I had occasion to warn you of your recklessness in the past? You were a wild and mischievous boy, a daring youth and are no wiser to-day; indeed I think you are——"

But at this moment the door opened to admit a slim, elegant youth whose pale, classic features exhibited sundry marks of violence, but whose golden curls, carefully brushed, fell upon snowy brow in an artful disorder.

"My dear Father," said he, "I trust you are not distressing yourself over a mere and ridiculous incident."

"Incident?" repeated Sir James. "Incident, Arthur. Look at your face, boy!"

"I have just done so, sir, and am relieved to find it less damaged than I ventured to hope—though to be sure, Cousin Jeremy's fists are devilish hard. Nay, never frown, sir, Jeremy did not mean to strike so hard, I'm sure."

"Ay, but I did!" growled Jeremy.

"And why did he assault you, Arthur?"

"Because he—is Jeremy—the best of fellows, of course, though a trifle hasty—very instant in quarrel, a word and a blow—good old Jeremy!"

"Ha!" murmured Sir James. "He recently knocked down one of the grooms, I hear?"

"Only my man, Sims, sir—the fellow was insolent, perhaps.'

"And to-day he beats and—throws you into the lake."

"Egad, no, sir—no, no, my fall into the water was quite—shall we say—fortuitous. Was 't not, Jeremy?"

"No, I threw you in!" growled Jeremy.

"For shame!" exclaimed Sir James. "What reason was there for such murderous outrage? Explain, Arthur!"

"'Pon my soul, I've forgot. 'T was some trifle—the veriest nothing. If Jeremy tells you the contrary——"

"Not I," quoth Jeremy.

"Why then, Father, pray let us all forget the foolish business. I am quite willing to let bygones be bygones and give old Jeremy my hand if he wants it."

"I don't!" growled Jeremy.

"Come, Jeremy, old fellow," Arthur persisted, his slim, white hand outstretched towards his cousins' morose figure, his fine eyes full of appeal, "if I angered you, I'm sorry—come, shake hands and be friends."

"No!" answered Jeremy, and turned his back.

"Spoken like a sullen, graceless oaf!" exclaimed Sir James. "On my life, Nephew, there are times when I scarce can credit that you are a true Veryan! Your speech, deportment and looks, God knows, smack rather of the *canaille*. 'T would seem Nature intended you for the howling obscenity of a ship's fo'castle rather than the boudoir or drawing-room!"

"Agreed, sir!" nodded Jeremy. "Nature should ha' made Arthur the heir; he at least looks a gentleman, I don't—I am a mistake—should be corrected."

"How so, Nephew? Precisely what do you suggest?"

But at this moment and before Jeremy could answer, the door opened and upon the threshold stood a tall, ruddy, smiling gentleman, at sight of whom Sir James' smooth brow wrinkled.

"Arrah, now!" he exclaimed in loud, jovial tones. "An' is it scowling y' are, me bhoys? Faith, then here's meself, Terence—poor Terence O'Leary to laugh ye into better humour!"

## CHAPTER II

### INTRODUCES AN EXTREMELY IRISH IRISHMAN

MR. TERENCE O'LEARY was a blond, shapely gentleman whose comely features were innocent of whisker; good nature seemed to clothe him like a garment, it twinkled in his eyes and buttons, it beamed upon his rubicund visage, it shone in his boots; it was in his voice, his every gesture, his very walk; thus, from head to foot he beamed, twinkled and radiated on obtrusive good-fellowship.

"My good Terence," began Sir James, frowning slightly, "you do not apprehend——"

"Faith, but I do, James. 'T was a bit of a scrimmage, they tell me. But, Gad love me, phwat's a foight betwixt friends—'t is the spoice of loife! If friends can't foight, friendship's a mockery, a hollow sham an' bad cess to 't, says I. Gimme the lad who'll foight whin necessary and kiss a pretty colleen whin occasion offers. Youth will be served, Jimmy, and bhoys will be bhoys! 'T is too severe y' are, James, too much of a martinit. After all, the bhoys are men and Jeremy's heir to vast possessions!"

"Very true, Terence, but for the next eleven months he is under my jurisdiction and indeed a great anxiety I find him."

"Anxiety is ut, James?"

"Precisely, Terence, as you must be sufficiently aware. For the last two months—to be exact, ever since he was expelled—and I use the word in its broadest sense—from his *alma mater,* Nephew Jeremy has misconducted himself——"

"Be aisy now, James! Ye can't put ould hids on young shouldhers——"

"He was always a sullen, quarrelsome oaf——"

"No, no!" exclaimed Mr. O'Leary in smiling good-tempered remonstrance. "Not sullen, James—let us say 'pensive'—it sounds kinder, and as for being quarrelsome——"

"Furthermore," continued Sir James, "he is for ever in some scrape, continually involving himself in some danger——"

"Ay," nodded Jeremy, "yesterday, sir, in the spinney, for instance!"

"The spinney?" exclaimed Mr. O'Leary, throwing up his large but shapely hands. "Och, me dear lad, will ye reproach y'r Terence? Is it me accursed carelessness ye're maning now?"

"No," answered Jeremy, "merely your gun, sir."

"Ah, me gun!" cried Mr. O'Leary, smiting himself upon broad bosom with white fist. "Oh, shure the damned thing moight have killed ye, Jerry! Troth, me dear lad—if ye had n't—chanced to stumble——"

"Then, sir," said Jeremy, "the Veryan heritage would have passed to—the next heir."

"And so," continued Sir James, delicately fingering his magnifying glass, "I propose sending Jeremy for a long sea-voyage."

"And I refuse to go!" growled Jeremy.

"Arrah now—an' refuse is ut?" exclaimed Mr. O'Leary. "Think, Jeremy, think, me bhoy! The noble ship! The bounding billow! Honest tars spinning yarns an' dancing hornpoipes in the dog-watches—and thin, me lad—the coral reefs, palm threes—coconuts an' dark-eyed, dusky belles——"

"Where," pursued Sir James serenely, "if he courts danger or incurs disaster, at least I shall not be at hand to worry."

"But, my dear Father," said Arthur softly, "if old Jeremy refuses to go——"

"Enough, sir! I have spoken!" retorted Sir James, "I am perfectly determined on it!"

"So am I!" quoth Jeremy. "I shall go a-walking sir, probably north towards Middlesex, or west through Sussex, or east through Kent, as the fancy takes me. But mark this, such evils as—may chance to beset me, I'll meet on terra firma."

Then Jeremy bowed ungraciously towards the elder gentleman, scowled at his cousin Arthur and plucking open the door, came face to face with a slim, pale-faced young man who shrank aside and bowed in the same movement.

"Ah, Sims, listening were ye?"

"No, indeed, Mr. Jeremy. I am but now from London, sir."

"London? Hum!" quoth Jeremy.

"With news for your uncle, Sir James—for his most private ear, sir."

"Eh—news?" called Sir James. "News for me, Sims?"

"Yes, sir, concerning a pocket-book——"

Sir James rose to his feet, staring at the speaker with an expression upon his aristocratic features that in any other might have been fear, a growing horror. "A small, red, morocco-covered memorandum, sir."

Sir James' stately form seemed to crumple and he sank back in his chair, head bowed upon his hands.

"Sir?" cried Arthur. "Father——"

"Faith," exclaimed Mr. O'Leary with his jovial laugh, "'t is but a turn o' Fortune's wheel and your father's a troifle dizzy. Lave him to me, me bhoy—off wid ye, now! Come in, Sims, and shut the door, me man." And Jeremy heard key turn in lock as he mounted the wide stairs. Reaching his bedchamber he packed such articles as he might require, which done he leaned from the open casement to stare away across trim gardens and undulating park to the blue distances beyond. Now as he stood thus, very full of thought, he beheld Sims hurrying stable-wards and wondered idly at the man's unwonted haste.

And after some while, Jeremy did on his bulbous knap-sack, took hat and stick and descending by a back stair, stepped out into a fragrant evening. He was standing to look round about him upon these familiar surroundings, all glorious with the first glow of sunset when upon the quiet, rose a sudden clatter of hoofs—a trot that became a wild gallop dying rapidly away; then he, too, turned stable-wards.

Thus, Tom Lacey the coachman looked up from his polishing to see Jeremy scowling in over the half-door, whereupon he grinned in welcome and stood at attention like the old soldier that he was.

"Art'noon, Mr. Jeremy, sir!" said he.

Jeremy's scowling brows relaxed, his grim lips curved to sudden transfiguring smile and he stepped into the stable.

"So, Tom," said he, his keen glance surveying the row of stalls, "Sims took the bay filly, I see?"

"Ay, sir, 'cording to Sir James' own orders—so 'e said."

"Sims seemed in a devilish hurry, Tom; I wonder why?"

"Can't say, sir. Sims ain't never been no friend o' mine, and keeps 'isself to 'isself since you give 'im wot for, t' other day—Comes in 'ere about ten minutes ago, 'e do, orders me to saddle the bay and off 'e goes at a gallop."

"Hum!" quoth Jeremy thoughtfully. "Did he say anything?"

"Ay, sir, 'e did so! Jest afore 'e rid off—'you Lacey,' 'e says, 'there'll be changes 'ere at Veryan as soon as your Mr. Jeremy's gone,' 'e says."

"Hum!" quoth Jeremy again. "So the fellow knows already! I wonder how?"

Now as Jeremy stood lost in thought, powerful hands crossed upon the stout stick he carried and bulbous knapsack strapped to his massive shoulders, the coachman stopped to peer into his rugged features with eyes suddenly anxious.

"But you—surely you ain't a-leaving Veryan, are ye, Mr. Jeremy?" he queried.

"I surely am, Tom!"

"What—afoot, sir, and a bundle on your back?"

"Walking is noble exercise, Tom. And this bundle is the knapsack you gave me years ago, the same you carried through your campaigns against 'Old Boney'."

"Lord, why so it be, sir. But—going away, sir? Oh, ecod, Mr. Jeremy, I know one as will miss ye woeful, and that's T. Lacey, late Corporal o' the old 'Buffs,' sir."

"Then, b'ged, Tom, you'll be the only one!"

"But—why go, sir? Axing your pardon, but is it by reason o' what chanced to-day 'twixt you an' Mr. Arthur?"

"No, Tom. 'T is for an all-sufficing reason."

"But—on your two feet, Mr. Jeremy, sir—in the dust, like a common tramping cove? You as was born a fine gen'leman!"

"Why, there's my misfortune, Tom—I'm out o' place. I detest your stately withdrawing-rooms and your perfumed boudoirs stifle me—pah! Your tight coats, choking stocks and cravats—oh, damn 'em! I never get into a pair o' gloves but I split 'em. There's my reasons, Tom—and enough too, I think. So, I'm off, Tom, east, west, north or south—what matter so I leave 'em all behind."

"Why, Lord, Mr. Jeremy, sir! Lord love my eyes an' limbs."

"Now look 'ee, Tom, I want you to give this letter to Lucy Western—into her own hand, mind!"

"Very good, sir."

"Then—good-bye, Tom!"

"Good-bye, Mr. Jeremy, sir—and may Fortun' go marching along o' you, sir, your true comrade ever and allus, sir!"

"God bless thee, Tom—shake hands!"

And so, having shaken the coachman's hand, Jeremy turned and strode upon his way. But hardly was he clear of the stable-yard than he heard a tread of light feet hastening after him and swung round, scowling, as his cousin Arthur came up.

"What now?" he demanded.

"Nothing, Jerry—only you held your infernal tongue and I'm duly grateful——"

"Keep your gratitude!" growled Jeremy. "But mark this! Live how you will, do what you will, but—leave Innocence alone."

"What?" exclaimed his cousin, falling back to view him in feigned amazement. "You too? Hath beauty stirred old Jeremy at last? Art bit likewise, mine ancient Sobersides?"

"Fool!" exclaimed Jeremy, with an angry shake of the head. "D' ye still measure every one by your own standards? I'm off and away!"

"What d' ye mean, Jerry?"

"What I say. But first, since you're here, you are going to promise me there shall be no more pursuit of that girl."

"But my dear good Jeremy, have n't I——"

"You are going to promise neither to speak nor communicate with her again. But you were an easy promiser even at school, I remember, so you had better swear an oath——"

"My dear fellow—tush! The whole ridiculous affair is over and done with——"

"And you will take that oath—now!"

"No!" exclaimed Arthur, in sudden heat. "Damme if I——" But even as he spoke he reeled and bent in Jeremy's strangling grip.

"Swear!" commanded Jeremy.

"Oh—curse you—I swear!" gasped his cousin.

"Why, then," said Jeremy, loosing his hold and stepping back, "good-bye, Arthur! Remember your oath! I shall come back maybe some day and—if you should have tricked me again—God help you!" Having said which, Jeremy tramped upon his way once more.

His course took him across undulating park to where, bowered in trees, rose the gables of the dower house. He was trudging past, when a voice hailed him in stentorian tones and he beheld Mr. O'Leary beckoning from the creeper-grown porch.

"Pwhat then, me broth of a bhoy, an' will ye be laving the Terence that loves ye, and nivver so much as a grip o' your fist, at arl, at arl? Faith, Jerry, will ye be breaking the heart o' me as is your friend?" And to him came Mr. O'Leary, both elegant hands outstretched, comely face beaming good nature. "'T is going away y' are—confiss now!" quoth he.

"I am!" answered Jeremy.

"That's me bould bhoy! 'T is roight y' are, Jerry—'t is meself would do the same in your place—freedom, me bhoy, 't is Heaven's fairest gift—But ye'll come in for a parting glass wi' Terence that loves ye like a brother, ay, and father and mother—ye'll step inside, Jerry?"

"Thank ye—no, Terence."

"Whisht, ye'll nivver deny me, Jeremy—no, no, 't would n't be Christian! Wan glass now, me bhoy—jist wan for luck and good-fellowship!" Then setting long arm about Jeremy's shoulders he turned and hailed the house:

"Oho, Pompey, ye black spalpeen, Pompey, ho!"

"Yassuh!" answered a voice. "Yas, Massa Terence—Pompey heah, suh!" And out into the sunset glow tripped a gigantic Negro, a huge creature who seemed to reflect his master's good nature, for his eyes rolled, his white teeth flashed and he bobbed close-cut woolly pate in a very ecstasy of welcome.

"Pompey berry momentously glad to see young Massa Jerry——"

"Thin hould your tongue, ye black omadhaun!" said his master. "Go set out the sherry."

"Yassuh—Yassuh!" and the huge Negro skipped back into the house.

"You'll take a glass with Terence, me bhoy—come!"

For a moment Jeremy hung back and seemed about to refuse, then glancing keenly into O'Leary's kindly face, he nodded.

"Thank'ee Terence, I will!" he answered and suffered himself to be ushered indoors and into a room as untidy as it was luxurious. Guns and fishing rods cluttered the corners, books and papers in French, German and English littered the table and no chair but sustained some incongruous burden.

"Sit down, Jerry, sit down!" said O'Leary hospitably, sweeping a hat and riding gloves from the chair he proffered. "'T is moighty lonesome I am here sometoimes, my bhoy—an old bachelor—though 't is koind in James to allow me the place rint-free. But thin I'm his fri'nd and he's my fri'nd and if fri'nd can't take from fri'nd graciously, why where the divvel's the virtue of fri'ndship?"

"I'm wondering," said Jeremy, crossing to the hearth, "why Sims was despatched in such a hurry, Terence, and—where?"

"Eh—Sims, d' ye say?"

"Yes. He galloped off on the bay filly—by Sir James's express order, so he said."

"Shure now and 't is news to me, Jerry—Aha, here's me rascal Pompey with the wine at last—on the table here, Pompey—no, on the sideboard yonder! Shure, Jerry, an' 't was the divil of a surprise ye gave Arthur to-day—'t is the ducking in the lake, I mane."

"He deserved it, sir."

"Faix and ye may say so! Arthur can be curst annoying, I'll admit. Arthur's my fri'nd and if a fri'nd can't spake truth of his fri'nd, the devil's in ut—sit down—me bhoy!"

But, instead of complying, Jeremy continued to lean against the carved chimney piece, apparently staring down the the empty fireplace like one lost in thought; but above the mantel hung a small Venetian mirror in an exquisitely wrought silver frame, and it was up at this his frowning gaze was directed while Mr. O'Leary, voluble as ever, proceeded to fill the glasses, above one of which Jeremy's quick eyes caught the momentary flutter of slim white fingers; then, as his host set down the cobwebbed bottle, Jeremy crossed to the window and stood with back turned, gazing out at the sunset.

"'T will be a fine night for walking!" said he.

"And good luck t' yiz!" quoth Mr. O'Leary, warm-heartedly. "Where are ye intending?"

"Nowhere in particular."

"Faith an' 't is woise y' are, Jerry, for nowhere is always somewhere if you go anywhere in this world." So saying, Mr. O'Leary crossed the room bearing two brimming wineglasses, one of which he tendered to Jeremy, who took it, raised it to his lips but, in the act of drinking, paused, his keen gaze upon his host's handsome face; and who so smiling, so jovial and debonair as Terence O'Leary.

"Phwat is ut?" he enquired.

"Name a toast!" said Jeremy.

"Shure, me bhoy, and phwat better than 'The Future'—your future, Jerry."

"My future?" repeated Jeremy, staring at the glass in his hand. "Hum! 'Tis the unknown quantity, Terence."

"Unknown, d' ye say? Tare an' ages, 't is the moighty rich man ye 'll be in a year from now."

"Shall I?"

"Av course! Ain't yez heir to the Veryan heritage, and is n't that a fortune?"

"Aye," nodded Jeremy. "I suppose many a crime has been committed for less."

"Ah—croimes, is ut?" exclaimed Mr. O'Leary, his fine blue eyes closing suddenly to open very wide.

"Come, let us drink! The Future!" said Jeremy, but turning from the window, his elbow struck the frame sharply and his wineglass shot from his fingers to fall and splinter on the floor.

"The devil!" he exclaimed, glancing from the fragments to his host's good-natured face. "I'm a clumsy fool, Terence!"

"Ye 're not!" laughed O'Leary, clapping him on the shoulder. "Neither one nor t' other, Jerry, no, no! As for the glass—'t was a throifle——"

"But a handsome one!" said Jeremy and stopped to pick up the largest fragment, but with a sudden movement of his shapely foot Mr. O'Leary sent it spinning into a distant corner.

"Ho, Pompey!" he roared. "Pompey, ye black divil, another glass for Mr. Jeremy!" Almost immediately the gigantic Negro reappeared, swift and light of foot despite his bulk.

So Jeremy took the new glass and having filled it, nodded to his genial host:

"To the Future, Terence!" said he.

"The Future, me bhoy, and may it be a path smooth as vilvit and gay wi' flowers——"

"Tush!" growled Jeremy. "Let it be paved with flints and strewn with thorns, I'll tread it so it bring me to my heritage——"

"Ay, Jerry, your acres broad, your golden——"

"No, Terence! The heritage of Veryan is to discover the black villain who slew my father sixteen years ago."

"Eh?" exclaimed Mr. O'Leary, his smile vanishing. "Is ut the man Openshaw ye 're meaning?"

"Who else? From all accounts, 't was bloody murder——"

"Be aisy now, Jerry; ye know 't was a duel——"

"I know it was without witnesses and altogether irregular!"

"But your Uncle James tells me——"

"No matter!" growled Jeremy, frowning. "Let us drink your toast and ha' done—The Future, and may it bring me to my heritage."

"The Future!" repeated O'Leary, and together they drank. "And 't is to seek Julius Openshaw ye 're going, is it, my bhoy?"

"Among other things!" answered Jeremy, taking up hat and stick.

"'T is long since he was heard of."

"Fifteen years!" growled Jeremy.

"He may be dead."

"He may," growled Jeremy.

"And how then, my bhoy?"

"He's probably in hell! Good-bye, Terence!" So Mr. O'Leary, having shaken both his hands and bidden him a hearty God-speed, followed him out to the gate, to stand, a tall imposing figure in the sunset, and wave him a smiling adieu. But Jeremy's scowl was black and his grim face grimmer than ever as he trudged heavily away.

## CHAPTER III

### DESCRIBES A CAUSE OF STRIFE, LUCY WESTERN

AMID the leafy shade of the spinney Jeremy paused all at once, arrested by sounds strange to hear in such a place, on such an evening. Guided by these sounds, he came to a little glade, very sequestered, and here beheld a girl who lay face down upon the grass, a very picture of despair. Young she was and daintily shaped, and when, suddenly aware of his approach, she lifted her head, it was to show a face that matched her form; indeed, despite rustic sunbonnet (woefully crumpled), despite tumbled hair and tearful eyes, she was of an extraordinary and unexpected beauty.

"Little fool!" quoth Jeremy.

"Ay, I know, sir, I know it—now!" she sobbed.

"Then why lie there and grieve?"

"Father's found out I meant to run off to London and he be—so hard on me—so bitter angry—him as never was cross wi' me all my days,—oh, Mr. Jeremy, what shall I do?"

"Does your father know everything?"

"Only what Joe Sims told him."

"Ha- -Sims!" muttered Jeremy.

"Oh, sir, what shall I do?"

"Go home, girl. Go to your father and ask his forgiveness."

"I have, Mr. Jeremy, indeed I have, sir—but he jest sets an' looks at me as if his poor heart were breaking—and 't is n't as if I had done anything wrong or s—shameful! Thank God, I found out and were saved in time."

"By an accident!" quoth Jeremy.

"Ay—I'd never ha' believed if he had n't sent that wicked letter by mistake—he seemed so good an' kind—such a splendid, great gentleman—and swore we'd be married the moment we got to London."

"Some men swear easily, girl."

"Ay, I know now, Mr. Jeremy—I know as grand gentlemen like him—don't marry wi' cottage girls like me."

"No," growled Jeremy. "Not his sort!"

"Ay, I know—I know—at last, sir!" she sobbed, rising upon her knees and looking up at him through her tears. "And it hurts me, Mr. Jeremy, it do so hurt me—here!" And she pressed shapely brown, hands upon rounded bosom. "My poor heart is broke, I think."

"No!" said Jeremy, looking down into her long-lashed, grey eyes. "I think your heart is too strong and cleanly pure to break for so small a thing——"

"Pure?" she repeated eagerly. "Oh, you know 't is pure—still. You be sure o' that, Mr. Jeremy?"

"Yes!" he nodded, gazing down into the eyes that met his so unflinchingly. "Of course it is, and always will be—ay, so long as you are Lucy."

Now at this she uttered a soft, inarticulate murmur, and with a sudden gesture wholly artless, caught his hand and would have kissed it, but he drew away almost roughly, and scowled down at her, his rugged features flushing.

"Why—why do that?"

"Because I am good and because you know it, and—and—ah, Mr. Jeremy, only a woman could understand all that meant—only a woman could know all my gratefulness and so—hush!" she whispered. "Oh—here's father!" And she was upon her feet as a tall, grey-headed man in velveteens stepped into the glade. For a moment he was silent, looking from one to the other.

his clean-shaven features pale in the half-light, his eyes fiercely accusing, yet when he spoke his voice was low and even:

"What—again?" said he, and Jeremy saw his muscular hands clench themselves. "Lucy—get ye indoors!"

Casting an appealing glance at Jeremy but uttering no word, the girl hurried off.

"Mr. Jeremy, sir," said the man, sternly, "I were head gamekeeper in your father's days and his father's days afore him, and I'd hoped, God willing, to be head gamekeeper when you come into the property next year—but, sir, I know now as I never can be—never!"

"Why so, Ben?" enquired Jeremy.

"Because me an' my lass be a-going away."

"Why so, Ben?" enquired Jeremy again.

"Sir, your father was an honourable gentleman, and I took you, nat'rally, to be the same—but you ain't—no, by God, you ain't!"

"Why so, Ben?" enquired Jeremy for the third time.

"What be all this I'm 'earing about you an' my Lucy?"

"Tell me!" said Jeremy.

"Why you—fillin' 'er silly head wi' notions o' marryin'——"

"Who says I have?"

"No matter, sir——"

"Was it Sims, my cousin's groom? Was it Sims?"

"Look'ee, Mr. Jeremy, I be only Ben Western, consequently my lass are n't the sort as a rich gentleman like you can make a honest wife of—and she ain't t' other sort!"

"She is not, Ben."

"And, by God, she ain't a-going to be—not whiles I live, she ain't!"

"Nor I, Ben."

"Then what so 'ee mean by meeting her—on the sly?"

"Who says I do?"

"I saw ye—the night afore last!"

"You saw me? Where?"

"Why here—on this very spot! You wore that same 'at and coat."

"The night before last!" repeated Jeremy, and glanced down at the bottle-green coat in question with eyes suddenly fierce. "Ah," he muttered savagely, "the night before last!" Then suddenly he raised his head and looked into the gamekeeper's troubled eyes. "Ben," said he, "I want you to believe that, so help me God, I have never intended any evil to your daughter Lucy, and never shall, so long as I live. I want you to know that she is as sweetly good and cleanly pure as ever she was; as for me, Ben, I'm a man born without the gift o' friends, it seems, for I never had one—and wish for none, much preferring animals. Consequently I am solitary and viewed askance; therefore—I am like the dog with the bad name who must hunt alone—and, on the whole, am content. Lastly, as for you, Ben, you need not leave Veryan, because I am going instead and Heaven alone knoweth when I shall return. Think of me as you will, but know that your daughter is all she should be and all you would have her. Egad, I never made such a speech in all my life—and so enough, Ben, and good-bye!"

So Jeremy trudged sturdily away into the gathering shadows, leaving Ben Western staring after him with thoughtful brow but eyes troubled no longer.

## CHAPTER IV

### WHICH INTRODUCES ONE, BILL

It was as he stood beneath the finger post that he became aware of two figures creeping towards him in the shadow of the hedge, dim shapes which, as he watched, halted and sank immediately from view.

Motionless stood Jeremy in the gathering dusk, eyes intent and ears on the stretch, very conscious of the menace of those stealthy, lurking shadows, though now he heard and saw nothing.

But here was something tangible, at last, to be met and overcome or—Jeremy's grim lips curled and he hummed softly as, turning from the high road, he hurried down a narrow, grassy side lane shut in by tall hedges.

And presently, sure enough, down this lane flitted two shapes on soft-padding feet, sinister shapes that peered and muttered together, that cast to and fro like hounds at fault, the one up the lane, the other down, running softly hither and yon.

"Oho, mate!" called a voice suddenly in harsh whisper. "What luck?"

"None, and be danged to it; I reckon we——"

A faint rustle in the hedge above, and down upon the speaker leapt something that staggered and smote him, groaning, to earth.

"Aha, ha' ye got 'im, Tom!" cried his fellow, and came running, but seeing Jeremy leap to meet him, stick eagerly a-flourish, he halted, turned and made off.

So back came panting Jeremy to drag his fallen antagonist from the gloom of the hedge, and thus saw him, for a powerful rough-clad man who groaned and blinked up at him with eyes dazed and wild.

"A sailer-man, ain't ye?" demanded Jeremy.

"Ay, ay!" groaned the fellow. "But don't 'it me no more, sir—I got enough for one trip!"

"Are there many of ye?"

"Four, sir."

"Who sent ye after me?"

"Cap'n did, sir—an' orders is orders, d' ye see."

"Captain who?"

"Johnson, sir. An' orders bein' orders, don't go for to 'it me no more."

"Hum!" said Jeremy and scowled down at the fellow until he blenched and cowered beneath protecting arm; then, to the man's amazement, instead of striking, Jeremy leaned upon his stick and laughed, harsh yet gleefully.

"I haven't hurt you much, have I?" he enquired.

"More than I like, sir!" the man answered.

At this Jeremy chuckled and drawing a coin from his pocket, tossed it to his late adversary and hurried off up the narrow lane, leaving the fellow to gape from him to the silver gleaming upon his open palm.

As for Jeremy, despite his haste, he hummed again cheerily, for life, it seemed, was good. Once or twice he paused to glanced about and listen, but observing no signs of immediate pursuit, fell to a long, easy stride, following a haphazard course that led him he knew and cared not whither; confident in his strength and filled with the high-hearted assurance of unconquered Twenty-Four.

On strode he through a fragrant dusk wherein stars paled to the ever-growing splendour of the rising, full-orbed moon.

Gradually the narrow lane dwindled to a winding track that led him upwards until, reaching the top of this ascent, he might look down over a wide prospect—field, hedgerow and sombre woods, to the looming swell of the Downs, vague and mysterious, beyond which lay the sea.

Thus stood Jeremy, leaning upon his stick, very solitary and therefore content; though, and for no reason in the world, he must begin to think of Lucy Western and of how she would have kissed his hand; lifting which hand, he viewed it in the clear light of the moon and beholding its unlovely, knotted strength, shook his head and sighed a little plaintively.

"Fool!" growled he to himself and trudged on down the hill.

It was a windless night full of a brooding quietude, with nothing to disturb this solemn hush but the sound of his own going; a night within whose awesome silence a man may hold communion with that mystery of mysteries—himself.

Thou Soul of me, mysterious Spirit so potent for good or evil, whence comest thou and whither shalt thou return? Thou force unseen whereby I live and breathe, source of my every thought and action, art thou of God, a power of good imperishable indeed?

With head full of some such thought (which since man learned to think has assuredly puzzled many an older and wiser head) Jeremy trudged on, troubling himself no more about his future than he did about his cold-eyed uncle, or the jovial, good-natured Mr. O'Leary.

All at once, the night's solemn quiet was broken by the shrill howling of a dog, a piteous yelping and whining that spoke of pain. Following these dismal sounds Jeremy hastened on and thus presently coming out upon the high-road, descried a lonely cottage standing in a small, trim garden; and here he beheld a large dog roped fast to a tree and a brawny fellow in shirt sleeves belabouring the helpless animal with a stout ash plant; so intent was the man and so loud the dog's complaint that Jeremy had approached quite unheeded and he now instinctively raised his stick and smote the smiter who, uttering a cry of pain and surprise, leapt back in scowling dismay.

"Ah—would ye!" he exclaimed, flourishing the ash plant threateningly. "Git out o' my gardin, an' quick about it!"

"Loose that dog!" growled Jeremy.

"Git out—an' be danged t' ye! Dog's mine, ain't 'e?"

"Loose that dog!" The fellow's answer was a whizzing cut at Jeremy, who parried the blow easily enough, but his stick, too light for such play, snapped short, whereupon, and before the man could strike again, Jeremy leapt in with ready fists; a flush blow with left, a swing with unerring right, and his antagonist pitched backwards and lay kicking feebly among his own cabbages.

Then, having loosed the dog which ceased licking its hurts to flick his deliverer's hand with hurried tongue ere skulking away, Jeremy took up the stout ash plant, tried it, nodded and turned to scowl down upon the man who, cherishing his hurts, scowled up at him, muttering curses under his breath.

"We'll change sticks!" said Jeremy, and away he strode, whereupon the man, grown bolder, ventured to curse aloud, and seeing Jeremy tramped on unheeding, grew defiant and shouted horrific threats, roared them until the welkin rang and his late assailant was half a mile down the road.

And presently, finding the knuckles of his left hand raw and bleeding, Jeremy sucked them; and forgetting the awesome solemnity of the night he began to whistle, soft yet cheerily, for life, it seemed, was exceeding good.

He had walked steadily for some half-hour when he heard a faint sound behind him and whirling about with stick poised for offensive action, saw the dog had followed him, a gaunt, woeful creature that watched him big-eyed.

"So it 's you, is it, my poor chap?" said Jeremy, leaning upon his stick.

The dog immediately sat down on bony haunches and cocked a stubby ear.

"And what might you want?" enquired Jeremy.

The dog cocked his other ear and smote the dust with scraggy tail, but seeing Jeremy approach, rose and slunk away, yet with tail feverishly a-wag.

Jeremy seated himself on the grass and reached out a welcoming hand.

"Come you here, my lad!" said he.

The dog advanced two or three cautious paces and halted, all anxious questioning from square muzzle to nondescript tail; and reading the wistful supplication in these eyes, Jeremy smiled suddenly and dropping his stick, reached out both hands.

"Come, then," said he in voice unwontedly gentle, "my poor lad, come to me."

Foot by foot, inch by inch the dog crept nearer until, being within reach, he cowered suddenly and shot out his tongue to caress that welcoming hand, then crouched suddenly, his ugly head in the dust at Jeremy's feet, but with his eyes upturned to Jeremy's face in an ecstasy.

"And you could n't," said Jeremy, pulling the nearest ear, "no, you could n't say more, old chap, if you had the tongue of Demosthenes! You're solitary, eh—and friendless? Well, so am I. And you're an unlovely brute! Well, so am I. We're neither of us lap dogs, nor boudoir pets all bark and no bite—no, b'ged, we're built for a rougher life, you and I. So it 's friendship you want? Well, friends we 'll be—eh, my lad?"

The great dog, emboldened by voice and caress, sat up and venturing to lay his muzzle on Jeremy's knee, thumped the dust with eloquent tail and whimpered softly.

"Very good!" quoth Jeremy, scratching the big, ugly head. "So be it! The question now is—what shall we name you? You look no more the fine gentleman, the proud and supercilious aristocrat than I do! Aha, and what's more, my lad, the bar sinister is writ large all over you! There's mastiff in you, a suggestion of the sheep dog, a touch of the bull, a hint of the spaniel, a suspicion of the hound—and heaven knows how many more! You're *multum in parvo,* my fellow. And how can one name fit so many of you? Ha, despite Bill Shakespeare, there's much in a name—you're so various, and you're big and going to be bigger, I judge, and we must have a name to suit you—and b'gad, we have it—a name, *the* name of all names for us Britons—'Bill.' There was Bill of the Avon, and Bill the Conqueror, BILL MILNES, and there are and will be thousands of other Bills, Bill being a common, great name and greatly common. How d' ye like 'Bill,' my lad?"

The dog lifted his head, cocked an ear and staring up into Jeremy's face, uttered a short whine.

"So be it, Bill!" nodded Jeremy. "Bill art thou henceforth. Give me thy paw on it, Bill—this one, so! And now you're hungry by your looks and b'gad, so am I. Well, presently our needs shall be satisfied, but first, mark this—and heed me well, Bill. We are out upon the high adventure, you and I; battle, murder and sudden death, Bill; blood, fire and stricken field are all one to us. Show me your teeth—excellent! Look at these fists—sufficient, I venture to think! They did well enough at school and university and shall do better, I trust. Meanwhile, Bill, my boy, let us seek some hospice where we may refresh and shelter us—though indeed a barn were better suited to your true adventurers; to sleep in a barn would be a novelty to me, Bill, and therefore hath its attractions—Come!"

So saying, Jeremy caught up his tough ash plant and rising to vigorous limbs, strode cheerily onward with the great dog at his side who looked up at him ever and anon with eyes of adoration.

## CHAPTER V

### CONCERNS ITSELF, AMONG OTHER THINGS, WITH A LADDER AND A LADY

It was a villainous-looking little tavern: remote and solitary it stood, half-hidden behind gaunt trees as though lying in wait for the unwary traveller; a place to be avoided at all times, more especially at night; therefore, Jeremy approached, viewing it over from steep-pitched roof to the worn step before the low-arched door.

"A regular death trap, Bill!" quoth he. "A very murder hole and consequently the place for us. Let us investigate." So saying, he approached and tried the door only to find it locked, whereupon he saluted it with lusty blows of his stick; but this proving of no avail, he turned to the uncurtained window just in time to see its heavy shutters swing suddenly into place.

"Hum!" said he. "This promises, Bill, this promises, I think. Come, let us explore."

Behind the tavern he found a little dismal yard where stood a post chaise dusty with recent travel while from tumble-down stables came the snort and stamp of horses.

He was staring at this vehicle when a lattice under the eave creaked open and glancing up Jeremy saw a woman looking down at him, a young-seeming woman —an oval face framed in dusky hair, the gleam of round throat, a slim hand; this the moon showed him. When at last she spoke her voice was soft and of that mellow richness called contralto.

"Are you a man?" questioned the voice.

"I have ventured to believe so," answered Jeremy, lifting his hat.

"Then get me out."

"With pleasure!" answered Jeremy. "So soon as I can get in."

"Spare yourself the trouble."

"'T will be a joy."

"Then deny yourself—there is a ladder lying along the wall yonder, if you will look."

So while Bill, seated upon his haunches, watched with patient, canine eyes, Jeremy brought the ladder and rearing it up to the narrow window, began to mount forthwith, but above him was the gleam of white, imperious hand.

"Stay where you are!" said the voice.

"The lattice appears very narrow!" demurred Jeremy.

"I shall manage if you will keep the ladder steady—and—look the other way!"

"Oh, madam, assuredly!"

Jeremy heard a rustle above his head, felt the ladder shake, and down she came, swiftly, sure-footed and with a surprising ease—a tall creature, slender yet shapely from slim ankle to the jetty hair that framed her handsome face; with one dainty foot upon the lowest rung of the ladder, she paused to frown up at the lattice above.

"It was painfully narrow!" she admitted and turned to glance at Jeremy and from him to Bill, who sat thumping the earth with welcoming tail and one scrawny ear cocked.

"Heavens, what is that?" she enquired.

"My friend Bill, madam."

"He is very hideous!"

"He is, madam, and my esteemed and worthy comrade who condescends you a welcome."

"I am duly honoured!" said she, reaching out slim hand. "You may come here, Bill."

The great dog advanced with a certain stateliness, despite gaunt and bony carcass, looked up into the speaker's face, sniffed at her hand, licked it once and, sitting down, glanced from her to Jeremy enquiringly.

"I think you might occasionally feed your friend, sir."

"I propose doing so immediately, madam."

"But not here!"

"So soon as I can get into this villainous den."

"You'll do no such thing, sir!"

"On the contrary, madam!" retorted Jeremy and, taking up his stick he advanced to the small back door of the tavern with evident and purposeful intent.

"Sir," said the lady, placing a restraining hand upon his arm, "you are very foolhardy."

"I am," nodded Jeremy. "Also my mind is made up."

"Then unmake it, sir."

"Impossible, madam! Bill needs supper and your chaise, horses."

"Bill shall sup at my house—let us go."

"But your chaise?"

"I'll walk—besides the chaise is not mine—Come!" she said with an impatient gesture. "Why will you delay?"

"The landlord," said Jeremy, scowling at the weather-beaten door, "the landlord must be a scoundrel——"

"He is, sir."

"Why, then——" began Jeremy, but at this moment the door opened and a tall man appeared, an ill-favoured, hairy fellow with one eye, who flourished a blunderbuss.

"Out of it!" quoth he truculently. "Get out o' my yard or I'll fill y'r carcass wi' slugs—an' be damned!—

Oho, lads," cried he suddenly, catching sight of Jeremy's companion, "your wench is away! Y'r fine mort's a-flittin'!—A ladder, by Goles!" At this, came two faces to peer over the hairy man's shoulders, staring faces and one of them crowned by the leathern cap of a postboy. "Come, lads," cried the hairy man, his one eye glaring, "you lay 'old o' the wench —I'll look arter the cove. Step to it, mates, and lively!"

But as he advanced upon Jeremy, very threatening of aspect, out from the deeper shadow a gaunt shape launched itself and uttering neither bark nor growl, the great dog was upon him; the blunderbuss fell, clattering, and with it the hairy man, writhing and screaming with terror; thither sprang Jeremy and after some moments' desperate work succeeded in wrenching the animal away.

Freed from his grim assailant, the hairy man staggered towards his blunderbuss but seeing Jeremy had reached it first, stood pointing where the dog crouched, silent as ever.

"'T is Bill Tranter's cur!" he panted. "I know 'im—a devil!"

"And he seems to know you!" retorted Jeremy.

"A dangerous beast—I tell ye!" gasped the man. "Shoot 'im—he's mad—shoot 'im——"

"I'd sooner shoot you!" said Jeremy.

"Ha—would ye, my buck?" snarled the hairy man. "Put down my blunderbuss an' I'll punch your face in, so I will!"

"Get into your villainous tavern while you 're safe," quoth Jeremy.

"Wait!" said the lady, pointing to the one-eyed landlord. "Could you knock this creature down?"

"If necessary," answered Jeremy.

"Then pray do so—I'll hold the dog."

"With pleasure, madam, but why?"

"Surely you heard him call me 'wench'?"

"True!" answered Jeremy and with a swing of powerful arm, sent the heavy blunderbuss hurtling over the stable roof; but the landlord, observing Jeremy's alacrity, stayed not the onset but dodging back into the tavern, locked himself in and cursed there in security.

Jeremy blinked at the door, tried it and finding it fast, sighed and turned to see the lady regarding him with a smile.

"I grieve for your disappointment," said she. "And now, let us go."

"Where, madam?"

"To Bill's supper."

"Hum," quoth Jeremy, picking up his ash plant, "Bill has taken to you, it seems."

"Are you surprised, sir? Bill, though hideous, is a creature of intelligence."

So they presently went forth from the dismal little yard, the dog walking sedately between them.

## CHAPTER VI

### IN WHICH THEY PROCEED SUPPERWARDS

AFTER they had proceeded some distance, she spoke, her sombre gaze fixed on the winding road before them:

"I am Mrs. Revell!"

"Indeed?"

"Yes—Olivia Revell! The name is familiar, of course. You have heard of me, I suppose?" And he wondered at the bitterness of her tone.

"No, madam."

"You must be a stranger hereabouts."

"I am."

"Then before I permit you to enter my house," said she in her smooth, soft voice, "I must warn you that I am suspected of killing—of murdering my husband."

"I've heard the world is full o' fools," said Jeremy.

"Thank you!" she murmured. "And yet, to be just, I think these fools have some excuse—I must tell you that I married my husband because I hated him."

"Which is one reason for wedlock!" said Jeremy.

"And upon the day I married him—he died!"

"Which, under the circumstances, was remarkably obliging of him!" said Jeremy.

"He died because he was—shot."

"An awkward complication!" said Jeremy.

"Consequently I have lived very much alone."

"I too prefer solitude," said Jeremy, but here she turned to frown at him and he was struck by the fierce, dark beauty of her.

"Solitude?" she repeated. "I hate solitude because it is forced upon me—it is my doom, I suppose. I am an outcast—people shun me."

"Which leaves you birds and beasts!" said Jeremy.

"I might have fled away to some place where my story was unknown, but I determined to stay and outface it."

"Yes," he nodded, "you look courageous."

"And am shunned!"

"Well," he answered, "I have always found animals more friendly than humans and infinitely less dangerous."

At this, she stopped suddenly and faced him.

"The moon is very bright!" said she. "Tell me, do you think I look a murderess?"

"No!" answered Jeremy, gazing into the dark eyes that met his so searchingly. "Neither does Bill—look at him!"

Seated between them as they stood, the dog was staring into her face with his wise, grave eyes, one ear cocked and tail thumping gently. All at once, swift and graceful, she sank to her knees and laid her two slim hands about Bill's ugly, square head.

"Oh," she murmured, "oh, I have been a very—lonely creature! To find such faith, such trust is—almost a pain——" Then with the same supple grace she rose and reached Jeremy her hand.

"Who are you?" she enquired.

"Call me—Jeremy," he answered.

"'T is an odd name."

"A fool of a name!" he nodded. "But there's been a Jeremy in the family for generations."

For a moment she stood eyeing him expectantly, then, freeing her hand abruptly, walked on again, but silent now and keeping her head averted; whereupon Jeremy wondered and, after some while, ventured to question her:

"Have I offended you?"

"Oh no!"

"I wonder how?"

"'T is no matter!"

"But how?"

"Why seek to conceal your other name?"

"Oh—Veryan!" he answered.

"Of Veryan?"

"Yes, madam."

"Veryan is scarcely ten miles from here—you told me you were a stranger in these parts."

"I have lived at Veryan but seldom," he explained. "My boyhood passed at school in London and these latter years at Oxford."

"How old are you, Mr. Veryan?"

"Twenty-four, Mrs. Revell."

"Don't!" said she, frowning at him. "Don't call me—that!"

"Then don't call me Veryan."

"Pray why not?"

"Because it don't suit me; I was meant for a Tom Smith or Dick Brown."

"Veryan is a great heritage, I've heard."

"I believe it is!" Jeremy admitted.

"And you are the heir?"

"Unfortunately."

"Why so?"

"Because I'd rather achieve than inherit."

"You are a remarkably strange youth, I think!" said she, viewing him grave-eyed.

"On the contrary, I'm as ordinary as I look, madam, and, moreover, I'm twenty-four."

"Why do you tramp abroad with a pack on your shoulders?"

"Bill and I seek the High Adventure."

"And what is that?"

"Anything which usually is to be avoided."

"Because you are a very young youth and so remarkably strange."

"Hum!" quoth Jeremy, pondering this. "Then let us say that I am extraordinarily ordinary."

"Yes," she nodded, "I think that describes you more correctly. And why do you seek what more ordinary folk avoid?"

"Because I conceive I am not suited to luxurious ease, but to hard usage."

"Because you have never known real hard usage."

"Hum!" quoth Jeremy again and went on a while pondering this in turn until he was aware of tall iron gates giving upon an avenue of sombre, stately trees beyond which rose a goodly house.

"There is my prison!" sighed she.

"Which looks like a mansion!" said Jeremy as they approached.

"And full of ghosts!"

"And you live here alone?"

"No, I merely exist."

She led him across a wide terrace, past a great front door, to a side entrance and so to a chamber where shaded candles glowed softly; a dainty, luxurious chamber breathing an elusive fragrance. Upon the threshold of this truly feminine apartment Jeremy halted and instinctively glanced down at his dusty clothes and boots.

"Upon second thoughts," he began, "I think——"

"Do you drink wine, Mr. Veryan?" she enquired, reaching slim white hand to silken bell rope.

"Yes. But indeed—but what of Bill?"

"He may drink whatever he please."

"But," demurred Jeremy, "he—I—we feel entirely out o' place in such a room as this."

"Speak for yourself, sir!" she retorted. "Come, Bill!"

Obediently the great dog advanced into the candle-light, a creature of truly unlovely aspect and looking very much out of place by reason of his shaggy hair, obtrusive bones and the marks of hardship and ill usage; and yet notwithstanding all this, there was about him a stately dignity, an ineffable repose that stamped him a dog of character.

"The poor thing!" exclaimed Mrs. Revell, and sinking to her knees the better to cherish the dog she frowned up at the man with accusing eyes. "Whatever have you been doing to him?" she demanded.

"Stealing him!" answered Jeremy "I thieved him from his master this evening."

"Was the brute beating him?"

"With this ash plant."

"Then I hope you were—sufficiently violent."

"Hardly!" murmured Jeremy. "And yet (here he glanced at his broken knuckles) perhaps I was."

"Then you may close the door, sir, and have the goodness to ring the bell yonder, thank you! And now, pray sit down."

Thus Jeremy, able now to observe her more particularly and at his leisure, saw she was younger than he had thought; generously formed she was, long-limbed and shapely and with a vigorous life that glowed in cheek and vivid lip and was manifest in her every supple movement. Viewing her with the dispassionate appraisement of experienced Twenty-four, Jeremy had just decided that her chin was too pronounced, her hair too black and straight, and her eyebrows too thick, when he was disturbed by a soft rap on the door and there appeared a person of poise, a being of unshakable calm from grizzled hair and small, neatly-trimmed whiskers to the toes of his neat shoes.

"Madam," said he, glancing at Jeremy and the dog as if they were not there, "you rang?"

"Yes, Bryant. Let supper be served for three, in the morning room."

"Certainly, madam!" saying which, the being bowed, turned and went forth, closing the door tenderly behind him. And presently Mrs. Revell spoke, though with her attention still focussed upon the dog:

"So you are travelling in quest of adventure? You are very strong, I think!"

"Beef and bone!" muttered Jeremy.

"You look like a fighting man."

"That's the worst of a face like mine!" he sighed.

"Oh, boy!" said she with sudden smile that matched her voice for gentleness. "You are very strange—and very much a boy!"

"Boy?" he repeated. "Why, I never remember being a real boy like the rest of 'em."

"Why not?"

"Well, you see, I was always solitary—never had any playmates—folk did n't take to me as a child; they don't now. Perhaps I'm too rough in my ways as I am in looks."

"And you are not in the least inquisitive, are you?"

"Perhaps not."

"I mean," said she, glancing up at him beneath her brows, "you have n't asked me how I came to be shut up in that very detestable little tavern."

"Because," he answered, "you'll tell me yourself if you want me to know; if not—'t is no business of mine."

"I'll tell you—after supper," said she.

## CHAPTER VII

### TOUCHING UPON MR. RICHARD ARMADALE, HIS WOES

THE dog Bill, fed to repletion for perhaps the first time in his experience, dozed blissfully upon the hearth-rug, yet opening a bright eye ever and anon (as in duty bound) to glance from his master, who sat at the supper table, square chin on square fist, to their hostess who, leaning back in her chair, seemed lost in unhappy thought, judging from the droop of her lips; heedful of which Jeremy sought to distract her; quoth he:

"I like your butler; he 's been a soldier, I think?"

"A sailor," she answered, "he was with my father at Trafalgar and has remained in the family ever since. . . . Mr. Veryan, I told you I was shunned because of what happened here four years ago, shunned by all people of any position in the county, which leaves me a prey to—the other sort—women who seek me for my hateful notoriety and men who pester me because I am rich. And chief among these—three, one whom I almost fear, one I despise, and one I neither trouble to despise or fear—a fool and yet I think a sincere, well-meaning fool who has persisted in his attentions for months. To-night I agreed to run off and marry him——"

"Why?" growled Jeremy; at which abrupt question she leaned suddenly towards him, her eyes bright in the candlelight, and threw wide her arms with a gesture that had in it something wild and despairing.

"To escape the ghosts!" she answered. To be free of my prison! This house is full of hateful memories that haunt me—and so, to be rid of it all, I ran away with a fool—but we had gone scarcely three miles before I changed my mind——"

A hoarse growl from Bill's shaggy throat and turning swiftly, Jeremy saw him crouched, the hair upon his neck bristling, his head raised and eyes glaring towards a corner beside the wide hearth; now glancing from the dog to his hostess, Jeremy was amazed to see her deadly pale, her two hands tight-clenched upon her chair arms, her eyes fixed in a horrified stare towards that self-same corner beside the great, carved chimney-piece; and in those beautiful wide eyes, Jeremy thought he read an anxious expectancy.

The dog growled again and rose, his lips curled back from gleaming fangs, his whole gaunt body quivering. In voice scarcely above a whisper, Jeremy commanded him to lie down, whereupon the dog seated himself obediently but with eyes turned always in the one direction; so thither looked Jeremy also, but with hand fast gripped in Bill's bristling mane. And presently upon the stillness was a whisper of sound, indefinable and hard to locate—a sudden, sharp click, and Jeremy saw a long panel slide from view and in its place a pallid, hairy face blinked in the candlelight.

"Richard—eh, Richard!"

"Yes, 't is I—what's left of me!" answered a pettish voice. "And the dooce of a time I've had getting here!" And into the room stepped a young man who, smoothing back his long, curly hair, showed a handsome, lean face, haggard with hardship or dissipation and lighted by long-lashed eyes too beautiful for a man. Closing the panel behind him he advanced, a trifle unsteadily, and beholding Jeremy for the first time, started violently.

"Damnation!" he exclaimed and frowned, while Jeremy scowled back at him and grasped Bill the tighter.

"This, sir," said Mrs. Revell, upon her feet and turning towards the stranger with both hands outstretched in eager welcome, "this is my brother, Richard Armadale——"

"And dev'lish hungry I am!" exclaimed Mr. Armadale, favouring Jeremy with a jaunty bow. "So with all submission, Olivia, though grieving to intrude thus, I 'll sit down and peck a bit—though, sir, I should esteem it a favour if you 'd send that lap dog o' yours out of th' room; he don't seem to like me."

There was a strident note in the speaker's voice, a brilliancy of the eyes, a nervous quiver of the delicate hands which, together, told their tale.

"Sir," said Jeremy, rising, "my friend Bill and I were about to take our departure——"

"Oh, b'ged," laughed Mr. Armadale, seating himself at the table in his sister's place, "pray don't disturb yourself on my account. I 'm a shadow, sir—I come and go. I flit hither and thither, unheralded and unsung. Olivia, ha' the goodness to pass the bottle."

"Why, 't is a fair night for walking, sir," answered Jeremy, "and the road calls me." But as he turned to reach hat and stick, he found his hostess beside him and read in her look an appeal so eloquent that he hesitated, and for a moment her cool, slim fingers touched his; Jeremy sat down again.

"Ha—excellent!" exclaimed Mr. Armadale. "Pray fill your glass, I abhor drinking alone! And I don't think I caught your name, sir."

"Because it was not mentioned," answered Jeremy.

"Then favour me."

"My name is Veryan, sir."

Mr. Armadale immediately spilled his wine and turned swiftly to stare at Jeremy with eyes more brilliant than ever.

"Eged, can it be possible!" he exclaimed. "Veryan, d' ye say? Not the Veryan—not the famous Jeremy?"

"The same, sir,—though as to famous, I fear——"

"Dooce take it, Mr. Veryan, can't ye shoot the spots off the five o' spades at twelve paces—eh? Did n't you stand up to the French *maître-d'armes* and knock out the Bermondsey Pet—eh? Ged, sir, they still talk o' you at Oxford! To be so expert with foil, fist and hair trigger—highly useful accomplishments, sir. I'm dooced proud to know you—I hear you are living at Veryan nowadays?"

"I was, sir."

"Ha!" exclaimed Mr. Armadale, holding his wine glass to the candlelight with hand that trembled despite its youth. "You'll be wondering at my highly melodramatic entrance, sir—'t is because my life is all dem'd melodrama, ay—from my curst cradle! And this old house, full of secret passages and chambers, is an effective back-ground. Mr. Veryan, you see before you a man curst by the Fates—the very plaything of Destiny—'pray pass the bottle, sir," he continued, filling his glass and making an awkward business of it, "the hand of mankind has been ever against me, the forces of Nature inimical to me from boyhood's hour, the what 's-a-name Sisters who rule our fates, dem'd hags, scowled upon my prattling infancy! I am a being apart, ay, b'ged, the very mock and sport of Circumstance, consequently Despond is my associate and Dejection my bedfellow!"

"Indeed!" quoth Jeremy.

"Veryan, my dear sir, from the fatal day, four years ago, that a devoted sister sacrificed herself to a villain to save an unfortunate brother, that brother has been that sister's sworn slave—would die for her, my dear fellow—mount the dismal, dem'd gallows for her if necessary—Veryan, you don't drink—fill, sir, fill!"

But instead of so doing, Jeremy glanced across at his hostess to find her regarding him; and seeing the stricken look in her eyes, turned to scowl down at Bill who sat beside his chair, very wide-awake now; and then Jeremy was conscious of Mrs. Revell's smooth, soft tones:

"Richard, I want you to tell Mr. Veryan everything—everything!"

Mr. Armadale set down his glass and leaned back with a jerk, to stare from his sister to Jeremy and back again.

"You—you mean about—Revell?"

"Yes, Richard."

"But Veryan is a—a stranger; I hardly know him——"

"I hope—I most earnestly hope he is going to be your friend—your best friend, Richard."

Jeremy glanced from Mr. Armadale's twitching fingers to his handsome, pallid features and scowled: but, chancing to meet the wistful entreaty in Olivia Revell's eyes, he muttered:

"Honoured!"

Hereupon, having tossed off his glass, Mr. Armadale bowed.

"My dear Veryan," said he, "I've known of you for some time—you see—I was at Oxford—and besides, I'm acquainted with your cousin Arthur Trevor and on bowing terms with your Uncle Sir James—I suppose Arthur has never mentioned my name to you?"

"Never."

"Arthur's a dem'd secretive fellow, up to every dodge, and well known about town—you are seldom in London, I believe?"

"Very!" answered Jeremy.

"B'ged now, Veryan, how you can endure the country passes my comp—comprehension! For your dandy bucks and true sportsmen there 's no place like town, sir."

"That 's why I prefer the country!"

"Then you have never plumbed the—ah—deeps o' life, sir?"

"Enough to find them distasteful!"

"You 're a dem'd strange fellow, Veryan!"

"I begin to suspect so!" nodded Jeremy.

"And you want to hear about the cursed, ugly Revel affair?"

"No!" said Jeremy.

"But I want you to tell him, Richard," said Olivia's smooth, soft voice.

Mr. Armadale refilled his glass, emptied it and leaning elbow on the table turned towards Jeremy.

"So be it, sir," said he, "since Olivia commands—I obey! And to begin with, I'll frankly own the whole dem'd business was the outcome of my folly—frankness is one of my too few virtues, sir, a virtue my worst enemy would not deny me. Well, sir, I had been a fool—and worse—wild oats and such—and was in debt up to my dem'd ears. Revell, merciless devil, had me in his power to ruin utterly and for ever, and to save me Olivia married him before I could prevent—and would consequently have sacrificed herself to the fellow's brutality but for me! For, sir, on that very day, goaded to desperation by my troubles, I rode down here with a friend, determined to fight the fellow and end it one way or the other, little guessing it was his wedding day. I found him here and, learning he had actually married my beloved sister, I grew frantic and insisted on fighting him on the spot—I had brought the necessary tools with me, you'll understand! But Veryan, the abject villain refused until I spat upon and struck him—at which he sprang upon me like a madman—I had a pistol in my hand—we fought and wrestled brutally together—and then, Veryan, I heard the crash of a shot—and he was down—lying at my feet—stone dead, and my pistol beside him——"

"And where was your friend standing?"

"My—my friend, sir?"

"A friend was with you, I understand."

"To be sure, De Ravenac was with me."

"Where was he standing at the time?"

"Where?" repeated Mr. Armadale, blinking and knitting smooth brow. "Why, very close to us—just behind me, if I remember aright—but I was very excited—I'll frankly admit I'd had a glass or so, and my memory is hazy. But these are the facts of the case, sir, but for De Ravenac things would ha' gone precious hard with me—I stood in the shadow of Tyburn tree—and a dem'd cold shadow it is, sir!"

"How did Mr. Ravenac save you?"

"Swore at the inquest that the pistol was in Revell's hand."

"Perjured himself!" muttered Jeremy.

"'T was a curst sordid business altogether, Veryan! Olivia and I ha' been cut by the county ever since, which, though unjust to me, is dem'd unjust to Olivia!"

"And who is De Ravenac?"

"Ged, Veryan, 't is very evident you're a stranger to town! Who is De Ravenac? Enquire at any of the most exclusive clubs! Oh, demme, any one in the Fashionable World or sporting *bon ton* will tell you."

"Yes!" nodded Jeremy, scowling thoughtfully at Bill's ugly head. "But who is he?"

"He is—De Ravenac, the one and only! He is every one's acquaintance—and my friend, sir—and a dem'd fine fellow, too!"

"Hum!" said Jeremy.

"And—dooce take me but the wine's out! Olivia, pray ring the bell and let 's have up another bottle."

"No, Richard, I think not."

"Why, very well—I see brandy yonder—I prefer brandy—we'll drink that."

"No, Richard, I 'm sure not."

"Eh—not?" ejaculated Mr. Armadale, with a febrile, pettish gesture. "Good Ged, girl, what d' ye mean?"

"Dear boy—what I say."

"Ha, madam, d' ye dare suggest I 'm drunk? And if I were—can carry it like a gentleman, I hope—What,

Veryan, you 're never going? The night's too young to part yet."

"Thank you," answered Jeremy, as for the second time he reached for hat and stick, "but I think——"

A knock at the door interrupted him and, in due season, the stately Bryant presented himself, who, bowing to Mr. Armadale with unshaken calm, cleared his throat to announce:

"Mounseer the Chevalier de Ravenac!"

"Now by all that 's lucky!" exclaimed Mr. Armadale, a little too boisterously. "Show him in, Bryant, show him in, man!"

Once again Jeremy glanced at Olivia and, once again obedient to the mute appeal in her eyes, he laid aside hat and stick.

## CHAPTER VIII

### OF BOWS, SNARLS AND SCOWLS

MONSIEUR the Chevalier de Ravenac was a tall, superlatively elegant, extremely languid gentleman, whose arresting features were ornamented by a profusion of whisker which, like his curling hair, was of a glossy black; a handsome sinister face, the more so perhaps by reason of the eyes so palely blue in such striking contrast with the raven hair.

"Madam!" said he, bowing profoundly to Olivia, "*Je suis enchanté!*" Then turning to Mr. Armadale with both white, be-ringed hands extended: "My friend!" he exclaimed.

"My dear Gaston," cried Armadale as they shook hands, "I present you to Mr. Veryan of Veryan—Mr. Veryan—Monsieur the Chevalier de Ravenac!"

"Charmed, sir!" said the Chevalier bowing, hand on heart. Now as Jeremy acknowledged this salutation, something stirred within his consciousness like the vague memory of a long-forgotten dream. A snarl from Bill and Jeremy's iron fingers had grasped the scruff of his neck only just in time; yet Jeremy's keen eyes had recognised in De Ravenac's sudden start, in the instinctive motion of the hand that gripped be-tasselled cane, the balanced poise of the fencer.

"'E is not pretty, your dog, sir, though with teeth the most admirable!" smiled the Chevalier. "But do not trouble, monsieur, 'e not annoy me p'raps. Also I 'ave my cane!"

"'Pon my soul," exclaimed Mr. Armadale, "I rejoice to see you, Gaston. But what in the world brings you here?"

"*Eh bien*, I pass on my way, I learn at the inn my friend Richard is 'ere—I come. 'T is the excuse to pay my so 'umble respect to Madam Olivia who is always more beautiful!" Here the Chevalier bowed profoundly, his glance upon Olivia's half-averted face; observing which glance, Jeremy's thick brows drew together and his powerful fingers clenched themselves upon Bill's shaggy coat until that much-enduring animal whined.

"And what takes you to London to-night, De Ravenac?" enquired Mr. Armadale.

"Not to London, my Richard, no, no—to Brighton for the box fight——"

"What?" cried Richard. "A mill is it? A prize fight?"

"*Parfaitement!* Mr. Thurtell 'ave backed his man against a Captain Despard his man for five hundred pounds. Monsieur le Prince will be there—all the ton—*tout la mode*—everybody!"

"By heaven!" exclaimed Richard, rising from the table a little unsteadily, "I 'll not miss it—no, no, demme! You must take me, Ravenac, positively, I insist!"

"My friend!" exclaimed the Chevalier, reaching out both hands, "I shall be charmed—oh, perfectly! My curricle is at the inn—yet, no, *hélas!*—Madam Olivia she sigh, she frown her so beautiful eyebrow! No, no, my friend—I go alone!"

"No such thing, De Ravenac; I 'm determined on 't. And when my mind is made up, I 'm iron! As for Olivia," here he turned upon her, "egad, you know how desperately determined I can be! I 'm going, I tell you! There, there, child, never shake your head, and pray don't plead or attempt to thwart me; 't is useless, what is to be must be——"

"But Richard," said his sister, laying her hand upon his shoulder, "remember last time you were Monsieur de Ravenac's guest! And you are not—well, to-night. Dear boy, stay with me——"

"But yes, my Richard," murmured De Ravenac; "be you persuaded—to stay with your so beautiful sister—oh, what a rapture most extreme! Indeed, my friend, the wish of Madam Olivia is my law—I go alone."

"Demme if you do!" exclaimed Richard, and shaking off his sister's detaining hand with a pettish gesture, he made towards the door; but there she stayed him to whisper in his unwilling ear.

"Tush, madam!" he exclaimed, "I 'm well enough! And besides, I 'm not a child. There, there—kiss me! I 'll be back with you in a day or so, never fear—come, De Ravenac!"

"Richard, *mais non!* I drive alone——"

"Then, by heaven, I'll walk!" cried Richard and strode from the room. Hereupon the Chevalier sighed, frowned, shook his handsome head and burst into a torrent of rapid French.

"Pray speak English, sir," said Olivia.

"Pardon, madam!" he answered. "But I 'ave not enough of your language so eloquent, to speak all my regrets—no! *Je suis désolé!* But your brother 'e is so passionate, so—'ow you say?—So 'ead-strong! Richard 'e leave you and for you I grieve myself!"

"Then send him back to me, sir. It seems your influence with him is greater than mine."

"Ah, but no, madam. You—so beautiful, Olivia—so tender——"

"Send him back to me!" she repeated. At this the Chevalier advanced and made to take her hand, but she drew back. Whereupon he smiled and bowed again; and Jeremy thought his face, thus smiling, more sinister than ever.

"Madam," he sighed, "your servant so 'umble and most devote, will do his best to oblige you, now as evermore. *Au revoir*, madam, I return soon p'raps, but I carry your beauty in my dreams!" And with a final obeisance, he sauntered from the room. For a long moment after the door had closed upon the Chevalier's stately form Olivia Revell sat lost in troubled thought.

"Mr. Veryan," she said at last, "how do you like that man?"

"I don't!" answered Jeremy, smoothing Bill's shaggy head.

"I think he 's a devil!" she exclaimed. "My brother's evil genius—oh, if ever a man needed a strong, true friend, it is my poor Richard! I wish—I do wish you could be such a friend to him."

"Impossible!" answered Jeremy. "I have n't the faculty for making friends, especially with—such as your brother."

"Ah—you—dislike him?"

"No, I pity him."

"That is worse, sir."

"It is!" answered Jeremy, taking up his hat and stick. "Also it takes two to make friends."

"And you refuse to try?"

"Of course!" he nodded. "The idea of thrusting my friendship on any human is repugnant—no, pray don't look at me like that, mam, I did n't mean to offend or grieve you—ask of me any other service—anything in reason."

"I will!" said she, rising from the luxurious divan with an effortless ease. "You are in quest of The High Adventure, you tell me, and this means, I think, the attempting of all manner of dangers and difficulties. Is this so?"

"Yes!" nodded Jeremy. "More particularly 'difficulties.'"

"Are you truly a brave man?"

"I hope so."

"A resolute and determined man?"

"I think so."

"Then you shall prove it."

"How?" he enquired, his sombre gaze upon the symmetrical curves of her lithe shape and finding therewith no fault whatever.

"Bring Richard back to me!" And now his roving gaze was upon the soft, creamy roundness of her throat, her dimpled chin, red mouth and delicate nostrils and, reaching her eyes, so various of expression, saw that which held him oblivious of all else until their sudden-drooping lashes hid them; to be sure her hair was very black and straight with no coquettish frizz of curls, yet was it very fine and glossy and would be soft to the touch; and if her eyebrows were too thick yet their low arch lent her a certain serene majesty, a certain——

"Will you adventure this?" she questioned.

"Surely!" answered Jeremy, starting.

"Do you think you can succeed?"

"Why not?" said he and laid his hand upon the door.

"The Chevalier may be armed."

"Hum!" quoth Jeremy, and opened the door; but as he did so, she was beside him, her hand upon his arm.

"This danger will not deter you, then?"

"No!" he answered.

"Then I forbid you to make the attempt!" Jeremy very nearly gaped. "I 'll not permit you to risk your life."

"I don't intend to——"

"But I tell you the Chevalier is a dangerous man."

"Quite so!" nodded Jeremy. "'T is why he interests me."

"Then I utterly forbid you to run any risk for

my brother's sake since you can feel no friendship for him."

"I don't!" answered Jeremy. "I do it for his sister."

"Very well!" she answered, catching up her cloak. "Then I'll go with you."

# CHAPTER IX

## GIVES SOME DESCRIPTION OF A WALK BY MOONLIGHT

FAST strode Jeremy yet, despite the pace, his companion kept beside him easily, though to be sure they spoke but seldom. Thus went they swiftly, silently, the dog plodding after them until they were come out upon the open road. And presently, rounding a sharp bend, they espied Richard and the Chevalier some distance ahead walking leisurely arm in arm; at sight of them Jeremy halted and turned to his companion:

"You will please wait here!" said he.

"No——" she was beginning, when he checked her with a gesture and pointed to the dog:

"And you will pray keep Bill beside you."

"Very well!" she answered, suddenly submissive, and seating herself beneath the hedge, set one arm about the dog's shaggy neck. Then Jeremy strode on again, but had not gone very far before Bill was beside him, whereupon Jeremy smiled a little grimly and went on faster than ever.

He was close upon the two gentlemen when the Chevalier glanced back over his shoulder and halting his companion, they swung round to watch Jeremy as he approached.

"Mr. Armadale," said he, ignoring the Chevalier, "I come from your sister who desires you to return."

Richard Armadale frowned, Bill growled, the Chevalier bowed and smiled; quoth he:

"And monsieur is a messenger the most zealous—oh, very!"

"Sir," said Mr. Armadale haughtily but with speech a little blurred, "your presence here is a d-dem'd impert'nence!" And, folding his arms, he surveyed Jeremy from head to foot with an air of extreme dignity, though he rocked a trifle on his heels.

"Are ye coming, sir?" demanded Jeremy.

"No, sir!" answered Mr. Armadale, becoming suddenly fierce. "And as for you—get about your business and be d-dam'd!"

"Precisely!" nodded Jeremy. "My business is to take you back! Do you come?"

"Most cert'nly and decid'ly not, sir!"

"I think you'd better."

"Ha—d' ye dare to threaten me, sir?"

"No!" retorted Jeremy. "Only you 'll go back if I have to carry you——"

"Carry me?" repeated Mr. Armadale, his voice shrill with anger and amazement. "Carry me, by heaven——"

"Or drag you!" growled Jeremy.

"My dear friend Richard," smiled the Chevalier, "your charming sister desires! Her messenger, this so brusque gentleman, commands! 'T is yours to—obey!"

"Obey?" cried Mr. Armadale, raising clenched hands in an ecstasy of passion. "Obey? Ten thousand devils seize me first! As for you, sir—you, Veryan, come a step nearer and I—I'll knock you down!"

"So be it!" said Jeremy grimly, and dropping his stick, he advanced with step surprising light and buoyant; but as he did so, the Chevalier interposed his tall and splendid person, and smiled upon Jeremy, serene and superbly assured; whereat Bill, growling, showed his formidable fangs and was promptly tapped on the nose by Jeremy's open hand.

"*Doucement, mes amis, doucement!*" said the Chevalier, gently. "You, monsieur, perceive my friend

Richard 'ave make up his so determined mind to go with me, is it not? *Eh bien*, we wish you good night, sir!"

"Mounseer," quoth Jeremy, scowling, "out o' my way!" The Chevalier laughed softly.

"You will tell our so beautiful Madam Revell that I—I, Gaston de Ravenac, will myself bring back my dear Richard as soon as he desire——"

"Mounseer," quoth Jeremy, clenching knotted fists, "walk off before I hurt you."

"'Urt me, sir?" repeated the Chevalier softly. "Oh la-la! Is it blow me wiz the fist, you mean? *Mais non! Peste*, I am not the—how you say?—prize fighter, I! You have your fist and I—regard, monsieur!" And out from be-tasselled cane he whipped three feet or so of narrow, murderous steel that glittered evilly in the brilliant moonlight. "Observe, dear sir," smiled the Chevalier, "your so bad dog or yourself I stick him with a pleasure the most perfect!" Here he made the triangular blade whistle through the air. "Beautiful, is it not?" he laughed. "So now, monsieur, now you make your instant depart or——" Here, the vicious point darted so near Jeremy's face that he recoiled instinctively, whereat the Chevalier laughed again, "*Violà!*" said he, and raised the weapon in airy salute; but even as the blade swept upward, Jeremy sprang in under De Ravenac's elbow and seized that upraised arm, found it an arm and wrist of steel; but the Chevalier's delicate fingers were no match for Jeremy's iron claws, and with a vicious wrench, he possessed himself of the weapon.

"The dog!" cried Mr. Armadale at this moment, "Oh, demme——" Jeremy turned, in time to see Bill crouching, fierce-eyed and teeth agleam, and to seize him before he could spring; recognising which masterful grip, the great dog cowered and slunk aside. Then Jeremy bent the fine-tempered blade across his knee until it snapped and tossing aside the pieces, glanced up to meet the Chevalier's dazzling smile.

"*Sapristi!*" he exclaimed, bowing gracefully. "Sir, my congratulations! Monsieur is most adroit and *hélas*, I do not commit the box! The *epée, mais oui!* The *pistolet*, oh, yes—*enchanté*, but——"

"Mounseer," growled Jeremy, picking up his ash plant, "walk!"

"Sir," answered the Chevalier, with another stately reverence, "adieu! We meet again—oh, be sure, yes!" And, turning upon his heel, Monsieur the Chevalier Gaston de Ravenac strolled away leisurely and serene as usual.

"Why, demme," gasped Mr. Armadale, staring after his retreating form with incredulous eyes, "dooce take and confound me if he—has n't actually—gone!"

"So let's go too!" said Jeremy.

"Oh, Ged!" ejaculated Mr. Armadale, staring at Jeremy with very wide eyes. "Ged love me!—I tell you there is n't a man in London—no, demme, nor out, could ha' made De Ravenac turn tail——"

"Come, let 's go!" repeated Jeremy.

"I tell you, sir, I tell you De Ravenac's a devil when he 's roused! I 've seen him quell a whole roomful before now—ay, b'ged, and bucks at that, sir, sportsmen all!—Demme but he might have pinked you just now with that toothpick of his!"

"But he did n't!" said Jeremy.

"You can be an ugly customer, Veryan!"

"Like my dog!"

"Why, so he is—but you 're dooced quick on your pins, Veryan."

"Come, your sister's waiting you——"

"Good Ged, man—where?"

"Sitting under the hedge, yonder."

"And what the dooce does she mean by it? Demme, sir, I 'll have you know I 'm not to be badgered by her nor bullied by you!"

"Why, then," said Jeremy, "will you walk, sir, or——"

Mr. Armadale drew himself haughtily erect and crossed his arms, but meeting Jeremy's scowling perplexity, laughed suddenly.

"Veryan," said he, "I'll walk."

"Wise Richard!" said a smooth voice and, wheeling about, they beheld Olivia within a yard of them stooping to fondle the dog.

"Ha, madam!" exclaimed her brother. "So you 're there, are you? You 've been watching, I suppose?"

"Of course!" she answered. "And I congratulate Mr. Veryan upon his powers of persuasion."

"Persuasion, d' ye call it?"

"To be sure, Richard. You are here and the Chevalier has gone."

"The Chevalier!" repeated Richard. "B'ged, Olivia, let me tell you Veryan has made a dooced dangerous enemy. De Ravenac never forgets!"

Now at this she turned to look at Jeremy with troubled eyes.

"And I am to blame!" said she. "Oh, forgive me!"

"Impossible!" growled Jeremy. "There 's nothing to forgive. As for the Chevalier, I 've a feeling we were—fated to meet and shall again—the sooner, the better!"

"And may I be there to see!" exclaimed Richard. "B'ged, but you 're a cool customer, Veryan, and—I like you and demme, sir, I 'm not ashamed to avow it!"

"Honoured!" muttered Jeremy, as they went on together.

"You 've heard of Jessamy Todd 'the Nonpariel'—quick as lightning and hits like a thunderbolt! You've heard of the famous Jessamy?"

"Of course!"

"Ever seen him fight?"

"No!" sighed Jeremy regretfully.

"Well, I 've boxed with him, Veryan."

"*You* have?" exclaimed Jeremy, and halted to stare at the speaker.

"And why not, pray?" demanded Richard, frowning. "Why such vast astonishment, Mr. Veryan?"

"You don't look it!" answered Jeremy.

"Oh, don't I, sir, don't I?"

"No," answered Jeremy, "you don't! To box with such a man as Jessamy Todd would be impossible in your condition——"

"You 'll find I 'm stronger than I look."

"You need be!"

"Ha—demme, what d' ye mean, sir? Curse and confound it, what d' ye mean? I 'm game to tackle anything on two legs——"

"You drink too much!" quoth Jeremy.

"Exactly true!" murmured Olivia.

"Now by all that 's demnable!" ejaculated Mr. Armadale, his handsome, youthful features distorted with passion. "You 're infernally offensive, sir——"

"But perfectly right!" said Olivia in the same soft, sweet voice.

"Madam," exclaimed her brother, "be good enough to hold your tongue!—Nay, leave us! Mr. Veryan, I repeat that I find you peculiarly offensive!"

"I don't mean to be so," answered Jeremy.

"Tush, sir, this shall not save you from my just resentment! I repeat, you are offensive and dem'd impertinent! Is this enough, sir?"

"Quite!" answered Jeremy, and taking off his hat, he bowed to Olivia. "I bid you good night, madam——"

But, as he spoke, the hat was dashed violently from his grasp and Mr. Armadale's pale, distorted features were thrust within a foot of his own; quoth he:

"Mr. Veryan, do you find this sufficient provocation, or must I strike you?" Saying which, Mr. Armadale tossed aside his own hat and, stepping back, buttoned his coat and stood poised for instant action. Jeremy looked at him, sighed and picking up his hat, was in the act of putting it on when Olivia's soft voice arrested him.

"I 'm afraid my brother is determined to be knocked down, sir!"

"Impossible!" answered Jeremy, putting on his hat. "It would be like hitting a woman or defenceless child——"

The hat spun from his head and Mr. Armadale's fist thudded into the breast of his bottle-green coat.

"The next will be a facer, sir!" warned Mr. Armadale.

"Regrettable!" muttered Jeremy. "But—if I must——" and he sprang to action.

But if Jeremy was supremely quick, Mr. Armadale was elusive and cunning; thus they feinted a while and danced to and fro in the moonlight while Olivia, seated upon the grassy bank hard by, with one restraining arm about Bill's quivering carcass, watched, chin in hand.

Three times in as many moments Mr. Armadale's fist had got home without a return, but the blows were light and already his breath laboured painfully.

"Oh, demme——" he gasped, "will ye—fight man! Don't—play at it! Hit and—be curst—hit me if—you can!"

"There 's no need!" quoth Jeremy, parrying a lightning blow.

"Is n't there,—B'ged! Then—here's for you——"

A thud of feet, the flash of vicious fist but, ducking the blow, Jeremy struck at last and Mr. Armadale spun round, staggered and fell; thereafter, propped on an elbow, he blinked up to see Jeremy smiling kindly down on him and a trickle of blood upon his cheek.

"Hope I did n't shake you too much, Armadale?" he enquired in a tone that matched his smile.

"Thanks—no!" panted Mr. Armadale. "But—dooced wind—all gone——"

"Yes, naturally!" nodded Jeremy. "You drink."

"D' ye—believe me now, sir?"

"Of course, I did all along—though I must repeat you drink too much. You 'd be a toughish handful otherwise."

"Perfectly true!" murmured Olivia.

"Oh, b'ged and are ye there, madam?" said Mr. Armadale and sitting up, he blinked about him ruefully.

"Sir," said Jeremy, reaching him his hand, "I should like to put the muffles on with you—six weeks from now, say."

"'Pon my soul, but that's dooced handsome of you, Veryan! But why six weeks?"

"You would doubtless be in better condition, sir. Your footwork is admirable."

"Ha, d' ye think so, Veryan, d' ye think so? Eged, sir, such praise from you—demme, but you 're bleeding, sir—your face—must ha' been my ring—I should have removed it, of course. Oh, curse and confound it! Believe me, my dear fellow, I'm very heartily sorry—"

"Merest scratch!" growled Jeremy and, having wiped the cheek in question, reached out his hand to aid the other to rise; grasping which hand, Mr. Armadale got somewhat unsteadily upon his legs. Now standing thus with hands still clasped they looked at each other eye to eye; suddenly Mr. Armadale smiled, whereupon Jeremy's grim lips curved also.

"Veryan, I should like to know you better."

"Then begin by calling me Jeremy."

"And I 'm Richard—Dick, if you will."

"Then, Dick, allow me to present my friend Bill."

"Ha—the dog? But he don't like me, Jeremy."

"He will! Come here, Bill."

The dog approached in his leisurely fashion, looked at Jeremy, surveyed Richard, snuffed at his legs and, having licked the hand outstretched to him, wagged his tail.

And presently they went on again, slow of pace and hushed of voice by reason of the warm, stilly splendour of the night.

Quoth Jeremy, glancing from Richard on his right to Olivia on his left:

"Have you, by chance, ever heard the name of Julius Openshaw?"

"No!" answered Richard.

"Yes!" said Olivia. "I once heard—*him*—mention such a name."

"Who—Revell, d' ye mean?" enquired Richard. "Julius Openshaw—an uncommon name—wait a bit! Yes, b'ged, Olivia's right! I remember now, I remember hearing Revell very heartily curse Julius Openshaw for a scoundrel—what of him, Jeremy?"

"Nothing, except I think Mr. Revell was right."

"Was he? Well, let me tell you, Revell was a villain, a debauched scoundrel, the very prince of blackguards."

"Hush, Richard," sighed his sister, "the night is too beautiful—look!"

They had left the dusty highroad and now trod soft, springy turf, shaded, here and there, by mighty trees of immemorial age, smooth turf that sloped before them down and down to where, bosomed amid leaves, rose an ivied ruin, a jagged outline of crumbling wall with the gracious span of fluted arch, broken column, the delicate tracery of window, yet all etherealised into things of faerie by the magic of the full-orbed moon.

"The old priory!" murmured Olivia. "They say 't is haunted and, on such a night—it may be."

"Tush!" exclaimed Richard. "They do say there was a secret passage from the priory to the house, but no one has ever found it if there is; and there 's Priory Dene yonder, Jeremy, beyond the trees about half a mile away."

"Priory Dene?" enquired Jeremy.

"Olivia's house, and a dem'd dismal, secretive place it is, with unexpected stairs to tumble up or tumble down, with hidden passages and rooms and dark corners everywhere. Olivia, why don't you sell the dem'd place and come up to town?"

"Because I will never run away, Richard."

"You would n't!" said Jeremy. "And here Bill and I wish you good-bye——"

"No such thing!" exclaimed Richard, clasping his arm. "Positively you must accept our hospitality, Jerry—demme, you owe it to me—confound it, man, you knocked me down, remember!"

"Because you are out o' form——"

"So you' ll sleep at Priory Dene to-night."

"I 'm very grateful," answered Jeremy awkwardly, "but——"

"Please do," said Olivia.

"But Mrs. Revell——"

"My name is Olivia."

"Why then, Madam——"

"My name is Olivia."

"Mrs. Olivia, I thank you heartily, but the road calls me."

"But my dear fellow," demurred Richard, "you must sleep somewhere, demme!"

"There is a small tavern——"

"No," said Olivia, "it is mere discomfort and dirt!"

"Well, then, I noticed a very likely barn——"

"Oh, Ged—a barn!" ejaculated Richard. "The man's mad! On my soul, Jeremy, what an uncommon queer fellow you are!"

"No," answered Jeremy, "merely common*place*. Just at present I 'm a tramp and shall live as such. I mean to exchange these clothes for others more tramp-like as soon as possible."

"In heaven's name why? What for? Where's your reason?"

"I 'm my own reason," answered Jeremy, "a careless, rough, very commonplace reason and fit at present for only commonplace things and people. And what so common as the highway? So I 'm for the road."

"The road is dangerous at night," said Olivia, looking from Jeremy's rugged features and squarely powerful figure, round about upon the quiet countryside. "Yes, there is danger sometimes!" she repeated. "And to-night I—have a feeling——" here she shivered suddenly and glanced at Jeremy, sombre and wistful.

"And when my sister has 'feelings,'" added Richard, "well, caution 's the word, my dear fellow. So be advised and come home with us."

"Thank 'ee—no!"

"Then is this indeed good-bye, Jeremy? Oh, the dooce! You 're not a chatterbox and you don't precisely sparkle but b'ged, Veryan, I feel we might have been friends—confound me if I don't!"

"Why, so we may, Dick. I shall come back again, you may rest assured—that is, we shall—Bill and I."

"It 's getting late and you'll have a curst lonely walk of it, Jeremy."

"I' m used to loneliness, Dick, and I like it—besides I have Bill."

So, having shaken hands with brother and sister, Jeremy turned and went his way, now striding apace, now sauntering, his head bowed, himself lost in profound reverie wherein Lucy Western, Veryan, and all within it had no part.

Now as he walked thus, the night's placid calm was vexed by a fitful-breathing air, a wind soft and stealthy that made sudden stir and rustling in hedge and thicket and filled leafy glooms with vague whisperings: a wind this, that seemed to trouble Bill's canine soul strangely, for he halted more than once to snuff uneasily, his scrawny ears a-cock, and once he uttered a short, fierce bark and was sternly bidden to silence, whereupon he slunk into the shadow of the hedge and Jeremy pursued his dreamy way communing with himself, something on this wise:

"Not beautiful according to his preconceived ideas, not in the least—and yet! A woman's eyes should be a limpid blue and her hair golden or brown and with a curl in it—instead of black and lankly smooth as an Indian's—and yet! To be sure the voice was beautiful, so mellow and richly soft with a wistful note in it that might haunt a man. . . . Indeed such voice might hold a magic——"

A sudden wind gust seemed to smite the near-by hedge to violent rustling—a savage snarl from Bill—and glancing up, Jeremy saw a shadow upon the white dust of the road before him, a black, monstrous shape hugely squat and menacing, and he whirled to see the moon as it were split asunder, riven to fragments—and the whole firmament go out in roaring flame.

## CHAPTER X

### HOW JEREMY CAME UP OUT OF THE DARK AND FOUND A GREAT LIGHT

A DREADFUL stillness. An awful darkness that throbbed—no, this throbbing was in his brain—or was it his heart?

Slowly upon the pervading quiet grew a whisper of sound, a low whimpering; something touched him, something clammy and cold, yet in this touch he somehow sensed a world of friendliness and comfort; the light gradually increased (or his sight grew less misty) enough to show him eyes, very round and bright and wistful, set in an ugly, shaggy head, a head which bowed itself and bored at him to thrust cold nose beneath his nerveless hand—and after many futile efforts, he contrived to lift this hand sufficiently to pull feebly at a scrawny ear—and a voice very faint and seemingly far away muttered:

"Bill!"

At which murmur, faint though it was, the whimper changed to a whine of ecstasy and this, in turn, to a ringing, joyous bark.

And thus slowly Jeremy's consciousness returned from the dark unknown to find himself lying half-buried among dried twigs and withered leaves that rustled to his least movement.

He lay in a dim twilight, though somewhere above him was a radiance he thought must be sunshine; yet this light was enough to show him crumbling walls patched with moss and lichen, and the great dog crouched near by, watching him eager-eyed, yet turning, now and then, to lick at an ugly wound in his flank.

"Oho, Bill," sighed Jeremy at length, "so they got you too, did they! 'What enemy hath done this thing?' Poor old Bill! No, I can't get up, Bill—B'ged, Bill, I can't even pat you. I'm floored, lad—knocked completely out o' time, Bill!"

And closing his eyes, Jeremy sighed and sank down again into black nothingness.

When next he awoke it was to a sense of bitter thirst and of pain that grew, racking him with every breath but, worst of all, Bill was gone; turn his eyes where he would he could see nothing of that gaunt, shaggy form, that wistful-eyed, ugly head.

"Bill!" he whispered. "Oh, Bill—oh, lad!"

But he heard only the leafy rustle as he strove vainly to raise himself—and his thirst was agonising—and the pain. And Bill had deserted him! Thus Jeremy, racked with pain and parched with raging thirst, groaned and closed his smarting eyes; but the sob that shook him was for the dog's desertion.

And now he was beset and haunted by visions and dreams, some evil and some beyond thought wonderful: he was indeed Veryan of Veryan, rough and uncouth no longer but of patrician stateliness, a potent, impressive personality of vast achievement. No longer the solitary wayfarer but blessed with friendship and an infinite love.

"Jeremy—speak to me—speak to me! Oh, God, he's dead!"

"Not I!" whispered Jeremy and felt his heavy head lifted for him to tender pillow, and opening his eyes, beheld a tress of hair unwontedly near—and this was black hair which, though very straight, looked very smooth and silky. So he stared at this glossy tress and wished greatly that he might touch it but, knowing this beyond his strength, sighed plaintively and closed his eyes.

And now the voice came again, stirring memory, a voice of that soft richness called contralto:

"Can you move?"

"Afraid not!" he whispered. "Been lying—and lying—for days—can you get me—water? Why, here's Bill—the old lad—he was hurt too——"

"Hush!—Drink this!" said the voice.

Jeremy drank and closed his eyes in an ecstasy. "Thanks!" he gasped. "Oh, my—my—blessed angel!" And lifting drowsy lids, he looked up into the face so near his—and—yes, her brows were thick, but beautifully, proudly arched, and the eyes beneath them, so dark, so deep, so heavily-lashed—so ineffably tender and pitiful.

"My angel—of mercy!" he sighed.

"Are you stronger now?"

"Yes—brandy and water—was n't it?"

"Yes, I came prepared—can you, dare you move?"

"For you, angel, yes."

With valiant effort and her strong supporting arm, he contrived to sit up; but the universe swung and swayed about him, and through enveloping darkness he whispered brokenly:

"I'm—going again—damnation—Hold me, angel! Hold me fast—beside you—Olivia——" But with the word, his head rolled upon her bosom. "I can't," he muttered, "if I 'm going—I shan't mind if—you will hold me—in your arms—angel——"

And, closing his eyes, Jeremy sank back into those terrific deeps, all unconscious of the tears that fell so fast upon his blood-bespattered brow.

* * * * *

When next Jeremy awoke it was to behold snowy, lace-edged sheet, satin quilt and silken bed hangings, beyond which he caught a glimpse of a chamber whose dainty luxuriance smote him; hereupon a hoarse voice croaked:

"This is dam' preposterous!"

At this, the curtain was drawn aside and Mr. Armadale's face looked down at him; for it seemed the croaking voice was his own.

"What, are you awake at last, Jeremy? B'ged, but this beats everything, demme if it don't!"

"Laces!" croaked Jeremy bitterly. "Frills and fluffs—what 's it all mean?"

"Oh, my dear old fellow," answered Richard gently, "ha' you forgot? Some dem'd scoundrel laid you out. Olivia found you lying in the ruined priory. Your dog Bill showed her the way. And now here you are safe and sound in bed—Olivia's bed. B'ged, Jerry, it has been touch and go with you—you very nearly hopped the twig, my dear fellow."

"Olivia's bed?" repeated Jeremy. "That should account for the fluffs and frills."

"To be sure—she 's nursed you night and day when we thought you a 'goner'—would n't trust the nurses—used to sleep in the chair here and b'ged seemed to thrive on it—women are queer creatures!"

"Night and day!" echoed Jeremy. "Pray how long have I been here then?"

"Ten—no, eleven days."

"Good Lord!" exclaimed Jeremy.

"Did you see anything of the dem'd rascals who attacked you?"

"No, they struck from behind, Dick—and eleven days, is it!"

"Well, the affair has raised the devil of a rumpus; y' see you 're a dooced important person—we 've had runners and law officers from London, Lewes, and God knows where, and all to no purpose!"

"Does my—kinsman, Sir James, know?"

"To be sure! The whole country knows. Your uncle was for removing you to Veryan but Olivia would n't permit; demme, sir, not she; and Doctor Wilbraham vowed 't would be murder to attempt it."

"Murder?" croaked Jeremy. "Ha!"

"Sir James drove here yesterday with Arthur to learn how you did, and to-day a Mr. O'Leary called, an Irishman, Jerry, and most dooced Irish! An old friend of your uncle's and knows you well, it seems?"

"Since he camped at Veryan a year ago!"

"Talked as if he 'd known you all your life."

"He talks!" croaked Jeremy in something approaching a growl.

"Olivia's with him now. Day nurse is out, night nurse is asleep, that 's why I 'm here and—curse it, you 're looking a bit flushed, a trifle glittery in the eye, Jeremy, and Olivia's bound to blame me! So close your peepers, old fellow, and try to sleep."

"No!" croaked Jeremy. "I want to get up!"

"Oh, dooce take and confound everything—impossible!"

"Where are my clothes?"

"Ged knows!"

"Then if you are friend o' mine—find 'em!"

"But, Lord love you, man, you couldn't walk!"

"I mean to try——"

But at this moment the door was opened gently, Jeremy heard the soft rhythmic whisper of draperies and Olivia stood looking at him.

"Richard," she murmured reproachfully, "why did n't you fetch me?"

"'Pon my soul, I was just about to—but you see, Olivia, my dear, he positively demands to get up, b'ged!"

At this a cool hand laid itself upon Jeremy's brow; slim but imperious fingers clasped his wrist.

"You are a little feverish, Mr. Jeremy," said she, smoothing the hair above his bandages. "Thank God you are better, but you must sleep again; pray close your eyes."

"No!" said Jeremy and opened them their fullest to stare up at her defiantly. "I desire my clothes, Mrs. Olivia!"

Here, endeavouring to sit up, he found it a labour beyond his strength, and lying back on the pillows, glanced up into the dark eyes above him with fretful amazement.

"You have been very ill, Mr. Jeremy," said she gently; "close your eyes and go to sleep again—sleep just now is life to you." And because of his weakness, and the touch of that so soft yet so imperious hand, what could he do but obey?

And now ensued a time of uneasy slumber and drowsy wakings within a world peopled by vague shapes as: first, nurses two, the one large of person and lethargic who snored gently through the midnight hours; the other a small energetic creature who sewed perpetually or clicked knitting needles. Second, a diminutive gentleman with enormous fob seals that jangled, and a mild face whose meekness was enhanced by a pair of the most ferocious whiskers. Thirdly, a Shadow monstrous and ever threatening, always behind him just out of eyeshot; this it was that most troubled his slumbers and haunted his wakings—this squat, black shadow with monstrous arm upraised to smite him down, as he had seen it for one brief moment upon the white dust of the road.

Waking one day with the horror of it, he found Olivia bending over him, anxious-eyed:

"What is it?" she whispered.

"The shadow!" he muttered, "The shadow of—the thing—as I saw it that night—I dream it always behind me—waiting to—strike again——"

"There, there!" she murmured, soothing him like a frightened child. "You are safe here, quite safe!"

"Yes!" he muttered. "Yes—you are here—my angel."

But upon one evening he awoke to see the open window all glorious with sunset, to breathe an air fragrant with flowers from the garden below whence rose the rich, liquid notes of a blackbird; and drinking deep of this sweet air, hearkening to the birds' joyous piping, Jeremy felt himself thoroughly alive again. Now suddenly he became aware of another sound and lifting himself on an elbow (with scarce an effort) he beheld Olivia, her face hidden, her shapely form bowed across a small writing table in the abandonment of her woe like a grieving goddess.

"Olivia?" said he; and his voice was no longer faint and far away. "Olivia!"

At this she started and raised her head and her eyes were bright and her lips smiling despite her tears.

"Oh, but you are better!" cried she, and rising with the supple ease which had in it something of the animal, she crossed to the bed and laid her hand upon brow and pulse. "Yes, you are better!"

"Much!" he answered. "Thanks to you. But why——"

"And Doctor Wilbraham!" she added.

"Tush! But for you I should be dead! But why were you——"

"And Bill!" said she. "Don't forget your friend Bill—'t was he came and led me to you, and himself all bleeding."

"Ay, to be sure, the old lad! How is he?"

"I have bathed and combed him until he begins to look—something like a dog," she smiled.

"Like half a dozen dogs, rather. But tell me——"

"Would you like to see him?"

"Greatly—but not now! Pray sit down—no, not on the chair, here on the bed! Now, tell me why you were crying?"

"Richard has left me," she answered softly, "gone back to London, back to the evil which is wrecking him—body and soul!"

"You mean the Chevalier de Ravenac!"

"Yes!" she answered. "Yes!"

"And I lie here like an accursed log!" said Jeremy bitterly.

"Hush!" she commanded. "Oh, pray don't excite yourself! I should not have told you yet—pray hush, Mr. Jeremy!"

"I 'll not hush!" he retorted. "How can I! And pray don't mister me!"

"There, there! Pray compose yourself! Thank heaven nurse will be here in a minute——"

"I 'll not see her! Send her away——"

"But it 's time for your arrowroot——"

"Arrowroot!" snarled Jeremy. "I 'll not touch it!—I want steaks! I could eat beef—roast, with parsnips——"

"So you shall—next week, sir!"

"But I 'm hungry—famished!" he wailed.

"Splendid!" said Olivia, her eyes glowing—Here a knock at the door and the small nurse entered, bearing a tray.

"The arrer root, mem!" said she.

"Throw it away!" growled Jeremy.

"Give it to me, nurse!" said Olivia. "Thank you. You may go!"

"The pore young gentleman's a bit obstropolous to-day, mem, the dear soul, but it 's a good sign, mem!" saying which the small nurse curtseyed energetically and departed; then Olivia, seating herself upon the bed again with the utmost determination, ministered to him herself, whereupon, after divers moans and growls, Jeremy swallowed the decoction and lay back on the pillows, sighing like the martyr he knew himself to be.

"And now, tell me about Richard!" he commanded.

Olivia set by the tray, smoothed sheet and pillow and sat looking at Jeremy a little dubiously.

"First of all you must not blame Richard!" said she.

"Not I!"

"You see it is very quiet here at Priory Dene, for as I told you, no one ever calls—and Richard is fond of society, which is only right and natural, is n't it?"

"I suppose so!" growled Jeremy.

"And so, being deprived of all society here he seeks it in town——"

"And leaves you to solitude!" growled Jeremy.

"Pray don't interrupt me, Mr. Veryan!"

"Very well, Mrs. Revell!"

"The Chevalier de Ravenac is a great personage in London, a friend of the Prince, a man of fashion and a duellist and consequently is much sought after—especially by young men."

"Ha—a duellist?" repeated Jeremy.

"He is reputed a deadly shot—and has killed men——"

"Then 't is time some one winged him!" growled Jeremy.

"Don't—ah, don't talk so!"

"Very well," said Jeremy, "though 't is true enough! And Richard admires him?"

"Yes, poor boy. He has singled out Richard from the many because he is my brother!"

"Ah!" growled Jeremy, clenching pallid fist.

"The Chevalier knows I hate him—so he means to ruin my Richard and break my heart—unless——"

"Unless?" growled Jeremy.

"I marry him——"

"Did the scoundrel tell you this?"

"Not in so many words, but oh, I know—I am sure!"

"You sacrificed yourself for Richard once; well now, it were damnable folly to do it twice!"

"Never—oh, never again!" she exclaimed, with a sudden, passionate gesture.

"I wonder?" said Jeremy, scowling at her averted face.

"So do I!" she murmured. "Richard is dearer to me than myself! And yet——"

"No man is worthy such frightful sacrifice!"

"He is my brother!"

"No matter!" growled Jeremy. "No matter! We must each of us work out our own salvation or be deservedly damned——"

"Hush, Mr. Veryan."

"Very well—only pray don't mister me! To marry De Ravenac would mean misery and degradation—and how should this help your brother? Absurd! Preposterous! Utterly damnable! Not to be thought of!"

"The Chevalier has such influence with him and I—I am powerless! Richard needs a friend—a strong man, brave and determined. This was why I had hoped—you might prove such a friend."

"Was the Chevalier acquainted with the man Revell?"

"It was the Chevalier who introduced him to Richard."

"Hum!" quoth Jeremy and stared up at the silken bed tester so long that at last she must needs question him; whereupon he smiled up into her wistful eyes, though his jutting brows were knit a little grimly.

"I was thinking," he answered, passing thin fingers across stubby chin, "that I must look a gruesome object with all these bristles."

Suddenly from the garden below rose a loud bark, a deep, harsh note with a fierce ring in it.

"Bill!" said Jeremy.

"A visitor!" nodded Olivia. "And Bill does n't sound pleased."

In due season was a tap on the door and the demure and solemn Bryant appeared to announce:

"Mr. Terence O'Leary waits below, madam."

Olivia glanced enquiringly at Jeremy who frowned and nodded.

"Ask Mr. O'Leary to step upstairs, Bryant," said she.

"Now I wonder," said Jeremy as the door closed, "I wonder what he wants?"

A light-treading, vigorous foot upon the stair, a soft knock upon the door and Terence O'Leary entered, handsome, debonair and radiating clean health and smiling good-fellowship. Softly he closed the door, and softly he advanced, his look, his voice, his every gesture admirably suited to a sick chamber, a smile of eager welcome for Jeremy, a look of admiration tempered with gentle deference for Olivia.

"Ah, Mrs. Revell," said he gently, as he bent to kiss her hand, "shure 't is a deloight to the eyes y' are. Faith an' indade, me dear soul, compared wi' ye'self Juno was an ox and Vanus a blowsy hoyden! Your humblest servant, mam! And Jerry, so thin and wasted—och me dear lad, it wrings me heart!" And taking Jeremy's wasted fingers he clasped them gently between his two warm, vital palms, while his kindly blue eyes were the brighter for the tears that suffused them. "'Tis moighty near dith ye were, they tell me, Jerry! But ye 're going to get well again——"

"I am!" said Jeremy grimly.

"And yet not too soon, I 'll wager! Eh, Jerry—ha, ha!"

"Why not?"

"B'ged, me bhoy, but is n't it lucky y' are to have a goddess to nurse ye! The hand o' lovely woman to soothe our fevered brows, beauty's eyes to watch o'er our ristless slumbers, her tinder prisence——"

"I intend to get up to-morrow!" quoth Jeremy, scowling.

"If Doctor Wilbraham permits!" said Olivia.

"I'm quite strong enough——"

"Faix an' so y' are, me bhoy, strong enough to appreciate the true beauty of a lovely woman's tinder care——"

"To-morrow I get up!" growled Jeremy.

"And shure that 'll mane going to bed again!" laughed Mr. O'Leary. "But how did it happen, me poor bhoy?"

"Somebody struck me down and threw me into the ruined priory."

"The distardly murtherin' villains!"

"Singular number, sir!" said Jeremy. "There was but one."

"Aha, did ye see him, Jiremy?"

"Not a glimpse."

"Bad cess to it!" exclaimed Mr. O'Leary with despairing gesture. "If yez had glimpsed him—even his hand or foot——"

"I saw his shadow."

"An' did ye so, Jirry? What of it?"

"It has haunted me ever since."

"And small wonder! Och, me poor bhoy! And have you anny idea what like the villain was—anny suspicions?"

"Plenty!"

"On me soul now, ye surprise me!"

"Do I, Terence?"

"Faith, Jiremy, 't is a charmed loife ye bear!"

"I have thought so—of late. As it is, I should most surely be dead but for Mrs. Revell—she rescued me!"

"B'ged an' 't was wise ye were to choose such a rescuer."

"But indeed," said Olivia, smiling at Mr. O'Leary's courtly bow, "Bill was the real rescuer."

"Bill?" repeated Mr. O'Leary. "Thin I must beg the honour of meeting and thanking him."

"Bill is a dog," Olivia explained.

"Ha, a dog, d' ye say? Shure ye don't mane the ugly blackguard that showed his fangs at me, downstairs?"

"To be sure he is not very handsome," Olivia admitted. "But he makes up for that in fidelity and affection—'t was he led me to poor Mr. Jeremy in time to save his life; indeed but for Bill, I fear——"

"Pray," said Jeremy, "how is Sir James?"

"Sir James?" repeated Mr. O'Leary, his eyes suddenly intent. "Shure your uncle is well, though anxious on your account when last I saw him, but I 've been in London for a few days, d' ye see."

"London?" said Jeremy thoughtfully. "Hum! D' ye happen to know the Chevalier de Ravenac?"

"Indade an' I do!" answered Mr. O'Leary, with a bright nod. "We travelled together in the West Indies, years ago—and we quarrelled and fought together too! But why d' ye ask—have you met him?"

"The other night!" answered Jeremy.

"What—hereabouts? De Ravenac?"

"In this house!"

"The divil! Then perhaps ye 'll know if he still has his nigger servant—a great, black fellow as big as my Pompey."

"What, has he a negro servant too?"

"Indade and he has, me bhoy—or did have. But 't is long since we met, which is just as well, for, as I say, we quarrelled and nothing would do but we must take a pop at each other. Well, I foired first and hit him in the hat, bad cess to it! 'O'Leary!' says he, 'ye 're a careless divil and life or dith is all wan to ye now. I 'll reserve my shot!' says he, 'until loife manes more to yez, and I 'll be happy to kill ye then at me own convenience!' says he. A merciless enemy is De Ravenac."

"Hum!" quoth Jeremy. "So I judge!"

"And a crack shot, Jirry, with either hand—dith sits in the crook of his fingers! Which reminds me—they do say you 're gifted that way, me bhoy?"

"I can shoot a bit!" nodded Jeremy.

"At a mark, Jirry?"

"At a mark, yes."

"Good! But, b'ged, 't is a different matter whin ye 're aiming at a man—a man who 's aiming at you! The Chevalier has fought often, I belave, and shot three men stone dead to my knowledge——"

"Horrible!" exclaimed Olivia.

"Arrah now—forgive me, me dear, swate creature! 'T is me tongue run away wi' me——"

Suddenly from regions below came a fierce baying, a loud and furious clamour followed by the slam of a door; hurried feet sped up the stair without, to the accompaniment of a voice woefully uplifted.

"Oh, Massah Terence—Massah Terence, for de lub of Gawd!"

Up started Mr. O'Leary, but in that moment Olivia had crossed to the door and opened it. Upon the threshold stood Pompey, the gigantic Negro, his huge frame shaking, his eyes rolling wildly, his mouth agape.

"Oh, Massah—Terence," he gasped. "Oh, Massah, a hugeous, big, monstrodious an'mal go for bite poor Pompey to deaf——"

"And serve ye right, ye black omadhaun!" exclaimed his master. "Pray forgive this black scoundrel's intrusion, me dearest Mrs. Revell——"

"Indeed," said Olivia, shaking her head, "I fear the dog is to blame!—I never heard him so fierce! Something has driven him wild . . . Oh, hark!" And truly the dog still raved and clamoured fiercely as ever.

"Shure an' 't is mad he sounds!" nodded Mr. O'Leary, taking up his heavy cane and turning towards the door. "If you go down to the brute I go with you, me dear soul."

"No, no," answered Olivia, "I can manage him, I can quiet him, I 'm sure—and much better alone." So saying she hurried away; whereupon Mr. O'Leary turned upon the trembling Pompey who seemed still overcome with terror, for his white teeth chattered and his eyes rolled, staring wildly here and there about the luxurious chamber.

"Well, ye sooty scoundrel, ye black slumgullion, an don't yez see Mr. Jiremy?"

"Yassuh, yassuh! Pompey berry glad to see Massah Jeremy ain't no corpse——"

"Corpse is ut!" exclaimed Mr. O'Leary in horrified accents. "An' will ye talk so in a sick chamber, ye benighted haythin? The curse o' Cromwell on y'r black carcass! Out with ye——"

"Wait!" said Jeremy. "Pompey meant well enough. And I want to know what he did to anger the dog——"

"Nuthin', Massah Jeremy! Pompey him talk to Massah Bryan'—den come de great, big debbil dog an' go for bite poor Pompey—so Pompey run berry momentously quick an' Massah Bryan cotched hold o' de dog."

"Hum!" said Jeremy, surveying the Negro languidly from his pillow. "It seems my dog objects to you—I wonder why?"

"Shure, Jiremy, 't will be by raison of his black nigger's hoide!"

"Ha!" mused Jeremy. "Have you ever seen the dog before, Pompey?"

"Nebber, suh! Nebber in all ma whole entire life, suh!"

"And now—be off!" said his master. "Get down to the stable yard and wait me there. Come, away wid ye!" And Mr. O'Leary advanced, cane a-flourish, whereupon the big Negro cowered, whimpered and vanished.

"A choild o' Nature, Jerry!" smiled Mr. O'Leary. "Strong as sin, ugly as the devil, and harmless as a suckling dove!"

"Hum!" quoth Jeremy for the third time, while Mr. O'Leary, laying by his cane, crossed to the open casement and leaned there, a stalwart, graceful figure, the sun making a glory of his blond hair.

"Faix, but 't is the illigant quarters ye have here, Jeremy," said he, surveying the dainty chamber with appreciative eye.

"The sooner I 'm out of it the better!" growled Jeremy.

"And a bewitching, handsome, enticing craythure to nurse ye, Jerry, young, rich, beautiful and—a widdy! And what could ye desire more?"

"Tush!" growled Jeremy.

"Now if she should fall in love wi' you——"

"She won't!" said Jeremy.

"Or you wid her, me bhoy——"

"Bah!" growled Jeremy.

"What? D'ye tell me ye 're not a throifle smitten already, me bhoy?"

"I do!" growled Jeremy. "Preposterous—damn ridiculous and curst presumptuous!"

"Aha!" laughed Mr. O'Leary merrily, but with eyes suddenly keen. "Methinks ye do protest too much!" Here he glanced out of the window. "And yet," he continued, "if 't is her riputation balks ye—what o' that, me bhoy? She 's young, beautiful, wealthy,—'t is hersilf that matters, not her riputation——"

"The devil!" exclaimed Jeremy. "O'Leary, what are you saying? I 'll thank you not to put words in my mouth!"

"No, no, Jirry; no, no! 'T is all me accursed tongue, d' ye see? Forgive me, lad——"

"Not I!" growled Jeremy, and rang the bell.

"What, have I offended yez, me dear bhoy?"

"'T is no matter! But I suspect you have wounded her!"

"The holy saints forbid!"

"Pray," said Jeremy to the small nurse who answered the bell, "ask Mrs. Revell to be good enough to come here."

"Me poor Jiremy!" sighed Mr. O'Leary as the nurse departed, "'t is moighty quick y' are to quarrel wid your frind Tirence—oh, wirra! And arl I meant was——"

"No matter!" quoth Jeremy.

"All your poor Tirence meant was that I 'd try me fortune wid the lovely Olivia if I were yoursilf——"

"But you 're not!" growled Jeremy.

"Well, well!" sighed his companion gently. "If ye should win her 't is mesilf will be foremost to wish ye joy o' such a charming conquist——"

Almost as he spoke, Olivia appeared on the threshold where she paused to glance enquiringly from one to the other.

"You want me, Mr. Jeremy?"

"You were in the garden, I think?" he demanded.

"Yes."

"Then of course you heard Mr. O'Leary mention the word 'reputation'?"

"Yes."

"Mr. O'Leary will perhaps oblige me by explaining how he came to mention it."

"No, no, Jirry!" laughed Mr. O'Leary, taking up his cane. "No, no, me dear bhoy! Explanations are awkward and beyond poor Tirence entoirly—so I'll run off and lave ye to do your own explaining, b'ged! Au revoir, Mrs. Revell—heaven bless ye, my dear soul! Good-bye, Jiremy, I'll call again in a day or so——"

"Then you won't find me!"

"No?"

"No! Mrs. Revell is dismissing the nurses to-day——"

"Am I?" said she.

"You are! I intend to be gone very soon."

"Why then, I must trust to luck. Good-bye, Jirry, until we meet again. Think a troifle more koindly o' your poor Tirence—Good-bye, me dear bhoy!" And crossing to the door he paused there to smile a little wistfully and went away, closing the door softly behind him.

"And what," enquired Jeremy suddenly, "what do you think of him, Olivia?"

"I like him—I think!" she answered. "His courtly manners, his gentleness, his warm-hearted kindliness—and yet——"

"Exactly!" said Jeremy and stared up at the silken canopy above his head.

"Well?" she enquired at last.

"Well?" he repeated.

"You wished to explain something, I think?"

"The word 'reputation'!" said he.

"Yes," she nodded.

"Yes!" he growled.

"Well?" she enquired again.

Now meeting the wistful directness of her gaze he hesitated and finding himself at sudden loss, was silent.

"Well?" she persisted.

For a moment Jeremy scowled at the be-laced sheet then, lifting his head, scowled at her.

"Will you marry me?" he demanded.

At this she started and gazed at him with dilating eyes, while up from chin to brow surged a wave of hot colour.

"Marry you?" she repeated, a little breathlessly; then turning suddenly, she stared out of the window for a long minute. "No!" she answered at last. "Certainly not!"

"Ha!" quoth Jeremy and scowled at the sheet again. "I suppose I should have waited until I was shaved!"

"It would have made no difference," she answered.

"No, I suppose not!" he muttered. "I have n't annoyed you, I hope?"

"You have honoured me!" she answered softly. "I am grateful."

"Is there any other man?" he enquired with a sudden new diffidence.

"Heaven forbid!" she answered.

"And I," said Jeremy, scowling up at the canopy blacker than ever, "I 'm not the sort to attract a woman, I know—not the proper cut for a lover or lady's man and never expected or meant to be one. But I am! I 've told you! You 've said 'no' of course and there 's an end on 't and—oh, dammit!" Jeremy turned and scowled at the wall.

And in that moment she was beside him, bending above him, her hand upon his bristly cheek, her voice murmurous in his ear.

"Foolish, fretful boy! Wait—wait until you are well again." Then he turned, eager to clasp that soft, slim hand, but she fled from him across the room and on her cheek a glow and in her eyes a light he had never beheld until now.

"Olivia!" said he. "What do you mean——"

And then was a loud rap on the door and Doctor Wilbraham entered, his meek face peering forth of his enormous whiskers, his fob seals jingling as he tripped towards the bed.

"Well, sir," he enquired, "and how are we to-day?"

"You should know that!" growled Jeremy.

"We are better!" nodded the doctor. "We are distinctly better, I perceive. Our fever is abated though our pulse—ha—hum! A leetle too rapid."

"I could eat a large steak!" quoth Jeremy.

"Good! We may indulge ourselves with beef tea and a rusk, and perhaps a fragment of fish. We have slept well, I trust!"

"I've done little else!" sighed Jeremy.

"Good again! We may discourage the sedative, my dear Mrs. Revell."

"To-morrow, sir," said Jeremy, "I mean to get up."

"Ha-humph!" quoth the little doctor. "We may think about it in a day or so, perhaps. We must not hurry ourselves, my dear sir. We must be patient! We must allow Dame Nature every chance. We have taken our medicine regularly, my dear madam?"

"Yes, Doctor."

"Then in a day or so—say a week, sir, we may venture to get out of bed——"

"A week," snorted Jeremy.

"A week, sir! Our legs will wobble and our back feel like a rush. But, by perseverance, sir, we shall succeed. We shall acquire strength with effort. Effort is life, sir, and vice versa. Ha-humph! We need patience and effort, sir——"

"And food!" added Jeremy. "At once, sir! Roast beef and parsnips buttered——"

"Fish, my dear young sir, fish boiled in milk, and a rusk! Mr. Veryan, I congratulate you 'pon a marvellous recovery—our physique, sir, is phenomenal, our vitality stupendous; but for this we were a corpse—days ago. Good day, sir! Patience, sir, remember patience is a virtue! Mrs. Revell, mam, I beg a word with you." So saying, the little doctor bustled and jingled away with her and Jeremy was left to scowl up at the bed canopy, but presently, remembering the glow on Olivia's cheek, the glory in her eyes, he smiled and turned to look at the radiant sunshine pouring in at the open lattice.

And from this moment, Jeremy mended apace.

But——

## CHAPTER XI

### DESCRIBING A HORROR BY NIGHT, WITH PARTICULARS OF A GREAT GLORY BY DAY

He was lying, gagged and bound cruelly, hand and foot, in a ruined cottage for, through holes in rotting thatch, he could see stars and a moon which filled the place with ghastly light. And he was sick with terror and an ever-growing dreadful expectancy, though of what, he but vaguely knew. Surely it was not the dismal aspect of the place wherein he lay; nor the great rats that skipped and darted all about him, pausing now and then to peer at him with small, evil eyes? Nor was it the shadows that hemmed him in—yet stay! What shadow was yonder, vast and squat and black, looming above him with spectral giant arm upraised to smite him down, that crept towards him near and ever nearer? A shape beyond words hideous and yet somehow vaguely familiar.

Jeremy awoke and, glancing towards the window, saw the dim radiance of a clouded moon, a radiance which, as he gazed, was suddenly blotted out by a stealthy, creeping, slow-moving something—a monstrous head, gigantic shoulders—and a face ghastly beyond description—a flat, white face having no features except eyes that glared within black, cavernous sockets. Jeremy lay frozen with horror as slowly, stealthily, this hateful thing crept towards him—to turn suddenly and crouch, for upon the door was a soft beating, a loud snuffle, the scratch of furious claws, a whimper changing to ferocious growl.

Jeremy groaned and, breaking the spell which had numbed his faculties, sat up in bed and stared about the great, shadowy chamber but saw nothing and heard nothing save the furious growling and scratching at the door. So out of bed he slipped and, stumbling across the room, opened the door and in leapt Bill, a dim-seen, fierce creature but who now, beholding Jeremy, forgot all else in the world and fawned upon him, licking his hands, his face, and whining for pure joy.

Jeremy locked the door and having quieted Bill's exuberance, lighted a candle and with the dog beside him, began a very thorough and systematic examination of the room, this wide and lofty bedchamber that was hers.

To and fro they quested together, the dog and the man, Bill snuffling here and there suspiciously and growling ever and anon; Jeremy scanning every crack and crevice in floor and ceiling, tapping gently at each and every individual panel of the walls, peering high and low—and all to no purpose.

"A dream, Bill!" said he at last, setting down the candle and seating himself wearily upon the bed. "Yes, it must ha' been a dream, my chap! And yet—if so, why were you in such alarm? Hum! I 'll swear there 's no sliding panel here, Bill! And could any one or anything get in here? This is her bedroom, Bill, d' ye see! And even supposing something did or could—what was it? A dream, Bill—it must have been! What, you don't agree? But, my chap, I tell you it must ha' been—Good Lord, you don't think she 'd sleep in a room that any one could steal into, do you? Of course she would n't—at least—not knowingly—Hum! Supposing, then, it was not a dream! Supposing—oh, Bill—the devil! We must make very sure, my fellow; let 's try again."

Once more dog and man fell to their search, once more Jeremy made a complete circuit of the room, tapping softly at every panel, and once more stood doubtful and puzzled, when Bill, crouching before the hearth, growled suddenly. So thither went Jeremy, candle in hand; thus he presently espied that which chilled him, yet this is no more than a thin sprinkling of soot upon the hearthstone. Stooping with candle before him, Jeremy peered up the wide chimney and saw that which resolved his doubts, once and for all.

"You were right, Bill!" said he, scowling at the candle flame, his eyes very bright, his lips grimmer than usual. "Here was no dream! No, nor ghost, either! To-night, but for you, Bill . . . Ay, but for you, the Veryan heritage would ha' passed from one who don't care a jot for it, to—one who does! Battle, Murder, and Sudden Death, Bill! 'T is the High Adventure, my chap, and what more could we ask, you and I? . . . If they can win—let 'em! Meantime, let us sleep; to-morrow we'll enquire into matters—thoroughly, Bill, for her sake."

Next morning Jeremy awoke late and, learning that Olivia was out for her morning gallop, summoned Bryant, who presented himself in due season, grave, sedate and imperturbable as ever.

"Bryant, I think you were a sailor once," said Jeremy, "one of Nelson's men?"

"I had that honour, sir."

"Consequently you can climb?"

"Climb, sir?" repeated Bryant pensively. "It all depends, Mr. Veryan. Climb what, may I venture to ask?"

"Say, a chimney."

"A chimney!" murmured Bryant, his tone as expressionless, his air as immutably calm as usual, though Jeremy fancied his eyebrows twitched. "Why, Mr. Veryan, sir, I might climb a chimney if necessary, though, not being a sweep, sir——"

"By means of an iron ladder affixed to the wall, Bryant. There's such a ladder in the chimney yonder."

"Dear me, sir!" ejaculated Bryant. "I know there are some secret passages in this old place but I did n't know of this——"

"Go and look at it!" Bryant obeyed. "Well, what d' ye think of it? Did you notice anything?"

"Why, sir—it almost looks as if somebody——"

"Exactly!" nodded Jeremy. "Somebody did—last night! This is Mrs. Revell's bedchamber, is n't it?"

"In summer, sir. In the winter she generally occupies 'The Queen's Chamber' on the other wing——"

"But she sleeps here in summer?"

"Yes, sir."

"Hum!" quoth Jeremy. "You and I are going to climb that chimney and explore—you see the necessity, Bryant?"

"I do, sir! But are you quite strong enough?"

"Quite! Pray bring my clothes. And get candles—a lantern—and—yes, hammer and nails—the longest you can find."

"Very well, sir."

Jeremy was dressed when Bryant returned with the articles in question; gravely he lighted the lantern and gravely surveyed Jeremy's grim visage.

"And are you quite well enough, sir, to climb?"

"Of course!" answered Jeremy. "Let us hurry and be done before Mrs. Revell returns."

So together they stooped and entered the wide chimney where the light showed them four stout iron stanchions socketed into the wall, one above another.

"By your leave, sir!" said Bryant, and swung himself nimbly up to an opening in the masonry of the chimney whence he stooped to reach a powerful hand down to Jeremy, who, scrambling up in turn, found himself in a narrow passage thick-carpeted with the dust of years; but upon this dust, plain to be seen, were the marks of feet, while here and there gleamed a spot of congealed tallow.

"Dear me!" murmured Bryant, stooping the better to examine these betraying splashes. "These look very recent, sir."

"They are!" growled Jeremy. "Come on!"

The passage led them round sharp corners, up sudden steps and down again, sometimes so narrow that they must edge themselves along sideways; they peered into unexpected recesses and odd-shaped holes and corners and once, opening a small, complaining door, they beheld a tiny panelled chamber where stood rotting a bedstead, its mouldering blankets wild-tossed and thick with the dust of immemorial years. Closing this door, Jeremy hurried on again until they reached yet another door, but vastly different this, being of stout oak reinforced with rusty iron bands; and this door gaped upon another wider passage, beholding which Bryant spoke.

"Sir, this is the passage your dog Bill found, the passage as I carried you along; it leads from the ruined abbey to the secret panel in the morning room."

"Then we 've come far enough; this is what I want!"

So saying, Jeremy closed the heavy door, shot the bolts and turned to his companion.

"Hammer and nails!" said he.

Then, while Bryant held the lantern, Jeremy nailed up this door very securely.

"Ha!" quoth he, as he drove the last nail. "Nothing less than a battering-ram will open it now. She may sleep secure!"

"She may, sir!" murmured Bryant. "And I keep my old cutlass to hand with a brace o' pistols always loaded!"

"Excellent!" nodded Jeremy. "And now let 's get into the clean daylight!"

Back in his bedchamber Jeremy glanced from his own dusty garments to Bryant's serene, smudged face, and laughed.

"Bryant," he enquired, "do you ever smile?"

"Frequently, sir."

"Then look at me and, for heaven's sake—laugh, man!"

Hereupon Bryant's neat whiskers twitched and turning away, he emitted a discreet chuckle.

"Fair, Bryant!" nodded Jeremy. "Some day I hope to hear you laugh—properly. Now could you find me the wherewithal to shave?"

"Cer-tainly, sir. Pray follow me, Mr. Veryan."

Thus after some while, new-shaven and feeling himself immensely the better therefor, Jeremy stepped out into the sunshine and following shady walks, presently found himself before a little arbour bowered in roses.

Seated within this fragrant shade he glanced about him, at blue sky, at burgeoning tree and blooming flower, glad-eyed, and breathing deep to the sunny air joyed to be alive.

And after some while he saw Olivia coming towards him, tall and shapely in her riding habit and, like her flowers, a-bloom with vigorous health that glowed in rounded cheek and vivid lip; but when at last she paused before him, her eyes were sombre beneath puckered brow.

"Mr. Veryan!" said she reproachfully. "What folly!"

"Mrs. Revell," he retorted, rising to bow. "What beauty!"

Now at this, she turned to pluck a rose and he saw the colour deepen in her cheek.

"You should be in bed, sir!"

"You called me 'Jeremy' once!" said he wistfully.

"That was—ages ago, sir."

"Yesterday, mam."

"Yes!" she nodded. "I said—ages ago."

"Hum!" quoth Jeremy, viewing her with puzzled eyes where she stood frowning at the rose in her fingers. "Won't you come in and sit down?"

"No, thank you!" she answered, without deigning him a glance; and then, to Jeremy's wonder, she entered the arbour and sank down upon the rustic bench, still frowning at the rose.

So Jeremy sat down too, and immediately became aware of that subtle fragrance that was not of the flowers about them but rather of herself, an elusive sweetness that was of her hair, her garments, her whole vivid being, a fragrance this, had soothed his fretful waking hours, had been within his dreaming slumbers, and was to become part of his memory of her.

"Olivia," said he, leaning towards her across the little table, "you bring your fragrance like the flowers—but sweeter, I think."

"'T is probably the soap I use," she answered.

Hereupon Jeremy leaned back and scowled at a butterfly hovering in the sunshine near by; and she, glancing slyly at his scowling visage, smiled suddenly and spoke in her softest tone:

"Thank you, Jeremy!"

His thick brows grew smooth, his deep-set eyes glowed and his grim mouth was transfigured by its infrequent smile.

"Always I 've hated my name," said he, "but your voice makes music of it."

"Why, Jeremy," she laughed, "you are a poet and much more poetical than——"

"I look?" he growled. "Looks, b'ged! In mercy don't judge me by my looks——"

"Indeed but I do!" said she, viewing him, chin in hands. "Of course I do!"

"No wonder you said 'no' the other day!" he sighed. "I 'm born out of my sphere. Nature intended me for something plain and strong and useful—a ploughman, say—egad, there 's nothing o' the patrician about me—inside or out, it seems."

"Is n't there, Jeremy?"

"Well,—look for yourself."

"I am."

"Well, madam, do I strike you as an aristocrat? There 's a hand for you—all knuckle!"

"And prodigiously strong, Jeremy!"

"Ay, like a blacksmith's. Look at my face!"

"I know it by heart!" she nodded.

"Like a pugilist!" he sighed. "You said so yourself!"

"I said 'fighting man'!"

"Where 's the difference? I was ugly as a lad and used to make faces at myself in the glass—and I never shave now without wondering at myself and the trick Nature has played me. And so, being born out o' my class, I 've generally been pretty lonely yet fairly content—until now."

"And now—you are not?"

"No!"

"I wonder why?"

"Because I 've fallen in love with a goddess! And myself in love must seem very ridiculous to every one except myself."

"I think you are too egotistical!" said she. "And over-sensitive."

"Yes," he nodded, "these last few days, lying in bed, I 've thought too much about myself and the more I 've thought, the more discontented I am with myself—and so to-day, I 've decided to take myself off."

"You mean—go?"

"Yes."

"Where to?"

"Anywhere."

"You still seek 'the High Adventure'?"

"That always. But I 've another purpose."

"What, pray?"

"Something I 've determined to achieve if possible."

"Won't you tell me, Jeremy?"

"Not now. You 'll know later—perhaps."

"Is it to do with Richard?"

Jeremy's grey eyes opened wide.

"How in the world should you guess?"

"It was not difficult," she answered, turning to glance across the sunny garden. "You mean to save him from—himself?"

"I mean to try."

"This is brave—generous of you——"

"No!" said he gruffly "I—you see I am hoping that—if I succeed you may perhaps answer me—a little—differently."

"A little differently?" she repeated.

"Change 'no' to 'yes'."

"That would be very differently."

"Yes," he nodded. "Not that I should be very hurt or surprised in the least if your 'no' must remain 'no'."

"You would n't mind then, very much?" she asked softly.

"I 'd get over it—somehow."

"When do you propose to start?"

"To-day."

"No!" she exclaimed. "Preposterous and quite out of the question."

"Oh!" said he meekly.

"You are not strong enough yet."

"I 'm stronger than I look, Olivia."

"I doubt it!" said she, viewing him with keen, feminine eyes which, for the moment, were wholly maternal. "You are much too pale and thin! Let me feel your pulse. Indeed—yes, much too quick!"

"But can you wonder?" he enquired; whereupon her eyes, very far from maternal all at once, drooped before his and she flushed, though to be sure, he made no attempt to touch or imprison the hand upon his wrist.

"Besides," said she, her gaze upon the sunny garden once more. "You may be attacked again!"

"Bill and I have our hopes," he answered, grim-lipped.

"Such hope is sinful," she pronounced.

"Yet natural!" he answered.

After this they sat awhile, neither looking on the other, and there fell a silence broken only by the twitter of the birds and the soft, drowsy hum of insects, a pregnant silence that held for both a conscious intimacy far beyond words.

"Always," sighed Jeremy, at last, "always I shall remember this hour!"

Then Olivia sighing also, turned and looked at him.

"Who is Lucy Western?" said she.

Jeremy raised his head and looked back into the eyes that searched his.

"My head gamekeeper's daughter," he answered.

"Well, it seems she has disappeared."

"You mean—run away from Veryan?"

"Yes."

"Foolish child!" growled Jeremy. "I wonder why?"

"Rumour says you are the reason."

"Ha—does it!" quoth he, scowling. "Pray what is Rumour's proper name?"

"It seems you were—kind to her?"

"I tried to be."

"You used to—meet her—in the spinney."

"Never in my life!"

"Her father—saw you!"

"He never did! He saw another—in my hat and coat—this very coat! Olivia, who told you this? Was it O'Leary?"

"And another."

"My cousin Arthur?"

"Yes."

"So you know Arthur?"

"Oh yes."

"Hum!" quoth Jeremy. "And do you believe this of me?"

"I—don't know. Men can be such—liars."

"Look at me."

"I 've no desire to."

"Olivia—look at me!"

"No!"

With a sweep of the arm he spun the table from between them—seized, lifted and swung her across his knee so that perforce she must look up into his eyes:

"Do I look the kind of animal that would blast Innocence—take advantage of a young, defenceless girl —do I?" he demanded.

"No!" answered Olivia, a little breathlessly. "No—only——"

"Only what?"

"Only of a defenceless—widow!"

Now as she spoke, her lashes drooped, her vivid lips curved to the ghost of a smile—Jeremy stooped, hesitated. Next moment she was back upon the seat and he was reaching to pick up the fallen table.

"You see," said he, a little unsteadily, "'spite o' my sickness I 'm stronger than I look."

"Yes," she answered, viewing him with eyes that held wonder and something more. "Yes, you are indeed strong—stronger than I dreamed, so strong that I do believe you—absolutely, Jeremy!"

"Thanks!" said he simply and sat watching the butterflies again, wholly unconscious that she still watched him with that same look of wonder and something more.

"Olivia," said he at last, "I very nearly—kissed you a moment ago."

"Oh, did you, Jeremy?"

"Yes! I—" here he paused to scowl down at his big, tight-clenched fist, "I—wanted to—meant to—indeed I think I 've yearned to kiss you from the very first."

"Have you, Jeremy?"

"But as you lay in my arms you looked so helpless——"

"I was!" she murmured.

"And so I—well, I could n't—could I?"

"No!" she answered. "You could n't and did n't because you are—Jeremy. And I 'm glad—Oh, I 'm very glad you did n't although I—meant you to——"

"You—you meant——" Jeremy gasped.

"Of course!" she nodded, flushing beneath his look, though her eyes never wavered. "Perhaps because I wished to prove you—perhaps just because——"

"Because of what? Olivia, tell me, pray tell me!"

"Because you are—Jeremy!" she answered softly.

Then Jeremy reached out eager arm but, swift and supple, she eluded him. "Not now!" she whispered. "There comes Bryant—no, it 's Mr. O'Leary——"

"And Arthur!" growled Jeremy. "Why are they here?"

"Because I asked them, sir. And pray endeavour to look a little pleased to see them."

"No," he answered, "I 'm not strong enough—just yet!"

## CHAPTER XII

### BEING DESCRIPTIVE OF NOTHING IN PARTICULAR

THUS, sullen and aloof, sat Jeremy to scowl upon the visitors as they greeted Olivia; his handsome cousin Arthur all slim elegance in blue riding frock, spotless moleskins and resplendent spurred boots; and contrasting his graceful form and easy bearing with his own heavy person and general awkwardness, Jeremy sighed and his gloom deepened.

And yet despite handsome face and figure Arthur paled into insignificance beside his companion's subtly masterful air and compelling personality (or so thought Jeremy) as Mr. O'Leary stooped in turn to kiss Olivia's white hand, keeping it much too long (or so thought Jeremy); a hand which struggled vainly to free itself and was drawn gently, yet masterfully, within Mr. O'Leary's arm. So up rose Jeremy and stepped forth of the arbour, scowling like a thundercloud, to be hailed joyfully by Arthur who hurried to meet him.

"My dear fellow," he exclaimed, seizing Jeremy's hand, "so you are out and about again——"

"It seems so!"

"This is a joy—a great occasion, Jerry!"

"Is it?"

"My dear Jeremy, can you doubt it——"

"Why d' ye lie about me, Arthur?"

"Lie? My dear fellow——"

"And Lucy Western?"

"No, no, Jerry——"

"I say yes!"

"Oh, b'ged, man, don't wrangle here, for decency's sake——"

"Decency?" repeated Jeremy. "Hum!"

"Also, my good fellow, pray don't hold me responsible for village gossip. If a lot of bumpkins choose to say the girl has run off to join you, am I to blame? Dammit, man, be fair!"

"So they say that, do they?"

"They do, my dear fellow—and for heaven's sake don't look at me so murderously! Hush—here are the others!"

Jeremy swung away from his smiling cousin only to come face to face with Mr. O'Leary who forthwith clapped his two hands upon Jeremy's shoulders and surveyed him up and down with eyes brimful of affection.

"'Pon my soul," said he in his strangely pleasant voice, "ye 're beginning to look quoite ye'silf again—eh, Arthur?"

"So I was telling him, sir," answered Arthur, glancing from Jeremy's frowning brow to Olivia's deep, watchful eyes. "We all owe Mrs. Revell a vast debt of gratitude for her—more than sisterly care."

"Thrue for you, Arthur! Faith and 't is the lucky invalid he's been, as I tell him—eh, Jiremy?"

At this, Jeremy merely snorted and shook the speaker's white, caressing hands from his shoulders.

"Och, me dear lad," nodded Mr. O'Leary, "and don't I understand yez now! Mrs. Revell, me swate soul, our Jeremy finds his gratitude beyand expression; phwat he manes ye to believe is——"

"Thank you," answered Olivia, "but I think I know!" And turning, she walked on with Arthur beside her.

"Shure she knows! 'T is the officious yet well-meaning fool I am!" sighed Mr. O'Leary. "Trust a woman to fathom a man's secret moind—eh, Jerry? But faix, me bhoy, 't is a wonderful recovery ye 've made of it! Bedad, but ye 'll take a monstrous dale o' killing, Jerry!"

"I mean to!" said Jeremy, a little grimly.

"And 't is not loikely ye 'll be leaving here yet awhile."

"Why not?"

"Because 't is no fool y' are."

"I hope not, Terence."

"So ye 'll stay here? Say a week or so, me bhoy?"

"Shall I?"

"Shure, 't is yourself should know."

"But I don't."

Here, chancing to glance round, Jeremy saw his companion regarding him with eyes remarkably keen.

"'T is a strange lad y' are, Jirry!"

"So they tell me," nodded Jeremy.

"You 've heard Western's lass has run off?"

"Yes."

"A lovely craythur, Jirry—remarkably so!"

"Yes. And there is ugly talk concerning her and myself."

"There is, Jirry, bad cess to it!"

"Which you repeat to Mrs. Revell!"

"Indade and I did, Jirry. Says I to your charming hostess ''t is scandalous shame the village folk should blame me dear Jeremy for the girl's disappearance, and him as innocent as mesilf!'"

"Hum!" quoth Jeremy. "They say also that I used to meet her secretly."

"And phwat thin, lad? And she so lovely! Who 'd blame you? Not I, Jerry, never your fri'nd Tirence, me bhoy; I 'm not too old to feel me heart leap at the glint o' beauty's eyes."

"How old are you, Terence?"

"Forty-four, me bhoy, and niver felt younger!"

"And why must you endeavour to blacken me to Mrs. Revell?"

At this, Mr. O'Leary paused to turn and look at Jeremy, blue eyes gently reproachful, to sigh and shake his head.

"Jeremy," said he, "ye hurt me! Ye wound me in me tinderest feelings. Tirence O'Leary is your fri'nd—to Tirence O'Leary fri'ndship is a sacred tie, a holy bond—Jeremy, me tongue may wag over freely sometimes, I 've lived a troifle woild belike in woild places, Tirence O'Leary is no angel maybe alas, but his heart is sound and none ever doubted his fri'ndship before—Jeremy, I'm hurt, me bhoy."

"So am I!" growled Jeremy.

"Faith and indade," sighed Mr. O'Leary, "there are occasions when I sometimes almost doubt your regard for me and it rinders me distressful, Jiremy!" So saying he sighed again, shook his head and left Jeremy to scowl at his stately back.

Returning to the arbour Jeremy seated himself within its welcome shade and became oblivious to all but his troubled thoughts until, roused by a light footstep, he glanced up to see his cousin Arthur.

"The devil!" exclaimed Arthur pettishly. "Two's company it seems, with a vengeance. The devil take O'Leary! 'T is no wonder he rides this way so often o' late!"

"What d' ye mean?" growled Jeremy.

"I mean your handsome widow's a deuced alluring creature!"

"Who?"

"Mrs. Revell, of course. A glorious armful! A dark-browed Juno—pride and passion! A stately goddess and yet with such eyes, such a shape she could grow deliciously human, ay—by Venus!"

"Ha, d' ye think so?"

"Any man would, except yourself, old Jeremy. She' s all bewitching enticement from handsome head to pretty fool! If O'Leary has roused the game b'ged I follow! She shan't lack for company, by heaven!"

"Yours and O'Leary's?" enquired Jeremy.

"Oh, the devil may take O'Leary and his curst Irish assurance!"

"I 'm wondering," said Jeremy slowly, "I' m trying to imagine who could have started these lies about Lucy Western."

"How the deuce should I know? And why distress yourself about the pretty fool—unless—aha, you too, eh? B'ged, it seems she 's as kindly free as she 's pretty; I 've heard she——"

"Liar!" growled Jeremy and over went the table again whereupon Arthur leapt back but not quickly enough to avoid the blow which drove him reeling across the path to fall limply into an adjacent flower bed.

A hurry of quick, light feet, a flutter of petticoats and Olivia stood between them.

"Mr. Veryan——" she panted, "in heaven's name—what is this?"

"Man's a liar!" growled Jeremy.

"Oh, madam, pray, pray don't distress yourself," said Arthur, rising gracefully and dabbing at bleeding lips with dainty handkerchief, "my cousin is one of those unfortunate persons who has no command over his brutish feelings—even in the presence of beauty it seems! He is quite—quite ungoverned, poor fellow!"

"Arrah now!" quoth Mr. O'Leary, hastening forward all solicitude. "Don't disthress our lovely hostess, me dear bhoy—be aisy now——"

"Gentlemen," said Olivia, frowning, "I dine early, let us go in. Mr. Veryan, pray give me your arm."

Jeremy obeyed, supremely conscious of his own awkwardness, of his cousin Arthur's smile and unshaken serenity, of Mr. O'Leary's pleasantly smooth murmur, and of Olivia's cold aloofness; her silence, her disdainful, drooping lashes, even her hand upon his arm, all seemed to rebuke him; thus, by the time they had reached the house, he felt himself a sordid creature of the deepest dye whose presence was suffered and misdemeanours passed over and condoned for the sake of mere politeness.

At the table he ate and drank perfunctorily, glowering at his plate, hearkening to O'Leary's witty sallies, to Arthur's soft and murmurous asides, to Olivia's light laughter; and painfully conscious of the contrast he made, he grew sullen; and finding himself so very much at a disadvantage, presently rose, mumbling an excuse, and went forth to look for Bill.

And surely never did eyes, human or canine, hold a look of more adoring, rapturous welcome than those of the great dog who came bounding across the stable yard to greet him.

But what transformation was here! Bill's gaunt form had filled out, his coat, shaggy no longer, showed sleek and glossy; save for his plebeian, nondescript tail, Bill was a changed creature.

"Why, Bill," sighed Jeremy, as he fondled the dog's sleek head, "Lord love me, Bill, she 's turning you into an aristocrat o' sorts! And you 'll be getting fat soon! 'T is time we took the road, my lad—'the High Adventure'—and the sooner, the better!"

# CHAPTER XIII

## IN WHICH MR. JASPER SHRIG, OF BOW STREET, MAKES HIS APPEARANCE

JEREMY sat in the arbour unheeding the pleasant, sunny world about him, and regardless even of Bill, who, crouched hard by, watched with eyes of patient devotion and thumped the floor with his tail, ever and anon, as a gentle reminder; but Jeremy, elbows on table and head in hands, sat oblivious, being lost in gloomy introspection.

His uncle had called him "an oaf" and assuredly oaf he was! Yes, a sullen, awkward, ill-mannered, unlovely creature——

Here Bill, doubtless worried by Jeremy's indifference, crept nearer and ventured to slide square jowl upon his master's knee and to emit a protesting snuffle, whereupon Jeremy glanced down and, laying a hand upon this inviting head, spoke from the depths of his self-abasement:

"I 'm an oaf, Bill, as ugly as yourself but with none o' your dignity. I 'm a scowling, sullen oaf, fitter for the howling obscenity of a ship's fo'castle than the withdrawing-room or the society of such as—you know who, Bill. There 's Arthur looks a young martyred saint—but is n't! And O'Leary who looks angel and devil and may be neither, but both are aristocrats—fine gentlemen, Bill, while I—? Oh, damme! Is there any hope, any chance, think ye, for this graceless sullen oaf? Well—I'm what Nature made me, and

I can't pretend, Bill, any more than you can. We don't fit here, my fellow, and the sooner we 're out of it —Ha, what now?"

The dog lifted his head and growled, then, changing his mind, uttered a short bark of welcome as out from behind an adjacent yew hedge stepped a man. A shortish, wide-shouldered man this and very soberly clad from neat top-boots to broad-brimmed hat which shaded his genial face; a powerfully built yet mild-seeming man, though possessed of a peculiarly bright and roving eye.

"Arternoon, Mr. Weryan!" said he, touching hat brim with the knobby stick he carried. "Werry glad to see ye pretty much your own self again, sir."

"Thanks!" said Jeremy. "How d'you know my name?"

"Obserwation, sir."

"I've never seen you before."

"No more you ain't, sir." Here the stranger stooped to caress Bill whose greeting was of the friendliest.

"Hum!" quoth Jeremy. "My dog knows you?"

"Sir, I've took partic'lar good care as 'e should. Dogs the like o' Bill is to be treated respectful, d 'ye see, though I generally gets on wi' dogs—ditto birds."

"Who are you? What d 'ye want?"

"Why, Mr. Weryan, sir, you know a gent as I knows —name o' Gillespie, sir."

"My lawyer and very good friend. Well?"

"Pre-cisely, sir. Now con-sarning the late, windictive attempts on your life, sir, Mr. G., your lawyer and friend, not being able to travel by reason o' sarcumstances warious, sends me instead."

"And who are you?"

"Shrig's my monnicker, sir—baptismal name Jarsper."

"And what are you? Your business?"

"A law officer, sir, werry much at your service."

"Which I don't require."

"And I 'm 'ere, first, to look into the aforesaid murderous——"

"Don't trouble. The affair is done with and I shall be none the worse in a day or so."

"Meaning as you don't want the matter took up, sir?"

"Exactly."

"Werry good!" murmured Mr. Shrig with a placid nod. "But then there 's another little matter, sir. 'Twixt you an' me, Mr. Weryan, I 'm enquiring for a gent name of Julius Openshaw——"

Jeremy sat up and stared into the speaker's mild face with suddenly awakened interest.

"Come in!" said he. "Come in and sit down!'

"Thank 'ee, sir!" answered Mr. Shrig, and stepping into the arbour he removed his hat and placing it carefully under the table, sat down.

"Now why," demanded Jeremy, leaning forward across the table, "why do you seek Julius Openshaw?"

"Well, sir, same being a official matter, my lips is sealed accordingly, though I dunno as I von't tell ye a thing or so—on a condition."

"What condition?"

"That you allows me to ax a few questions—and answers 'em."

"Go on!"

"And first, sir, about that there shooting?"

"What d' you mean?"

"That there gun—as vent off so accident'l-like in the spinney on the fifth ultimo."

"You mean when I and—a companion were out shooting?"

"Yourself and a gent, name of O'Leary—eggs-ackly, sir!"

"How d' ye know of this?"

"Observation, sir. You 'appened to be stepping over a fallen tree, ven the aforesaid gent's vepping 'appened to go off behind you, I think?"

"Yes."

"And if you 'ad n't 'appened to stumble over said tree, ewents might ha' proved—disastrous, sir?"

"Yes."

"Pre-cisely! Vich nat'rally brings us to the night o' the sixth o' this month, when you vas the wictim of a most determined attack as werry nigh succeeded. 'T is in ewidence as you vas struck down from the rear and consequently did n't see assaulting party or parties?"

"True."

"Having struck you unconscious and thinking you a corp', said party or parties took an' dragged you to a ruinated building and there deposited you? My fax is all correct, sir, I think?"

"Quite! You've been busy, it seems."

"As a bee, sir—as a nant! I 've took the ewidence o' your respected uncle, Sir James Trevor, Baronet, of your cousin, Mr. Arthur Trevor, Esquire, and a good many others, in and out o' Weryan, not forgetting your friend Mr. Terence O'Leary, such a fine gentleman. A Tippy, a Go—a reg'lar Nob! And so affable an' pleasant spoke!"

"He is!" growled Jeremy.

"'T were a j'y to 'ark to 'im, sir."

"And now what do you know of Julius Openshaw?"

"Why, Mr. Weryan, sir, I 'll tell ye, plain and p'inted, I don't know nothing—beyond the plain fax, nothing at all; I only suspects, and suspicions is best not spoke of unless backed up by fax, and fax depends on proof, and though my fax is, my proofs ain't—and there y' are, sir!"

"Well, what are your facts?"

"Ugly, sir! In my time, Mr. Weryan, I 've had the

good fortun' to 'andle some ugly cases—murder an' what not, but none uglier than the case o' Mr. Julius Openshaw and your unfort'nate feyther."

"I know that he was killed twenty-three years ago," said Jeremy, "and, as I believe, murdered."

"Murdered!" repeated Mr. Shrig, rolling the word upon his tongue. "You believe as your pa vas murdered—good! And v'y d' ye so believe, sir? Have you any proofs?"

"None!" replied Jeremy. "Tell me your facts."

"Twenty-three years is a goodish stretch, sir," quoth Mr. Shrig, "but I 'ave the case all dooly wrote down, and vich is better, in my nob, sir. And here it be! Twenty-three years ago, your feyther vas young and rich and conseqvently had many friends, and chief among 'em Mr. Julius Openshaw and your mother's only brother, Sir James Trevor, Baronet. One day—no, evening it was—your feyther drives up to Mr. Gillespie's chambers in a terrible state. 'Gillespie,' says 'e, all of a tremble, 'Gillespie, I vants to alter my will—cut out my damned brother-in-law,' says 'e, meaning Sir James Trevor, d' ye see, 'and not a penny to that scoundrel Openshaw!' says 'e. 'And Gillespie, I mean to make you executor an' sole guardian o' my child!'—yourself—Mr. Weryan, sir, aged one. 'Set about it, Gillespie,' says your feyther, stamping up an' down the room, 'draw it up at vunce. I'll be back in an hour to sign it,' says 'e, and avay 'e goes. So, Mr. G. draws up the noo will according, but your feyther don't come back to sign it—not 'e! And because why? Because he vas a-laying stone dead in his own libree, a pistol in vun 'and, a fob seal in t' other, a bullet in his brain and your mother laying a-top o' his corp'——"

"My mother!"

"As ever vas! In a dead swound! And vot's more, she never spoke again—leastvays not as nobody never heard."

"You mean—she was dead?"

"No, Mr. Weryan, but in a most extryordinary swound. Took to 'er bed she did an' never spoke more, so far as the ewidence shows—— So they buried your feyther and there vas an end o' him, pore gent!"

"Go on!"

"Being great folk, the matter vas hushed up, d' ye see——"

"And my mother—was she alive?"

"Ah! In bed, staring at nothing an' talking to none. Your pore mother's case vas stranger than your feyther's and—uglier!"

"How d' you mean?"

"I mean as for three veeks she lay abed, alive and no more. Then vun night the nurse, 'aving gone to sleep, of course, vakes up and finds your mother gone—bolted! So they searched the grounds, and, sure enough, they find 'er at last in her bed-gown and you in her arms sleeping 'eavens 'ard, sir, and her, pore lady, wi' a mark across her face like the mark of a vip——"

"God in heaven!" gasped Jeremy, and shrank back, covering his face with shaking hands.

"I told ye 't was a extryordinary case an' ugly, Mr. Weryan, sir, and so it be!" quoth Mr. Shrig, shaking placid head.

"And this—mark on her face was—was it the only mark of violence?"

"The only vun, sir. But that same night she died."

"Can you tell me—anything more?"

"There 's only vun as can, sir, and that 's Mr. G."

"Yes!" nodded Jeremy. "I must see him—as soon as possible."

"Us might start to-night, Mr. Weryan, sir."

"To-night?" repeated Jeremy, glancing up at Mr. Shrig's placid face.

"I 've a fast-trotting hoss and gig in the willage, sir, all ready if you 'll say the vord."

"To-night, then!" nodded Jeremy. "Half-past nine at the lodge gates."

"Werry good, sir! Mr. G. will be dooly pleased. 'Shrig,' says 'e to me, 'votever you do, bring 'im back vith you!' says 'e."

"Tell me, do you think Julius Openshaw is still alive?"

"Sir, I suspects as he 's werry much alive, ah—and kicking, sir, kicking!"

"Why d' ye believe this?"

"I don't, sir, I only suspects. I never believe nothing but fax as is proved, Mr. Weryan, sir."

"Where do your suspicions point?"

"Sir, I 'll tell you. They p'ints north an' south an' east an' west, according to sarcumstances. But there 's Mr. Gillespie, he may know a lot (as I believe) or precious little (vich ain't likely) for Mr. G. is as keen as a razor, as deep as a vell, and as close as a noyster!"

"And the only friend I ever had!" said Jeremy. "I think I begin to understand why he wished me to travel abroad until my twenty-fifth birthday."

"Life," sighed Mr. Shrig, shaking his head, "life is a slippery article, sir, at the best o' times—like a eel, ah, and a damp eel, at that!" Here Bill rose, growling fiercely, but at a touch of Mr. Shrig's hand he subsided, and glancing up, Jeremy saw Olivia approaching, accompanied by Mr. O'Leary.

"If," sighed Mr. Shrig, shaking his head and glancing down at Bill, "if coves in my line o' business only had the sense of a dog!" So saying, Mr. Shrig rose respectfully and lifted forefinger to placid brow.

"Mam an' sir, your servant!" quoth he.

Olivia acknowledged his salute silently and frowning a little; not so Mr. O'Leary:

"Why, shure, 't is me enquiring fri'nd from Bow

Street," said he, smiling in kindly greeting. "And faix, it seems ye 've made fri'nds with Mr. Veryan's divil dog as readily as with me black spalpeen Pompey."

"I generally gets on wi' dogs, sir, ditto blackymoors—sometimes," answered Mr. Shrig.

"This man, me dear Olivia," explained Mr. O'Leary with a graceful wave of his hand towards Mr. Shrig, "is a Bow Street officer here in the interests of our Jiremy."

"So I understand," answered Olivia. "He seems to pervade the place."

"Aha, has he questioned you too, me dear soul?"

"Several times. Let us hope he may soon bring his enquiry to a successful issue."

"A—men!" sighed Mr. Shrig so dolefully that Mr. O'Leary clapped him cheerily upon the shoulder.

"Phwat luck, me fri'nd?" he enquired.

"Sir," answered Mr. Shrig, "since you ax so kind-like, I 'll tell you fair and free—more than you might expect!—And vot 's more, Mr. Weryan is a-going to London along o' me."

"Eh—eh, is this so, me dear bhoy?"

"Yes!" growled Jeremy, frowning at the distance yet very conscious that Olivia had turned and was looking at him.

"And whin d' ye go, Jerry?"

"That is my business!" he muttered.

"This werry night, sir," said Mr. Shrig, reaching for his hat and stick.

"Why, then," said Mr. O'Leary after a momentary pause, "good luck go wid ye, me dear Jeremy—and remember, come what may, Tirence O'Leary is ever and always your fri'nd!"

"Thank you for nothing!" answered Jeremy, scowling. And calling Bill to follow, he trudged sullenly away, leaving Olivia to stare after him with troubled eyes.

But he had not gone far before Mr. Shrig was at his elbow, whom Jeremy angrily questioned forthwith:

"Why must you tell 'em of my departure?"

"For reasons, sir, as may appear in doo course."

Hereupon Jeremy strode on, frowning blacker than ever, while Mr. Shrig sighed and sucked meditatively at the knob of his knotted stick. "Sir," said he at last, "men is werry like animals, I think. There's yourself f'r instance—like, if I may say so, werry like your own dog; here 's me, werry like a nox, and your friend Mr. O'Leary—so extryordinary friendly and good-natur'd—now vat may he be like, d' ye think, sir?"

"I don't know!" growled Jeremy. "Nor care!"

"No more don't I!" nodded Mr. Shrig. "But all the same, he is remarkably like a certain animal as I knows on. But talking o' dogs, sir, 't is a great pity as their lives is so short nacherally. Six, eight, ten year and they 're old bones. Now take your dog Bill—Bill ain't a-going to make old bones unless you 're werry extryordinary careful."

"What d' ye mean?" demanded Jeremy, a little fiercely.

"Guns, Mr. Weryan, sir! Though they mostly prefers pizen! Pizen being surer and quieter, d' ye see?"

"Poison?" exclaimed Jeremy. "What are you suggesting?"

"Nothing, sir. I 'm only, as you might say, taking Time by the foreleg!"

"Who would kill my dog?"

"'Oo tried to do same for yourself, sir?"

"Shrig," said Jeremy, laying a compelling hand upon his companion's arm, "I'm inclined to like you, which is strange, for I usually prefer animals, but if we're to get along, pray remark that when I ask a question I desire an answer. What d' ye mean by poison?"

"Windictiveness, sir; it comes out in all manner of odd ways an' shapes: afore now I 've met it in the form o' bludgeons, knives, brickbats, barkers, and a occasional chimbley pot! And to-day—a beef bone!"

"A beef bone?" repeated Jeremy, halting to stare in amazement.

"As ever vas, sir, whereof the gardener's terrier is a-laying dead this minute. Ye see, sir, this pizened bone was a-laying just outside Gregory's pantry vinder, vhere your dog vas sure to find it, but Bill's been along o' the lady or you and conseqvently Bill Dartle's dog got it instead. Gregory depones 'e see Dartle's dog a-gnawing of it."

"I must see Gregory."

"Then come this way, sir—he 'll be in the kitching garding."

"Hum!" quoth Jeremy. "You seem to know all about things."

"Not at all, sir," sighed Mr. Shrig. "Ye see I 'm only a huming being."

Sure enough, they found Gregory sedately at work among the vegetables, his snowy shirt sleeves rolled above forearms whose solid brawn woke in Jeremy a certain feeling of comfort.

"Happy to see you about again, sir," said Gregory with a salute reminiscent of the quarter-deck.

"Thanks!" answered Jeremy. "What d' you know about the attempt to poison Bill?"

"No more than I told Mr. Shrig, sir."

"You have no idea, then, how that bone came here?"

"None, sir. The first I saw of it was when Dartle's terrier had it in the yard."

"How did the poor creature die?"

"Conwulsions, sir!" said Shrig. "I chanced to be by at the time."

Jeremy stood awhile lost in frowning thought.

"You've a powerful arm, Gregory!" said he at last.

"Pretty tidy, sir."

"And you're not a man to be intimidated, I'm sure."

"Thank 'ee, sir."

"You see—I'm going away."

"Indeed, sir? Soon?"

"Yes. And—this house is a—curst lonely place."

"It is, sir."

"Mr.—De Ravenac, now—what d'ye think of him?"

"Being an Englishman, sir, I don't hold wi' foreigners—on principle——"

"Is he often here?"

"Very seldom, sir."

Again Jeremy became lost in frowning thought; at last, plunging sudden hand into a pocket, he drew thence certain monies and thrust them into Gregory's unready grasp.

"Pray take this," said he, "and my thanks. And now, give me your hand; I may not see you again to speak with before I go. I shall come back again—maybe—sooner of later—until then—good-bye! You—keep a brace of pistols always ready loaded, I think you said?"

"Also my old cutlass, sir! Good-bye, Mr. Veryan, sir, and I hope you'll come back sooner than later, sir, and to—to stay longer, sir."

So Jeremy gripped the powerful hand, nodded to Mr. Shrig and strode off with Bill at his heels. But presently he paused to turn and stare up at the house now bathed in the glow of sunset; and yet, despite this glory, it seemed to him that a shadow hung about it, creeping down from twisted chimney and roof and gable and red-bricked wall like an omen of approaching evil, a menace of that which was to be. And as the house seemed to scowl at him, Jeremy scowled up at it and thereafter went his way, very full of gloomy thought.

Approaching the rose garden, he saw Olivia seated alone in the arbour, her stately head bowed over her tambour frame and straightway he turned upon his heel.

"The fields for us, Bill!" quoth he. "We're no fit company for a dainty lady just now—at least, I'm not, so—the fields for us."

## CHAPTER XIV

### TELLS HOW JEREMY SAID GOOD-BYE

STARS were peeping when Jeremy re-entered the house, there to be met by Betty, Olivia's buxom maid.

"Your supper be a-waiting, sir," said she, curtseying, "but madam's in the rose garden!" Here came a dimple in her cheek.

"Thank ye!" answered Jeremy and strode away to the garden forthwith.

He found her leaning against the old sundial, nor did she trouble to turn as he came up.

"Where have you been?" she questioned.

"Walking."

"Have you had supper?"

"I was not hungry."

Silence, wherein he viewed her loveliness as well as he could in the half-light while Bill, crouched on the grass between them, yawned prodigiously.

"Are you indeed a brutal man?" she demanded suddenly.

"I begin to think so."

"Yet you love your dog."

"He is a brute also."

"And you said you loved me."

"You are an angel——"

"No!" she exclaimed. "Ah, no—a woman. Oh, a very woman, God help me!"

"Why call on God?"

"Because I am so helpless."

"And therefore stronger than a man!" he answered. "Woman's weakness is her power, her best protection——"

"Only to a good man!" she retorted. "There are male creatures so debased and vile that woman's weakness is weakness indeed——"

"Do you know any such?" he growled.

"Two."

"Name them."

"No."

"Is De Ravenac one?" But of course! Who is the other?"

"The man you struck to-day."

"Arthur?"

"Yes. This is why I was so glad, so very glad you knocked him down."

"Glad?"

"Of course."

"Lord!" gasped Jeremy and stood mute with surprise.

"I told you I was no angel," said she a little pettishly.

"But—but I thought——" stammered Jeremy.

"Of course you did!" she exclaimed. "Just because I didn't dance and sing and clap my hands, you thought I was shocked, shamed and altogether outraged. So you grew sullen and stalked off and hid yourself—and now—now I think you have come to say good-bye?"

"Yes."

"What did that law officer want? The stout man in the arbour!"

"Mr. Shrig brought a message for me."

"A message?"

"From my lawyer—and only friend."

"And you are going to London to-night—to see your friend?"

"Yes."

"So then it is not on Richard's account?"

"Not altogether."

"Your business is important?"

"Beyond words."

"More than Richard's salvation?"

"No!" answered Jeremy, coming a pace nearer. "So soon as I've had word with Gillespie, I mean to find Richard and bring him back to you, sooner or later."

"Then I pray God to prosper you."

"Amen!" said Jeremy. "Good-bye!"

"Good-bye!" she answered without looking at him.

But instead of going, he drew a half-pace nearer and stood viewing her averted face, while Bill, glancing from one to the other, yawned audibly.

"Have I offended you?"

"Oh, no!"

"Or grieved you?"

"No!"

"Then—good-bye, Olivia!"

"Good-bye."

Jeremy took four steps away from her and turning, took five back again.

"Well?" she enquired, glancing up at him over her shoulder. "What is it now, pray?"

"You've forgotten to say good-bye to Bill."

At this she laughed, though somewhat uncertainly, and stooped to caress the stately creature.

"Good-bye, Bill!" said she softly. "I shall miss you—Oh, be sure of that! Come back again soon."

Then, with the dog at his side, Jeremy strode away grim and resolute; but hardly was he out of the rose garden than he halted to pause and look back

"Bill," said he, "I—did n't! I wanted to—I meant to, but—I didn't! What about it, my fellow?"

Heedful of which appeal, Bill stared up at him earnestly, cocked an ear thoughtfully, wagged his tail sympathetically and finally, having evidently considered the matter dispassionately, turned and trotted back again, whereupon Jeremy turned back also.

Olivia had fallen upon her knees the better to welcome the dog and thus, glancing up, saw Jeremy looking down at her.

"Why are you—come back?" she questioned a little breathlessly and quite unnecessarily, since she read the reason in his look. Thus, instead of speaking, Jeremy knelt also to clasp her to him, to kiss her hair, her eyes, her quivering mouth.

"Olivia," said he at last, "I shall return; nothing can keep me from you but death, and perhaps not even that."

Then up he rose and went his way without another word or so much as one backward glance.

"Bill," said he at last, "by heaven, I did it! And—oh, by heaven, Bill—she kissed me back."

# CHAPTER XV

## TELLS HOW JEREMY RODE FOR LONDON

HALFWAY along the avenue Jeremy halted, for Bill had growled suddenly, then out from the shadow of an adjacent tree stepped a shortish, broad-shouldered man.

"Is it you, Shrig?"

"That i-dentical, sir."

"Where 's your gig?"

"At the 'Acorn' in the willage, sir, along o my misfort'nate nag. Us 'll have to foot it a bit, if you don't mind."

"Why?"

"Because my mare ain't in no condition for the road, sir, having been 'ocussed, d' ye see! And no conweyance to be had, sir!"

"Ha! You suggest foul play?"

"As ever vas, Mr. Weryan, sir. My mare von't be compus mentus again for two or three days, I reckon."

"Any suspicions?"

"Oceans, sir! Windictiveness is in the werry air, conseqvently caution's the vord, sir, and wrote in capital letters. Foller me, sir."

"But our road lies the other way."

"Ah, but then us ain't a-going by the road, sir—back lanes and fields and paths 'll be safer to-night."

"D' ye mean there 's danger on the road?"

"Lord, Mr. Weryan, sir, don't I tell ye——"

"No, you tell me nothing!"

"Then, sir, there 's a party or parties unknown as be werry anxious you sha' n't reach London in an 'urry. And because why, says you? Because said party or parties is partick'ler anxious to keep you from 'aving speech wi' Mr. G. And because why, says you again? To vich I answers—Rome not being built in a day—I can't tell you—yet, sir. But talkin' o' my mare nat'rally brings us to your dog Bill."

"How?"

"Why, seeing as us must travel fast and light, I thought p'raps you might prewail on yourself to leave him behind 'ere at Priory Dene, Mr. Weryan, sir."

"Never!"

"Werry good, sir——"

"Bill 's my friend—and saved my life!"

"Ah—same as 'e might save—'ers!"

"What d' ye mean? Whose life, man—whose?"

"Mrs. R.'s, sir."

"Ha!" exclaimed Jeremy, grasping his companion by the arm. "D' ye mean she 's in danger too?"

"Why, you never know, sir. Priory Dene's a lonely place, a werry bee-utiful place for a act o' wiolence—say arson, say feller de see, say—murder——"

"Great God, Shrig!" gasped Jeremy. "D' ye think so?"

"Ah!" nodded Shrig. "Though you need n't twist my arm off, Mr. Weryan."

"By heaven, if you think she is in danger——"

"I don't, sir—Lord love you, no! I'm only suggesting as she might be—and she 's oncommon fond o' Bill! And sich a dog might be a companion, ah and more—a guardian angel on four legs, sir."

"True!" nodded Jeremy, frowning down at Bill's lithe, powerful shape. "Hum—I never thought o' this!"

"Bill's trusty an' a fighter, sir. Vith a animal like Bill at her 'eels all day and a-sleeping not too fur away all night long, she 'd be as safe, and 'appy almost, as if you vas there yourself, sir!"

"Hum!" quoth Jeremy again: and glancing keenly at the speaker's placid face, nodded. "You 're right, Shrig!" said he and, facing about, began to retrace his steps immediately, with Mr. Shrig at his elbow and Bill trotting sedately before.

Finding the rose garden deserted, Jeremy turned towards the house, whose chimneys and gables rose dark against the splendour of a rising moon.

"A pity Oliver's in town!" sighed Mr. Shrig, jerking a thumb moonwards. "Gimme a black night when Windictiveness is abroad. Moonlight's werry nice for lovers, but it gives Murder a extry good chance to shoot or stab, and being a nat'rally cautious cove myself, I——"

Uttering a sudden, fierce snarl, Bill leapt a flower bed, bounded up the terrace steps and next moment the night hush was broken by a cry, an angry shout and the dog's ferocious baying.

Forward sprang Jeremy in turn and, reaching the terrace, saw Olivia on her knees, both arms about Bill's quivering form who, snarling and with teeth agleam, strove to come at the Chevalier de Ravenac.

"Don't!" panted Olivia. "Don't shoot—pray don't shoot—he sha' n't hurt you, Gaston——"

Jeremy halted suddenly at the word, and when he spoke his voice sounded harsh and fierce, almost, as Bill's savage growling.

"Gaston—is it!" quoth he. "Lie down, Bill! And you, Monsieur de Ravenac, put away your pistol!"

"But *certainement!*" answered the Chevalier, bowing, "Monsieur himself comes at the moment most necessaire, as usual! *Hélas*, madam she is disturb by monsieur his so bad dog, but—monsieur shall himself console 'er p'r'aps—oh, yes, *alors!* But first I bring to madam a message from her so loving brother, my friend Richard, it is therefore that she should answer first, *n'est-ce pas ?*"

"Pray tell Richard that I cannot, will not—unless he comes himself!" said Olivia, still on her knees beside Bill.

"But if it is that our poor Richard is *malade*, sick, ill —how then, madam?"

"Please tell him what I say."

"*Fort bien, ma toute belle !* I shall do so. And now I go, I leave you with this so 'appy Monsieur Veryan. But I 'ave your mos' lovely image in my 'eart. *Mon cœur est toujours à toi.* Adieu, Madam Olivia, I come back soon, ah, but yes. Monsieur, your mos' 'umble!" And with an elaborate bow to each in turn, the Chevalier made to go, but as he did so, Bill snarled evilly and crouched to spring despite Jeremy's restraining hand. "Eh, monsieur," said the Chevalier with his dazzling smile, "I do not love your dog alive, someday p'r'aps 'e is dead—then, *ma foi*—I love 'im the so much bettaire." So saying, the Chevalier strolled away, a graceful, stately figure in the moonlight. Jeremy watched him out of eyeshot then, glancing round, saw that Mr. Shrig had vanished also.

"Why did you come back?" enquired Olivia, sinking upon the marble seat that stood near.

"So it's 'Gaston', is it?" growled Jeremy.

"It was then," she answered. "By accident."

"Accident!" he repeated bitterly.

"Accident!" she nodded serenely. "I was distraught."

"Why must you use his accursed name?"

"I tell you I—was not myself," she answered, frowning.

"'T is no excuse——"

"Don't be foolish, sir!" she retorted. "I make no excuse."

"Do you often call him 'Gaston'?"

"No!"

"How long have you known him?"

"Years—longer than I have known you."

"Why was he here—so soon as my back was turned?"

"You heard why, sir! You begin to grow offensive——"

"Did—did he—kiss you too?"

"Mr. Veryan!" she exclaimed, rising majestically. "You become insulting! You may go."

"Ha!" growled Jeremy, turning to scowl up at the moon. "What a devilish world it is!"

"'T is what we make it," she said scornfully.

"Yes," groaned Jeremy, "so am I in hell!"

"Then—oh, poor soul—come out!" cried Olivia, all suddenly tender. "Don't suffer needlessly when life holds so much real sorrow—look at me! Oh, Jeremy, do I seem the sort of creature your words suggest—do I?"

So he drew near and looked deep within her eyes and seeing them so steadfast and truthful and so full of pity for himself, beholding the quiver of her mouth, sensing all the mothering tenderness and comfort of her, Jeremy sank upon his knees to kiss her hands and bow his face upon them.

"Forgive me!" he muttered. "I'm a dog—no, Bill's a dog—I'm worse! To be jealous of such a man—to doubt you, my angel! I'm not worthy—clumsy—a coarse oaf——"

But here, her soft, cool palm closed his lips and stooping down to him she rested her cheek upon his coarse hair.

"Have faith in me, Jeremy!" she whispered. "Oh, have faith and trust me always! I think perhaps—some day I may need all your faith, all your trust. Should that black day ever come, remember this hour and trust me, Jeremy, oh, trust me!"

"I'm such an unlovely fellow!" he groaned. "Such a curst jealous brute——"

"I would not have you otherwise."

"With no good looks to help me, Olivia—no ready wit——"

"But you are, Jeremy!"

"Unpolished—rough o' tongue."

"Don't!" she whispered. "You hurt me."

"But I 'm so unlike what I would be," he muttered. "And so—so very different to you, my angel."

"Angel—ah, no!" she whispered. "Say your woman, rather—your very own woman, Jeremy!" And lifting his head she kissed him as his long-dead mother might have done, on brow and eyes and mouth.

So, clasped within her arms, Jeremy came up out of hell, filled with a blissful wonder to find these clasping arms so strong to hold him, Jeremy, who knew himself so lacking in all the graces of your lover of romance—and herein was a singular ecstasy.

"That you, my angel, my beautiful woman, can love such as me! Here is the wonder of the world!"

"Oh, foolish Jeremy!" she sighed and held him closer.

Now as they clung together thus, came Bill to thrust his head between them, to rest square jowl upon her knee, to whine softly, reproachful of their forgetfulness and to be fondled by each.

"Why did you come back?" she asked again, at last.

"To bring you Bill to watch over you in my absence. Will you keep him always by you, day and night, Olivia, until—I—come back?"

"Oh, Jeremy, how kind!" she murmured, tender-eyed. "How like you——"

"No!" sighed he. "It was Shrig's idea—I should never have thought of it—not I!"

"Yet you brought him!"

"I ought to warn you that some scoundrel tried to poison him——"

"I know—I know!" said she, frowning. "Gregory told me. Oh, but I 'll watch over him, he sha' n't leave me day or night until—until you——"

"Axing your pardings, sir and mam!"

Starting, they turned to behold a small, apologetic man, clad somewhat like a post boy, who stood, leathern cap in hand, bobbing at them with meek head, knuckling an eyebrow and making a leg all at once and with an air of the utmost humility.

"Who are you?" demanded Olivia, rising to her stately height, while Jeremy glanced from the intruder to Bill who lay crouched, one ear cocked in languid interest.

"I ain't nobody at all, mam, not o' no consequence I ain't," answered the meek man humbly.

"And my dog did n't notice you!" said Jeremy.

"But why are you here?" questioned Olivia. "What do you want?"

"No 'arm, lady, no 'arm—only Jasper Shrig, axing your pardons both, I'm sure. So if you could tell——"

At this moment was heard a soft and dulcet whistle, whereupon the small, meek person bobbed mild head again, knuckled apologetic eyebrow and, moving off in a noiseless, sliding fashion, vanished silently down the terrace steps. Now, staring after him, Olivia shivered suddenly.

"Jeremy," she whispered, "oh, Jeremy, what does it all mean?"

"I don't know," he answered thoughtfully.

"Who was that hateful little man?"

"I never saw him before."

"And the other—Mr. Shrig, can you trust him—do you?"

"Yes. So does Bill!" he answered and taking her hands he drew her nearer. "Why, how cold you are—shivering—and the night so warm!"

"Yes!" she whispered, and clung to him with the abandon of a frightened child, so that Jeremy, holding her close, stood dumb with a joy unknown till now. "Jeremy," she murmured, her head bowed beneath his lips, "I feel as if the night were full of evil—of danger for you and—oh, Jeremy, I have only just found you—must you go to-night?"

"Yes," he answered, kissing her hair—that hair which was so black and straight, so soft and smooth and altogether lovely.

"Dear, you will be very careful—you will run no needless risk—for my sake?"

"For your dear sake," he promised.

"And do you—love me—truly?"

"Most truly!" he answered and yearned to say more yet could not.

"And always will love me, Jeremy?"

"Always!"

"And never—oh, never doubt me?"

"Never!"

"And even if you should ever doubt me, you—you will love me still?"

"Yes, my Olivia," he answered, striving to find adequate words. "I—I love you, and shall—always, because I—don't you see—can't help loving you—so much I can never tell you—I have n't words—a poor dumb creature—a pitiful sort of lover for such a beautiful thing as you. I could never say much—less than ever now, it seems. Do I disappoint you, Olivia?"

For answer she raised her head to smile up into his eyes, to draw him down to her lips.

Thus stood they lost in each other, forgetful of all else in the world until, roused suddenly by a sound that was neither a sneeze, cough nor groan, and yet each and all in one.

Once again they started and turned, this time to behold Mr. Shrig seated upon the terrace steps, apparently lost in profound contemplation of the moon; him Jeremy addressed forthwith:

"There was a man here enquiring for you—who was he?"

"Only Dan'l, sir—vun o' my lads. And now, Mrs. Revell, mam, I 'd like to ax you a question or so, if you 'll obleege?"

"Well, sir?"

"First, mam, who 's your fine furrin' wisitor, vot might be his name, or as you might say, his monnicker, mam?"

"He is Monsieur the Chevalier de Ravenac."

"Moosoo the—Lord!" sighed Mr. Shrig. "He 's a tidy mouthful! A French gent, I think?"

"A French gentleman, yes."

"And a friend o' yourn, mam?"

"No."

"No," repeated Mr. Shrig, nodding at the open pocket-book on his knee. "Certainly not! You've know'd him long, mam?"

"Five years—about."

"Good!" said Mr. Shrig and made another laborious entry. "Friend o' your brother, Mr. Richard Armadale, I think?"

"Ye-es!"

"Might moosoo ha' been acquainted vith Mr. Revell, your deceased——"

"He was!"

"Good again, mam. And 'e was present, I think, along o' your brother, Mr. R. A., when Mr. Revell took an' died along of a pistol ball?"

"Yes. But why must you ask——"

"Mam, by your kind leave, two or three more answers an' I 'm done. D' ye know if moosoo lives hereabouts?"

"No, he lives in London, I think."

"Street an' number you don't know, p'r'aps?"

"No."

"Does 'e often come a-wisiting here, mam?"

"No!"

"Thank 'ee, mam, kindly! And you, Mr. Weryan, sir, about how long ha' you know'd this French gent?"

"Only since the night of my—accident."

"Ha!" quoth Mr. Shrig and, closing his memorandum, he rose. "Now, sir, if you 're qvite ready and don't mind, us 'll be getting along; we ought to reach Lewes in a hour."

"An hour?" repeated Olivia. "Pray, how are you going?"

"Afoot, mam. Needs must, it seems."

"No!" said she. "No, indeed, not while I have horses in my stable."

"'Osses?" repeated Mr. Shrig. "'T is oncommon handsome o' you, mam; 'osses is the vord. But are you fit for the saddle, Mr. Weryan?"

"Of course," answered Jeremy.

"Werry good, sir. I don't favour saddle exercise myself, but, sir, v'en I cocks my leg across a nag I generally rides—'ard!"

Very soon the horses were brought round and Jeremy, having mounted, turned to look his last where stood Olivia with Bill beside her.

"Good-bye, Jeremy!" said she softly. "We shall be waiting!"

Then glancing from the wistful eyes of the dog to the tender, yearning gaze of the woman, Jeremy bowed his head and rode away.

## CHAPTER XVI

### CONCERNING A PAIR OF BLACK WHISKERS

MOON and stars and a soft wind, a night whose solemn hush was apt for thought; and thus, astride easy-pacing horse, Jeremy, dreaming always of Olivia, imagined all those tender vows, those fine speeches, those burning words he had left unspoken and scorned himself bitterly for a dumb fool.

Avoiding the main road, Mr. Shrig piloted him by devious ways, crossroad, by-lane and cart track; past darkling wood and open meadow, past lonely farmstead and silent hamlet, up hill and down, until Jeremy grew faint with weariness and felt his head throb painfully to every hoof stroke of his horse.

At last, having climbed a grassy upland, Mr. Shrig checked his steed to point where lights winked in the valley below.

"Lewes, sir!" said he, and then, seeing Jeremy droop in his saddle, "Vot, sir, you ain't sick——?"

"No, but I 'm not so strong as I thought."

"Then easy does it, slow an' easy. Us 'll take a drop o' summat comforting at the 'White Hart.' This vay and easy, sir, easy!"

On again, down grassy slopes, through narrow, rutted lanes and so, at last, into an echoing street, up a steep hill to the hospitable door of an inn where Jeremy stiffly dismounted.

And here in cosy room, seated in deep elbow-chair beside a grateful fire, sat Jeremy wondering at his own weakness and yearning mightily for Olivia.

To him presently re-entered Mr. Shrig, followed by one bearing a tray whereon stood glasses and a steaming jug which gave forth a fragrance most delectable.

"Sir," said Mr. Shrig, so soon as they were alone and the door closed, "here 's a jug o' comfort vith a slice o' leming peel, brewed by my werry own 'ands, as 'll varm the werry cockles o' your 'eart! Smell it, sir! Taste it!" So saying, he filled two of the three glasses and, holding his own aloft, nodded: "Mr. Wee, sir, here 's long life, true love and a smiling fortun'!"

"Thanks!" said Jeremy and they drank together.

"And how d' ye find it, sir?"

"Most excellent!"

"Then drink 'earty, sir. You need it, seeing as you 're low by reason o' your cracked nob, or as you might say 'tibby'—and I needs it because I 'm flummoxed and conflummerated by reason o' this here French moosoo. Sir, I can't make 'im fit in, nohow! 'Oo is he, vot d' ye know of him?"

"Nothing beyond hearsay."

"And vot might you 'ave heer'd?"

"That he 's rich, popular in society, a friend of Royalty and a notorious duellist."

"Pretty good, sir! And might 'e chance to be a friend, or say ackvaintance, o' your uncle, Sir James T.?"

"Not that I know of."

Here Mr. Shrig sighed and shook doleful head.

"Might you ever ha' seen him at Weryan, sir?"

"Never."

Here Mr. Shrig sighed again and his gloom deepened until, his thoughtful gaze chancing upon his glass, he raised it to his lips, emptied it and was in the act of refilling it when a soft tattoo sounded upon the window.

"Some one's rapping—outside!" said Jeremy, turning to peer.

"Ah!" nodded Mr. Shrig placidly. "That 'll be Dan'l!" And crossing to the lattice he opened it; whereupon ensued a brief scuffling and into the room slipped the small apologetic man; there was a streak of blood upon his face, also his clothes were dusty as from a recent fall.

"All 's bowmon, Jarsper!" said he, knuckling an eyebrow at Jeremy.

"Ditched, Dan'l?" enquired Mr. Shrig.

"Ah!" nodded Dan'l, glancing shyly, yet yearningly, at the steaming jug; whereupon Mr. Shrig filled and tendered him the third glass.

"Drink, lad!" Dan'l obeyed. "Now speak—ditched, eh?"

"Ah, 'bout two mile down the road, Jarsper. I come down a bit heavier than I meant—and so did they."

"And damage?"

"Nothing to matter. Bruk' chaise winder and lamp. Near 'oss bolted, so I rid 'ere on t' other 'un. French gent's a-coming on along wi'——"

"French?" repeated Mr. Shrig in a kind of gasp, his round eyes goggling. "The French gent? Black 'air and viskers?"

"Ah, 'im, Jarsper——"

"Love my eyes!" exclaimed Mr. Shrig and sat down heavily in his chair. "Black viskers?"

"Ah—wot's wrong?"

"Everything, Dan'l! You 've got the wrong party."

"Blow my dicky!" exclaimed Dan'l. "It were the party as ordered the chaise, Jarsper."

"Well, 'e 's wrong, 'e don't fit. The party as I reckoned on vas clean-shaven, Dan'l, no viskers an' gold 'air!"

"'Ows'ever, Jarsper, the French gent's a-limpin' here along wi' 'is mulatter——"

"His 'oo?"

"His mulatter, blackymoor, nigger servant, Jarsper."

"By Goles!" ejaculated Mr. Shrig, reaching for hat and stick. "Then I must get a peep at this blackymoor. Mr. Weryan, sir, dooty calls, and I must ax you to vait a bit. I sha'n't keep you long, sir, but dooty is dooty. Step lively, Dan'l, lively!"

So saying, Mr. Shrig hurried away with Dan'l at his heels, leaving Jeremy to his thoughts. And of whom should he think but Olivia, her divine tenderness, her beauty and all the indescribable allurement of her. Now dreaming of her thus and she out of his reach, she became ever the more precious, and his love, worship. "That she should love him!" here was the undying, never-ending wonder of it all,—that she could possibly love such as himself! Unfeigned in his humility, simple of heart, he sought an answer and found none. Only he yearned mightily for the sound of her voice, a glimpse of her eyes, the touch of her hand, until longing became a pain.

From this he was roused by a sudden stir and bustle in the inn, a running to and fro, a voice that called, "Show the Chevalier into the Primrose! Horses and chaise for the Chevalier de Ravenac!"

Jeremy scowled and turned sharply as the door opened to disclose Mr. Shrig.

"Now, Mr. Wee—if you 're ready, sir!" said he.

Without a word and frowning still, Jeremy followed him out of the inn to where stood a post chaise, its lamps gleaming, horses stamping and postillion ready mounted. "In vith you, sir!" said Mr. Shrig. "And postboy, don't spare 'em!" So saying, he followed Jeremy into the vehicle and with a clatter of hoofs they were off and away before he could shut the door.

"And now," said Jeremy as the lights of Lewes sank behind them, "perhaps you 'll explain what it all means?"

"Mr. Weryan, sir, I only vishes I could!"

"Do your best."

"Vell, sir, seeing as some vun had 'ocussed my mare I nat'rally opened my peepers, axed questions and found as some gent had ordered a chaise for London in a precious hurry. Vhereupon, 'aving dooly bribed and corrupted the postboy of said chaise, I put my man Dan'l in said postboy's 'at and boots vith orders that said chaise vas not to reach London afore you and me——"

"Why should n't they?"

"Sir, the word being 'Caution' with a capital 'C', I acted according. But Dan'l, being a very thorough cove, spills 'em into a ditch—vich is perhaps just as well, considering. A werry zealous cove is Dan'l, wi' more o' the owdacious Old Adam in him than you might expect from his looks."

"Hum!" said Jeremy. "Your methods are original."

"As original as ever vas, sir."

Jeremy yawned and leaning back in the fast travelling chaise, watched flitting trees and hedgerow until roused by his companion's placid tones.

"You 've knowed Mr. Gillespie a long time, I think, sir?"

"All my life!" answered Jeremy thoughtfully. "He used to visit me when I was a very little, lonely lad at school—and always brought me some present or other—and if he could n't come, he would send his clerk Lockett."

"Ah, so you also know Mr. Lockett, eh, sir?"

"Very well."

"And Mr. G. vas good to you, eh?"

"Most kind—most generous. He was and is my only friend."

"And him a Scotsman! Sap-rising!" murmured Mr. Shrig. "Ah, and a werry Scotch Scotsman too! Now this here French gent, Mr. Wee, sir?"

"De Ravenac—what of him?"

"I can't fit him in nohow."

"What d' you mean?"

"Sir, I 'll tell ye—it 's his viskers!"

"Be serious!" growled Jeremy.

"Serious, sir?" sighed Mr. Shrig reproachfully. "So I am—as a judge—as a nowl! Sir, I could almost veep by reason o' them viskers; they spile my theory, they make my deductions all wrong! Serious, Mr. Wee, sir? I tell you them black viskers has humbled Jarsper Shrig to the dust, sir, to the werry dust!"

"Why?"

"Because, sir, according to con-cloosions drawed, they ain't, they can't be, and yet—they are!"

"You talk in riddles, Shrig."

"And no vonder, sir. Life's vun riddle a-top of another—'specially my life. Flowing raven locks and black viskers ain't entered into my calkilations, d' ye see. Now smooth cheeks and golden hair I was prepared for."

"Golden hair? D' ye mean Mr. O'Leary?"

"I might, sir—mind now, I don't say I do, but—I might. And vot then?"

"Hum!" quoth Jeremy, turning to view his companion's placid face.

"Ah!" murmured Mr. Shrig, looking serenely out of the window. "To be sure I know as Mr. O'Leary's your werry good friend, I heered him say so—ah, more than vunce! The question is—are you a friend of his, sir?"

"Hum!" said Jeremy again.

"And then, to be sure, there was the little matter o'—his gun, sir!"

"Accidents will happen, Shrig!"

"Werry true, sir, and it 's my dooty to see as they don't 'appen too frequent! Vich brings us back again to them black viskers!"

"Dammem!" murmured Jeremy, and closed drowsy eyes.

"Vith all my 'eart, sir!" nodded Mr. Shrig. "Regarding Mr. O'Leary, sir, 'e come to live at Weryan about a year ago, I understand. Now, where did 'e live afore?"

"I don't know."

"You vas n't acqvainted vith him afore he came to Weryan, then?"

"No."

"Werry good!"

Here, lulled by the sound of wheels, the jingle of harness and rhythmic beat of hoofs, Jeremy nodded, settled himself comfortably, folded his arms and presently fell asleep, to dream of—nothing at all. Nor did he wake from this deep and dreamless slumber until roused by the loud rattle of the wheels upon unending cobbled ways and, peering forth of the window, saw rows of houses and buildings which sped past phantom-like in a misty dawn. Shivering, he sat up and turned towards Mr. Shrig who promptly opened his eyes and nodded.

"And the vord is—breakfast, sir!" quoth he. "Here we are in the Borough; the 'George' is over yonder! Ham-and-eggs, coffee, sir, all 'ot vith a dash o' brandy or rum—eh?"

"And the sooner the better!" answered Jeremy, stretching cramped limbs.

Almost as he spoke the chaise swung suddenly to the right, clattered beneath an echoing arch and pulled up in a wide yard where, despite this so early hour, ostlers and others bustled to and fro among a jumble of vehicles of all and every sort from dashing chaise and stagecoach to huge, lumbering country wains and wagons.

"This vay, sir," said Mr. Shrig; "they knows me here." Sure enough, even as he spoke, a man approached, a burly fellow who, not seeming to so much as look at Mr. Shrig, yet hearkened attentively to such words as Mr. Shrig softly uttered and, still appearing not to glance at Mr. Shrig, nodded slightly and lounged away.

"Now, Mr. Wee, sir, breakfast being the vord, foller me!" quoth Mr. Shrig.

Thus, very soon, Jeremy found himself seated in a snug room, beside a blazing fire, where stood a table upon whose snowy cloth was laid such a breakfast that Jeremy rejoiced in his hunger; but with knife and fork poised, he glanced across at his companion.

"Shrig," said he, smiling, "the word is 'whiskers'—black whiskers—what about 'em?"

Mr. Shrig set down his coffee cup and beamed.

"Sir," he answered, "since you ax so p'inted, I takes leave to tell you as said viskers druv' into this here yard not ten minutes ago!"

"But why? What's it all mean? And how d' ye know?"

"Sir," sighed Mr. Shrig, "you'll find this here coffee werry good, 'specially vith a drop o' rum in it!"

## CHAPTER XVII

### OF BLOWS, BRUISES, AND MR. GILLESPIE, OF CLIFFORD'S INN

It was still very early and the streets more or less deserted when Mr. Shrig stopped the hackney coach and, having paid the driver, stood to watch him out of sight; then, nodding to Jeremy, he walked on westwards.

"Sir, have you ever wisited Mr. G. at his chambers?" he inquired.

"No."

"Then, here ve are!" And pausing abruptly before a sort of wide passage, he pointed to a pair of high, forbidding doors set beneath a frowning arch. "Clifford's Inn, sir," said he. "Though 'oo Clifford might be or when, I——" Here Mr. Shrig broke off to glance keenly towards a large and handsome chariot which stood some distance up the street, its mettlesome horses pawing impatiently, its coachman hunched somnolent, upon the box. "A bang-up, rifle-green chariot wi' yaller wheels!" he murmured. "And so werry early in the morning too!"

"What of it?" said Jeremy a little impatiently and turned towards the frowning arch of the Inn. Almost unwillingly Mr. Shrig followed, and lifting knobbed stick, rapped loudly upon those tall, forbidding doors. And in due season, bolts creaked, chains rattled, one of the heavy doors opened slowly and Mr. Shrig entered with Jeremy close on his heels—

to hear the great door clap suddenly behind them—to find himself beset by murder—four men armed with bludgeons who, uttering no word, sprang upon him swift, determined and always grimly silent.

In an instant Mr. Shrig's hat was smitten from his head to fall with resounding clang and Jeremy reeled back to the door and leaned there half-stunned. But now, above the murderous scuffling and sound of blows he heard a groan, caught a momentary glimpse of Mr. Shrig upon his knees, his convulsed face upturned, one arm raised feebly to ward off the blows that battered him. Thither Jeremy sprang, closed with his nearest assailant, took a blow that staggered him, but, at the same moment, had gripped an arm, a wrist, a hand wielding murderous bludgeon; awhile he wrestled, shielding himself with his opponent's body as well as he might, then—a bone-racking twist of his powerful hands and the bludgeon was his.

And now in the gloomy arch beside the gate was a battle fierce and fell and always grimly silent, except for the shock of blows, the hoarse gasping of breath, the quick, ceaseless shuffle of feet. Broad back to the wall, Jeremy fought, blow for blow. Men fell and rose again, leaped to smite and be smitten, groaned and cursed, swore at and encouraged one another, for, sheltered now in the angle of wall and door, Jeremy fought as one born to it, swift of foot and eye, of parry and counterstroke, judging speed and distance with the passionless calm of the true fighting man.

But a random blow caught him below the knee—for a moment his head was undefended—then blood was upon his tongue, trickling into his eyes, blinding him. And now, being hurt at last, Jeremy laughed, loud, harsh and fiercely exultant and, cunning no longer, sprang among his would-be slayers, raging in baresark fury. A mad hurly-burly of failing blows, shouts, cries, a scurry of feet and Jeremy, staggering in a red mist, felt powerful arms about him and the mist clearing somewhat, saw these for the arms of Mr. Shrig and found himself half-sitting, half-lying upon the steps of the porter's lodge.

"Lively—eh, Shrig?" he gasped.

"As ever vas, sir!"

"Are they—all—gone?"

"'Ide and 'air, sir! You smote 'em like Goliah o' Gath, 'ip and thigh, sir—and laughed a-doing of it! Ecod, Mr. Weryan, sir, I don't vant to 'ear you laugh again—not that vay, sir—by Goles, but you can fight!"

"It 's about all I can do!" sighed Jeremy, a little bitterly. "Had I been in better condition, Shrig——"

"You 'll do, sir, you 'll do! If you had been any better you 'd ha' killed 'em all—stone dead!"

"Are you all right?"

"As a trivet, sir—thanks to you!—I 've took a nap, d' ye see——"

"Eh—a nap?"

"Ah, they put me to sleep, sir, but just afore I dropped off like any babby, one o' them windictive coves kicked me as I lay and swung his bludgeon to finish me, but you leapt on that there cove and downed him, and conseqvently the word 'twixt you and me is 'pal'!"

"Pal?" enquired Jeremy, sitting up.

"Ah, Mr. Wee, sir. Pal's flash for friend but means a sight more! And now, can ye stand, pal?"

"Of course!" and Jeremy rose forthwith, though somewhat unsteadily, to be sure.

"Then if you 'll step inside I 'll untie Bob, the night watchman." Following Mr. Shrig into the lodge, Jeremy beheld the unfortunate Bob trussed securely in a chair and gagged with his own neckcloth, the which was no sooner removed than he burst forth into peevish complaint:

"Kicked me, they did! In the stummick, blast 'em! Jumped on me while I were asleep and trussed me up like a perishin' chicken! So blast 'em again, says I!"

"Vich sentiments, Bob," said Mr. Shrig, loosing the prisoner's bonds, "is dooly shared by us. But now the vord is—water, a bowl o' same for this 'ere gen'le-man's damaged tibby, and if so be you chance to have summat comforting in a bottle—rum, say, or a drop o' blue ruin, I'll thank ye!"

So, while Mr. Shrig ministered to his inner man, Jeremy doffed coat and waistcoat and did as much for his outer, laving such hurts and abrasions as were most accessible.

"They volloped you a bit—'ere and there, sir," quoth Mr. Shrig, observing the bruises on Jeremy's muscular forearms. "Will ye take a spot o' rum, pal? Eh, no, is it? Werry good, sir, then, if you 're ready, foller me."

Forthwith Mr. Shrig conducted Jeremy across the uneven paving of the silent old Inn, through an open doorway and thence up a creaking and dingy stair to a small gloomy landing where he rapped at a certain door, a stout oaken door black with age, on which in faded lettering dim with years, Jeremy deciphered the word:

GILLESPIE

"Not much to look at, sir," said Mr. Shrig, nodding at this time-worn oak, "but 't is sap-rising the queer lot o' fistes ha' knocked on this yer door—big and little 'uns, old and young 'uns, rich an' poor, men, vomen and children—every kind an' sort o' fist and some on 'em reekin' red wi' murder! Mr. G. used to live in the rooms downstairs, but 'e sleeps up here now—it 's safer, d' ye see."

"How safer, Mr. Shrig?"

"Sir, Mr. G. is almost as much a wictim o' windic-tiveness as I am—and here he comes at last."

A slow, shuffling step drawing nearer beyond the stout door, then a querulous voice upraised in imperious questioning:

"Who knocks? Speak out—who is it?"

"Only me, Mr. Gillespie—Jarsper Shrig, sir."

"You 're confoundedly early, Shrig!"

"So early, sir, that we werry nearly ain't here at all."

"Eh—eh? What 's that, Shrig? Bide a moment!"

Ensued a sound of bolts and chains and the door opened cautiously, discovered a head in betasselled nightcap which framed a lean face narrow of brow, prominent of chin and lighted by a pair of keen, quick eyes in whose depths lurked a twinkle.

"Now, Shrig—why, who 's that behind you? Eh, is it Jeremy? My dear lad—Shrig, hold this!" As he spoke, Mr. Gillespie drew a long-barrelled horse pistol from the folds of his dressing gown and, thrusting it upon Mr. Shrig, reached out both hands to Jeremy in eager welcome.

"How long since we last met, Jeremy—six—nine months?"

"All o' that, sir," answered Jeremy, clasping the bony hands that grasped his.

"Ay, ay—it would be! And ye 're pale, lad, pale and thin—and no wonder! Come in, come in! And—ha, Shrig, though so confoundedly early, I think the occasion warrants—nay, demands—eh, what d' ye say, Shrig?"

"Sir," answered Mr. Shrig, removing his battered hat, "I says ditto with all my 'eart!"

"Why, then, there are lemons in the corner cupboard, you know which bottle, Shrig, and if Mr. Jeremy will oblige by blowing up the fire while I get into some clothes, you shall mix and we 'll celebrate—— But, my certie, man, what 's chanced to your face—Jeremy's too?"

"Windictiveness, sir, in the shape o' bludgeons—four on 'em!"

"Ha!" exclaimed Mr. Gillespie as he carefully re-chained and bolted the door. "So soon, Shrig, so soon? Tell me about it—no, wait until I'm dressed."

Straightway he brought them into a cosy room where a heavily banked fire smouldered, pointed Mr. Shrig to the cupboard, thrust a bellows into Jeremy's grasp and vanished into his bedroom adjacent.

And now, while Jeremy blew the fire to a blaze, Mr. Shrig, as one perfectly at home, set forth a china bowl, a silver ladle, bottle, glasses, sugar and a lemon and fell to work with dexterous hands and brow of heavy portent.

Yes, a cosy room with its mellow panelling and wide, generous hearth, and comfortably furnished with its high old-fashioned press in the corner, small yet solid table, and deep-seated cosy chairs; yes, indeed, a very cosy room—except for one thing, and this, a great irregular stain in the plaster of the ceiling and immediately above Mr. Gillespie's favourite chair, an ugly blotch that seemed to Jeremy very like a monstrous hand with clutching fingers and which filled him with an unaccountable and wholly unreasoning aversion. Thus, as he puffed at the fire, he must needs lift his head every now and then (and almost despite himself, it seemed) to stare up at this unsightly blemish; and always he read in it a nameless menace, so that he wondered at himself.

He was stealing yet another look at this thing when a hand clapped his shoulder and Mr. Gillespie spoke:

"Ye're looking at yon stain, Jeremy? Years ago some poor wretch cut his throat in the chambers above—that's his blood! I've had the ceiling whitewashed often but it always comes through—and always will! And now, Shrig, if that toddy is ready, fill the glasses and favour me with an account o' your adventures."

And presently, seated round the fire all three, glass

in hand, Mr. Shrig entered into a detailed relation of his latter doings, while Mr. Gillespie sipped, nodded now and then, his keen eyes half-closed, his long, slim legs crossed; and Jeremy glancing from one to the other, spoke not at all.

"And there y' are, sir!' said Mr. Shrig at last, shutting his notebook with a snap and thrusting it carefully into an inner pocket. "And vot d' ye say to that, Mr. Gillespie?"

"That you have interested me, Shrig, particularly as regards your researches at Veryan and your mention of the Chevalier de Ravenac."

"Ha, you know Moosoo Black-Viskers, sir?"

"Let us say—I live in hopes."

"And what might you know o' same, sir?"

"An extraordinary and most interesting gentleman, Shrig."

"And vot might you be thinking, Mr. G. sir?"

"That you brew a most excellent toddy, Shrig! I'll try another glass—if there is any left." His glass being duly refilled, Mr. Gillespie turned to the silent Jeremy.

"Dear lad," said he, "I pledge you my love! Here 's joy and prosperity and—brighter days."

"Ditto here, sir," quoth Mr. Shrig, "if I may make so free!"

"Thanks!" said Jeremy.

"Yes," continued Mr. Gillespie, gazing thoughtfully at the fire, "brighter days, for, Jeremy, you have walked o' late in the very shadow o' death! And this shadow is over me also, very dark and imminent, yet I see a light beyond—I am upon the eve of my greatest achievement, my greatest triumph or——" Here Mr. Gillespie paused to shake his head at the fire and there was that in his look which compelled even Mr. Shrig to silence. "If," he went on in the same hushed tone, "if I succeed, I destroy a monster; if I fail, my work will be ended for good—in this sphere."

"Sir," enquired Mr. Shrig, his voice less jovial than usual, "eggs-ackly vot might you mean?"

"Death, Shrig!"

"Eh—eh—the 'Capital Act'? Murder, sir?"

"Murder, Shrig. You and I have seen death in many grim aspects; you and I have sent many a rogue to the gallows; we have pitted ourselves against monsters obedient to no laws and must consequently run the risk of a violent end."

"True enough, sir!" nodded Mr. Shrig placidly. "Windictiveness is all about us—I can smell it!"

"I have lately," continued Mr. Gillespie, sipping his toddy, "come upon unimpeachable evidence of crimes past and, possibly, to be, of such a nature that I—yes, even I, who have known so much of evil—am appalled!"

Mr. Shrig hitched his chair nearer to the speaker, his eyes rounder than usual, as, setting down his empty glass, Mr. Gillespie went on:

"Man is naturally prone to evil and we are all of us potential rogues and rascals. But now and then, perhaps once in a generation, is born a monster beyond our human conception, a Genius for Evil no laws can bind, a stranger alike to fear, anger, pity, and all the humanities, and therefore beyond all human understanding." Here, leaning back in his chair, Mr. Gillespie stared up at the ceiling and, by chance, his gaze rested upon that dark and ominous stain, so like a monstrous, clutching hand, whereat he frowned suddenly as he continued:

"This Inhuman Thing I have set myself to destroy or —yes, perish in the attempt. For years I have suspected, have planned and schemed with small success, but at last—and almost by accident, I have stumbled upon the needed clue, the chain is almost complete, there needs but one more link, only one, and to-night that link will be forged and this pestilence in human form destroyed, or I shall be . . . well—interested in nobler things, let us hope—And now, Shrig, since we have him safe, what are we going to do with Mr Veryan?"

"I can answer that, sir," said Jeremy. "But, first, pray why did you summon me to London?"

"Because this case that I speak of touches you very nearly."

"Ha!" exclaimed Jeremy, suddenly eager. "How so, sir?"

"Heark 'ee, Jeremy," sighed Mr. Gillespie, shaking his head; "since that evil day when, most unhappily, you learned the tragic fate of your parents, I know you have lived with the sole purpose of hunting down their slayer, have cherished the thought of exacting full vengeance. To which end you have devoted yourself to all manner of violent exercise and perfected yourself in the use of sword and pistol—and I have feared for you and grieved because you are—dear to me. For, Jeremy, this idea of personal vengeance is all wrong, lad, folly and worse! Should you kill your enemy, what remains? Emptiness! Remorse for the wasted years—misery! And so, Jeremy, to save you from this, to keep you clean from bloodshed, I have been working upon this case all these years and at last can promise you the untimely deaths of your parents shall be avenged to the very utmost—but—by the hand of Justice!"

"Then, sir——" Jeremy rose to his feet, pale and trembling, "then, sir, you—you know the murderer of my father—my mother? You can—prove his guilt beyond all—all shadow of doubt?"

"I shall do—to-night!"

"Then I entreat you to—name him!"

"Not until I have the final proof, Jeremy! Not until he is safe in the hands of the Law——"

"When—when will this be?"

"To-night, I hope! Come here with Mr. Shrig at ten o'clock and you shall know all. Many things will be revealed then—strange, terrible things! You shall see the end of my achievement!"

"To-night, at ten o'clock, sir!" nodded Mr. Shrig. "Werry good!"

"And now, pray go. My clerk will be here soon and I have a busy day before me."

"One other matter, sir," said Jeremy, a little diffidently; "will you lend me some money?"

"Money—you?" exclaimed Mr. Gillespie, staring.

"A large sum, sir!"

"How much, Jerry?"

"Five or six thousand pounds at least, sir."

"Ha? And pray, what security can you offer?"

"Nothing, sir—except my chances of the Veryan heritage. And I want the money at once, sir—as soon as possible."

"Hoots! D' ye tell me so. And for why, Jerry?"

"I wish to become a—a man o' fashion!" growled Jeremy.

"Fashion!" exclaimed Mr. Gillespie. "A man o' fashion—you, Jerry?"

"Seems infinite ridiculous, I know," admitted Jeremy. "But I wish to make some stir among the—the sporting Bon Ton, dammem! But with a purpose. In short, sir, the—the brother of a—a lady of my acquaintance is going to the devil, along with others like him, by reason of a certain French gentleman who is esteemed to be unmatched in—in certain fashionable particulars—and I believe I can outmatch him—anyhow, I mean to try."

"Aha!" murmured Mr. Gillespie. "And does this gentleman happen to be the Chevalier de Ravenac?"

"Black Viskers!" muttered Mr. Shrig.

"Yes," answered Jeremy.

"A sportsman, Jerry, a buck, a reckless gambler, a notorious duellist, and unerring pistol shot—eh?"

"Exactly, sir!"

"And you desire to match yourself against this brilliant person, Jeremy?"

"Only in one or two particulars, sir."

"You 'll clip his wings—is that it?"

"Yes."

"That means fighting! A duel!"

"No, sir. At least I don't think 't will go as far after he has seen me shoot."

"Tush! Should I lend this money 't would be sending you to risk your life like the quixotic young ass y' are!"

"Sir, risk is everywhere. And this money cannot alter my determination to cross De Ravenac sooner or later."

"You were a dogged, determined young rascal as a boy, Jerry. I suppose this was why I made ye my heir——"

"Your heir, sir! Why—indeed I—I——"

"Ridiculous of me, considering you 're so rich already, lad, or will be soon, I hope. Aweel, if 't is ready cash ye want, I may as well advance it now as later." Saying which, Mr. Gillespie rose and crossed to a desk in the corner.

"Sir," quoth Jeremy, more diffidently than ever, "if you are busy there is no hurry, for a day or so——"

"How d' ye know that, Jerry? Who shall say what the future hides? And wills must be proved; that means delay. So, if you need the money, lad, you shall have a bill this moment."

"Sir," said Jeremy heavily, "you are very good—you were always my friend in the days when I was very lonely and—minded it! And, sir, I have never told you all your kindness meant to me then and—means to me now—never thanked you and—and——"

"Don't!" said Mr. Gillespie, busy with his pen. "Pooh—nonsense, Jerry; tush, man!"

"I can't!" said Jeremy lamely. "But pray know that without you, my desolate—my lonely boyhood would have been—lonelier——"

At this, Mr. Gillespie laughed and, thrusting the note into Jeremy's fist, rose and set his two hands on Jeremy's broad shoulders.

"My dear boy," he smiled, "I was a very lonely man with only my work and—you. The pleasure was mutual! And now, Shrig, what shall we do with him until to-night?"

"Why, sir, if Mr. Wee don't mind things a bit rough but homely-like, there 's the old 'Gun' and Corporal Richard Roe, late Grenadier Guards, my pal an' comrade."

"What d' ye say, boy?"

"Thanks!" answered Jeremy.

"Then off with you until——" but at this moment was a knocking on the outer door. "Ha, that should be Lockett! You remember Lockett, my clerk, Jeremy? Pray let him in, Shrig—and remember, Jerry, if you must enact Quixote—don't go tilting at windmills!"

At this moment Mr. Lockett entered, a small, slim white haired person whose movements were very quick and bird-like and whose age might have been anything from thirty to fifty.

"Lockett," said his master, "you remember Master Jeremy?" The little man stared at Jeremy, his head on one side, uttered a soft, cooing noise of surprise and, darting forward, grasped the hand Jeremy had extended.

"Master Jeremy, to be sure!" he exclaimed. "But oh, dear, gracious me, how altered! How very much changed from the little silent boy I used to visit at school!"

"And you look just the same!" said Jeremy.

"Have you any message for me, Lockett?" enquired Mr. Gillespie.

"Here, sir!" And drawing a sealed letter from the bosom of his somewhat threadbare coat, the little clerk handed it to Mr. Gillespie with a quaint, old-world bow.

For a long moment Mr. Gillespie stared at the missive as one in profound speculation, then suddenly breaking the seal he unfolded and read it through hastily and again, more slowly, then, tearing it up, set the pieces carefully upon the fire and watched until they were consumed; when at last he looked up, his eyes gleamed beneath knit brows, his grim mouth smiled and he nodded as one well content.

"So, then—to-night, Jeremy!" said he. "At ten o'clock. To-night will be—fateful!"

## CHAPTER XVIII

### CONCERNING, AMONG OTHER THINGS, THE TEMPTATION OF ONE JESSAMY TODD, A FIGHTING MAN AND BROTHER

"As deep as a vell, sir, and as close as a noyster!" quoth Mr. Shrig, as they stepped out into Fetter Lane, which narrow thoroughfare was already astir with an ever-growing traffic, hurrying feet and rumbling wheels. "His plans all laid, Mr. Weryan, sir, his de-ductions drawed, his case com-plete, but not a vord, pal, no—not a nint until the right moment! A deep cove is Mr. G., as prefers to vork in the dark, burrer like a mole and—allus alone!"

"D' ye think he 's running any risk, Shrig?"

"Ay, I do! Risk o' the riskiest! But Lord, sir, vot o' that?" For Jeremy had stopped to glance back as if minded to return. "He 's used to risks, is Mr. G.; he 's took 'em all his life—so have I! Risk is our trade, as ye might say."

"D' ye think he 's in immediate danger?"

"As ever vas, sir! Ain't I in danger? Ain't you? We are, says I, ay—all on us. I can feel it, smell it—ah, taste it! There 's blood about, Mr. Wee, pal, sure as you 're born, sir! Some vun is a-going to die soon and sudden—and I 'ope 't is the right 'un and in the right fashion—on a gallers!"

"You sound devilish creepy, Shrig! Have you any idea of what is to happen to-night?"

"No more nor you, sir!"

"Hum!" quoth Jeremy; and they walked on in silence awhile, each busied with his own thoughts.

"You 've heered tell o' Jessamy Todd, sir?" enquired Mr. Shrig, as they turned into Holborn.

"Of course! What of him?"

"Having give up the fighting game 'e's a-staying at 'the Gun.'"

"Ha, then I shall see him?"

"You will, sir—and 'ear him too! Ye see, he's training werry 'ard."

"But if he 's done with fighting——"

"True enough, sir, he 's given up the game since 'e killed a cove accidental. But he 's a-training of hisself now for a finish fight wi' Old Nick, d' ye see!"

"What d' ye mean?"

"He 's a-larning the Scripters—Psalms, Matthew, Mark and the rest on 'em. Ye see, he 's turned hisself into a preaching cove—brands from the burning—out into the 'ighways and 'edges, sir."

"And does he never spar, even with the muffles?"

"Werry seldom, sir. Calls even boxing a wanity, nowadays—but——"

"But?" repeated Jeremy.

"But, sir, Jess is a champion never beat by none; a nat'ral born fighter is Jess, and since he 's cut hisself off, as you might say, in the middle of his career, and though denying hisself the pleasure o' pounding coves black and blue, 'e misses it crool."

"Ha, d' ye think so?"

"Sure of it, sir. Why, afore now I 've caught him all alone, 'opping about and a-punching of the empty air for lack o' summat better to use his fists on."

"Keeping in condition!" nodded Jeremy. "I'm wondering if he could be induced to spar with me?"

"Sir, there 's dozens o' young gents, reg'lar 'eavy—toddlers eager for it—ah, comes vith golden guineas in their hands, begging and beseeching Jessamy to knock 'em about a bit, but Jess only sighs and begs to be excused—but——"

"But?" repeated Jeremy again.

"Seeing as Jess is a partic'lar pal o' mine and you 're a pal o' mine, I should n't vonder as us can prevail on Jess to knock you down as frequent as you desire—though to be sure you can fight, Mr. Wee, pal—ay, by Goles you can, sir!"

By this time they had turned out of busy Holborn into Gray's Inn Lane and now Mr. Shrig swung sharp to the right into a quiet alley, at the end of which stood an ancient, cosy-looking building with a neat sign above the door whereupon the following was set forth:

THE GUN
ALES, SPIRITS & TOBACCO
BY
RD. ROE

Leading the way down a narrow passage, Mr. Shrig stopped suddenly before a small, insignificant door to grope beneath its worn step, whence he drew a ponderous key and, opening this door, ushered Jeremy into a room very small and dark but full of a fragrance delicious beyond all description, a savour so appetising that Jeremy's mouth watered and his weariness was forgotten.

"Oh, Mr. Wee, pal," sighed Mr. Shrig passionately, "is there anything as goes to a man's marrer like the smell o' fresh coffee—'specially if it comes, as you might say, 'and-in-'and vith frying bacon?" So saying, he opened yet another door and led the way into a room long and low, with black beams overhead and red tiles under-foot, a room full of odd nooks and corners and with a vast open hearth where blazed a cheerful fire before which a man was stooping, very intent upon a Dutch oven whence came the pleasant hiss of toasting bacon.

"Aha, Dick, and 'ow goes it?" enquired Mr. Shrig, whereupon the man stood up, a gigantic figure whose curly pate well-nigh touched the rafters, whose smiling, comely features were adorned by a pair of neatly trimmed whiskers, indeed a very trig and soldierly figure from newly polished shoes to carefully ironed shirt frill, despite the steel hook that replaced his left hand. "How goes it, Corporal Dick?"

"All the better for seeing you, Jarsper," answered the Corporal as they shook hands.

"Mr. Wee, sir, this is my pal an' comrade Corporal Richard Roe, late Grenadiers—Dick, this here young gent is Mr. Weryan o' Weryan as I've felt bound to take the liberty o' naming 'pal'!"

"Is that so, Jarsper? Then, sir, I beg to say as a pal o' Jarsper's is a pal o' mine. Vindictiveness again, Jarsper?"

"In the shape o' bludgeons, Dick. If it 'ad n't been for Mr. Wee—but I'll tell you about it as us eats. Where's Jessamy?"

"Out in the yard there, a-working off some o' the old Adam."

Crossing to the window, Mr. Shrig beckoned Jeremy and pointed to one who, stripped to the waist, was fighting an imaginary antagonist with the utmost spirit and gusto; a lithe, shapely man whose muscles rippled beneath a glossy skin; a man marvellously quick and nimble, who feinted and smote, ducked imaginary blows, dancing lightly on twinkling feet, and all with such graceful ease, such deftness and celerity that it was a wonder and joy to behold.

"Lord!" ejaculated Jeremy enraptured.

"Pore cove!" quoth Mr. Shrig.

"Magnificent!" exclaimed Jeremy.

"'Eart-breakin'!" sighed Mr. Shrig.

"Why so?" demanded Jeremy.

"'Aving nobody to fight 'e 'as to content hisself wi' the empty air—pore Jess!"

"Hum!" quoth Jeremy thoughtfully.

"And breakfast 's ready!" said the Corporal. "So, Jarsper, if you 'll give Jess the office I 'll dish up!"

And presently, in reply to Mr. Shrig's stentorian bellow, Jessamy Todd appeared, buttoning his coat as he came; a man of no great stature he, but clean-limbed and close-knit, a keen-eyed, short-nosed, square-jawed fellow whose mouth had a humorous twist. And now, the introductions spoken, he touched an eyebrow in respectful salutation, but seeing Jeremy's hand outstretched, grasped and shook it heartily.

So they sat down to breakfast all four and a cheery meal they made of it, for as they ate they talked on this wise:

*Jeremy:* So you are "The Thunderbolt!"

*Jessamy:* (*Sighing*) I was, sir!

*Jeremy:* And you 've done with fighting?

*Jessamy:* Ay, I have, sir—everybody an' everything, except Old Nick, an' he keeps me busy enough; we 're at it mornin', noon an' night, sir. A tough customer is Nick and up to every dodge—and when he hits he hits hard! Fair or foul all 's one to Nick and he 's here and he 's theer—like a flash; his footwork is astonishing! Ah, and he 's a glutton for punishment too! If I stops him wi' my left and floors him wi' my right, up he comes again, smiling and eager for more.

*The Corporal:* (*Skewering a piece of bacon on his fork and shaking his head at it*). Nick's a rum customer and no error! What d' you say, Jarsper?

*Mr. Shrig:* (*In the act of blowing the coffee in his saucer*) Vich I says, Dick, that seeing as Old Nick can't nowise be appre'ended, nor jailed nor gibbeted, I don't trouble about him; I leaves him to Jessamy.

*Jessamy:* (*Bolting a mouthful of toast*) Aha, but if all folks tackled him hearty and willing as I do, Jarsper, there 'd be no need for your jails or gibbets.

*Mr. Shrig:* Vich don't bear thinkin' on! A country without a jail—ain't—never vas and never vill be.

*Jessamy:* Let's hope so—some day—a world without crime, Jarsper, think of it!

*Mr. Shrig:* Crime being my meat, I 'd rather not.

*Jeremy:* (*A little hastily*) And how do you pass your time nowadays, Jessamy Todd?

*Jessamy:* I 'm a-marching, comrade, with a fair wind, shipmate, and all for the glory o' the Lord—ever and allus ready, sir, to diddle Old Nick out o' what don't belong to him—immortal souls. Sir, there 's some as steals jool'ry—gold and what not, there 's some as has to content theerselves wi' filching the humble "wipe"—but I steals souls, snatches 'em from Old Nick's claws to the everlasting Glory, brother!

*Jeremy:* Then help me to snatch a soul.

*Jessamy:* As how, brother?

*Jeremy:* (*Eagerly*) By teaching me all I can learn of the "Game."

*Jessamy:* (*Sighing and shaking his head*) The Game is "vanity and vexation o' spirit," sir!

*Mr. Shrig:* Ye see, Jess, Mr. Weryan's honouring the old "Gun" for a day or so, and him 'aving a nat-ral gift for the noble art, I good as promised you might be kind o' per-suaded to put the muffles on vith him occasional, all in the way o' kindness an' good-fellowship, eh, Jess?

*Jessamy:* (*Sighing sadly and shaking his head at the coffee-pot*) No, no, Jarsper. I 'm main sorry to disoblige but—it can't be. The Old Adam's oncommon strong in me still, and when I claps eyes on a likely cove as looks an' moves as a fighting man should, the Old Adam rampages inside o' me to that degree 't is all I can do not to toss my castor at that cove and say "Oh, brother, for the sake of love an' kindliness, put up your mauleys." For though now a man o' peace I was born an' bred to the Game, and when I meet a likely cove it comes easier to say "brother, let us fight" than "brother, let us pray."

*Mr. Shrig:* And vot might you think o' this young gentleman, Jess?

*Jessamy:* (*Sighing*) Brother Jarsper, never in all my days did I see a likelier!

*Mr. Shrig:* And I don't vonder! S'pose I tell you as 'e downed four windictive coves 'smorning—an' saved my life a-doing of it? S'pose I tell you 't is in ewidence as 'e vas throwed out o' Oxford College for thrashing a dook's son as nobody else could? S'pose I tell you as 'e beat the "Paddington Splasher" in six rounds? S'pose I tell you as, bar yourself, Jess, Mr. Weryan o' Weryan is the out-an'-outest fighter I ever see—how then, eh?

*Jessamy:* (*Viewing Jeremy with kindling eyes*) The "Paddington Slasher!" Why, sir, are you—that Mr. Veryan?

*Jeremy:* (*Smiling, though a little uncomfortable*) Yes!

*Mr. Shrig:* And vot d' ye say now, Jess?

*Jessamy:* (*Shaking head dolefully*) That you 're a-making it very 'ard for me! That Old Adam's a-rampaging inside o' me most unmerciful—what I says is—"Deliver us from temptation"—for there 's no glory nor grace in fighting for the j'y of it.

*Jeremy:* (*Shaking his head*) Not a whit! This is why you are going to teach me the Game, I hope.

*Jessamy:* Oh! And wherefore, sir?

*Jeremy:* Because I also want to snatch a man's soul from the devil. Will you help me, Jessamy Todd?

*Jessamy:* Brother, I surely will! Though how teaching you the "Game" is a-going to save some other cove's soul I don't exactly twig.

*Jeremy:* Trust me for that, Jessamy.

*Jessamy:* Right, sir! Dooty 's one thing and Pleasure's another, but when they comes both together, my soul sits up and sings merry as any lark, brother. And now, Dooty calling me Hungerford Market way, I 'm a-going chock-full o' loving kindness——

*Mr. Shrig:* And why Hungerford Market, Jess?

*Jessamy:* On account of a butcher, Jarsper, a very big, strong cove and therefore a oppressor o' the weak, him being remarkable prone to violence and bloodshed and who, though a child o' God, don't know it, Jarsper. So I 'am a-going to argufy with him, preach an' pray over him, and snatch his soul from Old Nick by hook or by crook, d' ye see.

*Jeremy:* (*Rising from the table*) I should like to go with you.

*Jessamy:* So should I, sir, only you ain't fit, brother, judging by your looks, and if I 'm to teach you the "Game" you must be ruled by me now and then, and my word to you is—bed, brother, shut eye, sir—and plenty on it!

And thus presently Jeremy followed the Corporal upstairs to a small chamber as clean, as neat and trim as the Corporal himself, and was very soon between the cool sheets. And now as he drowsed he thought of Olivia and sighed, of Bill and smiled, of the morning's affray and frowned, of Mr. Shrig, the Corporal and Jessamy Todd, and felt within himself a glow wholly unknown hitherto—and Jessamy had called him "brother!" Well, surely the comradeship of true men, whatsoever their rank or station, is a great and thrice-blessed privilege.

## CHAPTER XIX

### WHO BEING DEAD YET SPEAKETH

SAINT CLEMENT the Dane was striking the hour of ten as, halting beneath the gloomy gateway of Clifford's Inn, Mr. Shrig turned to glance at Jeremy's alert figure.

A wind was abroad, a complaining wind that wailed fitfully, that sank to a murmur, swelled to a roar and—was gone.

"Things looks innocent enough!" quoth Mr. Shrig. "But 'aving been bit vunce us should act cautious according. 'Ave you a vepping, sir?"

"No."

"Then take this stick o' mine; you'll find it play werry sweet if necessary." So Jeremy took the knotted stick, twirled it in powerful grasp and nodded. Thereupon from capacious pocket Mr. Shrig drew a formidable pistol wherewith he rapped loudly upon the stout door. And, after some while, a hoarse voice challenged them:

"'Allo! 'Oo's knocking? Speak up!"

"'Tis me, Bob, Shrig o' Bow Street to see Mr. G."

At this, after some delay, the door opened a foot or so and the porter's face appeared, together with the yawning muzzle of a blunderbuss.

"Aha!" he exclaimed nodding. "If 't is you, Mr. Shrig, so be it! Only I ain't a-going to be took an' trussed up again like a perishin' chicken—not me! I'm awake, I am, and powerful ready to kick if need be."

"Good!" quoth Mr. Shrig, pocketing his pistol. "Caution 's the vord, Bob! No signs of any rough customers to-night—eh?"

"Not so fur."

"Any person enquired for Mr. Gillespie to-night, Bob?"

"Nary a soul."

"Ha' you let in any strangers?"

"No."

"Rum!" murmured Mr. Shrig, blinking up at the swinging lantern whose feeble rays served only to make the darkness more visible. "So you ain't seen nothing nor nobody onusual—eh, Bob?"

"Nary a thing! Leastways, as I were a-crossing the Inn 'bout 'arf an hour ago I see summat like a dwarf peering down at me from Mr. Gillespie's winder."

"Eh—a dwarf, Bob?"

"Well, an 'unchback then, leastways the shadder of an 'unchback all crooked, it looked—one shoulder 'igher than t' other."

"Ha!" nodded Mr. Shrig. "A dwarf or 'unchback peering from Mr. G.'s vinder 'bout 'arf an hour ago! Werry good! Has his clerk Lockett gone, Bob?"

"Gone—ah, hours ago. But 'e come back about twenty minutes afore you and in a precious 'urry!"

"In an 'urry, vas 'e?" murmured Mr. Shrig.

"Ah! 'Bob,' says 'e, ketching 'old o' my arm, ''ave you 'eard anything?' says 'e. 'Only the wind!' I says."

"Rummer and rummer!" murmured Mr. Shrig. "Is the gate into Fetter Lane locked, Bob?"

"No, I don't lock no gate 'till——" Bob's voice was lost in a sudden flurry of wind, a fierce gust that boomed in the arch above them, clapping to the great door with reverberating bang, extinguishing the feeble lantern and rushing away to fill the night with clamour, near and far.

"Vind 's a-rising!" murmured Mr. Shrig.

"Wind?" exclaimed Bob, spitting fierce and loud. "I 'ates the wind—specially o' nights! Lord, I 've been 'earing creepin' futsteps an' shrieks an' cries—'ark to that now!" Again that rush of bellowing wind, fiercer, louder than before, and borne upon this swelling pandemonium another sound, faint, inarticulate, scarce to be distinguished, yet full of evil omen.

"'T were n't all the wind!" quoth Mr. Shrig, as the fierce hubbub subsided.

"Some one cried out!" said Jeremy.

"Then quick and cautious is the vord, sir!" and Jeremy heard the sharp click of Mr. Shrig's pistol as he cocked it. "Now, foller me, pal!"

Stepping from the shadow of the gateway, they began to cross the wide Inn where the rising wind rioted and presently heard the approaching sound of hasty feet and descried a dim form that tossed wild arms and moaned and cried:

"He won't answer me! Oh, he won't answer! I should n't ha' left him alone!"

"Mr. Lockett, be that you, sir?" At sound of Mr. Shrig's voice, the little clerk ran at him to grip his arm and shake it wildly:

"Oh, Shrig—Shrig——" he gasped. "I can't make him hear! His light 's a-burning—see, there it is yonder—but he won't answer—and yet his light's a-burning!"

Now glancing at this lighted window, Jeremy must needs bethink him of that great, clutching hand in the ceiling, and he shivered suddenly.

Side by side they hurried forward all three and, reaching the door, Mr. Shrig uncocked his pistol and therewith rapped loud and long, but without avail; hereupon he handed the weapon to Jeremy and, taking a clasp knife from his pocket, fell to work on the window and, having opened it at last, clambered through with Jeremy and Mr. Lockett at his heels. Then, the window closed against the racketing wind, they stood motionless, listening. A rat scampered in the wainscot, a distant casement rattled in a wind gust, but all else was silent; no sound reached them from that upper chamber where burned the light.

"Oh, God," whispered Mr. Lockett, "why is he so still?"

Fumbling in the gloom, Mr. Shrig led on, and presently they were climbing a dark and creaking stair and so to the landing above, lighted by a dismal lantern whose flickering beam showed that time-worn door that bore the word:

GILLESPIE

Here Mr. Shrig knocked, then recoiled suddenly with pistol levelled, for this door had swung open stealthily beneath his hand, revealing a passage dim-lit by a narrow beam of light where the sitting-room door stood ajar.

Now, staring upon this partly open door, Jeremy caught his breath, waiting for he knew not what.

"Mr. Gillespie, are ye there, sir, are ye there?" called Mr. Shrig, his voice sounding strangely hoarse and loud.

A long moment of dreadful silence broken at last by a groan from Mr. Lockett:

"Oh—why don't he answer? If he's there why—why won't he answer? Oh, God, I should n't ha' left him——"

Suddenly Mr. Shrig strode forward and, flinging wide that half-open door, halted upon the threshold, pistol in hand.

"Lord!" he gasped in sibilant whisper. "Lord love us!"

Mr. Gillespie sat sprawled in his armchair, his grizzled head prone upon the little table before him, and it needed but one glance at his unnatural posture to show that he was dead.

"So they 've got 'im at last!" said Mr. Shrig, removing his hat. And then Mr. Lockett had darted into the room to fall upon his knees beside that sprawling shape, wringing his hands.

"Oh, my poor master!" he whimpered. "My good, kind master! Oh, Shrig—Shrig, say he is n't dead!"

"Nobody 'll ever be deader!" sighed Mr. Shrig, lifting the dead man's nearest hand very gently. "But he 's still limber and varm! He vas killed say 'alf an hour, threequarters—say an hour ago, I reckon."

Trembling and sick with horror, Jeremy lifted his haggard gaze to the ceiling blotched by that awful stain which seemed more like a vengeful, grasping hand than ever now, its clutching fingers crooked above its dead. Dumb with grief, he turned away and, crossing to the hearth, leaned there, staring into the dying fire, dully conscious of Mr. Lockett's broken lamentations and of Mr. Shrig's heavy tread going up and down and to and fro behind him and in the bedroom beyond.

"Your woe, Mr. Lockett, does ye credit, sir," said Mr. Shrig after some while. "Deceased vas a gen'leman o' parts and vun as I regarded with a respectful admiration, familiarised by friendship! And now 'ere 'e lays, sir, dead by the Capital Act, vherefore it behoves me to be dooly prompt! So, Mr. Lockett, if vhile you veeps you 'll lend an 'and to our esteemed friend's cadaver, I 'll be obleeged."

Here ensued a confused scuffling sound with the creak of chair and table; and guessing the cause, Jeremy bowed his head upon his arm and shivered anew, while mingled with the old clerk's whimpering, he heard Mr. Shrig's placid tones:

"Pockets empty and the fatal vepping apparently wanished! Must ha' bled to death pretty qvick—here 's gallons on it, d' ye see—and yet—hum! Killed as 'e sat—a down'ard stab through the right breast—precious deep, too! Yet 'e went off werry peaceful, judging by his look."

Then Jeremy turned and, although Death was before him in dire shape, his horror gave place to wonder and a profound awe, for upon this lean, dead face sat a great and serene dignity.

They had placed him back in his chair, but even so, his right hand and arm still lay upon the table before him, a hand that gleamed whitely against the dark wood of the table whose polished surface was dulled, here and there, by ghastly stains and blotches; a bony fist, its pallid fingers clenched all save one, the long gaunt forefinger rigidly outthrust as if pointing. Now looking closer, Jeremy saw the nail and tip of this pointing finger stained with blood.

"Ah, you 've tvigged his daddle, pal, his 'and, sir!" said Mr. Shrig. "You see summat rum about it —eh?"

"Look," whispered Jeremy, "where is he pointing, and what at?"

"Sir, I 'll tell ye—at nothing in particular—not a thing! But vot *is* the corpse a-trying to say? Take a good peep at it! First it is a-saying, werry plain, as the blow come afore Mr. G. could make a move to defend hisself, 'im probably stooping over papers on the table afore him. Werry good! It likewise tells us as wictim did not die all at once."

"How—d' you know this?"

"Obserwation, sir!" sighed Mr. Shrig, nodding placidly at the stiffening form in the chair. "The murderer 'aving struck the fatal blow, vipes the reeking veapon on Mr. G.'s coat skirts, pockets it, takes said papers and—burns 'em werry careful—you can twig the ashes on the 'earth, sir. But——" and here Mr. Shrig paused to nod three several times, "while his murderer's back 's turned, Mr. G. tries to write us a message——"

"A message?" gasped Jeremy. "Where—where?"

"Sir, on the table afore you."

"I see nothing."

"You vill, if you look close enough—ye see 't is a bit 'ard to make out, being wrote by Mr. G.'s finger in his own gore."

"Horrible—oh, horrible!" cried Mr. Lockett.

"Admirable, sir—werry ad-mirable!" quoth Mr. Shrig with eyes agleam. "A truly wonnerful man were Mr. G.! Though to be sure I can't make 'ead nor tail of wot he 's wrote—yet. But 'ere goes!" So saying, Mr. Shrig very gently drew the table from under the dead hand with its pointing finger and, sinking upon his knees, began to examine the stained mahogany while Jeremy peered over his shoulder.

"Now, sir, d' ye see anything?"

"Yes!" answered Jeremy in awed tones, for what he saw was:

"'Ere 's vot looks like a O and a P and a S," said Mr. Shrig; "stop a bit and I 'll make a draft of 'em in my little reader—vatch an' see as I takes 'em down correct." And drawing forth notebook and pencil, he began to copy therein, slowly and with much painful care, such faint and irregular characters as that dying finger had found strength to trace:

"That 's all, I think, sir?"

"Yes, I see no more."

"You 'll ob-serve as letters begins fairly plain and ends werry shaky, sir? Vich is only nat'ral, considering as 'e vas a-dying vith every letter—gasping 'is life out and a-writing this here message to us—in his werry own gore! There 's stoopendious determination for ye!"

"Heroic!" said Jeremy.

"Heroic is the only vord for it, sir!"

"But what does it mean, Shrig?"

"Why, the beginning 's plain enough, sir: first a Capital J for Jeremy or Jarsper, then 'beware' next an O an' a P with SH, as don't make sense, and last, two or three marks as may mean anything. But this can bide a bit, the question now being . . . vot can you tell us, Mr. Lockett?"

"Little enough, I 'm afraid, Shrig—too, too little."

"First, sir, about that letter you brought Mr. G. this werry morning; 't was a letter 'e expected, I think —a letter as I see him read and tear up immediate—as you 'll remember, p'raps?"

"To be sure!" nodded Mr. Lockett.

"How did you come by that letter?"

"I was instructed by Mr. Gillespie to call for it this morning at a small, riverside tavern Blackfriars way, a very disreputable place called the 'Jolly Waterman.'"

"This morning?" repeated Mr. Shrig. "You must ha' got there precious early."

"Yes, Mr. Gillespie made it a point that I must knock at the door precisely on the stroke of five o'clock."

"And 'oo gave you the letter?"

"A woman."

"Young or old?"

"Young, I think—though her face was muffled in a shawl."

"Did she say anything?"

"Not a word. Nor did I; she just opened the door and thrust the letter into my hand."

"Was the superscription wrote in an eddicated fist or no?"

"The letter bore no superscription."

"And you don't know contents o' said letter?"

"No, Shrig—oh, deary me—not I!"

"Vot time did you leave Mr. G. to-night?"

"It would be about seven or a little after."

"And vot vas the last words 'e said to you?"

"His last words! Oh, dear, his last words indeed! Oh, Shrig, I shall never hear him speak again! His last words? Let me think! Yes, I remember: 'Very well, Arthur,' said he—always used my Christian name after business hours—'Very well, Arthur, come back if you must, though there's no need; but, if you will, come with the others at ten o'clock.' So I left him—went home to supper—but, Lord, I could n't wait until ten——"

"Why not?"

"Because I was uneasy—anxious——"

"Because 'e vas to meet some person or persons unknown, eh?"

"Yes."

"'Oo might they be, sir?"

"Ah, if I could only tell you that, Shrig—but I can't, I don't know—I don't know!"

"But you vas his con-fee-dential clerk, sir?"

"Yes, but only up to a point. There were some cases, generally the most dangerous, he worked alone—a secretive man always, Shrig."

"Vot time did you get 'ere to-night, Mr. Lockett?"

"About half-past nine."

"Might you 'ave 'appened to see or hear anything? Say a cry? Say a face peering down from Mr. G.'s vinder?"

"No, Shrig!"

"Did you knock at the door?"

"Not at once. Being so much before the appointed time I walked up and down and watched his light until St. Clement struck the three quarters, then I knocked and could get no answer."

"And you see nobody and heard nothing?"

"Nothing at all!"

"Hum!" quoth Mr. Shrig, pinching his chin and staring up at the ceiling. "You see nothin'—you heered nothin', and nat'rally can tell us nothin'! Vich brings us to the qvestion: Can this here room tell us anything? Werry little, seeing as Mr. G. died without a struggle—Vich is a pity, a great pity and werry 'ard on me!"

"How on you?" demanded Jeremy.

"A corpse as strives and struggles can tell more nor vun as don't, Mr. Weryan, pal! But vot says this room, now? First, it vants to tell me as the murderer wore spurred boots——the lowest stave o' the cheer yonder is noo-cut and scored, you can see the scratches if you 'll look! Could only ha' been done by a spur rowel—probably vhen the murderer jumped up to commit the fact. Next, it tells me as, 'aving burnt the papers every bit—vich is another pity—the murderer searches 'is wictim's pockets for more and, so doing, gets blood on 'is fingers and then 'earing footsteps below, 'e crosses to the vinder, and remembering 'is shadder—oh, 'e 's a werry downy bird is this Capital Cove . . . 'e turns hisself into an 'unchback; 'e crouches an' peeps."

"Horrible," gasped Mr. Lockett.

"Werry as-toot and remarkably downy, sir! But, being at the vinder, 'e leaves a smear o' blood on the blind—you can see it if you look."

"I see it, yes—yes!" whispered Mr. Lockett. "Though 't is very small!"

"Let 's 'ope 't ' is big enough to 'ang and gibbet 'im, sir," sighed Mr. Shrig. "Now finding 'is hands bloody, our Capital Cove looks for summat to vipe 'em on—the qvestion is—vot, and vheer?" Mr. Shrig's keen gaze roved from wall to wall, from floor to ceiling, into every nook and cranny while he pinched at his square chin and pursed his lips in a soundless whistle. "Ah, that's the qvestion!" he repeated. "The skirts of his wictim's coat—no, I 've looked! The cushions o' the cheers—no, ditto! The 'earth rug? No, I think not——" Mr. Shrig turned up a corner of the worn rug with the toe of his boot and stooped swiftly with a sudden exclamation. "By Goles—yes!" And he rose with a charred and blood-stained piece of linen in his hand. "Mr. G.'s 'ankercher! 'Aving wiped 'is daddles on it our Capital Cove throws it on the fire, but a puff of vind blows it off again and under the corner o' the rug, d' ye see! . . . Mr. G.'s werry own vipe—here's his monnicker in the corner!" So saying, Mr. Shrig spread out the pitiful stained thing upon the table and beamed down at it in mild satisfaction; then, having placed it carefully in his bulbous pocket-book, he stood pinching his chin and staring at that tragic form in the easy chair.

"A werry brave man vas yourself, Mr. G.'!" he apostrophised. "But then you vas also dooly cautious and not to be caught napping, sir! Yet there you sits, growing colder and colder, your intellects all gone, sir, seeing nothin', hearing nothin' and never to speak no more—a lump o' senseless clay——"

"Shrig, Shrig—for the love of God!" gasped Mr. Lockett in a strangled voice.

"Mr. Lockett, Death's only death, arter all, and the common lot, sir——"

"But not—not such a death as this, Shrig! Can you do nothing—find out and punish the fiend who did this? Is there no clue? Have you no idea, no theory or suspicion?"

"Why, I von't say 'yes' and I don't say 'no,' sir, but this I can tell ye—the party as killed Mr. Gillespie vas no stranger!"

"Ha—what d' ye mean?" demanded Jeremy.

"Sir, Mr. G. sits here alone to-night, expecting a desperate man, a dangerous cove and, being dooly cautious, is conseqvently prepared—see here!" And jerking open a drawer in the table, Mr. Shrig pointed to a long-barrelled pistol that lay there ready to hand. "Loaded and fresh-primed, sir, and never touched! And why, d' ye suppose? I 'll tell ye: Mr. G. has left the doors of his chambers open, and sitting here pistol to hand, 'e vaits. And presently 'e hears feet upon the stair, a knock at the door, shouts 'Come in'—vith his hand on this drawer—the footsteps comes on, the door yonder opens and Mr. G. stares and forgets all his caution, so soon as 'e sees 'oo his wisitor is, and then——"

Mr. Shrig stopped suddenly and stood staring towards the half-open door as, above the rumble of wind, above the rattle of that distant casement, came a sound of masterful feet upon the stair outside, feet that halted suddenly near by; and then was a loud imperious summons on the door of the landing.

Mr. Shrig's hand vanished into his pocket and they heard the sharp click of his pistol as he cocked it: "Come in!" he called.

Heavy feet that trod with dignified deliberation, a perfunctory tap on the half-open door that swung wide to show the tall, elegant figure of the Chevalier de Ravenac.

## CHAPTER XX

### MR. SHRIG TAKES UP THE TRAIL

"AH, pardon!" said he, blinking in the candlelight. "I commit the mistake, I fear—excuse! I come to see Monsieur Gillespie, but I come wrong, it seems!"

"No, right!" answered Mr. Shrig. "Step in, sir, peep about and you 'll see 'im."

The Chevalier stared in apparent surprise, then advancing into the room, stopped suddenly and, uttering an inarticulate exclamation, let fall his walking cane which Mr. Shrig picked up.

"*Mon dieu!*" gasped the Chevalier, recoiling. "Oh but it is 'orrible—mos' 'orrible!"

"Werry much so!" answered Mr. Shrig, and turning his back, gave a sudden, strong twist to the gold-mounted cane, then sighed and shook his head at it reproachfully.

"Sir . . . the poor Monsieur Gillespie, I am amazed . . . *il est atroce* . . . the poor Monsieur Gillespie! Pray 'ow come this so 'orrible affair?"

"Moosoo," answered Mr. Shrig, eyeing the cane a little wistfully as he returned it, "I don't know no more on it than you do."

"Ah!" exclaimed the Chevalier, glancing at Jeremy. "And do I see again Monsieur—Veryan, is it not?"

Jeremy bowed, and observing the other's handsome, sinister face and arrogant air, felt again that fierce, unreasoning abhorrence of the man.

"*Helas*, sir, but this is terrible! The poor Monsieur Gillespie! When did it 'appen? I come to talk the business with him and now—ah, but it is too 'orrible—I will go——"

"'Arf a minute, sir," said Mr. Shrig, pushing forward a chair; "since you are 'ere p'r'aps you von't mind me axing a few questions?"

"But no, my friend—only—that poor Monsieur Gillespie—it is too terrible to be seen!"

"Then don't look at it, sir! Sit vith your back to it—so!"

"Thank you, I prefer to stand—now, my friend, speak me your questions which I will take pleasure to answer as please me most."

"First then, your name, sir?" and out came Mr. Shrig's notebook.

"I am Gaston, Emile des Raux de Ravenac."

"Ha!" quoth Mr. Shrig, shaking his head. "You 're a furriner, I think?"

"A Chevalier of France, monsieur."

"And vot might you be doing in England, moosoo?"

"Sir?" exclaimed the Chevalier haughtily.

"Your trade, business or per-fession?"

"*Sacré!* Do I not tell you? I am a gentleman of France."

"Werry good, but vot beside, moosoo? Likewise, your present abode, domi-cile or 'abitation, sir?"

"*Tiens!*" cried the Chevalier. "Who are you to demand the so impertinent question so many?"

"I 'm a nofficer o' the law from Bow Street, moosoo. Come, vhere do you live?"

"An officer! *Alors!* Then I tell you, *Monsieur l'Officier*, I live in London."

"Vhereabouts, sir—your district, street and number?"

"This, monsieur, is my business."

"Werry good! How long have you known Mr. Gillespie?"

"For 'ow long? Two—three months, maybe."

"Then Mr. Lockett, you 'll 'ave seen this French gent afore?"

"Never in my life, Shrig."

"Hum!" quoth Mr. Shrig, staring wistfully at the Chevalier's elegant Hessian boots. "Quite sure o' that, Mr. Lockett?"

"Quite."

"And vot d' you say to that, moosoo?"

The Chevalier shrugged gracefully. "It is always that I see Mr. Gillespie—alone."

"And vot might you want wi' Mr. G. at this time o' night?"

"*Monsieur l'Officier*, it is my business."

"And vot is your business, sir?"

"Completely mine, *mon ami—tout seul!*"

"Tout vot, moosoo?"

"Ah, pardon!" sighed the Chevalier. "It is that I do not speak my business except to Monsieur Gillespie and . . . *hélas*—'e is dead!"

"As dead as ever vas!" nodded Mr. Shrig. "Murdered, sir, at about nine o'clock to-night! Did you come by app'intment vith Mr. G., sir?"

"But no, my friend, it is 'ow you say?—by chance. I am driving past Clifford's Inn and I think—ah, it is 'ere lives Monsieur Gillespie the man of law; I will call and talk my business and—violà, 'ere I am!"

"So then it vas n't to see Mr. Gillespie as you drove up so fast and fur'ous from the country this morning, moosoo?"

The Chevalier's blue eyes narrowed as they scanned the speaker's placid features, then he smiled with a flash of white teeth.

"*Sapristi*, sir, but in London I 'ave much business, many of affair."

"Still you 're often in the country, sir."

"But yes."

"In—say, Sussex—say, Brighton, or Brighthelmstone as some calls it—eh, moosoo?"

"I 'ave been there, yes."

"Then p'raps you might 'appen to know a werry Irish gent, name of O'Leary?"

Here, once again, Jeremy saw the Chevalier's eyes narrow as they scanned his questioner's heavily serene features.

"I 'ave met a Monsieur O'Leary many years since. But now, my friend the officier, I make my depart, I leave you to the business of this so unfortunate Monsieur Gillespie. You 'ave p'raps discover the—'ow you say?—the motive for the crime, yes?"

"Robbery, sir!" nodded Shrig. "Seeing his vatch is wanished, together with purse an' other wallybles, robbery, it is, moosoo. Ah, and vot's more, 'is murderer left 'is 'at behind 'im as a clue, vich on the whole vas werry thoughtful of him, con-sidering as 'is name is all dooly wrote into said 'at werry conspicuous!"

"*Ceil!*" exclaimed the Chevalier. "I felicitate you, *Monsieur l'Officier;* you p'raps bring the so guilty one to the justice soon?"

"Ah, p'raps sooner than some might expect!" nodded Mr. Shrig. "And, moosoo, my 'opes is rose according!"

"Let us 'ope so, monsieur, for the sake of our so poor, mos' lamented Monsieur Gillespie."

So saying, the Chevalier saluted them with stately bow and went his leisurely way.

"But Shrig," whispered Mr. Lockett, so soon as these slow footsteps had died away, "surely you know the motive of this dreadful crime was more than robbery?"

"But then it don't do to say all you knows—all the time, Mr. Lockett, sir."

"And I saw no hat, Shrig——"

"Howsomever I found vun, sir, a-laying in the corner yonder, a-vaiting to be found. I got it in my pocket at this i-dentical minute!"

"Show us!" said Jeremy.

Slowly and almost unwillingly Mr. Shrig drew from his pocket a cloth cap, a dingy, sodden-looking, greasy thing which he proceeded to smooth and straighten out with the tenderest care, as if it had been the most rare and delicate object in the world.

"And there y' are!" he murmured, turning the unlovely object over in gentle fingers. "And here, look ye, so as there can't be no mistake, tucked into the lining, this bit o' paper with owner's name all wrote out nice an' careful!" Saying which, he drew forth a stained and crumpled piece of paper whereon Jeremy deciphered these words:

JOS. SHIELDS 28, SAUCY NELL.

"And there y're again!" nodded Mr. Shrig. "'Joseph Shields,' vaterside character, '*Saucy Nell*' 'is boat, and tventy-eight 'is number. And nothing could be fairer than that!"

"Why this," cried Mr. Lockett, "this puts a different light on the dreadful business!"

"It do——" quoth Mr. Shrig, slipping paper into lining and rolling the cap up again with the same tender solicitude, "and it don't!"

"My poor master had many enemies among the riverside cut-throats, Shrig, as you know."

"Oceans!" nodded Mr. Shrig. "And there 's Clement a-chiming eleven, and I 've a tidy lot to do 'twixt now and to-morrow morning. So I 'll ax you, Mr. Wee, sir, to tell Corporal Dick as I sha' n't be 'ome to-night. Mr. Lockett lives close by 'The Gun' and can show you all the near cuts."

"Yes, yes!" murmured the little clerk, absently, smoothing the nap of his somewhat shabby hat. "And yet—my poor master! I—I don't like to leave him, Shrig!"

"Lord bless your 'eart, Mr. Lockett, 'e 's nice an' comfortable now, 'e ain't a-going to vorry about nothing no more, and that 's summat, arter all! That theer French gent now—Moosoo Black Viskers—you ain't seen 'im afore, you say?"

"No, Shrig, never before."

"Vot d' ye think of him, Mr. Lockett?"

"A dominating, a very arresting personality, Shrig."

"Arrestin'?" repeated Mr. Shrig with a thoughtful nod. "Sir, 't is the only vord as fits the case!"

"And in spite of all your questions, Shrig, he told you nothing."

"Nary a thing, sir, and my 'opes is a-soaring in conseqvence."

"Why?" demanded Jeremy.

"Sir, I 'll tell you. In all my days I never see a subjeck as drawed me so powerful strong. Ecod, pal, if all my subjecks vas like Black Viskers my profession vould be a continual capital J O Y—j'y, sir—and 'twixt you an' me, sir, I begin to think us 'll be able to fit him in werry comfortable, arter all! And now, sirs, if you 're ready!" So saying, Mr. Shrig, taking up hat and stick, blew out the candles.

The fire was dim, but its dying embers shed a rosy, a soft, comfortable light that served only to lend a new and indescribable horror to that awful, rigid form so grimly huddled in the easy-chair. But the last thing which drew and held Jeremy's gaze was the blot in the plaster of the ceiling, that monstrous hand whose fingers, talonlike, were clutched above its dead.

## CHAPTER XXI

### BRIEFLY DESCRIBES THE CONVIVIALITY OF MR. ARMADALE

SIDE by side through deserted, wind-swept streets went Jeremy and the little, white-headed clerk, their footsteps echoing forlornly, themselves speechless and busied with much the same gloomy thoughts.

"So passes a great soul, sir!" sighed Mr. Lockett at last. "These eyes shall never look upon his like again! My honoured master!"

"My only friend!" said Jeremy.

"And thus," continued Mr. Lockett mournfully, "ends for me a connection of thirty-five odd years! My working days are done, my world is topsy-turvy! And yet, even so, it seems impossible he is dead—where is now that keen intellect, that strong and dauntless soul of him?"

"Living a greater life, maybe," said Jeremy.

"Let us hope so, sir, let us pray it may be so indeed."

After this they walked again in silence, hearkening to the wind that filled the darkness about them with stealthy rustlings, the shrill complaint of swinging signboards, sighs, moans, softly desolate sobbing and a thousand such dismal sounds.

"Hark to it!" exclaimed Mr. Lockett suddenly. "If I believed in ghosts—which I do not—I should vow they were all about us very close, and closest of any—his, my poor master's, now at your elbow, now at mine, trying to tell us the name of his murderer—ah, sir, if only he had written the name instead of wasting his dying strength trying to warn you——"

"Warn me?" repeated Jeremy. "Lockett, what d' you mean?"

"Mr. Veryan," answered the little clerk, stopping to peer up into Jeremy's face, "I do verily believe my master spent his last breath trying to write a warning to you and you only."

"But J stands for Jasper also——"

"But he has kept guard over you all these years, Master Jeremy, according to the promise he made your father, and you would be the only one in his thoughts as death crept on him——"

"D' ye think so, Lockett—God in heaven, d' ye think he spent his last strength for me?"

"Sir, I feel positively assured of it. Your father meant to make Mr. Gillespie his sole executor and guardian to yourself; I know, for 't was I drew up the new will which was never signed. Since when Mr. Gillespie, busy man though he was, harassed by many affairs, and his life threatened more than once, still continued to watch over you, to be a kind of father to you, lonely child as you were, and as he tried to guard you from evil while he lived, so he did while dying!"

Jeremy strode on some distance in silence and when he spoke again his voice sounded harsher than usual.

"You think the warning was for me?"

"I do!"

"And of what would he have warned me—of whom?"

"God alone knows that, Mr. Veryan. But these latter months, ever since you—ah—quitted Oxford, sir——"

"You mean 'was expelled'!" growled Jeremy.

"Since then, sir, he has seemed to think some grave danger threatened you, which feeling increased upon him until at last he despatched Jasper Shrig to bring you up to London—though just too late to save you from the murderous attack you suffered."

"But why should he so suspect, and—whom? Surely he must have mentioned his suspicions to you? Come, speak, man!"

"This, Mr. Veryan, I may not even hint at—I dare not!"

"Dare not?" repeated Jeremy, turning to stare at his companion. "What do you fear?"

"No one, sir. But it is all too horrible—too unthinkable! And now, since all proof is destroyed, my lips must remain sealed."

"Man, what do you mean? What proof do you speak of?"

"The papers Mr. Gillespie's murderer burned to-night so carefully, sir. Without these papers—to hint at what little I suspect would be useless—worse than useless, sir."

Now beholding the speaker's determined face, Jeremy questioned no further and walked awhile in silence; but presently the little clerk ventured to lay a hand upon his arm and spoke in voice that somehow reminded Jeremy of his solitary boyhood:

"Dear Master Jeremy, has my reticence hurt you—offended you?"

"Dear old Keyhole—no!" answered Jeremy, drawing the little man's hand within his arm. "You mind how I used to call you 'Keyhole' when you visited me at school—graceless young urchin that I was?"

"Yes, yes, Master Jerry, to be sure I remember! 'T was I taught it you—'Without the keyhole you can't Lockett'—a poor enough joke, sir."

"Yet it served well enough!" nodded Jeremy. "It made us friends on the spot—and friends once, friends ever, eh, my Keyhole?"

"Thanks, Master Jeremy, thanks! 'T is kind in you to remember, and does me good, sir—especially to-night."

And now as they went, arm in arm, the streets seemed somehow less dreary and desolate and the wind less unkind.

"As to the man Shrig, you've known him some time, I think, Lockett?"

"These twenty-odd years. A remarkable character, Master Jeremy; he is what I may term a philosopher in crime, with nerves, like his hat, made of iron."

"Also he has a sense of humour," said Jeremy.

"True, sir. Indeed there is only one Shrig! Shrewd, fearless and utterly relentless in his methods, he has brought many a rogue to the gallows, as I know, and consequently is the most feared and hated man in London among the criminal community; bless you, his life has been attempted so often that he takes it as a matter of course, now. Yes, Shrig and I have been associated in many cases, but—that is all past and done; my working days are ended, alas!"

"And what," enquired Jeremy, as the little man sighed thus dolefully, "what shall you do in the future, my old Keyhole?"

"Dear Master Jerry, I propose devoting myself to one who is as solitary, almost, as myself."

"Who?"

"One who came into my life not long ago, a gentle, frightened waif, as pure and sweet as she is young and lovely, a girl who had fled a peril of temptation. She is the niece of my landlady, sir, herself not long for this life, I fear."

"And when she dies, you'll care for this girl—eh, Lockett?"

"God aiding me, sir. I've been a lonely creature all these years since my young wife died and left me childless. And I always longed for a daughter! And now, it seems, Heaven has sent me one at last. In these long years I have contrived to put by a little money, sir, and how use it better than in caring for this lonely young girl?"

"How like you, old Keyhole, how exactly like you!" exclaimed Jeremy, squeezing the little clerk's arm. "Don't I mind how you would spend your money on me when I was a forgotten, unlovely imp——"

"Never unlovely, Master Jeremy—ah, no! Good gracious!" ejaculated Mr. Lockett, halting suddenly. "Dear me, who can that be!" They had turned into Gray's Inn Lane and were close upon that narrow alley leading to "The Gun" whence issued a voice upraised in uncertain song, a rich, tenor voice that sang with excessive feeling and expression, albeit somewhat marred by hiccoughs, thus:

"Drink to me only (hic!) thine eyes
And I will (hic!) with mine.
Or leave a (hic!) within the cup
And I'll not ask for (hic!) . . ."

Hurrying forward, Jeremy presently espied the musician—hat over one eye, legs a-straddle and back propped against a wall—an elegant young gentleman though his rumpled finery bore signs of recent stress and strain, yet none the less a swaggering, devil-may-care young gentleman whom there was no mistaking.

"Armadale!" exclaimed Jeremy scowling.

Mr. Armadale broke off in the middle of a note, hiccoughed solemnly and removed his hat with a flourish.

"'S' me, sir!" he answered. "Rish-ard Armadale at your shervish—eh—what—why, b'ged, it's Veryan—iss Jeremy, demme if 't is n't! Well met, my tulip! Jerry, you (hic!) behold in me . . . devoted lover sherry-nading peerlesh beauty . . . livesh about here, she does, 't least if she does n't, I'll be dem'd! An angel, Jerry, an angel o' light——"

"Come with me!" growled Jeremy.

"You know the young gentleman, Master Jeremy?" enquired Mr. Lockett anxiously.

"Yes, Lockett, I'll see after him—call and see me at 'The Gun' sometime."

"I shall be honoured, sir—you are sure you can—er—manage the gentleman?"

"Quite!"

"Then good night, Master Jeremy, and thank you!" Saying which, Mr. Lockett hastened on down the alley.

"Now," said Jeremy, setting vigorous arm about Mr. Armadale's unsteady person, "Come on!"

"Shtop a minute, old f'ler . . . wanner tell you I . . . I tell you I wanna tell you I metanangelo' light-anlovlinesh——"

But despite Mr. Armadale's plaints, protests and reproaches, Jeremy hurried him on forthwith and into the hospitable shelter of "The Gun."

"So you've got him safe and sound, eh, sir?" said the big Corporal, shaking comely head over Mr. Armadale's tousled form. "Nigh got 'isself laid out by two raskels, all along of a young fe-male——"

"Not——" exclaimed Mr. Armadale fiercely, "not a 'female', Corporal Dick! A goddish, man! A sup-superlat-tively lovely creature! None o' your dem'd 'femalesh'!"

"Very good, sir. And now, wot d' ye say to bed?"

"I shay demmit!" answered Mr. Armadale promptly. "I say bed be curst! We're going to make a night on't!"

"You'd be better in bed, sir," the Corporal suggested gently, "more comfortabler like."

"Ha!" exclaimed Mr. Armadale, sitting up and speaking with evident care and effort. "D' ye dare in-insinuate I'm drunk? I could fight a round with the best of 'em! Where's Jess—where's Jessamy Todd?"

"Lord love ye, sir—in bed hours ago!"

"Then don't suggest I'm drunk! I'm sober as 'nowl—ain't I, Jerry?"

"No!" answered Jeremy.

"Eh—no?" sighed Mr. Armadale. "D' ye say 'no'?"

"I say you' re drunk!"

"That," quoth Mr. Armadale, rising with great dignity and clutching at the table to steady himself, "that's done it! Mr. Veryan, friendship is a bub-bubble, a hollow mockery, a dem'd sham! Mr. Veryan, sir . . . I leave you! May remorse gnaw your vitals like the dem'd Spartan fox . . . Good night, sir. Corporal Dick, oblige me with your arm."

And so, with the Corporal's assistance, Mr. Richard Armadale staggered upstairs to bed.

Very soon the Corporal was back again, to whom Jeremy duly delivered Mr. Shrig's message and thereafter briefly and baldly described the tragic incidents of the night, while the Corporal listened, wide-eyed and mute.

"So they got Mr. Gillespie at last, have they, sir?" sighed he, when Jeremy had ended. "They 've been arter him often and long enough, same as they have Jarsper. And they 've got him at last, eh! Well, then, let me tell you, sir, them as done it ain't got long to live if my pal Jarsper's on their track!"

"Unless they murder Jasper too!"

"Murder Jarsper? Sir, it don't bear thinkin' on! And wot's more, sir, Jarsper ain't born to be murdered —nohow!"

# CHAPTER XXII

## IN WHICH MR. ARMADALE IS ABASHED

NEXT morning, waking to sunshine and a cheery whistling, Jeremy arose and leaning from wide-flung casement, looked down into a small yard, grimy yet orderly; barrels were there and boxes, with a hundred and one other oddments, but all were marshalled in serried ranks and rows, while in an angle of the wall, roofed from the weather, by a wooden structure somewhat reminiscent of a sentry box, stood a pump with a trough before it, whereat stood Jessamy Todd, stripped to the waist, joyously performing his ablutions and whistling whole-heartedly.

Him, Jeremy hailed forthwith, whereupon the ex-champion turned to look up with water trickling from nose and chin.

"It looks good!" quoth Jeremy.

"And feels better, sir!" answered Jessamy.

"I'll come down."

"Ay, do, brother. There's nothing like water for a man—inside or out!"

So presently Jeremy steps into the sunny yard and standing beside Jessamy at the trough, strips off his shirt to plunge head and shoulders into the sparkling water, to splash and rub it over naked arms and powerful torso and gasp deliciously.

"You peel oncommon well, sir."

"You called me . . . brother a . . . moment ago!" gasps Jeremy.

"Then I took a liberty, sir."

"Take it again!" says Jeremy.

"Thank 'ee, brother, I will, for I like you better an' better, more especially your barrel."

"My what, Jessamy?"

"This, brother!" And the ex-champion taps Jeremy lightly upon the wide, high-arching ribs. "Plenty o' room inside here, which is good for the wind, and wind 's everything sometimes. As to your pins now?" Here he steps back the better to survey Jeremy's legs. "They look speedy! And them arms and shoulders? Ay, you ought to be good for a mighty per-suading wallop, brother! Taking you by and large, I likes you most oncommon. Natur' cut you out for a fighter, sir—ah, and a champion at that, brother."

"D' ye think so, Jess?" And the glow upon Jeremy's cheek was not altogether by reason of the towel.

And now, being dry, aglow with health and redundant vigour and stripped for action, they eye each other a little wistfully, viewing each other's points like the experts and enthusiasts they are. And in Jessamy's keen eyes beams a glad light as he nods his satisfaction, and upon Jeremy's grim lips dawns a slow smile.

"Jessamy Todd," says he, a little diffidently, "how about it?"

"Brother," answers Jessamy softly, "if you feel inclined for a bit o' fibbing afore breakfast, I 'll box ye a round or so with all the j'y in life, sir."

"Thanks," said Jeremy. One word quietly spoken, and yet whole volumes could not have said more; and Jessamy understood, for they smiled on each other while eye spoke to eye in an eloquent silence as is the way of Britons the world over.

"This yard is pretty quiet—what d' ye think brother?"

"Could n't be better."

"Then bide a minute, sir, while I fetch the muffles!" And away goes Jessamy at a run and soon comes running back with the articles in question.

"Sir," says Jessamy, as they don the boxing gloves, "no tapping! Hit 'ard, floor me if you can, go your best an' show me what you can do."

"Right," says Jeremy.

Naked to the waist they front each other, poised and watchful; Jessamy Todd smiling, eager and keen-eyed, his muscles rippling beneath a skin glossy with health; Jeremy a little taller, a little heavier, his white flesh discoloured here and there with traces of recent strife, calm of eye, very serious and immensely determined.

"Ready?" enquires Jessamy.

"Quite!" answers Jeremy.

"Then, brother—go!"

A quick, light tread of feet, a flash of white arms and, feinting cunningly, Jessamy leapt and struck, smote empty air, ducked Jeremy's return, danced away and nodded in smiling approval.

"You 're pretty fast, brother, tidy footwork!" quoth he and dodging Jeremy's left, smacked two light blows into Jeremy's ribs and was away again. But, silent and determined as ever, Jeremy followed him up, to be tapped here and patted there, while his own blows were either slipped, or eluded altogether, until he marvelled within himself at Jessamy's matchless speed, unerring judgment and profound cunning.

None the less he followed, dogged as ever, and spying an opening, shot over a lightning left-hander that staggered his elusive opponent and, rushing in to second the blow, took Jessamy's terrible right full upon his chin and went down to lie half-stunned. And then Jessamy's arm was about him and Jessamy's voice in his ears:

"Sir, sir, I ax your pardon? I shouldn't ha' let go my right—but you made me forget you was only a ammytoor! Forgive me, brother——"

"Heartily!" answered Jeremy a little breathlessly, as he got to his feet. "It 's what I need—only," and here he sighed despondent, "I used to think I was quick——"

"Why, so you are, brother—amazing! Only I'm a bit quicker, d' ye see."

"And I was never knocked off my pins before, Jessamy."

"Why as to that, brother, you ain't in your best condition, I can see; consequently you ain't up to championship form—it ain't to be expected yet. But fib wi' me reg'lar for two or three months, and I 'll make a wonder o' you—there won't be a man to beat ye, no, neither ammytoor nor professional—not one!"

"D' ye really think so, Jessamy?"

"Brother, I know it! You are hard, sir, and oncommon quick and can punch wi' both hands, which to a fighting cove is a precious gift—ah, beyond rubies, brother!"

"And now, Jessamy, what about another round?"

"To-morrow, brother!" said Jessamy, slipping off his muffles. "We 've done enough to-day, seeing as you ain't in your best form yet, I reckon, and small wonder!"

"Indeed, but you 're a wonderful fighter!" quoth Jeremy, viewing the other in unfeigned admiration, insomuch that Jessamy, reading the sincerity of word and look, smiled and flushed with pleasure.

"Brother, I was Champion of England!" said he. "And there's many a good man in England——"

"And the best of 'em all to-day is Tom Holt, the 'Hoxton Slasher'!" sighed a voice hard by, and glancing round Jeremy beheld Mr. Armadale seated upon a barrel, drooping in an attitude of pathetic languor. "'The Hoxton Slasher' is said to be the best man in England!" he repeated. "What d 'ye say to that, Jessamy?"

"Why, sir, he may be and he can be for all o' me—but I doubts it!"

"Ha—you think you could beat him, Jess?"

"Sir, I do."

"Well, Jessamy, my friend De Ravenac is willing to back him at any moment against you or any man in England. And what d' ye say to that?"

"What I said afore, sir—there 's many a good man in England—but as for me I 'm done wi' the Game for good an' all!"

"Tush, man, what 's to stop you——"

"My conscience, sir! The Game is vanity and vexation and I 'm done wi' it!"

Here Mr. Armadale moaned feebly and clasped hand to haggard brow, but meeting Jeremy's enquiring gaze, smiled wanly.

"Bit of a head this morning, Jerry," he explained. "Nay, grieve not, my friend, anon 't will pass and I shall carol with the feathered warblers o' the grove. Exercise is all I need, so if you 've done with the muffles, Jessamy shall spar me a round or so——"

"Mr. Armadale, sir—no!" quoth Jessamy. "Not on no account."

"Eh? Demme and why not?"

"Because you ain't fit, sir! Because if I 'ad the misfortun' to ketch you one you 'd lie a perishing corpse, sir."

"Eh—what?" exclaimed Mr. Armadale, rising and immediately clasping his head again. "Stuff and dem'd nonsense, man, I'm right as ninepence! Fight any man on two pins, b' ged!"

"Why, you 're game all right, sir," nodded Jessamy, tucking the muffles beneath one arm and draping the towel about him. "Your sperrit 's willing enough, I 'll allow, but your body ain't! Your poor flesh is weak, sir, and small wonder, seeing as you 're a-pizening of it—constant."

"Poison? What the dooce d' ye mean?"

"Brandy, sir!" answered Jessamy and nodding, strode off forthwith.

Mr. Armadale sank down upon his barrel and groaned.

"Todd 's a curst impertinent, dem'd insolent fellow!"

"Todd 's right!" said Jeremy.

"I tell you, Jerry, all I need is exercise!"

"'T will be a coffin if you don't give up the brandy!"

"Ha—brandy again, by all that 's demnable——"

"Exactly!" nodded Jeremy.

"Ye gods! And this man dare name himself my friend!"

"Also I mean to be, Richard!"

"Ha—d' ye think brandy 's the root o' my trouble?"

"I do!"

"Then you 're a dooced unimaginative, curst unsympathetic, addled-pated numskull. Brandy!" exclaimed Mr. Armadale in bitter scorn. "Veryan, I tell you the cause of my general lowness o' spirits is far sweeter, nobler, loftier and—and—well, demme if 't is n't!"

"What, Dick?"

"The divine passion!" sighed Mr. Armadale. "Sublime love, Jerry—I 'm smitten to the very soul! Her sweet image sits within my dreams, consequently the thought of breakfast is anathema! Oh, b' ged, in this dem'd material world there never was such a love, there never will be! I who fancied myself in love a score o' times have found the real article at last—it took me like a dem'd flash of lightning—blinded, dazzled and bowled me completely over—such a love as poets sing and I suffer infernally in consequence."

"What 's her name, Dick?"

"I don't know."

"Eh—you don't——"

"Not the faintest vestige of an idea! That 's the wonderful, the extraordinary thing about it, Jerry, lifts it above all ordinary loves, my dear fellow."

"Have you spoken to her——"

"Once, I told her to cut and run. You see, I 'd just floored one of her vile assailants and was hard at it with t' other——"

"And what happened?"

"She hopped off like a rabbit—no, I mean flew like a startled bird, fled like a what 's-a-name o' the woods, a nymph, a dryad, Jerry, and graceful as any thing-ummy—I mean fawn, of course."

"Have you seen her since?"

"No, but I shall."

"D' you know where she lives?"

"Not precisely, but I mean to find out. You shall help me like the true friend you are and mean to be."

"But are you sure she——"

"I am, Jerry, I am! Her eyes spoke to mine and her soul was in 'em—I mean her eyes, of course, not mine! For one deathless moment her eyes gazed in mine—I happened to have one of the villain's heads in chancery at that precise moment, and, Jerry, my avenging fist fell inert, for our souls were in communion and I was her slave and shall be henceforth and for ever. My hopes, ambitions, dreams—nay, my sole thought is—oh, dooce take it, here 's the Corporal!"

Sure enough Corporal Richard Roe, very spick and span, presented himself to announce:

"Breakfast is a-waiting, sirs—ham an' eggs or——"

"Horrible!" wailed Mr. Armadale.

"Kidneys an' bacon, coffee, toast and rolls, gentlemen!"

Mr. Armadale hid his face and cowered.

"Revolting! Dooced revolting!" he moaned.

"Wot, no breakfast, sir?" enquired the Corporal, shaking his head. "Stomach a bit queasy-like?" Wot d' ye say to a pickled onion, sir?"

"Leave us, Corporal, leave us!" sighed Mr. Armadale, shivering; the which, with a glance at Jeremy, the

Corporal did forthwith, shaking his head more gravely than ever.

"And you, Jerry," quoth Mr. Armadale bitterly, so soon as they were alone, "food appeals to you, I suppose?"

"Irresistibly, Dick!"

"Egad, it would! And it will until you know what love really is—but no, you never will, Jerry; I cannot even imagine you a lover."

"Hum!" quoth Jeremy, scowling.

"So go and feed, Jerry, go and feed while I, fasting, seek the habitation of my peerless fair!" So saying, Mr. Armadale arose, clapped hand to brow, moaned feebly and wandered forth upon his solitary quest, while Jeremy hasted incontinent to the breakfast table.

But hardly was the meal over than Mr. Armadale wandered in again, more woeful and dejected than before, and taking Jeremy by the arm, led him out into the seclusion of the yard.

"Jeremy, oh, Jerry, I've seen her!"

"Well?"

"Very well! She dawned upon me from a shop—the baker's shop down the alley—a goddess with a loaf! More beautiful than fancy painted! The sun making a glory of her golden hair! Her face an angel's face! Her form a budding Venus! I ventured to speak! We talked! She thanked me for protecting her from insult yesterday in voice sweet as her look, and then——" Here Mr. Armadale uttered a mournful noise, "called me a drunkard!"

"Ha!" exclaimed Jeremy.

"Precisely!" sighed Mr. Armadale. "Now my dear fellow, I'm no angel—frankly I confess it, I am the merest human, and subject to the ordinary human foibles, candidly I avow it! But, by Heaven, if there is one thing I am not—it is a drunkard!"

"Hum!" quoth Jeremy.

"For drunkenness, my dear fellow, is a sottish and disgusting sin, and a drunkard is a—a sot, of course, and a dem'd fool and profligate rapscallion into the bargain! Agreed?"

"Heartily!" answered Jeremy.

"Very good! Drunkenness, furthermore, besides being a sin in itself, opens the door to every other dem'd sin in the calendar. Consequently there 's not a dem'd soul on this confounded globe with a fiercer detestation of drunkenness than myself! Not"—he continued hastily as he met Jeremy's eye—"not that I claim to be altogether exempt—no, honour compels me to acknowledge myself human enough to err—now and then. But, my dear fellow, being a poor devoted wretch, whom a cruel Fate has pursued with the utmost dem'd relentlessness and merciless ferocity from my unfortunate cradle, b'ged, I claim some little extenuation for an occasional lapse. And now She, knowing nothing of all this, and with her pure eyes upraised to mine full of tenderness and melting pity—She herself names me—'drunkard'—oh, dem!"

"So you 'll see her no more, Dick?"

"Consequently, I love her more than ever, Jerry. Cruel and unjust though she may be, I adore her yet. Though her small fingers tear my heart, I 'll kiss 'em! Dooce take me, Jerry, I 'd love her little feet for stamping on me—yes, b'ged, these bleeding lips should kiss 'em as they stamped—and that 's the confoundingly amazing, unearthly thing about my love, m' dear fellow! Nobody ever knew such love as mine, demme if they did! And she named me a——! Now, Jeremy, as a man of the world, ay, b'ged, as between men, I ask you—am I a drunkard, yes or no?"

"Yes," answered Jeremy.

Mr. Armadale halted suddenly, glanced from Jeremy to cloudless heaven, from heaven to earth, and sinking upon an empty cask that stood adjacent, stared blankly at his own immaculate Hessian boots.

"Veryan," said he at last, "it was 'yes', I think?"

"It was."

"And—pray let me be sure—by 'yes' you mean—?"

"That I agree with the lady, and with Jessamy Todd; she names you 'drunkard' and he says you are poisoning yourself."

Mr. Armadale nodded and rose, calm, cold and excessively dignified.

"So be it, sir!" said he. "Henceforth the word 'Friendship' is anathema to me! Henceforth I walk my own way—alone! And as for you, Mr. Virtuous Veryan—be demned!" Then, cold, calm and more dignified than ever, he turned and walked away.

But before he had taken six strides Jeremy was beside him, Jeremy's arm was about him, and Jeremy's hand had grasped his.

"Dick," said he, "I came to London seeking you——"

"Ha—because my sister sent you, sir?"

"Because I wanted a friend."

"Because you desire to play 'saviour' to me, sir?"

"Because my only friend is lately dead! And if—if I hurt—offended you, Dick, I 'm sorry."

Gone in a moment was Mr. Armadale's so excessive dignity and he was calm and cold no longer; the arrogant young head drooped, the scornful eyes were abased, and grasping the strong hand that clasped his, Mr. Armadale spoke in a voice low and strangely broken:

"She 's—right, Jerry!— You—Jessamy Todd—you 're all quite—quite right! And I know it—the hateful truth has forced itself on me—more than once and—I 'm afraid, Jerry. Afraid of myself and—the future—what I may become. I 've fought against it—kept away from it for days, weeks sometimes—but it gets me again, do what I will. How can I help myself, Jerry—in God's name—how?"

"By helping me, Dick."

"You?"

"Yes. I intend living in town this season and I want a—fashionable establishment and I thought you might help if—if you don't mind, Dick?"

"You ask my assistance, Veryan—mine?"

"Yes, Dick—and your friendship."

Mr. Armadale, being humbled, was inclined to be abject.

"Egad, but my friendship 's a poor dem'd miserable affair and may prove a curse! And I 'm a pitiful, self-deluding wretch, laying the blame of my own weakness upon Fate, Fortune, Circumstance—anything but my curst self."

"We might start now, Dick?"

"Eh—start? Where for?"

"To find suitable chambers——"

"But my dear Jeremy, I feel myself altogether too——"

"Somewhere in the neighbourhood of St. James', Dick."

"But Jerry, dear fellow, I——"

"Also I must have clothes, horses, servants—on the whole a busy day, so the sooner we start, the better, Dick."

And thus, in a while, they set forth together, arm in arm, and as they walked, Mr. Armadale's gloom was lifted from him and long before they reached St. James', his humbled spirit was soaring.

## CHAPTER XXIII

### DESCRIBES A VERY SMALL DESPERADO

"A WILDISH night, sir!" said Corporal Richard Roe, turning, poker in hand, to nod towards the curtained window as it shook and rattled to the fierce buffets of wind and the spiteful lash of rain. "An ugly night, sir!"

"Very!" answered Jeremy.

Here the Corporal proceeded to poke the fire and did it with the neat precision characteristic of him in all things, plying burnished poker with such nicety of judgment, tapping the embers lightly here with such a deft and kindly hand, tickling them gently there (and so exactly in the right and proper places) that the fire, inclined to be sullen hitherto, brightened up immediately and presently found a small, merry voice that seemed to chuckle and laugh until the cosy kitchen was full of the comfortable sound.

"I never hear the wind and rain at night," said the Corporal, musingly, tap-tapping gently with the poker, "but I think o' the river, so cold an' dark an'—wet! Ecod, sir, is there anything in natur' so wet as the river on a rainy night—so dismal an' full o' secrets as 'll never be found out? Like the night as it would ha' got me! Conse-quently, sir, on such a night as this, I 'm oncommon glad to be a-sitting here and mighty thankful to my pal an' comrade, Jarsper Shrig."

"Why to him?"

"Because, sir, when I lost my hand at Waterloo, d' ye see, I lost everything else—'specially hope, and meant to end it all in the river, but Jarsper jumped in arter me and 'im not being able to swim, I nat'rally had to get 'im out again and—arter that—well, we've been pals and trusty comrades ever since and—here I am!"

The Corporal was silent, but the fire, crackling cheerily by this time, sent forth a leaping, dancing flame that lighted up the trim kitchen from red-tiled floor to the age-old, writhen beams overhead, a merry flame that capered and twinkled, shone and glittered on polished copper pans, on well-scoured pewter, and the crossed bayonets upon the wall.

"Hark to that wind!" said Jeremy at last. "I wonder where Jasper is to-night?"

"On the track o' murder, sir, as usual."

"It 's five days since we had word of him, I think?"

"Five days to-night, sir. Which means as he 's busy and when so—things is likely to 'appen, sir!"

"What?"

"Things in the gallers and gibbeting way, sir."

"You think he 'll find Mr. Gillespie's murderer?"

"Ay, I do, sir. Once Jarsper's set on a murderer's trail, there 's only one way o' dodging Jarsper and that 's by dying! There 's small 'ope for any criminal when Jarsper 's on his track."

"You 've immense faith in him, Dick."

"Sir, I 've watched him at work, many a time!"

"Has my old friend Lockett been here to-day, Dick?"

"Twice, sir, the first time 'sarternoon just arter you and Mr. Armadale had left, and then again this evening to see you very special—waited 'till arter nine o'clock."

"D' ye know what he wanted?"

"Well, sir, 'twixt you an' me, he 's a bit worrited."

"What about?"

"Why, sir, it 's all along o' Mr. Armadale."

"How so?"

"It seems Mr. Armadale's took to meeting Miss Ruth, Mr. Lockett's adopted darter, o' late—onexpected like!"

"Hum!" quoth Jeremy thoughtfully.

"Which, sir, considering as Mr. Armadale's a swell Corinthian, a buck and a bang-up blood, and Miss Ruth, though pretty as any pictur', is only Miss Ruth, nat'rally makes Mr. Lockett a bit anxious-like."

"Is the girl very pretty, Dick?"

"Ah—more than pretty, sir!"

"Hum!" quoth Jeremy again, and sat awhile scowling at the cheery blaze.

"I suppose," ventured the Corporal at last, "you 'll be a-marching off and leaving us soon, sir, setting up for yourself and Mr. Armadale in your fine noo lodgings St. James' way?"

"In about a week!" nodded Jeremy gloomily.

"The old 'Gun' 'll be sorry to lose ye, sir."

"I shall be sorry to go," replied Jeremy, shaking his head, "but I go with a purpose."

"And there 's Jessamy! Jess 'll miss his sparring wi' you of a morning——"

"I shall come here regularly three times a week to spar with him."

"I 'm glad o' that, sir—very!" said the Corporal in so hearty a tone and with such beaming smile that Jeremy's scowl vanished and he smiled also.

"Thanks, Dick! I suppose Jessamy's in bed?"

"Hours ago, sir. He tells me you 're a wonder, sir."

"Ha—did he so?"

"And improving every day, sir! Says you are nigh as quick as ever 'e was and can punch harder than any man he ever met!"

"Lord!" exclaimed Jeremy, his deep-sunken eyes glowing. "Did Jessamy say all that?"

"Every word, sir—and meant it too! He likewise told me this very morning——"

A sudden squeal outside the curtained window, a shrill, child voice upraised in fierce protest, and then a drumming on the outer door.

"That 'll be the little door in the entry!" quoth the Corporal, rising. "But it ain't Jarsper's knock! And so late too!" And away he strode, with Jeremy at his heels, bearing a candle.

"Who is it?" demanded the Corporal through the stout oak.

"What, ho, within there!" answered a gay voice. "Open the dem'd door and see!"

With his solitary but dexterous right hand the Corporal loosed bolt and chain, opened the door to a rush of blusterous wind and out went the candle; in which sudden darkness Mr. Armadale's merry voice greeted them:

"A dooced night! Close the door, Corporal, and shut out the curst wind! I 've caught a dem'd desperado, a spying scoundrel in the very act!"

Back they trooped to the warm, glowing comfort of the kitchen forthwith, to behold Mr. Armadale, his long, many-caped overcoat dripping rain, his gloved right hand grasping a twisting, writhing thing of tatters, that gasped and panted shrill oaths and foul invective in weeping childish tones.

"Aha!" quoth Mr. Armadale, holding this deplorable object at arm's length. "Hold still, my bold ruffian, stand still and let 's look at you! Examine it, Jerry! Behold it, Corporal!"

A small, unlovely creature indescribably tousled and grimy, whose dismal, rain-sodden rags clung, revealing the pitiful emaciation of the little shivering body they should have hidden.

"Lemme go!" he wailed. "I ain't done nothink—lemme go!" A weazened, undersized slip of humanity, a child who cowered, expectant of blows, a wild, furtive thing who stared about him with eyes ages old in experience of suffering and manifold evil.

"I caught the small scoundrel trying to peer in at the window," explained Mr. Armadale. "But, b'ged, he looks a dooced cold and famished little scoundrel!

Are you hungry, Mr. Bones?" The boy's answer was a dexterous twist that freed him from his captor's grasp; then retreating behind Jeremy's chair, he cowered, all pleading misery from tousled head to small bare feet.

"Don't let 'im 'it me, guv'nor!" he wailed. "I ain't done nothink——"

"Bread and cheese, Corporal!" said Jeremy.

"Or ham?" suggested Mr. Armadale.

"Beef!" nodded the Corporal. "Nothing like cold b'iled beef, sirs!"

"With a pickled onion or so!" nodded Mr. Armadale, removing his dripping hat and coat.

Thus very soon the pallid, rain-sodden, unlovely Imp, perched beside the fire and encouraged by the three, set to ravenously upon the goodly fare before him like the small, famished animal he was; and yet as he munched thus voraciously, he none the less kept his bright, sharp eyes on Jeremy.

"Why d' ye stare so, boy?"

"Well . . . becos'!" answered the urchin a little indistinctly by reason of the cold, boiled beef.

"Because of what?"

"Well, becos' you ain't got the look o' one o' them."

"One of who?"

"Them as 'its and kicks a cove for nuffink."

"What were you up to outside the window?" demanded Mr. Armadale.

"Nuffink!" answered the urchin promptly.

"How old are you, boy?" enquired Jeremy.

"Dunno."

"What's your name?"

"Ain't got none."

"Well, what are you called?"

"Anyfink."

"Where do you live?"

"Nowheers."

"But where do you sleep at nights?"

"Anywheer."

"But your father and mother——"

"Ain't got none."

"And what brings you here so late at night?"

"Well, this is the 'Gun,' ain't it?"

"Yes."

"Well, I got a writin'."

"D' you mean a letter?"

"Yus, a letter."

"Who for?"

"Well, it ain't for you, guv'nor."

"How d' you know?"

"Becos' you ain't got a 'ook."

"Then it must be for me," said the Corporal.

"Well, I dunno."

"But I 've got a hook—see here, my lad!"

"Well, wot 's your monicker?"

"I 'm Corporal Richard Roe."

"Then you 're 'im an' 'ere 's the writin'." And forth from some corner of his steaming rags the boy drew a wisp of crumpled paper; the Corporal took it, smoothed it out upon his huge knee, read it and starting to his feet, gave the paper to Jeremy, who saw thereon these hastily scrawled words:

Corporal Dick, follow the boy, Life and death. Your pal Jaspar.

"Who gave you this, my lad?" enquired the Corporal, staring down into the boy's impish, weazened features.

"A bull, guv'nor."

"Where is he?"

"Well, I ain't to say."

"Then show me!" And the big Corporal reached down hat and coat from the adjacent corner.

"Hold hard, Dick!" quoth Mr. Armadale. "You 're never going with Master Bones to dooce knows where—and on such a curst night, too?"

"Ay, but I am, sir—this moment!"

"But our scoundrelly infant may be a stool pigeon——"

"No matter, sir. When Jarsper calls I go."

"Then dooce take me, I 'll go with you, demme if I don't!"

"Are you sure this is Jasper's writing, Corporal," enquired Jeremy.

"Sartain sure, sir, and 't is wrote on a page tore out of his little reader; I' d swear to it anywheres."

"And now," quoth Mr. Armadale, "what about weapons?"

"Why, I 've got my hook, sir, which is apt to be pretty handy-like if and when needful."

"Egad, I believe you, Dick! This stick shall serve me. Are we ready?"

Hereupon Jeremy, who had donned hat and surtout, led the way out of the kitchen, the ragged urchin trotting beside him.

"Sirs," said the Corporal, pausing with his hand on the bolt of the outer door, "you 'll notice as Jarsper says 'Life an' death' and when Jarsper says so 'e means so!—And you, my lad, can ye run?"

"Yus!" answered the urchin. "I 'm allus a-runnin', I am!"

"Then, run your best! And now, sirs, quick march!"

So saying, the Corporal opened the door and they stepped out into the rushing dark.

## CHAPTER XXIV

### TELLS WHAT THEY FOUND AT THE "JOLLY WATERMAN"

THROUGH blusterous wind and driving rain they hurried behind their small guide, who padded along on his small, bare feet at a tireless jog trot, splashing prodigiously in miry places and making the very utmost of every puddle, insomuch that Mr. Armadale, wiping mud from his eye, felt called upon to utter a protest to which the urchin, without checking his pace or troubling to turn his head, responded with a breathless but derisive:

"Yah!"

He led them along dim thoroughfares wide and narrow; he turned disconcertingly sudden corners; he pattered across unexpected courts; he darted down narrow alleys, past noisome dens where Misery wallowed, teeming rookeries where dim lights winked and whence came a babel of unlovely voices that roared, chattered, sang or screamed, a discordant tumult. On he led them by dismal ways, short cuts known only to such as he, until the vast city lay behind and before them, showed a dark expanse, a silent mystery where sullen flowed the immemorial river. Turning sharp, the urchin trotted on, the river upon his right hand, upon his left a row of dim-seen buildings that loomed fantastic in the dark, until these too were behind and nothing to see but the muddy causeway beneath their feet and a rain-filled gloom where swirled the river's dark immensity.

"There y' are!" cried the urchin suddenly, and pointed ahead. And here, growing as it were from the very ooze and slime of the river, rose a gaunt and solitary building, vague and monstrous, its upper storeys jutting out above the sullen tide, a shapeless structure of unlovely angles and toppling gables whence unlighted windows, small and deep-set, seemed to scowl malevolently.

"Where are we?" enquired the Corporal. "What place is this, my lad?"

"The 'Jolly Waterman'!" answered the urchin shrilly.

"And a dem'd desolate, doocedly murderous hole it is!" added Mr. Armadale fervently, as he stumbled whither the boy led.

Halting suddenly, the urchin pointed to a door, deep-set and massive, whereon the Corporal promptly rapped, loud and long. And after a space, filled in by the moan of wind, the patter of rain and mournful lapping of the river, this door opened and an ancient crone appeared, bearing a small lantern—a bowed, mumbling, haglike creature who peered into the boy's face, sniffing and muttering to herself.

"'Sall right, Sal—'s only me!" piped the boy, whereat the old creature sniffed again violently and beckoning them to enter, closed the door and led the way along a narrow, crooked passage, tottering on before them upstairs and down, turning corners to right and to left until, pausing abruptly, she pointed to a small door, nodded, sniffed dismally and tottered away with the lantern, leaving them in the dark.

Groping for the door, the Corporal threw it open and following hard on his heels, Jeremy found himself in a long, low chamber, half kitchen, half cellar, dim-lit and full of dark nooks and corners whence peeped all manner of objects such as oars, spars, odd-shaped boxes and barrels; while from every blackened rafter hung nets, coils of rope, strings of onions, oilskins, dried herbs, and many other vague objects in the strangest confusion, and in a deep armchair before a cosy fire, steaming glass at elbow, pipe in mouth and notebook open on his knee, sat Mr. Shrig, wholly at his ease and placid as ever.

"Well, dooce take me!" ejaculated Mr. Armadale in amazed and indignant surprise. Mr. Shrig closed his "little reader" and nodded.

"So there y' are, Dick and gen'lemen! Mr. Wee, your servant, sir. Mr. Armadale, ditto, sir."

"Why, how goes it, comrade?" enquired the Corporal anxiously, glancing about, keen-eyed and expectant.

"Werry so-so, Dick!" sighed Mr. Shrig. "Werry so-so indeed, Dick—though it might be worse. Still, I 'm a disapp'inted man, Corporal Dick——"

"But—oh, demme, Shrig," exclaimed Mr. Armadale, wiping mud and rain from his face, "curse and confound it, but you look dooced comfortable!"

"Howsomedever, I'm a disapp'inted man, sir!" sighed Mr. Shrig with a doleful shake of his round bullet head. "And therefore you finds me a-puffing my steamer and takin' a drop o' comfort all for to cheer my drooping sperrits, sir."

"But—your letter, Jarsper?" said the Corporal in gentle reproach. "Lord, I've been that worrited—you wrote 'Life and death' Jarsper!"

"And Death 's been werry near me, Dick! It 's near me now! It 's near all on us! It 's in this here werry room! See yonder!" And Mr. Shrig pointed with his pipestem to something in an adjacent corner, something hidden beneath discoloured canvas whence oozed small, slow trickles of water; a covering this, so insufficient and scanty that it left exposed a pair of sodden, knee-booted legs. Beholding which, Jeremy shivered suddenly, and Mr. Armadale uttered a strangled exclamation of horror and disgust.

"A dead man, Jarsper?" enquired the Corporal in hushed tones.

"As ever vas, Dick!" quoth Mr. Shrig, puffing at his pipe and nodding mournfully. "My bird 's flew the coop, pal, hopped the perch afore I could, as you might say, catch an' cage same. Death 's gone an' diddled me, Dick, and I 'm a disapp'inted man according!"

"Drownded, Jarsper?"

"Drownded, Dick!"

"Eh—drownded?" repeated the urchin eagerly, approaching the grisly shape. "Wot, a stiff un? Lor! I seen a lot o' stiff uns took out of the river, I 'ave!"

"Boy—come here!" said Jeremy sternly.

"'Arf a minute!" said Mr. Shrig, rising and patting the urchin's tousled head kindly. "Come and take a peep at it, sonny, and tell me if you 'appen to know 'oo it is—look here!" And stooping, Mr. Shrig lifted a corner of the dingy canvas, whereupon Jeremy turned hastily to look otherwhere; and thus, by the merest chance, his gaze lighted upon a small, square opening or window high up in the angle of the opposite corner, a square of blackness, and yet it seemed to him that within this blackness something stirred.

"Ah!" exclaimed Mr. Shrig. "So you knows him, sonny?"

"Yus!" answered the boy. "That 's Jos Shields, that is! Kicked me last night, 'e did——"

"And there y' are!" sighed Mr. Shrig, and having covered the "thing" reverently, turned to behold Jeremy staring fixedly at the square opening in the opposite corner. "And there y' are, Mr. Weryan!" he repeated, laying his hand on Jeremy's arm. "Jos Shields, vater-side character. *Saucy Nell* 'is boat. Tventy-eight, 'is number! Come over 'ere, sir, an' I 'll write them particulars down for ye."

"But I don t want 'em!" said Jeremy.

"Ah, but you do, sir, seeing you 're inter-ested in the murder o' poor Mr. Gillespie. Look now, I writes down first J-O-S for Jos, and S-H-I-E-L-D-S for

Shields!" But to Jeremy's surprise and growing wonderment the words Mr. Shrig's pencil actually traced were these:

Keep your peepers on me, never mind the corner.

"So there y'are again, Mr. Wee, pal! And now p'raps you'll take a look at these 'ere?" And from an inner pocket Mr. Shrig drew a small, canvas bag whence he took certain articles which he named thus:

"Number Vun, a gold watch and seals bearing monny-gram T G. Number Tvo, a plain signet ring bearing monnygram ditto. Number three, a net purse containing six pound, three shillings, and a farden vith a nole in it. Now might you chance to recognise these same, sir?"

"Yes," answered Jeremy, "of course! This is Mr. Gillespie's watch, and this his ring, and this his purse, I suppose."

"Pre-cisely, sir!" nodded Mr. Shrig, stowing the articles away with the same tender care. "And all found on the drownded corpse yonder."

"Which means that he is the murderer, Shrig?"

"Sir, you'll mind the hat was found beside Mr. G.'s body? Werry good! On the morning arter the murder, I set out to find the owner of aforementioned 'at, said owner being Jos Shields. Werry good again! Sir, I located Jos Shields in this werry 'ouse and 'im flush wi' money—but afore I could apprehend him, afore I could get my daddles on Jos Shields, 'e goes and takes and gets hisself drownded under my werry nose, as you might say! All o' vich comes werry 'ard on me, seeing as I can't arrest a corpse and the law won't 'ang it if I do. And there y'are vunce more and lastly, pal!"

"Ah, well, the villain's paid the price, Jarsper!" said the Corporal, consolingly.

"And diddled me, Dick. Dodged the gallers and cheated the law. I done my best, but Fate and the river has been too much for me! I 'm conflummerated——"

"No, no, Jarsper!" said Corporal Dick, setting friendly hand on Mr. Shrig's drooping shoulder, "Arter all, you found your man, as I knowed you would, comrade. Your job 's finished——"

"Ah, Fate 's took it out o' my 'ands, Dick—and I may as well toddle back along o' you to the old 'Gun', and step in at the nearest office as I go to 'ave this here cadaver removed. Life's full o' 'downs', sirs, but then it has an occasional 'up' and that 's summat, arter all!" Having delivered himself of which, Mr. Shrig sighed, rose, and taking hat and stick, turned towards the door.

"But, demme, what about Master Bones?" enquired Mr. Armadale, staring down at the little urchin who stood rubbing one small, muddy foot with the other and watching them with great, wistful eyes.

"Ay, by Goles, I vas forgetting him!" said Mr. Shrig, thrusting hand into pocket. "A bright lad! Here 's a brand noo shilling for ye, sonny."

"Hum!" quoth Jeremy as the urchin snatched and bit the coin. "And when that 's spent—how then?"

"That 's the lad's consarn, Mr. Wee, sir."

"No, it shall be mine, Shrig. Will you go with me, boy?"

"Yus!" nodded the urchin.

"Come, then!" said Jeremy and held out his hand. For a moment the boy hesitated, half-sullen, half-afraid; then Jeremy smiled and the boy crept a little nearer.

"Ye won't go fer to twist me arm?" he demanded.

"No."

"Well, you ain't a-going fur to clout me, or pull me year?"

"No."

"Well, then"—and out came a grimy hand, pitifully thin and small and cold, to lose itself in Jeremy's big one, and they crossed the room together, but upon the threshold, moved by some impulse, Jeremy paused to glance once more towards that square opening in the corner, and again he thought to see a movement in the blackness beyond; so sure was he of this indeed, that he would have spoken, but Mr. Shrig's fingers gripped his arm and Mr. Shrig's voice whispered in his ear:

"Caution's the vord, pal! And step lively!" Moreover he saw that Mr. Shrig held a pistol half-hidden in the fold of his coat; wherefore, grasping the boy's hand a little tighter, he was silent and followed his companions, wondering, nor did he speak until they were out in the wind and rain and the inhospitable tavern of the "Jolly Waterman" had vanished in the murk behind them; then:

"Why the pistol, Shrig?" he enquired.

"For a remarkable good reason, sir."

"Name it."

"Why, then, sir, if the con-clusions as I've drawed is co-rect, Bloody Murder was a-peeping at us out o' that theer spy-hole, yonder, d' ye see!"

"Man, what d' you mean?"

"More than I say, sir."

"I don't understand you in the least."

"Sir, I did n't expect as you vould! And the less you knows the safer you'll be, so the less I tells, the better for you, so—mum it is, sir."

"As you will!" said Jeremy, and they walked in silence awhile.

"Sir," said Mr. Shrig. "I'm tryin' to think vot you're a-going to do with this here little, dirty lad?"

"Feed him!"

"And then, sir?"

"Shelter him!"

"Eh? D' ye mean as you intend to—keep him—for good?"

"I hope so."

"By Goles!" ejaculated Mr. Shrig and took three or four steps in silent amazement. "But why, sir—and him such a precious young warmint!"

"For that reason!" answered Jeremy.

"Ho!" said Mr. Shrig thoughtfully and then, "still I don't exactly tvig, sir."

"I did n't expect you would, Shrig. Devil take the wind!"

"Amen!" quoth Mr. Shrig.

# CHAPTER XXV

## IN WHICH, AMONG OTHER THINGS, MR. SHRIG ASKS QUESTIONS

JEREMY stood before the looking-glass scowling at the reflection of his splendour. And indeed this past week has wrought a stupendous change in him, at least as regards his attire. From snowy cravat to gleaming, gold-tasselled Hessian boots he is all that a fashionable young Buck could be, thanks to Mr. Armadale's assiduity and unerring judgment. His double-breasted coat, with its high roll collar and crested gold buttons, seems moulded upon him, his tight-stretched nether garments show scarcely a wrinkle, while his flowered satin waistcoat is a veritable glory. None the less, Jeremy's scowl deepened and he uttered a contemptuous sound between laugh and growl.

"Eh?" questioned Mr. Armadale from the sofa where he lay glancing over the *Gazette*.

"These clothes!" growled Jeremy.

"Perfection, my dear fellow!" nodded Mr. Armadale, viewing Jeremy's appearance with the eye of an expert. "Absolute works of art, demme!"

"They don't suit me, Dick."

"Eh—begad, what's that?" exclaimed Mr. Armadale, starting to a sitting posture. "Don't suit you——"

"Or rather, I don't suit them, Dick. I look like—like——"

"Like what, in Heaven's name?"

"A gamekeeper dressed in his master's clothes! And I feel about as comfortable."

"Oh, the dooce!" gasped Mr. Armadale.

"I 'm not built for finery, Dick——"

"Calls 'em 'finery'!" wailed Mr. Armadale, fanning himself with the *Gazette*.

"They're too—exotic and——"

"Exotic!" murmured Mr. Armadale. "The sublimest examples of sartorial genius and he names 'em 'exotic'! Oh, ye gods—ye avenging deities, hear him!" And crumpling up the *Gazette* he hurled it into a corner. Quoth he: "Jeremy Veryan, my good ass, I tell you Stultz never turned out finer creations; they are all and everything that clothes could possibly hope to be—did n't I choose 'em? Did n't I watch over the making of 'em as tenderly as a doting mother over her babe? Was n't I at every fitting? And you call 'em 'exotic'—oh, dem! Ingratitude, thy name is Jeremy!"

"Hum!" quoth Jeremy. "I think, having regard to my face and general looks, something a little plainer——"

"Face?" retorted Mr. Armadale scornfully. "What's a man's face matter? Not a dem'd jot! It 's birth that counts—an ancient and honoured name—suitably attired. And b'ged, you are as well dressed as any Corinthian in town and there 's no older or more honourable name in England than yours, Jerry!"

"I 'm glad you think so——"

"Of course I do!"

"Because it will be your sister's name one day, Dick!"

"Eh? The dooce! D' ye mean Olivia?"

"Who else?"

"Do you really mean——"

"To marry her, Dick—soon, I hope!"

"Marry? Olivia? You? Astounding!"

"Very!" nodded Jeremy.

"I mean—what I meant to say was, ye know, I—I never regarded you as a possible Benedict, Jerry."

"Neither did I, Dick. And you 're quite right—it is astounding and almost beyond belief that Olivia should have chosen—me! I shall never be used to the wonder of it! She is altogether beautiful and I——"

"The very best old fellow in the world!" exclaimed Mr. Armadale, and up he sprang to grasp Jeremy's hand, shaking it heartily. "And if she loves you, Jerry, why, God bless you, both of you. I wish you every happiness. And Olivia deserves to be happy at last, sweet soul, for a more absolutely devoted sister never lived and, b'ged, never will! But for her I should be gone to the dem'd dogs or blown my miserable head off, long ago! As it is, you behold me to-day regenerate, abounding in hope; and as for health, well—you saw me go three rounds with Jessamy yesterday morning. Nobody could name me 'drunkard' these days—eh, Jerry?"

"No!" answered Jeremy, looking into the speaker's clear, eager eyes.

"Which goes to prove what iron and relentless determination may achieve, Jerry. Wine? Yes, occasionally! Ale? Now and then! Beer? Sometimes! But spirits—brandy, curse it! Never! Not a spot! Not a dem'd drop! When my mind is once made up, b'ged, I 'm a rock! The adamantine crag is thistle-down compared with my stupendous determination, my dear fellow. If you should be writing to Olivia, you might mention something o' this! And pray, when do you propose to marry?"

"Whenever she is ready, Dick. And while we 're on the subject—when do you?"

Mr. Armadale started, his handsome, youthful face reddened, his glance wandered.

"What I—I marry?" he stammered. "Dooce take it, Jerry, what d' ye mean?"

"The girl Ruth!"

"Ha!" exclaimed Mr. Armadale, knitting delicate brows. "So you know her, it seems? When did you meet her? How? Where?"

"I have never seen her, Dick, but her guardian happens to be an old friend of mine."

"Eh—what—old Gruff and Glum? He watches over her like a dem'd ogre!"

"Have you ever met Mr. Lockett?"

"Not I, b'ged; the old monster hates me already, I 'll be sworn."

"Then the sooner you do, the better. I 'll invite him here to-morrow, or better still, we 'll call on him to-day."

"Thanks—no, Jerry! I prefer to do my wooing in my own peculiar fashion——"

"And cause my old friend needless anxiety and care!"

"How so, pray?"

"By meeting this girl without his permission, this child who is all he has to live for! Will she make you a suitable wife, Dick?"

"Wife?" repeated Mr. Armadale, staring very hard at the carpet. "Wife?"

"What else?" demanded Jeremy, beginning to scowl. "You tell me frequently that you love her——"

"Madly, my dear fellow, passionately, with all my confounded soul! There never was such devotion as mine, so dooced humble and adoring—never!"

"Does she love you?"

"I believe so, I hope so, but I don't know. So you see it 's a bit early to talk of—er—marriage—now is n't it? Besides——"

But at this moment, and to Mr. Armadale's very evident relief, was a knock on the door and an exceedingly grave and dignified person appeared, very soft as to tread, smooth as to voice and entirely unobtrusive as to manner, in fine, a very superior gentleman's gentleman indeed.

"Gentlemen," said he, "the Marquis of Jerningham and Major Piper are below."

"Then ask 'em to step upstairs, Moxon. That 's Piper of the 'Heavies'—a bit heavyish himself but a true-blue sportsman. And I think you met Jerny at White's or Boodle's, last week."

Meantime the gentlemen having duly "stepped upstairs," now presented themselves, the Marquis a slim, high-nosed, athletic exquisite, his square chin throned, as it were, in the folds of a stupendous cravat, a truly marvellous confection whose many and intricate convolutions baffled the eye.

Major Piper was a heavy dragoon in every sense, being heavy of tread, person, disposition, speech, chin and eyebrows.

"How de do!" said the Marquis, shaking hands. "Veryan, y' don't know my friend, I think. Major Piper—Mr. Veryan o' Veryan."

"Haw!" quoth the Major, bowing ponderously. "Honoured, sir—servant!"

"You were n't at the fight t' other night, Dick?" said the Marquis. "Private room at Jackson's—only a few amateurs present. I sent you word of it."

"B'ged, I forgot all about it, Jerny. Y' see, I was at my tailor's and that put everything else out of my head."

"Ah, well, a devilish poor affair, Dick, and soon over. My fellow lost and De Ravenac's won, of course. But no wonder; the 'Hoxton Slasher' is a perfect marvel. Such bewitching footwork and hits like a deuced thunderbolt! There is n't a pugilist in England to match him to-day—and, by Gad, I almost think he might have conquered even Jessamy Todd, at his best!"

"Then he must surely be the miracle of fighting men," said Jeremy.

"He is, Veryan, he is!" said the Marquis, pausing to shake his head with a pinch of snuff at his nose. "And that 's the dooce of it, for De Ravenac is his patron—he fights for nobody else, of course, and my ambition at present being to beat De Ravenac at something or other, I 'm on the constant lookout for some willing young fellow to beat this fellow of his—and with dev'lish ill luck so far."

"No one ever beat De Ravenac, my dear Jerny—at least not more than once!" said Mr. Armadale.

"'T would almost seem so, Dick!" nodded the Marquis gloomily. "Still I live in hopes."

"Jessamy Todd never met this 'Hoxton Slasher', I think?" Jeremy enquired.

"No, my dear Veryan, more 's the pity. Todd was before his time."

"But Jessamy 's as good a man to-day as ever he was!" averred Mr. Armadale stoutly. "I know, for I spar with him frequently."

"I wonder," murmured the Marquis dreamily, "I wonder if we could induce Jessamy to come back—to fight just once more?"

"No!" answered Jeremy. "Nothing would induce him."

"A great pity!" sighed the Marquis. "This would have been a titanic encounter—a fight of fights!"

Major Piper here removed the gold knob of his cane from his lips; said, "Haw! Homeric!" and put it back again.

"By the way, I suppose you 've heard about young Tommy Jardine?" enquired the Marquis.

"Not a word, Jerny."

"Blew his brains out last night, poor lad! Tragic!"

"Good God!" exclaimed Mr. Armadale, rising from his chair and sitting down again. "We were at school together. Poor Tommy Jardine! What was the cause, Jerny?"

"Jews and the cards, Dick! A deuced deadly combination—remember poor old Slingsby? Only Sling happened to get snuffed out in the Steeplechase."

"But Jardine!" sighed Mr. Armadale. "He was so dooced young, ye know."

"Haw!" quoth the Major. "And unfortunate! Always!"

"Yes," nodded the Marquis, "he 's been in the dam'dest ill luck of late, lost at everything, to everybody—even me! And last night De Ravenac finished him, poor, desperate young fool!"

"Ha!" said Jeremy. "De Ravenac again!"

"What! D' you know the *preux chevalier*, Veryan?"

"We are acquainted. The man's a public menace!"

"My dear fellow," said the Marquis, smiling indulgently, "the man's merely a lucky gambler."

"And has ruined others, I understand!"

"Who would have ruined him!"

"And most of these—callow youths!"

"Haw!" quoth the Major. "Y' are right there, sir! Hawk and pigeons! Just off the nest! Damnable!"

"Egad," nodded the Marquis, "he 's one to be reckoned with, however you take him."

"But the reckoning should be final!" said Jeremy.

"Dooce take it, Jerry, it 's easy to talk—you might tackle him yourself!" suggested Mr. Armadale.

"I intend to!" said Jeremy grimly.

The Marquis, who happened to be busied at the glass rearranging an intricate fold of his cravat, turned to glance at the speaker beneath raised brows.

"Ha, do you, b'ged!" he exclaimed. "I would venture to remind you that De Ravenac's good fortune is proverbial, Veryan, in every particular."

"It would seem so, my lord! And especially against youth and inexperience!"

"Why, as to that, you're not precisely a Methuselah yourself!" said the Marquis, with the ghost of a smile. "But if you have such profound confidence in your good fortune, why, the very best of luck to you. And now, Armadale," said he, having arranged his cravat to his satisfaction, "if you 're for a bout with the foils, we 'll stroll over to Angelo's. Will you accompany us, Veryan?"

"Thank you," answered Jeremy, "but I have letters to write."

"Why, then, some other time, I hope. Come, Dick!" And bidding Jeremy adieu, away they went, arm-in-arm, Major Piper marching heavily in their rear; but halfway down the stairs he halted, wheeled and strode back. And now, having something particular to say, he became heavier and "Hawed" more than usual.

"Haw—Veryan," said he, "—er—haw! You'll forgive the liberty, but if you seriously contemplate—haw—playing De Ravenac, I should—haw—most earnestly endeavour to—haw—dissuade you. One night's madness may mean years of—haw—You understand? I speak from experience! Hope you 'll forgive the liberty—haw—comparative stranger, but, b'ged, I feel—that is to say—haw——You understand, I hope?"

"And thank you!" answered Jeremy, grasping the Major's hand. "Should I play the Chevalier, it will be for a very definite purpose. And, sir, if you will step in again when you chance this way, I should be glad."

"Haw!" said the Major. "Honoured!" Here the Marquis roaring for him from below, he shook Jeremy's hand again, wheeled, and strode heavily down the stairs.

Thus alone, Jeremy sat down to finish his daily letter to Olivia, a screed of many pages for, if slow and unready of speech, his pen found eloquent expression for all those thoughts which were for him too sacred for utterance. Thus his quill sped screeching across the paper, unfaltering, scarce pausing as he set forth his hopes, his dreams, his ever-growing love in words so impassioned and yet so very reverently sincere.

But, after some while, he was disturbed by a gentle rap on the door, and, receiving permission, the dignified Moxon appeared.

"Sir, your pardon!" said he softly. "I regret to intrude, but really, sir, I must beg to lay complaint against the boy, sir!"

"Again, Moxon! What now?"

"Bodily anguish, sir! Inflicted upon the person of James, sir, by means of some sharp instrument introduced into the seat of his chair, sir!"

"Ha!" said Jeremy, grey eyes twinkling. "A sharp instrument, Moxon?"

"In the nature of a pin, needle or tin tack, sir."

"Who is James?"

"The footman, sir!"

"So we boast a footman, do we?"

"Yes, sir, Mr. Armadale engaged him yesterday."

"And James is hurt, you say?"

"He complained at the time—loudly, sir!"

"Are you sure the boy is guilty?"

"Indeed, sir! He admitted the fact—gleefully, sir. So much so that James would have chastised him—on the spot——but I esteemed it more proper to refer the matter to you, sir."

"Hum!" quoth Jeremy. "Bring the boy to me."

"Very good, sir!" And Moxon softly retired, leaving Jeremy to stare wistfully at his unfinished letter and finally to lock it away as the butler returned, ushering before him a diminutive person who hung back, glowering sullenly. His grime was gone, his tousled hair, cropped and combed, showed red-gold and curly, his dingy rags had given place to smart and comfortable garments; but in his eyes was the same wild look of elfish wisdom, and his face, though less pinched and wan, seemed more impish than ever.

"Boy," said Jeremy, "come here!"

With head sullenly bowed, the Imp sidled forward and scowling up in Jeremy's face muttered:

"Ain't done nuffink!"

"What 's this I hear of a pin in a chair?"

"Cussed lies!"

"Oh!" murmured Mr. Moxon. "What precocious audacity!"

"Boy, tell me the truth! Did you put a pin in the chair? Yes or no?"

"Yus."

"Then don't you think I ought to thrash you?"

"No, I don't, guv'nor! But everybody beats me sometime, so if yer wanter beat me I don't mind, seein' as it 's you. You won't 'urt me s' much as some on 'em did—you won't 'urt me no more than you can 'elp—I know!"

"How do you know?"

"Well, because you ain't got the look o' them as 'urts poor little coves as ain't done nuffink, you ain't."

"Hum!" quoth Jeremy. "Boy, how old are you?"

"Dunno!"

"Moxon, what age should you say?"

"Indeed, sir, it would be difficult to estimate with any precise exactitude but, judging by his size, I should say eight or nine; again having regard to his general configuration he might be eleven or so; but, from the extremely knowing expression of his eyes, he is probably years older, sir."

"Hump!" quoth Jeremy again. "Boy, look at me!"

Obediently the Imp raised his head and Jeremy saw a smear of blood upon his cheek.

"Hallo, what 's wrong with your face, boy?"

"Nuffink!"

"Fighting, sir!" explained Moxon. "He fights regularly with the boys in the mews behind us, sir, and being so small is usually beaten."

"You 're a liar! I ain't never beat, I ain't!"

"Hush, boy! Moxon, you may go."

"Thank you, sir. But first may I venture to beg you will not chastise him too severely, sir? Youthful high spirits, sir—though to be sure it may be my own chair next time."

"Moxon, you 're a trump! No, I shan't thrash him, he 's had too much o' that already. But there shall be no 'next time'."

"I am grateful, sir, for the assurance!" and bowing sedately, Moxon retired.

"Now, boy, did you copy out your alphabet?"

"Yus!"

"And the words I set you?"

"Yus!"

"Spell 'em!"

"Not me!"

"Spell 'cat'."

"Ain't a-goin' to!"

"I think you are!" says Jeremy, setting his chin.

"Well, I ain't!" says the Imp, setting his, and then quick to heed Jeremy's threatening mien he smiles with a look that quite transfigures his small, battered face, whereupon Jeremy smiles too.

"Come, spell 'cat' old fellow, to please me."

"Well, orl right, guv'nor—with a C an' a O an' a A then!"

"Quite wrong!"

"Well, I knows as theer 's a C in it somewheers, I do!"

"Did you try to learn your lessons?"

"No, I did n't!"

"Why not?"

"Well, becos' lessons ain't in my line, no'ow—'osses is my mark!"

"But you must learn your lessons; I want you to grow into a useful, intelligent man!"

"Well, I 'd rayther be a groom or a ostler. I ain't never a-goin' to be nothink else, I ain't—no'ow!"

"Why, boy?"

"Becos' I likes the smell of 'osses, an' 'osses likes me."

"I might make a jockey of you!" says Jeremy thoughtfully.

"I seen jockeys at the races, I 'ave!"

"What? Have you been to races, child?"

"Ah! Been everywhere, I 'ave. An' I ain't no child, I ain't!"

"I wonder?" said Jeremy, viewing the elfin face before him with puzzled eyes.

"I seen a man kill a woman oncet, I did! First 'e scragged 'er by the 'air, then——"

"Hush!" cried Jeremy.

"Whaffor must I 'ush, guv'nor?"

"It 's too horrible!"

"Lor! Wot 's killin' a woman? Lots o' women gets killed along wheers I come from——"

"I must send you to school. No—a private tutor might be better."

"Wot 's a tooter, guv'nor?"

"One who would teach you better than I."

"Don't you go a-sendin' o' me to no tootors—I 'll toddle off, I will!"

"B'gad, I believe you would!" exclaimed Jeremy, and sat staring at the big-eyed Imp in deepest perplexity. "And then again, what to call you? Did you never have a name, boy?"

"Ah, lots on 'em! Jem Timmins, wot was a sweep, uster call me 'Snifter' cos when 'e made me climb up the chimbleys, the soot uster make me sneeze. Black Dan, as was 'ung for crackin' a crib in 'Olborn Bars, uster call me 'Ratty' cos' I could crawl froo the littlest 'oles when 'im an' me was working a lay. But ol' Gammer 'Iggins uster call me 'Guts,' cos I were allus so precious 'ungry. So Guts 'll do, though I ain't 'ungry no more. Call me 'Guts,' guv'nor; I don't mind!"

"Lord love me!" exclaimed Jeremy. But at this moment was a knock and a smart young footman appeared, somewhat over-developed as to knuckles, ears and calves, who, expanding his chest, vociferated:

"Mr. Terence O'Leary!" And into the room stepped that gentleman forthwith, as handsome, as dashing and jovial as usual. Jeremy heard a terrified gasp behind him and glancing round saw to his surprise that the boy had vanished.

"Shure and it 's meself, Jirry!" cried Mr. O'Leary, laying aside hat and cane. "Being in town for a few hours, says Oi to meself, says Oi, phwat 's to stay me from shaking me dear Jirry's hand? Nothing at all, at all, barring di'th, says Oi—and here Oi am!" And seizing Jeremy's hand, Mr. O'Leary shook it heartily and, still grasping it, led him across to the window, whence he peered down into the street.

"'T is divilish odd, Jerry, but 'pon me sowl, there 's a spalpeen in top-boots and a belcher neckerchief been following me or I 'm a Dutchman!"

"But who should follow you, and why?"

"Faix, me bhoy, 't is more than Oi—— bedad, there is the rascal!"

Now looking whither his companion directed, Jeremy saw a man approaching on the opposite side of the way, a shortish, square-shouldered man, whose top-boots paced in leisured strides, whose head, crowned with shaggy-napped broad-brimmed hat, was bowed as in thought, and beneath whose arm was a remarkably knobby stick.

"It 's only my friend Shrig," said Jeremy.

"Faith an' 't is roight y 'are, Jerry—the Bow Street officer we met at Priory Dene, to be sure! And a friend of yours, is he?"

"Yes."

"Then a fri'nd o' yours is a fri'nd o' mine. Call him in, me bhoy."

"He 's coming of his own accord, I think!"

Mr. Shrig was, for even as Jeremy spoke, he crossed the road and a moment later they heard his knock.

"B' the powers, 't is a foine lodging y' have here, ye dog!" cried Mr. O'Leary, glancing about with appreciative eye. "And in the very heart o' things too—close t' all the theatres, clubs and most fashionable hells! It 's a rich man y' are before your toime, Jirry! Faix, 't is the lucky bhoy y' are!"

"Am I!" said Jeremy frowning.

"You 're sharing y'r illegant apartments with a Mr. Armadale, Mrs. Rivell's brother, Oi hear."

"Yes," answered Jeremy, setting before his guest a silver tray with decanters and glasses.

"'T is loike the koind, generous heart o' ye, me bhoy—he drinks divilish hard, they tell me."

"Then damn 'em, whoever they are!" growled Jeremy.

"With all me heart, Jerry!"

"And how are things at Veryan?"

"Your uncle James sticks pins into beetles and is blooming. Your cousin Arthur, having got himself into trouble about some pretty face or other, has come up to town for a change of air——"

"Arthur always was an infernal coward!"

"Why, no, Jerry, no—not a coward," said Mr. O'Leary, helping himself to the sherry; "scarcely a coward—no! Arthur 's a fri'nd of mine, and Oi cannot permit another fri'nd to miscall a fri'nd, me bhoy, for loyalty to fri'ndship is the breath o' loife to me! Arthur 's no coward; he 'd foight as gamely as the boldest. But Truth compils me to admit that Arthur 's a damned scamp where the sex are concerned and not to be trusted with a handsome woman, be she innocent or no. Very excellent sherry this, me bhoy! And talking of Arthur naturally brings me to the bewitching Olivia—our fair widow——"

"How?" growled Jeremy.

"Because Arthur 's sighing, dying—mad for her."

"Arthur!" exclaimed Jeremy in profound contempt.

"And divilish determined too, me bhoy! Ay, bedad, ready and eager to shed his blood for her. 'T was phwat Oi meant when Oi told you he was no coward. Arthur 's quite ready to 'go out' with the Chevalier de Ravenac on her account—and doubtless get himself shot—and all for her sake, Jerry!"

"Why—with De Ravenac?"

"Jealousy, me bhoy! The green-eyed monster!'

"O'Leary, what d' ye mean? Explain yourself!"

"Me dear bhoy, the situation is manifest. Whin two gintlemen woo the same lady and are constantly meeting on her doorstep, they 're bound to quarrel sooner or later."

"D' ye mean De Ravanac—visits at Priory Dene?"

"So report says."

"Report is a liar, as usual!" Jeremy retorted. "Besides, I happen to know De Ravenac is here in town."

"But there are certain contrivances, they call 'em chaises, me bhoy, that shall whisk off a man to Sussex and back again with astounding celerity!"

At this moment the discreet Moxon knocked and entered to announce that a person by the name of Shrig was below.

"Tell him to wait!" growled Jeremy.

"Bedad, me bhoy, but Oi should loike a word wid him, if it 's all the same to you?" smiled Mr. O'Leary.

"Moxon, ask him to come up!"

"On me sowl, Oi never tasted foiner sherry!"

"And is he—are they—frequent visitors?"

"Why, report says, Jirry, that——"

"Report's a liar! What do you know of yourself positively, O'Leary?"

But before Mr. O'Leary could respond, the door opened to admit Mr. Shrig, who touched an eyebrow to Mr. O'Leary and grasped the hand Jeremy extended.

"How are you, Jasper?"

"Hearty, sir!"

"And all at 'The Gun'?"

"Hearty likewise, thank 'ee, sir!"

"You remember this gentleman, I think?"

"Let me see!" said Mr. Shrig, glancing askance at the gentleman in question and stroking his clean-shaven chin. "Not Jones—no! Nor yet Smith——"

"Me name 's O'Leary, me fri'nd, and you remember me perfectly!"

"Ay, but do I?" murmured Mr. Shrig. "I sees a mort o' different faces vun way and another——"

"Mr. O'Leary imagined you were following him."

"Lord!" exclaimed Mr. Shrig, and turned to regard O'Leary with eyes even rounder than usual. "You ackcherally thought that, sir?"

"I did!"

"And wherefore did ye so imagine, sir?"

"Because having eyes, I use 'em!"

"And see me? A-following you?"

"Shure Oi did that!"

"Then, sir, that proves the werry contrary, for if I foller a man that man never does see me, and don't know nothin' about it!"

"And what brings you here, Jasper?"

"Why, things being slackish, sir, perfessionally speaking, I toddled along to pass the time o' day."

"Good! You'll take a glass of wine?"

"Thank 'ee, sir! Your 'ealth, gen'lemen. And talk-o' 'ealth, I just took my last peep at Jos Shields—all as they've left of him."

"And who's Mr. Shields now?" asked Mr. O'Leary, holding his wine up to the light.

"The scoundrel who murdered Gillespie," answered Jeremy.

"Och, the curse o' Cromwell on him! So they've proved his guilt on him, have they?"

"They 'ave so, sir!" nodded Mr. Shrig with complacent emphasis.

"Hurroo!" exclaimed Mr. O'Leary and sipped his wine with gusto.

"They've proved 'e done the deed or as you might say, committed the fac'," continued Mr. Shrig; "proved it out and out, through an' through, vich was werry satisfactory. But not bein' able to hang J. Shields, seein' as 'ow he vas a corpse already, they sent 'im along to the doctors at Surgeon's Hall, and they're a-cutting Jos up and a-taking Jos to pieces at this here i-dentical minute."

"The divil they are!" exclaimed Mr. O'Leary, setting down his empty glass and making a wry face. "Unpleasant fellows, doctors—unless you happen to be ill—nasty ways!"

"Vun man's meat 's another man's pizen, sir!" returned Mr. Shrig sententiously. "And, talking o' pizen, Mr. O'Leary, sir, 'ow 's that theer dog?"

"Dog?" repeated Mr. O'Leary, staring at his questioner's placid features in surprise. "Phwat dog will ye be maning now?"

"I means Bill, sir—Mr. Weryan's dog as was a-living—when last heered of—at Priory Dene, along o' Mrs. R."

"Och, shure the animal is well enough, so far as I know!" answered Mr. O'Leary, beginning to draw on his gloves. "Why do you ask me, man?"

"Why, sir, 'twixt you an' me, I 've almost—ah, werry nigh expected that theer devoted creetur to be—took off—sudden!"

Once again Mr. O'Leary turned to scan the speaker's placid features, the smooth brow, mobile mouth and round, non-committal eyes; and once again he asked a question.

"An' phwat 'll ye be after meaning now, at all?"

"Pizen, sir—or say, a bullet!"

"An' phwat scoundrel should be for murthering the poor baste?"

"Vell, there's vun I knows on as 'ud do it—French gent! Black viskers! Name o' Ravvynack—'im 'aving threatened same, as I can dooly bear witness! You 'appen to know this here Ravvynack, I think, sir?"

"We were acquainted years ago!" answered Mr. O'Leary rising.

"I 'spose you have n't 'appened to meet 'im o' late anywheres?"

"No!" answered Mr. O'Leary, taking up hat and cane.

"And I 'spose you ain't expecting to meet 'im anywheres?—— Here in London, say?"

"No!" answered Mr. O'Leary again; and turning from his so persistent questioner, he grasped and shook Jeremy's hand.

"Good-bye, me dear bhoy!" said he heartily. "B' the powers, it 's done me worlds o' good to see ye so full o' life and spirits, so dashing and illigant! Good-bye, Jirry! Have ye anny message for our bewitching Revell?"

"No!" answered Jeremy, opening the door and following his guest out to the stairs.

"Ah, well—— Good-bye! Think sometimes of your friend Tirince!— No, don't throuble to come down. God bless ye, my bhoy!" And with a final benignant gesture of white shapely hand, Mr. O'Leary descended the stair, humming gaily to himself and went forth upon his way.

Returning to the sitting-room, Jeremy beheld Mr. Shrig at the window, observed a motion of Mr. Shrig's fingers and, glancing down into the street, saw a small, unobtrusive and meek-seeming person in drooping whiskers who, emerging from nowhere in particular, nodded meek head despondently as who should say, "Well, well—what a world it is!" and moved unobtrusively away.

"Only Dan'l, sir!" said Mr. Shrig

"So then, you were following O'Leary?"

"Mr. Wee, sir—since you puts it to me so p'inted, I 'll tell ye—— Love my eyes—vot 's this!" he exclaimed, as from the heavy window curtains a small, curly head shot into view.

"Yah!" quoth the Imp, with hideous grimace.

"Vot are you a-doing of behind them curtings, ye young wagabone?" demanded Mr. Shrig, grasping the urchin's arm, yet not unkindly.

"Nuffink—only 'iding!"

"Vot for?"

"Well, becos' I knows 'im, I does!"

"'Oo, sonny, 'oo?"

"Why, 'im as just went out. A bad un, 'e is!"

"Nonsense, boy!" said Jeremy.

"D' ye mean the tall gen'leman, sonny, with the nice gold 'air?" enquired Mr. Shrig with growing interest.

"Ah—'im!" nodded the Imp.

"Are ye sure, sonny?"

"Yus! Pulled me year once, 'e did—nigh twisted it off, 'e did. 'E 's a bad un, 'e is!"

"By Goles!" quoth Mr. Shrig, pinching his chin and staring at the urchin round eyed. "Did 'e, though?"

"Yus, 'e did!"

"Preposterous!" said Jeremy. "How and where could this poor child have seen O'Leary?"

"Ay, that's the question, sir!" nodded Mr. Shrig, hitching his chair nearer to the sullen Imp.

"I ain't no pore child, guv'nor, I ain't!"

"And where might you ha' seen this here gen'leman, sonny?"

"'Long by the river!"

"Not," said Mr. Shrig, stooping forward to pat the urchin's curly head, "not anywheres near the 'Jolly Waterman'—come now?"

"Yus, I did!"

"Not," questioned Mr. Shrig, drawing the urchin nearer to him with large but gentle hand, "not inside of the 'Jolly Waterman?' Never there—no!"

"Yus, I did—many a time!"

"And when was the last time, sonny?"

"I dunno."

"Might it be—say a month ago? Five weeks? Six?"

"Well, I dunno!"

"Might it be about the time as you an' me met along by the river and I give you tuppence 'cos you vas hungry?"

"Yus, 'bout then, I guess—but I ain't 'ungry no more, I ain't!"

"And 'e pulled your ear, eh, son?"

"Ah—fort 'e 'd twist it off, I did."

"And wot were 'e doin' afore 'e pulled your ear, son?"

"A-maggin."

"'Oo with?"

"Free coves."

"Did ye know any o' these three coves—eh? Their names?"

"Naw!"

"Vould ye know 'em if ye see 'em again?"

"Yus!"

"Did ye ever see 'im—think 'ard, sonny—along o' Jos Shields? Think werry 'ard now, sonny!"

"Naw, I did n't. An' I ain't a-going t' say no more, I ain't!"

"Look 'ee, son! Here 's a nice, bright, round shilling——"

"Well, give it 'ere!"

"Ay, so I will, but first tell us 'ow you come to see this here gen'leman the first time."

"Well, when it rained I uster sleep under a old boat, see. An' one night I crep' under it 'cos it was rainin' an' along come free coves an' began a-maggin an' I sneezed, I did, so they dragged me out an' one on 'em twisted me year—an' it was 'im. Gimme the bob!"

"They y' are son. And don't go for to spend it all at vunce!"

"Yah!" cried the boy defiantly and darted from the room.

And now Mr. Shrig seemed to be lost in the profoundest abstraction. Motionless he sat, elbow on knee and chin on fist, staring before him, with eyes half-closed; so oblivious was he, indeed, that he began to whistle very softly at first, but gradually louder and louder until the room was full of the cheery sound.

"Ax your parding, sir!" said he suddenly. "But I was thinking werry 'ard and at such times I vistles—the 'arder the louder, d' ye see?"

"What were you thinking, Jasper?"

"That this here vas vun o' my lucky days, sir. Some days is 'down' uns and some days is 'ups'—and this is an up un!"

"Now tell me—do you believe the boy's story?"

"Ay, I do, sir."

"But," said Jeremy in frowning perplexity, "what does it—what can it possibly mean?"

"Sir," answered Mr. Shrig, shaking his head, "maybe I 'll be able to tell you that—vun o' these days if I ain't snuffed."

"Ha! Jasper, what are you suggesting?"

"Windictiveness, sir! How many times was your life attempted at Weryan?"

"We are not at Veryan."

"No more is Windictiveness—at present, sir. It 's on my track, unless I 'm mistook—ah, it 'll be a-creeping behind me, laying for me round every corner—unless I 'm werry much mistook! Hows'ever, Mr. Wee, pal, vot is to be, must be! But life without a bit of uncertainty is like toddy without leming, or a stoo' without a nonion, and there y' are. And now I 'll be toddling."

"But confound it, Shrig, you explain nothing—tell me nothing!"

"Because nothin' is exackly vot I 'm sure of, sir! And nothing being nothing, can't nohow never be told—now can it, I ask you? But if anything as is anything—meaning something—should turn up, I 'll let you know, sir."

So saying, Mr. Shrig grasped the hand Jeremy extended and turned to the door, but paused there to glance back over his shoulder.

"That there b'y, sir—are you a-goin' to keep same?"

"Yes, Jasper. Why?"

"Because if you don't—I would. A bright lad, sir!"

"Yes."

"With plenty of the Old Adam about 'im, sir."

"Plenty. How old would you think him, Shrig?"

"Why, sir, I should say as that there b'y ain't to be reckoned in years! He was a reglar old un afore he vas born and being nat'rally a smooth file, a downy bird, a knowing card and a reg'lar rasper, he 'd make a name for hisself in my perfession!" Having delivered himself of which, Mr. Shrig nodded and took his departure; and it was to be noted that, as he went, his lips were pursed in a soundless whistle.

## CHAPTER XXVI

### WHICH INTRODUCES LORD JULIAN MIDMARSH

THE days have numbered themselves into almost two months and upon this sunny morning, seated at the breakfast table before the open window, Mr. Armadale is helping himself to yet another slice of cold ham. And Mr. Armadale's erstwhile pallid cheek has become ruddy, his eyes keen and direct, his lips firm, his whole slender, shapely person alert of movement and vibrant with energy.

Beholding all of which, Jeremy, sitting opposite, nods to himself and his grim features (slightly puffed here and there by reason of Jessamy Todd's recent exertions), become wonderfully tender, none the less, for he is thinking of Olivia and the joy in store for her when she shall behold the change these latter weeks have wrought in her reckless, young brother.

"Jay," says Mr. Armadale, suddenly (thus has he shortened Jeremy's name), "Jay, my buck, pray observe my appetite! Breakfast is become an expected joy! And this, mark you, solely by reason of a clean and regular life!"

"Yes!" says Jeremy.

"There 's nothing like a Spartan sobriety, Jay!"

"No!" says Jeremy.

"B'ged," exclaims Mr. Armadale with an airy flourish of the carving fork, "when I think what a miserable dem'd dog I was becoming, Jay, the frightful doom that would have engulfed me but for myself—

I'm amazed at myself, astounded, I confess! When I ponder upon the strength of mind required to free myself from an accursed curse, the sublime determination, not to mention the profound mental effort, the inflexible purpose, the stern, heroic, unflagging, indomitable dem'd will to conquer or die, I am, as I say, astounded, astonished and amazingly surprised I should have successfully undertaken an achievement so vast! Pray pass the mustard! I suppose there is scarcely a parallel in the history of mankind! Thus, my dear fellow, I amaze myself most demnably!"

"And Olivia," said Jeremy. "Olivia will be glad!"

"She will, sweet soul, she will! I meant to write and tell her all about it but have been so infernal busy! I'll trouble you for another cup of coffee. Some sage and ancient cove once said or wrote: 'He that conquers himself is greater than he that taketh a city!' Fancy that's coming it a bit too strong, but if there's any truth in it, I go to Olivia a conqueror. By the way, when do we go?"

"In two days' time," answered Jeremy. "Two whole days!"

"She'll hardly recognise you at first, for you're doocedly changed, ye know, Jay—externally at least—and immensely for the better, thanks to my unremitting care—and, b'ged, now I look at you, I see you've tied your cravat divilishly——"

"I thought it was pretty well, Dick."

"It's a dooced!— You're a solemn old sobersides, Jay, and yet most confoundedly likeable—and amazing in your own way."

"How?"

"Well, for one thing, what makes you so dooced popular?"

"Am I, Dick?'

"Demme, of course you are! Already you have the entrée of all the most exclusive clubs—though your name might do that! No, what I mean is—why does everyone take to you?"

"Do they, Dick?"

"Demme, of course they do! Most remarkable and dooced singular, for you're not particularly lively, Jay, nor observably dashing; you've no arresting tricks, and dooce knows you're no talker, a dem'd oyster is an orator beside you! And yet, b'ged, your acquaintances all want to become friends and everybody wants to become acquainted! I fancy it must be your downright, dooced bluntness; anyhow every one seems to like it!"

"Do you?"

"Well—of course—now and then, my dear fellow——"

"Then," said Jeremy, "have you asked her to marry you yet?"

"Oh, the dooce—dooce take and confound everything!" gasped Mr. Armadale. "How sudden you are! No, I have not—most decidedly—no!"

"Why?"

"Because I'm not a dem'd bull at a gate to rush in where angels fear to tread, in the first place. And in the second, because she's as timid as a—a confounded what-is-it—no, I mean a fawn, as shy, as bewitchingly elusive as a dryad, my dear Jay."

"Does your wooing prosper?"

"To be sure it does. Yesterday I ventured to kiss her fingers."

"Fingers, Dick?"

"Fingers, Jerry. And b'ged, even this took some courage, for she positively—awes me! My dear fellow, believe me, I 'm no laggard—'t would have been any other woman's lips—weeks ago! But Ruth with her sweet simplicity, her shining purity and innocence looking up at me from her sweet eyes, makes me feel the unworthiest, dem'dest dog that ever howled! But yesterday, I kissed her fingers, such pretty, slim things though all roughened with her dem'd needle. To-day it may be her wrist, to-morrow her round, white arm—the very perfection of an arm, Jay! And next week, or month, or sometime, the dooce knows when, it may be her lips."

"You see her often?"

"Of course! Every day."

"Have you told her your love?"

"Thousands of times——"

"Does she know it is so reverent, so honourable?"

"Sir!" exclaimed Mr. Armadale, suddenly haughty, "D' ye dare suggest I 'm such an inordinate scoundrel, such a base black-hearted villain, such a monster of perfidy, as to dream evil against one so angelically holy?"

"No, but her guardian may!"

"Tush! The old wretch is an ogre——"

"And my friend!"

"He guards her against me as if I were a dem'd pestilence!"

"He probably thinks you are!"

"The dooce he does! Then let him and be dem'd!"

"Why not speak and undeceive him?"

"And spoil the sweetest idyll o' love that lover ever knew—Not I! Be asked into some stuffy back parlour to hold hands, sigh and languish while he sits by playing dem'd gooseberry? Not I! No, Jerry, when I have kissed her lips, when she has promised to wed me—which seems dooced impossible, considering my dem'd past and general unworthiness, then I 'll talk to Gruff and Glum, not before."

"Does she agree to this?"

Mr. Armadale laid down his knife and fork to stare across at Jeremy beneath brows and slowly gathered in a frown.

"You say you have never seen Ruth Trent?"

"Nor have I, Dick."

"And know nothing whatever about her?"

"Nothing—except that she is under the fatherly care of my old friend Lockett."

"Then the constant interest you manifest in regard to her strikes me as remarkable—so dem'd remarkable—that I naturally begin to wonder if——"

"So do I!" said Jeremy. "I am wondering what I should do were I in Lockett's place—an old man harassed by such anxiety as you are causing him—anxiety for one I loved better than myself—seeing her thus menaced by the attentions of a man so far above her rank——"

"Menaced, sir?"

"How should Lockett know any different? I think were I he, I should carry her off out of danger——"

"Ha—danger, sir! D' ye dare suggest——"

"Danger!" nodded Jeremy. "How should old Lockett know you are not the black-hearted villain you mentioned just now?"

"Enough, sir—I' ll have no more——"

"I think, were I old Lockett, I should at once carry her off out of danger——"

"Stop, sir!" And up sprang Mr. Armadale, quivering with passion. "By God, Veryan, you go too far!" he exclaimed between quivering lips. "Friendship has its limits——"

"I think not!" answered Jeremy.

"Oh, curse everything!" exclaimed Mr. Armadale and strode off to his bedroom, slamming the door behind him. Left alone, Jeremy sat awhile in gloomy thought, then going into his bedroom, closed the door gently and sitting down at his desk took thence his latest (and unfinished) letter to Olivia and glancing over the close-written lines came to these:

"Richard is well, indeed so very well, I begin to believe he has already outfought and conquered his particular devil. Every day but makes him more worthy of your tender love and abiding faith. Could you but see him to-day, his eyes keen and alert, his hands steady, himself brimful of vigorous life and the joy of it, you would behold the manifest answer to your prayers. Moreover, since taking up our residence here, we have seen no sign of De Ravenac, nor has Richard mentioned his name. Thrice a week regularly he spars with me or the wonderful Jessamy Todd (of whom I told you in a former letter). Truly, my Olivia, your Richard is regenerate and all by reason of his own determination, or because (as I think) of your prayers, for surely such supplications must——"

He had reached thus far when Mr. Armadale strode in.

"Jeremy," said he, more in sorrow than in anger, "you've the very dem'dest way with you at times—positively, y' know!"

"Then pray forgive me, Dick!"

Mr. Armadale's frown vanished and out came his hand to clap Jeremy's broad shoulder.

"Upon my soul, Jay, old fellow, that 's dooced handsome of you for, egad, I came to ask you to forgive me."

"Then let 's forgive each other, Dick!"

"With all my heart, Jay! And now come back and let us finish breakfast."

So back they went forthwith, arm in arm, but hardly were they seated than the door burst open and the Imp appeared; his clothes were dusty and dishevelled, his small face showed marks of recent battle, but in his hand he flourished an unlovely ragged object triumphantly.

"I got it, I did!" he panted.

"True," nodded Mr. Armadale. "But what is it?"

"Tommy Nolan's 'at—lives in the yard, 'e do!"

"And an uncommonly bad hat, Bones! Why did you take it?"

"'Cos 'e says as 'ow I couldn't, an' dared me to, so I punched 'im on the nose an' took it, I did!"

"Very right and proper, my Bones. Have some ham!"

"Boy, come here!" growled Jeremy. "To take another's property is thieving and——"

"Yah! Wot 's thieving, guv'nor! Everybody thieves from somebody sometimes, if they wants a thing bad enough——"

"And b'ged, that 's sure enough!" nodded Mr. Armadale.

"Dick," sighed Jeremy, studying the boy with all his old perplexity, "in heaven's name—what age is he?"

"Anything from eight to eighty, Jay."

"What on earth can we do with him?"

"That 's the problem!" nodded Mr. Armadale. "Our Bones would seem unpopular outside our immediate circle—they promptly expelled him from the school you placed him at, remember! And the tutor fellow said he was hopeless and complained of our lamb's violence——"

"Well, I only kicked 'im a bit," explained the Imp, "an' not 'arf so 'ard as wot I been kicked——"

"Precisely, my sweet child——"

"Yah—boo!" cried the indignant urchin.

"Silence, boy!" growled Jeremy.

"Well, you tell Mister Armystall as I ain't no child——"

"Mr. who!" demanded Mr. Armadale. "Pray repeat that remark, my gentle laddie——"

"Walker!" exclaimed the urchin.

At this moment the dignified Moxon appeared who, coughing discreetly behind his hand, begged to say there was a person below.

"Eh!" quoth Mr. Armadale.

"A somewhat violent person, gentlemen, though of the gender feminine, who loudly accuses us of purloining her son's hat. Whereupon, sirs, I denied the alleged larceny—strongly!"

"Quite right, Moxon!" nodded Mr. Armadale. "Nothing like denying—the stronger the better!"

"And here is the hat!" said Jeremy, twitching the object in question from the Imp's reluctant grasp and thrusting it into the astonished Moxon's hands. "Pray return it with expressions of regret."

"Certainly, sir, though it looks somewhat dilapidated, sir, and . . . considering the female in question is so vehement a personage, I would—er—humbly suggest——"

"I twig you, Moxon!" nodded Mr. Armadale, thrusting hand into pocket; "give Madam Virago this half-crown."

"And this also!" said Jeremy.

"On her behalf, gentlemen, I thank you!" murmured Moxon. "A sum so handsome should prove sufficient amelioration," and, coins in one hand, hat in the other, Moxon bowed and withdrew.

"Ah, Bones—my Bones," sighed Mr. Armadale, "thou pestilent Imp, thou 'rt like to become our affliction——"

"No, I ain't!" quoth the urchin; "'osses is my fancy!"

"What are we to do with him, Dick?"

"Well, we might make him our 'tiger'—little top-boots and buckskins, cockaded hat—dooced smart, y' know."

"I meant to find him a home, Dick, never having known one myself!"

"A home, eh? Then Olivia must take him!"

"Do you think she would?"

"Of course! Do anything in the world for me, my dear Jay! We 'll take him down to her. So that 's settled!" So saying, Mr. Armadale rose and crossing to the open window, leaned out into the sunny air. "Glorious morning for a gallop, eh, Jerry? Very good! Boy—you Three Feet of Iniquity, trot and tell Moxon to have the horses saddled and ready in ten minutes—Sharp, now!"

Waiting no second bidding, the urchin sped away on his errand, while Mr. Armadale, lounging gracefully in the window, surveyed the sunny world with an indolent appreciation of it and all therein, more particularly himself; but suddenly he uttered an exclamation and retreated from the window somewhat precipitately.

"B'ged, there 's Midmarsh in his curricle—pulling up here too! Now what the dooce can he want at such a confoundedly unearthly hour! And he's always so dooced dismal and low-spirited—especially after a night of it! Gives me the spleen, megrims, farcy and staggers all at once—so, I'm out, Jay! Say I 'm out or sick abed! Be a friend, Jay, a trump and a Trojan, and oh, b'ged, there 's his knock!" And out of the room whisked Mr. Armadale before Jeremy could find a word.

And presently appeared the young footman, knuckles, ears and calves very much in evidence to announce:

"Lord Julian Midmarsh!"

My lord was very young and extremely pale, a slim, languid youth with large, melancholy, brooding eyes and a too gentle mouth. Despondency clothed him like a garment, and therewith a dreadful weariness; it was in his voice, his air, his every gesture.

"Ah, Mr. Veryan," said he in soft, tired voice, "remember me—I hope? Met you—White's, last week—sometime."

"To be sure!" answered Jeremy, grasping the nerveless hand his lordship offered.

"Ridiculous hour to call, I know! But I 'm early because I 'm late. All night at Martinetti's—but it 's the last time—I 'm done with all the hells—yes, I 'm done—for good!" Here his lordship glanced out wistfully at the glory of sun flooding in at the window and, shivering violently, knit his brows as with some sudden pain or unutterable thought. "I came for a word with Armadale, but he 's dodged me, I see?"

"Dodged you, my lord——" repeated Jeremy awkwardly.

"Of course!" replied his lordship. "And quite naturally, for I 'm devilish bad company—yes, even for myself! So I 'll not aflict you for long——"

"My dear fellow!" said Jeremy heartily, moved by something in the speaker's look and tone, this desperately weary voice, the haunting care, the expression of nervous anxiety so very much out of place on such youthful features. "Pray sit down! Let me ring for some breakfast."

"Uncommon good of you, Veryan, but I seldom eat—never early in the morning. No appetite."

"A cup of tea or coffee?"

"No, no! Bed 's all I need. But y' see, hate bed—can't sleep, y' know. God, Veryan, it 's devilish to lie awake—counting the throbs of your heart—and thinking! Oh, by God, anything is better than that. To think and think . . . in the dark—of all that might have been . . . should have been . . . and is n't. So I don't go to bed very often now—naturally!"

"My dear fellow," said Jeremy again. "You need fresh air exercise, a friend to pummel you heartily."

"Perhaps I do—or did. But all 's one, now."

"Why?"

His lordhsip glanced at Jeremy, his slender brows wrinkled with that same look of sudden, painful anxiety, his eyes so wistful that Jeremy was reminded of the eyes of some animal in pain. Then, leaning forward, and laying his hand upon Lord Midmarsh's drooping shoulder, Jeremy spoke in that voice none but Olivia had ever heard; and what he said was:

"My chap, what's your trouble?"

At this, Lord Midmarsh shrank in the depths of his chair, covering his eyes with one hand but fumbling with the other until he had found and pressed Jeremy's fingers.

"Veryan," said he softly, "you 're a strange—good fellow! Why do you ask?"

"To help—if possible."

"But—you kardly know me."

"Enough to help—if you'll permit." Here his lordship turned to look at Jeremy and to shake his head with a smile that was worse than any tears.

"It 's too late, Veryan—quite too late! Six months ago—a month, yes—a week may be— But now——!"

"Is it ever too late?"

"Not for others, perhaps! Mine 's the story of a fool—a poor pigeon—tried to soar with eagles—no, kites! I 'm one whose desperate folly has blasted two lives, Veryan, d' ye know what it is to love with every thought, every breath, every heartbeat—do you?"

"Yes!" answered Jeremy.

"We were to have married, y' know, Veryan. Six months ago I wrote to break it off—point of honour—and my heart broke too. Yesterday I learned she was dead—and consequently——"

Lord Midmarsh turned to glance at the sunshine glory again and smiled. "Thus it becomes at once apparent, my dear Veryan, that all the friends on earth and all the angels in heaven cannot help me, y' see—She 's dead!" Here Lord Midmarsh rose, but with his gaze still upon the glory at the window. "By the way," said he, taking up his hat and staring at it absently, "d' you gamble?"

"Seldom!"

"Then let it be more seldom until—it is n't. D 'ye take me? Cards are the devil, hell and damnation, remorse, despair, and hatred all in one. And now I 'll go, and time too! Besides, my horses will be catching cold. Stay, though, I 've a letter for Armadale—unless I 've dropped it! No, here it is—invitation t' supper party—select! Devil's orgy! I shall be there, of course! When he's read it, tell him to burn it and forget!" But, instead of giving Jeremy the letter, he tossed it upon the table, and stood regarding it a while beneath furrowed brows.

"Good-bye, Veryan!" said he suddenly. "Had we met before, we might ha' been friends, I think—and I—happier! As it is, we meet only to part—you up into the light, I hope, my dear Veryan—I down into the outer dark—and yet—I may find—there may be a light beyond, eh, Veryan?"

So saying, he grasped Jeremy's hand, wrung it hard and was gone. And presently, looking from the window, Jeremy saw him climb wearily into his smart curricle and take the reins only to hand them back to the smart groom, and with head bowed and hands folded he was driven away.

# CHAPTER XXVII

## WHICH DESCRIBES A COMBAT

JEREMY was still at the window when Mr. Armadale's voice roused him.

"Gone at last, eh? And the dooce of a time you kept him, Jay!"

"Have you known Lord Midmarsh long?"

"Years! We were at school together."

"You had another schoolfellow, Dick—named Jardine!"

"Ay, b'ged, and the very opposite to Midmarsh; Tommy Jardine was the blithest bird that ever chirped—and yet—poor old Tommy, he killed himself y' know."

"Yes, Dick."

"But confound it, Jay, why must you remind me o' this? What did Midmarsh want?"

"He brought you a letter—it 's on the table."

Mr. Armadale took up the letter, glanced at the superscription, frowned, hesitated, and finally, breaking the seal, began to read; now as he did so, his gaiety seemed to be slowly quenched by a gathering shadow very like that which had haunted the haggard features of Lord Midmarsh.

"Bad news, Dick?"

"No, oh no!" answered Mr. Armadale, crumpling up the missive and thrusting it into his pocket. "Merely a line from De Ravenac—an invitation for to-night.

Midmarsh's house in St. James's Square—little dinner —just a sociable gathering, Jay."

"Lord Midmarsh said 'orgy'!"

"Midmarsh—pshaw!" exclaimed Mr. Armadale with a peevish gesture.

"You 'll go?"

"I must—er—that is—I mean, y' know, to refuse would not be exactly—well—polite."

"Why?"

"Oh, well—dooce take it—De Ravenac's my friend——"

"Is he?"

"Demme, of course he is!"

"D' you want to go?"

"Certainly! To be sure I do—dooce take it, of course!"

"Hum!" quoth Jeremy.

"I need a little relaxation. Jolly dogs, Jay, bucks and sportsmen all!"

"Hum!" quoth Jeremy again.

"What the dooce are ye humming for?" demanded Mr. Armadale, more peevishly than ever.

"Lord Midmarsh does n't strike me as a particularly 'jolly dog'!" said Jeremy, frowning thoughtfully.

"Midmarsh!" exclaimed Mr. Armadale scornfully. "He 's always as mopish as a dem'd owl—and getting worse."

"Why?"

"Dooce knows!"

"Is it any use asking you not to go?"

"No! I 'm determined on it. And you know when my mind 's made up I 'm iron, Jay, iron, b'ged!"

"For the sake of our friendship."

"I tell you my mind 's made up!"

"For your own sake."

"It 's for my own sake I 'm going."

"Then—for Olivia's sake!"

"Oh, confound it, what the dooce has she to do with it? Demme, I 'm my own master, I hope!"

"Are you?"

"Ha!" exclaimed Mr. Armadale suddenly haughty, "What d' ye mean by that, Veryan?"

"De Ravenac!"

"Sir, I repeat—Gaston De Ravenac is my very good friend!"

"Hum!" growled Jeremy. "Has the scoundrel any hold over you?"

"Sir!" exclaimed Mr. Armadale, magnificently disdainful. "Your disparagement of my friend is an affront to myself!"

"Has he any power over you, Dick?"

"If the deepest and sincerest gratitude be a power—yes, sir!"

"Gratitude for what?"

"If you must know—for the Revell affair——"

"He holds that over you still, does he, Dick?"

"Veryan, this conversation has gone far enough!"

"But, Dick——"

"Sir, your vilification of an old and tried friend such as Gaston offends me beyond expression."

"And your association with him grieves your sister deeply, constantly, as you are aware! Through you he can wring her heart and the damned scoundrel knows it."

"Veryan, you have twice named him scoundrel—behind his back! I suggest the next time should be in his hearing."

"I wait but the occasion, Dick. Meanwhile—for Olivia's sake—I beg you 'll destroy that letter and forget all about it."

"And for my own sake, Veryan, I 'll do no such thing! Confound it, sir, I 'm no schoolboy to be hectored and browbeaten! And I 'll thank you not to come the dem'd virtuous friend-o'-the-family over me. I 'm as wide awake as yourself, perhaps a little more so. Pray understand I 'm my own master and not to be dictated to by any man breathing!" So saying, Mr. Armadale turned towards the door which opened at that moment to disclose the dignified Moxon.

"Gentlemen," said he, "I knocked—thrice—to inform you the horses await your convenience and——"

"Horses be demmed!" quoth Mr. Armadale.

"Certainly, sir!" said Moxon, bowing. "Also there is a person of the name Lockett—Arthur Lockett, to see Mr. Armadale——"

"Is there, b'ged! Then tell him to go away and be dem'd! I 'll not see him——"

"Ah, but you will, sir, you must and shall!" And, thrusting the astounded Moxon aside, Mr. Lockett stepped into the room; but a very different Lockett from his usual deprecating self, for now his slight figure was erect, his white head high and his usually gentle eyes bright and fierce, like his words and tone. "I am here, Mr. Armadale, to warn you."

"The dooce, you are?"

"To warn you that unless you cease your persecution of helpless Innocence, you will have to deal with a desperate man!"

"And who may he be, pray?"

"Myself, sir!" answered the little man, trembling. "I who love her beyond all fear, Mr. Armadale, ay, beyond death itself."

"B'ged, but then so do I!" retorted Mr. Armadale with a grandiloquent gesture. "There never was such an adoring, dem'd determined lover as myself; there never will be! And I warn you that I 'll win the sweet soul in spite o' you and ten thousand like you! Sir, I have the honour to bid you good morning!" And with a mocking bow, Mr. Armadale went out, slamming the door behind him. Instantly Lockett made to follow, but was stayed by a long arm.

"Let him go, Keyhole, let him go!" said Jeremy, giving the trembling little man a comforting squeeze.

"But—oh, Mr. Jeremy, you heard what he said!"

"Never heed his vapouring, old friend!"

"I—I would kill any man who harmed her."

"I believe you would," nodded Jeremy, "but then so would Richard; his love for her is very deep and true—"

"Then why does he persistently avoid me? Why must he waylay her—on the sly?"

"I thought I 'd explained this, Lockett."

"Yes, yes, Mr. Jeremy, and I was ready to find comfort in your assurances, but why has he set ruffians to watch—to spy on her?"

"Ha, d' ye say so?"

"I do, sir. Two hangdog fellows have been prowling about us the last three days—with some evil purpose! Oh, indeed, indeed, I 'm not mistaken. When I ventured to question them, they jeered and threatened me——"

"What sort of men, Lockett?"

"They look like fighting men."

"And you think Mr. Armadale set 'em on?"

"Who else, sir?"

"Hum!" quoth Jeremy, scowling. "Let us enquire!" Forthwith he crossed to Mr. Armadale's door, knocked, received no answer and glancing into the room found it empty.

"Mr. Armadale is about to go riding, sir," said Mr. Lockett, at the window, and coming thither, Jeremy leaned out to behold Mr. Armadale in the act of getting to horseback.

"Dick," he called, "a word with you."

Mr. Armadale swung lightly to saddle, and removing his hat with a graceful flourish, bowed.

"Ah, Veryan!" quoth he, gathering the reins. "I 'm in no humour for more words at present. I bid you good morning!" And touching his mettled animal with the spur, he galloped off down the street.

"Well, perhaps we 're better alone!" growled Jeremy. "And now if you 're ready, my Keyhole, I am."

"For what, sir?"

"These men."

"But what is your intention?"

"That depends."

"On what, Master Jerry?"

"These men. We must learn their business and who employs 'em."

"I fear they may be—violent."

"Good! You say they threatened you, my Keyhole."

"Horribly, Master Jerry. I went and bought a pistol!"

"Hum!" quoth Jeremy, taking hat and cane. "You think we shall catch 'em?"

"Catch them, sir?" repeated Mr. Lockett, staring.

"I don't want to miss 'em, Keyhole."

"I fear there 's no chance of that, Master Jerry. They were there when I left, in the yard where we live, watching the house."

"And are they likely looking fellows, Keyhole?"

"On the contrary, sir, one has a broken nose and the other a monstrous ear——"

"Come on!" exclaimed Jeremy, slipping his arm within Mr. Lockett's. "Let 's go."

"But—Master Jerry—oh, dear me——" said Mr. Lockett, as Jeremy hurried him down the stair. "I do hope—beg—you 'll—not incur any risk? Sir, what is your purpose? Such haste?"

"Dear old Keyhole, I'm merely anxious to test my capabilities in certain particulars. I 've been studying under a very efficient master and wish to prove myself. What is it, Moxon?"

"Sir," said the sedate person, as he opened the front door to their exit, "shall you return for dinner?"

"No—yes, I may be late—no matter! And, Moxon, give an eye—and ear to that Imp o' mine."

"Pray rest assured, sir."

Then, arm in arm with Mr. Lockett, Jeremy stepped forth into the sunny air and set out at such a pace that the little clerk's short legs had much ado to keep up.

"Master Jerry," said he at last, a little breathlessly, "might I suggest—you moderate your—excessive speed?"

"To be sure, my dear old Keyhole, I beg your pardon! I was thinking. I suppose they 're pretty sure to be there, these fellows?"

"I fear so."

"'T would be pity to miss 'em. A most tempting opportunity."

"Do you think you can discover their employer?"

"We can try, old friend. Of this I 'm sure—his name is not Armadale."

"Do you think so, Master Jeremy?"

"I 'm sure! Richard would never stoop to such vileness."

Here Jeremy scowled; the little clerk sighed and they walked a while in silence.

"The gift of beauty is a dangerous thing!" said Mr. Lockett at last. "More especially when it goes hand in hand with poverty."

"And your Ruth is beautiful, I hear."

"Yes, sir. And sweet and gentle also. You have never seen her, I think?"

"Never," answered Jeremy and stepped from the pavement to cross the busy thoroughfare; but in that moment his companion uttered a warning cry and dragged him back only just in time to escape the lashing hoofs of a wildly rearing horse; even so the wheel of the vehicle brushed his sleeve, and turning he found himself staring up into the pale blue eyes of the Chevalier de Ravenac, beside whom sat Mr. Arthur Trevor, his handsome, aristocratic features distorted by an unwonted spasm of excitement.

"*Mille pardons,* monsieur!" cried the Chevalier, reining in his snorting animals. "Pray accept my excuse the mos' 'umble! Why, *pardieu*—surely it is Monsieur Veryan!"

"By—by God, Jerry," stammered Arthur, "that—that was a close shave, old fellow—a narrow squeak!" And his voice ended in a strange, high-pitched laugh.

"Very," answered Jeremy, scowling from one to the other, then, taking Mr. Lockett's ready arm, he went his way, thick brows knit in frowning speculation.

"You recognised him, Master Jerry? The gentleman driving?"

"Yes."

"A personality not easily forgotten, sir. I 'm wondering what should make his horses rear and swerve so—so very unexpectedly. To be sure they were very mettlesome, very nervous creatures—and yet——"

"And yet," said Jeremy, smiling down into the little man's puzzled face. "I 'm still—very much alive! Dear old Keyhole, you surely saved my life, and let us hope to some purpose."

After this Jeremy became once more lost in thought, walking with head bent and following the guidance of his companion's arm mechanically, nor did he wake from this profound abstraction until Mr. Lockett halted suddenly and spoke in low, troubled voice:

"Oh, dear me, there are three of them to-day!"

Hereupon Jeremy roused and glancing up, found they were in a small courtyard, very quiet and clean and full of sunshine. And here, in shady corner, lounged three men in growling confab, burly fellows all and each remarkably thick as to neck, square as to jaw and battered as to features; but now they hushed their talk to turn and stare at Jeremy in highly threatening fashion, eyeing him truculently from head to foot, while Jeremy viewed them severally with the eye of keen appraisement.

Mutely thus, the one and the three, they surveyed each other awhile; then the three issued their commands like the heavy-fisted autocrats they were:

Quoth Number One (in ferocious sarcasm), a brawny individual with massive blue chin and cauliflower ear: "Me lord dook—'op off!"

Quoth Number Two (laying blunt finger to broken nose): "Out o' this, an' lively, Your 'Ighness, afore we spiles y'r pretty toggery!"

"Toddle!" growled Number Three.

"My Keyhole," said Jeremy, "they promise well!" And he took off his hat, whereupon the Three stared wondering, and Number One, all menace from scowling brows to heavy boots, growled in fierce question:

"Come, me young tippy, wot 's y'r lay? Wot d' ye want? Speak out and speak sharp! Wot are you arter?"

"The name of your employer," answered Jeremy, whereat was a moment's amazed silence; then, "Do I get it?" enquired Jeremy.

Number One laughed in fierce derision. Number Two spat contemptuously. Number Three swore viciously.

"Hum!" said Jeremy, and thrusting hat and cane into the little clerk's trembling hands, he faced the menacing three. "Look 'ee, my lads," said he, "I 've never yet hit any man my hardest and I 'm anxious to try. This is an excellent opportunity because you are three to one and true pugs o' the ring by your looks, so when you 're ready—come on!"

"Well, blow my dickey!" quoth Number One.

"Smash 'is fice in, Ben!" suggested Number Two.

"Let 's kick 'is inside out!" snarled Number Three.

"Right!" nodded Jeremy, stepping lightly towards them. "One at a time or all together. I 'm your man. And I mean to pound you until you beat me or tell the name o' the scoundrel who employs you."

As one man the Three stepped forward, eager for the fray; but, laughing savagely, Number One thrust his fellows back; quoth he:

"Leave this pretty buck to me! I 'll give me lord all 'e wants—an' a bit more!"

So saying, he threw aside his dingy white hat and began pulling off his coat. Jeremy instantly removed his, and tossing it to the pale-faced Lockett, smiled into the little man's troubled eyes reassuringly.

"Watch now, my Keyhole," said he, rolling snowy shirt-sleeves over powerful arms, "watch and tell me how I shape! A heaven-sent opportunity this to prove how much I have profited by Jessamy's lessons."

Then he turned to meet Number One who advanced against him, massive shoulders hunched, head bowed, knotted fists up, a grim, scarred veteran of many a hard-smitten encounter and therefore supremely assured; with lips drawn in an evil grin, eyes half-closed yet keenly watchful, and feet wide and firmly planted he stands, danger in every line of him—in so much that little Mr. Lockett, burdened with Jeremy's coat, hat and cane, begins to pray in passionate whispers.

Once or twice Jeremy feints cautiously, but Number One, not to be drawn, merely swears contemptuously and bids him "stand and fight like a man!"

"Right," says Jeremy and is upon him, blocks a left lead, ducks a right swing, drives a powerful right and left into his opponent's ribs, and is away again.

Surprised and angered at this, Number One bores in savagely, takes a stiff left upon his bullet head, is shaken by a lightning uppercut, but counters heavily and grunts in triumph, for with just such a blow he has ended many a fight ere this; but Jeremy shakes his square head, laughs and is back again, hitting harder than ever, short-driven blows that yet sting and jar and shake Number One from heel to head—wherefore growing more wary, he becomes more dangerous, seeking a chance for the deadly tricks of butting head, smashing knee or goring elbow; but Jeremy is quick and watchful; thus the fight waxes ever the fiercer.

And Mr. Lockett, viewing these grim, blood-spattered faces, these quick moving forms, hearkening to the sickening impact of vicious-thudding blows, flinches from very sympathy and prays harder than ever. For now Number One, inured to hard blows and brutally strong, knowing the best defence is attack, rushes his man with hard-driving left and mighty right swings, but these are either ducked or slipped or blocked, while time and again he is rocked and shaken by Jeremy's unerring counters—blows judged to a hair and timed to the fraction of a second. Before Number One's glaring eyes is a grim-smiling face, now here, now there, but always just out of reach; wherefore, growing desperate, Number One covers up and, wise from much experience, changes his tactics once again, endeavouring to close for a fall. And Jeremy, reading his purpose, meets him foot to foot, breast to breast, and secures a wrestling hold; and thus they strive desperately together, brawny arms locked, mighty shoulders bowed, swaying, stumbling, but always grimly silent until Mr. Lockett (grown sick at the sight) may be heard praying aloud above the harsh pant of breath and ceaseless scrape of feet:

"Lord, help him! Oh, Lord, help him!"

And, even as he prays, Jeremy breaks free, reels and stands a moment panting; and in this moment, uttering a hoarse gasp, Number One leaps to end him, is met by a staggering left—and then Jeremy leaps in turn—out shoots his terrible right—and Number One whirls backwards with arms upflung and goes down headlong, to lie a motionless heap.

And now, as Jeremy blinks down at this inert form, Mr. Lockett screams a warning lost in the clatter of feet, and Jeremy is borne down beneath the rush of Number Two and Number Three, but before they can kick his life out, he is up again. And then a voice is heard, a voice singularly clear and rich and very jubilant:

"I 'm with ye, brother, I 'm with ye!"

But at the sound of this cheery voice Jeremy's assailants, checked, turned and fled incontinent, leaving him to stare after them a little dazed; and then Jessamy Todd was beside him.

"Oh, brother!" says Jessamy, and grasps his bloody hand. "Oh, brother." says he again, and hugging Jeremy in mighty arms, pats him with caressing hands, finding speech beyond him.

"You saw, Jessamy?"

"Every blow, brother. Every shift and feint."

"How do I shape?"

"Like the archangel Gabriel! There ain't a man in all England—nor nowheers else—could beat ye—no, not one!"

"D' ye think so, Jessamy?"

"Brother, I do! And what 's more, he 's scarce touched ye. Lord love ye, brother, I 'm that proud o' ye I can't say."

"And now," says Jeremy, moving towards his still prostrate antagonist, "will you lend me a hand with this fellow?"

"To be sure, brother. I was forgetting Ben—and small wonder!"

"What, d' ye know him, Jessamy?"

"I do, brother, and a rare bad un is Ben and consequently, a 'brand' with an immortal soul waiting to be snatched to glory."

"He lies very still!" says Jeremy, stooping above the inanimate form of Number One.

"And, brother, no wonder! That last leveller o' yourn would ha' dropped a bullock. But Ben 's precious tough, and though, to be sure, you've cut him about a bit, he 's right as a trivet, breathing sweet and soft as a sleepin' babe, though 'e don't look quite so innocent. We 'll take him to 'The Gun' when you 're ready."

Jeremy wiped the stains of combat from face and hands as well as he might and thereafter, with Mr. Lockett's eager help, got himself into his tight-fitting coat, though somewhat stiffly to be sure. Then Jessamy and he raised the unconscious form of Ben between them and bore him out of the quiet court into the alley, to the no small excitement of such folk as they chanced to meet.

"Oh, the pore, unfort'nate creetur!" exclaimed a prodigiously stout woman in a remarkably small bonnet. "Look at 'is pore fice!"

"Unfort'nate!" repeated a very small woman, whose sharp little face peered from the profound depths of an enormous construction of the coal-scuttle variety. "Unfort'nate, mam? My eye an' Betty Martin, Mrs. Noggins, mam! The man ain't a creetur', being a bloodthirsty rapscaylion—"

"Oh, indeed, Mrs. Maggles!"

"Yes, indeed, mam. Threatened to do for my pore 'usband this very mornin', an' 'im a cripple wi' the rheumatics! Ah, an' wot 's more, last night 'e insulted me—me, mam!"

"Well, that ain't no reason for murdering of the pore soul so shockin'!"

"Oh, ain't it, mam! To be sure you ain't likely to be insulted by none, wot wi' your shape an' size."

"Oh, mam, oh? Let me tell you a fine upstandin' woman o' my comfortable figger stands more chance o' catching the masculine heye than a starved scrimp, mam—a little bag o' bones like some as I could name——"

So ensued a wordy strife, bitter and fell; little bonnet bobbing disdainful, large bonnet flapping derisively, while the unconscious cause was borne into "The Gun."

Here, responding to Jessamy's skilful ministrations. the man Ben presently moaned, blinked, sat up, and becoming aware of his many bruises, swore fervently.

"That 's it, Ben!" quoth Jessamy, patting bullet head kindly. "Spit out y'r venom, and when you 're rid of it, you an' me will pray together."

"First," said Jeremy, "he's going to tell me the name of his employer."

"No, I ain't!" growled Ben, getting upon wavering legs.

"You are!" said Jeremy, clenching his fists; seeing which, Ben instantly dropped into the nearest chair.

"You 've give me enough for one day, master."

"Then tell me who set you to watch that girl? Was it a French gentleman named De Ravenac?"

"No, it were n't!"

"Then who was it?" demanded Jeremy fiercely.

"Why, then," answered Ben, cowering, "since you 've beat me so crool, and me pals 'as left me, and me a sick man this day along o' you, an' not wantin' no more o' sich medicine, though not wishful to give away a gen'leman as pays so 'andsome, and not wanting to name no names to none, yet name 'im I must—vich name is Mr. Arthur Trevor."

"And now, Ben," said Jessamy, "come and wash away that blood of unrighteousness, for you an' me are a-going to wait upon the Lord." Perforce Ben rose and tottered out into the yard upon Jessamy's arm, leaving Jeremy to stare blandly out of the window; nor did he move until roused by the voice of Mr. Lockett:

"Arthur Trevor! Surely that name is familiar, sir?"

"Hatefully."

"He is your cousin I think?"

"Yes. But at least Mr. Armadale is exonerated!"

"Fully, Master Jerry. I ask his pardon. Yet the danger is imminent; my course is clear."

"What?"

"I must take her away. We must go at once."

"Tush!" growled Jeremy. "Give me ten minutes with Cousin Arthur and I promise he won't——"

"No, no!" cried Mr. Lockett. "No, no, Master Jeremy, my way is best! Though indeed I thank you humbly. And for some time we have contemplated leaving this neighbourhood."

"However, I must see Cousin Arthur," growled Jeremy.

But here the little man caught Jeremy's battered fist between his two hands, holding it as if it had been some rare and lovely object.

"Good-bye, Master Jerry," said he. "Good-bye!"

"Why, my old Keyhole," said Jeremy, drawing the little man within his arm. "Lord love you, we are n't parting forever. You 'll write to me——"

"Yes, yes, Master Jerry, so soon as we are settled."

"And should you need any help, at any time, old Keyhole, you 'll call on me—privilege of friendship—and once friends always friends—eh, Keyhole?"

"God bless you, Master Jeremy!" said Lockett and bowed white head above Jeremy's knotted fist much as if he would have kissed it. "Such friendship heartens one—inspires hope and courage; it is a light in the dark—so, God bless you, Master Jerry!" Saying which, Mr. Lockett crossed to the door, but there Jeremy stayed him.

"Remember, old friend, Richard Armadale loves her truly."

"Then, Master Jeremy, if she wishes, he shall surely find her."

Long after Mr. Lockett had gone, Jeremy sat upon the great oak settle, staring moodily into the fire until the Corporal entered, to grasp his hand in hearty welcome.

"Kneel down, Ben, here alongside me!" said a voice beyond the open lattice.

"Jessamy 's a-going to pray, sir," explained the Corporal. "And Jess prays as hard as 'e hits! Hark now!"

Sure enough and almost as he spoke, Jessamy's clear rich voice was heard upraised in solemn invocation:

"O Lord, because Thou art the Father of infinite mercy, look down upon this Ben o' Thine, this Thy wayward child as looks more like a man o' blood! Regard now this poor lost lamb as seems so uncommonly like a ravening wolf to every eye but Thine. For this Ben, Lord, is very sore in regard to his carcass, having been beat and well thrashed and all for the good of 'is soul, and Thy glory. Therefore we praise Thee for his two black eyes; we thank Thee for 'is split lip and for every bruise inflicted on 'im, since, being in the sake o' righteousness and Thy glory, they must be for the good of his soul. And as by the fists o' Thy servant, Jeremy, Thou has bruised his body so sore, do Thou also touch his soul that he may awake to the knowledge o' Thy mercy and know himself Thy son, the child o' Thy Spirit, and walk in Thy Light hereafter, until through death, and by Thy love, he comes at last to Thy everlasting glory. Amen!"

"Say, 'Amen', Ben!"

"Amen!" growled Ben.

"And now," says Jessamy, "up with ye, brother Ben, and I 'll give ye an arm along home, but first a drop of old ale won't do ye no 'arm—eh, Ben?"

"Lord love ye, Jessamy. I 'm that dry! Thank 'ee, pal, thank 'ee!"

"That 's Jessamy's way, sir!" said the Corporal.

"A wonderful man," nodded Jeremy.

"Second only to my comrade, Jarsper, sir."

"Where is Jarsper?"

The Corporal hesitated, glanced about almost furtively, and leaning forward, whispered:

"Gone, sir."

"Out of town?" questioned Jeremy, whispering also.

"Priory Dene!" breathed the Corporal. "Hush, sir, the walls ha' growed ears lately."

"When did he go? And why—why there?"

"Last night, sir. And why he went I don't know. Y' see they 've been arter him again, sir—three men—along th' alley—t' other night! And next night some one shot him in the dicer!"

"Dicer?"

"Cady, sir—'at, Mr. Jeremy. Also 'e left you a message, sir—come a bit closer an' I 'll tell ye. First I was to say wherever you go, day or night, don't go alone—but things is moving and Jarsper's hopes is rose in consequence. Second: Look out for Dan'l, he 'll be along wi' news for you when least expected. Third: if the little lad as you found should get lost, don't worrit—and that 's all, sir!"

"But Dick, what 's it all mean?"

"Mr. Jeremy, only the Lord knows—and Jarsper, o' course, and now, if ye don't mind, I 'll get on wi' my cooking, sir."

"What?"

"Shin o' beef, sir, stooed."

"Nothing could be better, Corporal Dick."

"Then p'raps you 'll stay an' pick a bit wi' me and Jess, sir?"

"Thank'ee, I will," said Jeremy.

## CHAPTER XXVIII

### TELLS HOW LORD MIDMARSH WENT HOME

It was late when Jeremy returned to his chambers, there to be met by Moxon who hastened to relieve him of hat, cane and gloves.

"What o'clock is it, Moxon?"

"It has struck the half after eleven, sir!" Here Moxon stifled a yawn behind discreet finger tips.

"Has Mr. Armadale returned?"

"Not as yet, sir."

"Hum!" quoth Jeremy. "Boy behaved himself?"

"I have no complaints to urge, sir."

"Then you may go to bed."

"Thank you, sir. Good-night, sir!"

"Good night, Moxon!" So saying, Jeremy took his bedroom candle and went upstairs, but not to bed, for unlocking escritoire he took thence his letter to Olivia and sat down to finish it.

And what better season for the writing of a love letter than night? For in this hushed and solemn hour the consciousness, freed from the thralling rush of tumultuous, material day and scornful of distance, may project itself, unerring, across the dark and slumberous void and, in some measure, hold communion with that one being beyond all others loved.

". . . This letter, Dearest Beloved, has been over-long a-writing, but I have suffered many distractions. To-day, for instance, has been a busy one, and I the better therefore, I hope. The hour is late and as I pen these lines you will be lying asleep. Yet the night is kind for in the dark you seem more near. And my love is all about you, bending above you like a guardian angel, my Olivia, a love which is indeed the very best and noblest part of me. And I am to see you soon—it grows now to a matter of hours. And, oh, my dear, when I think of the past weary weeks, I marvel how I have endured them. But, as I hope and think, my promise to you is fulfilled, Richard is indeed your brother, and comes back worthy of your love as you will know when you see him for yourself."

Thus wrote Jeremy and much beside, in the lonely midnight hours, his pen scurrying across the paper, setting forth his love, his dreams, his abiding hope and faith in the future; at last, having signed, sealed and directed this letter, he glanced at his watch and scowled to see it showed close upon the hour of two. Therefore he donned hat and surtout and choosing a stout, serviceable stick, set forth upon his quest.

There was no moon and the gloomy streets seemed only the more desolate for the dim light of the infrequent oil lamps that flickered dismally here and there; overhead a black void, a deep immensity where no friendly star twinkled; to right and left buildings, vague and mysterious, whence came no sound of life, no ray of light; and over the vast city this same brooding quiet, a deathly stillness; and all so dark, so dreadfully hushed and still, it might, verily, have been a city of the dead where none moved save only himself—Stay, though!

Was that a shadow flitting after him on the opposite side of the street?

Jeremy lengthened his stride; but when, having covered some distance, he glanced back again, he saw this shadow had become two. Thereupon he grasped his heavy stick more firmly and found a certain comfort in its formidable weight and balance, so that he was greatly minded to turn and try its effect upon these dim-seen followers; to discover what manner of men were these who dogged him, and learn their reason. But remembering Mr. Shrig's warning and bethinking him that a stick might little avail against firearms, he began to run, and, holding his breath, fancied he caught the muffled pad-pad of pursuing feet. Settling his hat firmly, Jeremy raced at the top of his speed, clenched fists aswing, head back, breathing smooth and regularly through his nose; and, being in prime condition, thoroughly enjoying it.

Swiftly he sped, running upon his toes until, turning a sudden corner, he saw before him a light that bobbed and swayed in the hand of a much be-shawled and top-coated watchman. Espying Jeremy's flying figure the watchman halted, set down his lantern and prepared for instant battle. Jeremy slowed to a walk, gratified to find himself in no wise distressed or short of breath, and saluted the watchman with an airy flourish of his stick.

"A fine night!" said he.

"Oh, is it?" quoth the watchman.

"Well, is n't it?" enquired Jeremy.

"I ain't s' sure," answered the watchman, lifting his lantern the better to scan Jeremy's person. "You looks a gent, you talks like a gent, but then you runs! And a gent don't never trouble to run unless 'e 's up to summat. So wot might you be up to?"

"Running," answered Jeremy.

"Whaffor? Where to? And why?" demanded the watchman.

"Footpads."

"Where are the scoundereels?"

"Behind."

"'Ow many are they?" enquired the watchman, glancing back uneasily.

"More than we can tackle."

"Lord love ye!" exclaimed the watchman, preparing to spring his rattle. "I ain't a-going to tackle 'em—not me! I may be a watchman but I ain't no fool!"

"Then never mind sounding your rattle; walk along with me."

"Why?"

"For company."

"And wheer to?"

"St. James' Square."

"What for?"

"Five shillings."

"Show us the blunt."

"Here!" said Jeremy, drawing forth certain coins.

"Done for fi' bob, sir!" quoth the watchman promptly. "St. James' Square ain't far, so come on, young gent."

Now glancing back, after they had gone some way, Jeremy saw he was followed no longer.

"And wot might you want wi' St. James' Square, young gent?"

"Lord Midmarsh's house."

"I knows it, sir. Rare doings there to-night! A cock party, sir, nary an 'en among 'em, all breeches an' no petticuts, an an 'igh old time they 're a-makin' of it! I 've see two or three gents carried out a'ready—tight as aldermen—ah, bee-utifully drunk, they was, sir!"

"Hum!" growled Jeremy.

"Lord!" sighed the watchman. "To be a real gent—a nob or a nobleman, able to drink all you wants, when you wants, and servants to carry you when you can't toddle! Lord—'oo would n't be a noble gent, like them?"

"I 'd rather be a watchman!" said Jeremy.

"Lord love me, sir—and because why?"

"Because when you 're eating your breakfast and

enjoying it, these noble gentlemen will be wishing themselves dead."

"Then, sir, a 'air from the tail o' the dog as bit 'em 'll soon put 'em right again! And yonder 's my Lord Midmarsh's 'ouse, the one wi' the lights an' the carriages afore it."

And now, having paid the five shillings and bid the watchman good night, Jeremy mounted the broad steps of my lord's great house and knocked; and after some delay the door was opened by a sleepy footman, who, hearkening to Jeremy's request, yawned, frowned, shook powdered head and, a little uncertain as to legs and voice, gave it that:

"'T was too infarnal late—his ludship could n't be sheen—no—not even by the P-pope o' Rome!"

But setting this bemused and protesting menial aside, Jeremy stepped in, closing the door behind him.

Now from the regions above came a voice upraised in dolorous song, a tenor voice infinitely woeful that broke off now and then but always to recommence and always woeful.

Guided by this, Jeremy ascended a wide and handsome stair, crossed a broad landing and halting at a partly open door, beheld the object of his search.

At a long table, its rumpled cloth much stained by spilled wine and littered with bottles and glasses, many of them broken, sat Mr. Armadale, beating time to himself with an empty bottle as he sang:

"I only saw her passing by
Yet must I love her till I die."

Upon his right hand sat a young gentleman who wept, upon his left a young gentleman who snored in unison with three or four others who lay where they had fallen, while at the head of this disordered table, his face ghastly against the dark upholstery of his high-backed chair, his large, haggard eyes full of a sick weariness, sat young Lord Midmarsh.

"Oh, Di—Dicky——" sobbed the weeping gentleman, "ss-nuff—ss-nuff, I c-can't bear it!"

"Eh, Bob, eh?" questioned Mr. Armadale, breaking off in the middle of a long-drawn, minor note. "Demme and why not? Wasser marrer?"

"Iss so—so infernal plaintive, Dick——"

"Demme if 't is n't, Bob! Wake Jack Hawley, somebody; his snoring puts me out!"

"H—heart-rending, Dicky! Y—ye see, he only s-saw her p-passin' by—poor d-devil! I can't b-bear it, Dicky!"

And laying his head upon the table, the young gentleman wept harder than ever; whereupon Mr. Armadale, with the utmost solicitude and most elaborate care, poured over him the dregs of such wine glasses as chanced within reach. Then Jeremy stepped into the room to be hailed by Mr. Armadale in rapturous acclaim:

"What, Jay, my pippin—my dear ol' f'ler——"

"Where 's De Ravenac?" enquired Jeremy ungraciously.

"Gone, Jay, gone—hours ago!" sighed Mr. Armadale, waxing lugubrious. "Vere Manville an' H-Hawley an' two or three more o' the poor s-souls are under th' t-table—we 're all 'ss left—but jolly dogs all—except Midmarsh 'n' he 's always gloomy as—dem'd funeral bell!"

At mention of his name Lord Midmarsh started and rose a little unsteadily and supporting himself against the table with one hand reached out the other in greeting.

"Aha, Veryan," he cried in strange, high-pitched tones, "welcome to these, my ancestral halls, which have sheltered good, bad and indifferent for generations. But all things must—must end—even we Midmarshes, thank heaven! See, there are some o' my ancestors staring down at us!" And he waved a slim hand towards the dim canvases upon the panelled walls.

"My ancestors, Veryan, and—dead, every one o' them, lucky dogs! All dead!"

"D—demme Julian," stammered Mr. Armadale. "What—what the dooce!"

Here the weeping gentleman rolled curly head upon the table and moaned dismally.

"My dusty ancestors!" laughed his lordship. "Dry bones, Veryan! See how they scowl on me—the last of 'em. And why? For if they built up an honoured name and great fortune, I did the next best thing and—lost it! And yet, see how they scowl on me, dammem! But I've a picture—above a shrine, Veryan, smiles on me, do what I will, come good fortune or ill; she smiles as her angel may in heaven, and makes death the more lovely——"

"Dooce t-take everything, Julian," quavered Mr. Armadale. "Why b-babble o' death? We're 'live enough—jo-jolly dogs——"

"Alive?" repeated Lord Midmarsh with another strange laugh. "That's the irony o' the joke—to live when we might be comfortably dead! Who'd choose life rather than death? Who'd remember when he might forget?"

"Ju-Julian, I pro-test!" stammered Mr. Armadale with extreme dignity. "I bid you goo-good night!" Here, having made three unsuccessful attempts to rise, he sat where he was and scowled. "P'mit me t' tell you I c'sider you a g-ghoul, a dem'd skeleton at the feast, sir! I strongly resent having d-death hurled in my teeth—death 's for graveyards, sir, not con-vivial circle! I bid you goo' night! Jay, old f'ler, if you'll lend me a fin I'll hop along t' roost."

Lord Midmarsh stared from the speaker to the grim pictures on the wall, from these to the wild disorder of the table and shivered violently. Now, beholding this and the dreadful weariness of these sombre eyes, Jeremy set an arm about his lordship's shaking form and spoke in his strange, gentle voice.

"Midmarsh," said he, "come home with us."

His lordship's haggard face became suddenly youthful in a smile, his twitching fingers closed on Jeremy's hand.

"Veryan," said he, shaking his head. "You 're a strange, good fellow. I feel we are friends awhile and therefore venture to tender you the advice of a friend, for even I am grown a little wise at last—*Experientia docet!* Piper tells me you mean to try your fortune against—him!"

"De Ravenac!" nodded Jeremy.

"Well—don't, Veryan, don't. But, if you will, then be wiser than I and shoot yourself first—not after!"

Here, looking into the big eyes that looked so earnestly into his, Jeremy drew that slender form closer.

"Midmarsh," he repeated, "come home with us to-night."

"Too late, Veryan, it 's too late!" whispered his lordship and then, freeing himself from Jeremy's hold, he laughed and pointed again to the pictures on the wall. "How? D' ye think I 'd leave 'em?" he cried. "They were hard-fighting old fire-eaters, some of 'em, and honourable gentlemen all. And shall I run off, steal away and leave 'em to sneer at me on this, the greatest night in the history o' the family—I, the last o' the Midmarshes? No, no, Veryan! To-morrow another shall rule here—b'gad, they 'll scowl then, poor wretches! —But to-night I 'm still master here, and here I stay because I am a Midmarsh and the last of 'em! Gentlemen all," he cried, "I bid you a very good night and —good-bye!"

So saying, Lord Midmarsh sprang to the bell rope and tugged it furiously until footmen came running.

"These gentlemen to their carriages!" he commanded. "You 'll find some asleep under the table—carry 'em down. Hurry, there, I 'm tired!"

Spurred to activity by their lord's terrible eye and voice, the footmen obeyed. Somnolent gentlemen were hauled from beneath chairs and table and borne away, snoring; drowsy gentlemen, peevishly rebellious, were half led, half carried downstairs until there none remained except Mr. Armadale and Jeremy.

"Midmarsh," said he gently, "friend Julian, if ever you loved, if ever you respected that one who has gone forward—to the greater living, come home with me."

For a long moment Lord Midmarsh continued to pace feverishly up and down the great room.

"No, no!" cried he at last, halting suddenly. "Our ways part here—you into the light, I down into the dark—the cool, sweet dark! Leave me, Veryan; my course is set and nothing can turn me now. Go—go and remember me for all that I—might have been! Go!"

Slowly Jeremy turned and slowly he left the room, arm in arm with Richard, who muttered drowsy imprecations on everything in general. Slowly he descended the wide stair and reaching the entrance hall, paused there so long that Mr. Armadale, having donned hat and coat, broke out into peevish complaint:

"What th' dooce are we waiting for, Jay?"

But Jeremy's gaze was upon the broad stair, his thick brows knit in dire perplexity.

A footman stood ready to let them out and at last Jeremy signed him to open the door; the footman obeyed and then, to the man's gaping wonderment, Jeremy shut it again with reverberating bang.

"Oh, b'ged!" exclaimed Mr. Armadale. "What in the name of all the——"

"Hush!" said Jeremy fiercely and stood again rigidly tense, listening. And after some while, like a long-delayed echo to that banging door, was another sound, short, sharp, that came and was gone but seemed to leave the great house full of a new and dreadful silence.

"Oh, Jay—Jerry——" stammered Mr. Armadale. "Oh, God, Jerry——" But Jeremy had turned and was racing back up the stair.

"His lordship's bedroom—quick!" said he to the pale-faced footman who had followed. Speechlessly the man pointed to a door that, yielding to Jeremy's hand, showed a luxurious chamber; now upon the wall was a painting, the picture of a girl's face virginally sweet and pure, and before this picture was a kind of altar where candles burned and fresh-cut roses bloomed; and below this altar, outstretched upon the floor lay my lord Julian Midmarsh, a duelling pistol in his right hand; but upon his dead and mutilated face was the smile of one whose troubles were all forgotton.

Day was breaking as they stepped into the street where a chilly wind met them; but it was not this only which caused Mr. Armadale to gasp and shiver so violently as he walked beside Jeremy, stumbling a little uncertainly every now and then.

"A dreadful business!" said he, at last. "Oh, a hateful, ghastly business!"

"Yes!" answered Jeremy.

"He was so—so young!"

"So you said of your other schoolfellow—Jardine!"

"And his face, Jeremy! All blacked with the powder and—God, I shall never forget his face!"

"Nor I," said Jeremy.

"By heaven, Jay, I'm—sick—faint!"

"Too much brandy!" said Jeremy, reaching out a supporting arm as his companion stumbled.

"No, no—I'm sober enough now, 'spite o' the brandy. And I did n't take s' very much, Jay, ol' f'low. No, no, 't is the memory o' poor Midmarsh's face."

"Your friend Jardine looked much the same, I expect!" said Jeremy grimly.

"Yes, but—I did n't see him! But—poor old Julian, I can't bear the thought of him."

"Then think o' something else."

"What, Jay, what?"

"Your friend De Ravenac!" growled Jeremy.

"He brought a cousin o' yours with him to-night; they left early."

"Ha, my damned cousin Arthur!"

"A p-particularly elegant f'low—I took t' him amazingly, Jay."

"People do!" nodded Jeremy.

After this, Mr. Armadale's conversation languished, he moaned softly at fitful intervals and stumbled more than ever.

"Oh, Jay—oh, Jay," he gasped suddenly. "Poor Julian's face—it 's—turning me—sick——"

Mr. Armadale was.

Reaching their chambers at last, Jeremy carried his miserable companion upstairs and put him to bed.

"Ah!" sighed Mr. Armadale, stretching luxuriously between the cool sheets. "I feel better already—right as a trivet in the morning, you 'll see! All the better for it to-morrow. But Jay, my dear fellow, I—yes, I was a curst fool to go to-night."

"You were!" nodded Jeremy.

"Poor Julian! A hateful—a ghastly business, Jay."

"Yes!" nodded Jeremy. "And yet, maybe, he is happier than he was. Yes, I'm sure he is!" Then clasping Richard's extended hand, he closed the door and went into his own bedchamber, slow and heavy-footed.

It was the dayspring, for in the east was a radiance that filled the room, an ever waxing glory; therefore he made to extinguish the candle, then paused, and drawing forth his letter to Olivia, that oft interrupted, voluminous love letter so very full of fond hopes, of joyous faith in the future, he thrust it into the candle flame and watched until it was utterly consumed.

Then, scowling upon the new day, he undressed and went to bed.

## CHAPTER XXIX

### WHICH DESCRIBES A CHASE

"WAKE up, Jay—wake up, man!"

Jeremy started from sleep, blinking in the strong sunlight, to see Mr. Armadale bending over him, wild of eye and distraught of gesture.

"What 's o'clock, Dick?" he yawned.

"Past three in the afternoon!" cried Mr. Armadale idignantly. "And here you lie snoring while the whole dem'd universe totters to crashing and irretrievable ruin about my dem'd ears, b'ged!"

"Eh?" said Jeremy, stifling another yawn.

"Oh, Jay—Oh, Jeremy, I 'm the most miserable dog in the world, my hopes everlastingly blighted, my dreams shattered, my soul prostrated in the dust. She 's gone!"

"Who—what?" enquired Jeremy.

"She 's gone, Jay—my Ruth! They 've all gone! They 've snatched her from me. She 's gone!"

"Yes, I know," answered Jeremy, yawning.

"You know?" Mr. Armadale reeled and sat down upon the bed. "You know?" he repeated. "Thank heaven! Then, where is she?"

"I don't know."

"Eh—what 's that? You do know—you don't know. What the dooce do you know?"

"Only that Mr. Lockett has taken her away."

"Has he, b'ged! Then ten thousand devils——"

"To escape a villain."

"Ha! name the scoundrel!"

"No, Dick!"

"Eh, you won't? You mean to say you positively refuse?"

"Positively!"

"And why—why, in the name of all that's demnable?"

"Because you 'd fight."

"Of course."

"And get yourself shot."

"That 's my affair."

"And mine, Dick."

"I 'll thank you not to dry-nurse me, Jeremy! So you won't tell me the name o' this scoundrel?"

"I will not!"

"Then, by heaven, you 're no friend o' mine!"

"I try to be!"

Mr. Armadale swore bitterly, sighed disconsolately and tramped about the room feverishly.

"Oh, Jay, no curst lover in all this demn'd world suffered as I suffer! No hand may bind up my wounded spirit, no power mend my broken life! Oh, dooce take and confound everything, I 'm a walking misery!"

"Then sit down," said Jeremy.

Mr. Armadale groaned and cast himself into a chair to droop dejected.

"Egad, it 's easy for you to lie there so dooced smug!" he moaned. "But what o' me? Think o' my breaking heart! The only woman I ever truly loved—found but to lose! Think man, think, and tell me what the dooce I 'm to do?"

"Find her again!"

Mr. Armadale leapt to his feet and pounced upon his hat which had rolled into a corner.

"To be sure!" he cried. "Yes, by Heaven! I 'll find her if it takes all my confounded life! I 'll search every street in London—every city on this round globe; b'ged, I 'll tramp the world till I find her—like the dem'd Wandering Jew! And I start this moment!" Here Mr. Armadale clapped on his hat and striding to the door opened it, but paused there to droop and sigh despondent. "London 's such an infernal vast place to look about in! A curst human ant hill! Hopeless!"

"I 'll help you, Dick."

"Will you, Jay, will you? Monstrous kind of you, I swear it is! But get up, man, in heaven's name get up and let 's—— What the dooce?"

From below Moxon's voice was heard upraised in dignified protest; there was a sound of hasty feet upon the stair, and with no ceremony of knocking, Mr. Lockett entered, breathless with haste, his looks wild and disordered.

"Oh, Master Jeremy," he gasped, "they 've carried her off—my Ruth!" And sinking into a chair he covered his face.

"Eh, what—what?" stammered Mr. Armadale. "Ruth? Ruth gone? Carried off?"

"Tell us what happened, Lockett!" said Jeremy; and, getting out of bed, he began to dress hastily.

"About twenty minutes ago a letter was brought to her; she read it and ran out of the house—then I heard her scream and hurried out. I saw her forced into a carriage—brutally—brutally!"

Mr. Armadale swore passionately.

"What sort of carriage?" enquired Jeremy, pulling on spurred boots.

"A four-horsed chaise, rifle-green with yellow wheels! Oh, God protect her!"

"Ten thousand curses!" cried Mr. Armadale, raging up and down the room. "What can we do, Jerry?"

"Which way did they go?" questioned Jeremy, tying his cravat.

"I followed as far as the Oxford Road and lost them there—so I came to you."

"Dick," said Jeremy, getting into his coat. "Order the horses!"

"Horses!" cried Mr. Armadale, leaping for the door. "Ay, to be sure—horses!" And they heard him clatter downstairs, shouting as he went.

"Oh, Master Jeremy, can you—can you save her? Is there any hope?"

"If 'tis my damned cousin—yes! He has a tumble-down house out beyond Croydon. If they are taking her there—— However, wait you here, my Keyhole—and hope!"

Staying for no more, Jeremy hurried downstairs, where stood Moxon to tender him hat, gloves and riding whip.

"Mr. Armadale has gone round to the stables, sir; he desired you to follow immediately."

"Ha!" quoth Jeremy, clapping on his hat. "Can't you find me something heavier than this?" And he tossed the light, gold-mounted whip into a corner. "This is better!" And snatching a heavy hunting crop from the rack, he hurried out to the stable yard, where all was stir and bustle; spirited horses stamped, grooms ran to and fro, Mr. Armadale roared and cursed, while the Imp, who seemed to pervade the place, darted here and there, uttering shrill catcalls and capering like a gleeful, smutty-faced sprite.

Mounted at last, they were off and away with a clatter of eager hoofs.

"Where to?" cried Mr. Armadale, as they swung into the wide street.

"Croydon!" answered Jeremy, settling feet in the stirrups.

"Why there?"

"Ride!" said Jeremy.

They made good speed when they might, Mr. Armadale fuming and fretting at every check; but soon they were clear of the denser traffic, and their pace increased.

At the first toll-bar Mr. Armadale questioned the keeper passionately:

"A chaise—chaise, d'ye hear, with yellow wheels, going Croydon way! Have ye seen a chaise?"

The man spat thoughtfully and nodded:

"Ah!" quoth he. "I've seed plenty o' chaises with all manner o' wheels, red uns, black uns, blue uns——"

Mr. Armadale swore; Jeremy tossed the man a half-crown.

"A four-horse chaise," said he, "rifle-green and yellow?"

"Ah, to be sure, sir!" nodded the toll-keeper. "Rifle-green body, yaller wheels and a young woman inside——"

Spurring his eager animal, Mr. Armadale dashed away.

"How long ago?" enquired Jeremy.

"About 'alf an hour, sir—mebbe a bit more——"

Giving his horse free rein Jeremy bounded forward, galloping hard in Mr. Armadale's dust.

Soon they were out upon the open road that wound away between blooming hedges, a white dusty highway shaded, here and there, by stately trees.

Stooped low in the saddle, with loosened rein and goading heel, rode Jeremy, his scowling gaze upon that rolling dust cloud where, some half-mile ahead, galloped Richard Armadale. It was whip and spur up hill and down, a headlong, wild career; past crawling country wains and lumbering waggons whose sleepy drivers lifted heavy heads to watch them thunder by; past plodding wayfarers who took to the hedge to give them room, cheering them on with stick or hat a-flourish or cursing them for the swirling dust they raised; past shady wood and purling rill they raced; past fragrant rickyards where busy fowls clucked and smock-frocked figures turned to stare. On they spurred at the same wild speed, their flying hoofs muffled in thick dust, now ringing upon paved ways, now waking the echoes of sleepy village street.

But spur how he would, Jeremy lost ground. Mr. Armadale's lighter weight told, and the distance between them gradually increased; and stare how he might, nowhere was there any sign of the vehicle they sought, wherefore Doubt assailed him and Fear shook him.

And now before them was another toll-gate, but Richard, scorning such barriers, set his horse at it, cleared it and galloped on, nothing heeding the keeper's indignant roars.

Drawing rein, Jeremy accosted the man, half-crown between finger and thumb:

"A rifle-green chaise with yellow wheels—four horses?"

"Why, yes, sir," growled the man. "Her went through not a quarter of a hour——"

A stamp of hoofs and Jeremy was away again, leaving the man to pocket the coin and stare after him open-mouthed. On again by open heath; splashing through miry ford; between high banks where wild flowers bloomed, on until they reached a hill, a long ascent, and spurring his horse at it, Jeremy watched where Richard galloped, his speed unabated, up—up until he was upon the summit outlined against the blue. Then Jeremy heard him shout—a wild, fierce "view hallo," saw him flourish his hat ere he vanished down the farther slope.

Reaching the summit in turn, Jeremy beheld at last what he had yearned for, a four-horsed chaise that rolled and lurched downhill in a smother of dust, 'mid which he descried the gleam of yellow wheels. Down—down the hill it plunged, rocking and swaying, but with Richard in hot pursuit, plying whip and spur. Jeremy saw the post-boys' arms rising and falling, flail-like, and then Richard was beside them, striking at them with his whip and shouting. The chaise slowed down and stopped in a swirl of dust in which horses reared and plunged, and men strove together, while upon the air rose the sounds of fierce conflict.

And then Jeremy rode up to see Mr. Armadale beset by four men, beheld him beaten to his knees, only to struggle up again, fighting the fiercer.

"Hold 'em, Dick—I 'm with ye!" cried Jeremy, and leaping from panting horse, plunged into the fray with smashing fist and whizzing crop. And there upon the dusty road was fierce and desperate work awhile. But Richard fought like one possessed, and a heavy hunting crop wielded by a powerful arm is a most convincing object. Thus very soon two men lay groaning in the dust, two were limping off across adjacent field, and Jeremy, grasping a broken hunting crop, stood peering.

"Dick!" he panted, "Dick—where are ye?"

"In the dem'd ditch, Jay—and dooced muddy!"

And then was a sudden glad cry, a cry indeed of wondering rapture:

"Mr. Jeremy! Oh, Master Jeremy—thank God!" A rustle of flying petticoats and Jeremy felt himself caught and embraced by two soft arms that clasped and clung, and turning in startled wonder, he stared down into the lovely, tear-stained face of Lucy Western.

"Oh, Mr. Jeremy," she sobbed; "dear Mr. Jeremy—hold me tight! Keep me safe——"

"Damnation!" said Mr. Armadale, rising out of the ditch, torn, mired and bloody. "Ten thousand curses!"

At this Lucy started and turned, and clasping Jeremy tighter, stood all flushed, trembling, dishevelled, yet distractingly beautiful, viewing Mr. Armadale with eyes of horror:

"You?" she cried in passionate reproach. "Oh—is it you, sir—then may God forgive you!" And shrinking before Mr. Armadale's grim aspect, she hid her face on Jeremy's breast.

"Yes—'t is I, madam!" quoth Mr. Armadale, dabbing blood from his face, "I myself, madam, and—one too many it seems!"

"No, no, Dick——" began Jeremy.

"Tush, sir!" retorted Mr. Armadale contemptuously. "As for you, madam, embrace your Mr. Jeremy and hear me name him perfidious liar and perjured friend. As for yourself——"

"Hold hard, Dick, let me explain——"

"Silence, sir!" cried Mr. Armadale so fiercely, with such wild and furious gesture that Lucy sobbed again and clung to Jeremy faster than ever. "As for you, madam," continued Mr. Armadale, scowling at the girl's lovely drooping form, "I do confess your prudish airs, your mock modesty and studied innocence ha' deceived me, hitherto. But I 'm grown wise at last, madam, and bid you farewell for ever! To-morrow I shall laugh heartily at my folly in believing any woman pure and true!"

"Richard—wait!" cried Jeremy, supporting the weeping, half-swooning girl. "Don't be rash, Dick—hear me——"

"Enough, sir!" said Mr. Armadale haughtily. "Your lies, your treachery, nauseate me! Your very sight is a reproach! I shall demand due satisfaction of you at a place and time more convenient."

So saying, Mr. Armadale stumbled to his horse, mounted and galloped away, leaving Jeremy to stare after him with troubled eyes, and the postboys to stare at Jeremy and the weeping girl, and at each other, to scratch their heads and shake them at each other, and all with never a word. And now, freeing herself from Jeremy's hold, Lucy sank down on the grass that bordered the road and burst into a very passion of weeping, while Jeremy stood watching her in the utmost perplexity.

"Mr. Jeremy," she sobbed at last, "what did he mean? Oh, to think he could be—so wicked! To treat me so—those dreadful men——!"

"Why, child," said Jeremy, seating himself beside her. "You never imagine this was Richard's doing?"

"Who else, sir? Indeed, Mr. Jeremy, I do know how determined, how headstrong and wilful he can be——"

"But never dishonourable!" said Jeremy. "I believe he loves you truly and most reverently."

"I began to—hope so——" she sobbed. "But now—Oh, what am I to think?"

"Has he ever asked you to—to marry him, Lucy?"

Now at this she shrank and covered her face like one shamed.

"No!" she whispered. "Oh, Mr. Jeremy, if he only had, I—could forgive him carrying me off—almost!"

"But, child, I tell you this was none of Richard's doing——"

"Are you sure, Mr. Jeremy. Oh, are you quite—quite sure?"

"Certain. Child listen! If my suspicions are just, these men were taking you to my cousin Arthur Trevor!"

Here, to Jeremy's wonder, she uttered a soft, glad cry and looked up at him, her lovely face transfigured with a great and sudden joy, her tearful eyes radiant.

"Thank God!" she whispered. "Then Mr. Richard is good and true and so brave as I dreamed him!"

"Child, do you love him?"

"Yes, sir!" she whispered. "Ah, Mr. Jeremy, I could n't help it. I just had to! And I know I allus must—so long as I do live!"

"Why did you run away from Veryan, Lucy?"

"To escape Mr. Arthur—and worse. Y' see, sir, father found out the truth and threatened t' shoot Mr. Arthur, and would have. So I got father to bring me to London to his sister, and changed my name. And then I met—him—Mr. Richard! And oh, sir, to-day I did doubt his goodness! Called him 'wicked' I did—him that fought for me so brave! Him that saved me! And his dear face all bleeding! Oh, Mr. Jeremy, what shall I do?"

"Let me help you into the chaise and take you home to old Lockett. Come, child!"

Mutely she obeyed and at Jeremy's command the postboys turned the chaise, Jeremy mounted his horse, and back they went to London town.

Reaching his chambers, Jeremy beheld Mr. Lockett, who ran to greet him, to grasp his hand and kiss it before Jeremy could prevent.

"Master Jerry," said he brokenly. "Oh, Master Jerry!"

Hereupon, having dismounted, Jeremy took the little man by the shoulders and opening the chaise door, gave him to the arms outstretched in such eager welcome.

"God bless you, Master Jeremy!"

"And you!" answered Jeremy, shutting him into the chaise. "Both of you! Drive on!" he cried to the postboys, who forthwith cracked their whips and the dusty vehicle rolled away.

A discreet cough in his immediate vicinity and Jeremy turned to behold Moxon upon the steps, dignified, sedate, and inordinately grave:

"Sir," said he, "Mr. Armadale has departed—in the greatest dudgeon!"

"Oh!" said Jeremy.

"Indeed, sir, he seemed quite—transported—an ecstasy of indescribable fury, sir—his look most frenzied, his speech infinite—more so!"

"Ah?" said Jeremy.

"He bade me give you this letter, sir, the instant you arrived."

Jeremy took the letter and strode upstairs, his spurs jingling, and scattering dust at every stride. Seated in his favourite armchair, he opened the letter and saw this:

"Sir,

My first and most pressing duty is to write and warn my sister Olivia of the deceitful hypocrite who professes to love her, my next to employ the services of a trusty friend to help arrange our inevitable and I trust, final meeting. Words are too weak to express the indignant loathing with which your duplicity has filled me. Needless to say all communication between us ceases for ever, nor do I wish again to behold your abhorred face until I see it behind your weapon.

"Your obedient Svt.

Richard Armadale."

Having read this letter through twice, Jeremy lay back in his chair and stretching dusty, weary limbs, scowled up at the ceiling and said:

"Hum!"

# CHAPTER XXX

## TELLETH HOW JEREMY RECEIVED A CHALLENGE AND LAID A WAGER

AMONG those ranks of the Sporting Bon Ton which Mr. Armadale adorned, there was stir and there was flutter. Gentlemen of his acquaintance, particularly the younger, snuffed blood upon the air and condescended to become excited. In shooting galleries and fencing schools—such as the famous Angelo's, where gentlemen were instructed in the polite art of slaughter, how best to exterminate one another with steel or bullet in the most approved and elegant fashion when Honour (that extremely nebulous but very uncomfortable thing) so demanded—in such academies of the duello, was much discussion pro and con. anent "sharps" and "hair triggers," with keen arguments as to the relative merits of Mantons and Wogdons; and Mr. Armadale, arm-in-arm with the Chevalier de Ravenac or surrounded by noble sportsmen of his own age, laughed and chatted gaily yet contrived to look slightly grim the while.

And Jeremy, seated alone in his chamber, poring over his bank book, found himself possessed of some thirty thousand pounds, the legacy of his dead friend, Mr. Gillespie.

Having ascertained which fact, Jeremy got up to ring for Moxon, but, before he could reach the bell rope, that dignitary appeared to announce:

"Major Piper, sir!"

The Major entered a little more heavily than usual and having shaken hands, took the chair Jeremy proffered and began to polish the gold knob of his cane very industriously.

"Haw!" said he at length. "M' dear Veryan, I hear there 's trouble between you and—haw— There 's even talk of a—haw—a meeting?"

"Hum!" quoth Jeremy, frowning.

"Under the circumstances, m' dear—haw—fellow, should you need a—haw—a friend, beg t' offer my services."

"And I 'm grateful!" answered Jeremy heartily. "But there 's no possibility of any such folly."

"Haw!" quoth the Major. "Rejoice t' hear it! Duels are the—haw—the devil—'specially between friends." Here the Major began to polish the knob of his cane once more. "It 's a dooced world, Veryan," said he suddenly, "particularly as regards—haw—nephews! Mine 's the dooce and driving me to the—haw—the dooce, y' know! You 've met him, I think—Bob Stukely?"

"I saw the Honourable Robert at Lord Midmarsh's tragic supper party, sir!"

"Haw!" nodded the Major. "He was probably under the table. Bob can't drink, will drink, drinks and is drunk—instantly! Young fool—wild oats, Veryan, and—haw—there y' have it. I believe nephews are born merely to be curses to their—haw—unfortunate bachelor uncles; mine was, and is, b'ged! Mother, my sister, father dead, Bob just of age, myself sole uncle and consequently—haw—responsible. Plague o' my life, 'ssure you! Wild, Veryan, wild and growing wilder—every minute!" Here the Major became so despondent that his very whiskers seemed to droop and languish.

"Have you lost all authority over him?"

"Of late, yes. Young fool flouts my advice—had audacity to disobey me o' late—frequently! Wild, a wild set, d' ye see—Chisholm, Denby, Vere-Manville, Hawley—all—haw—youngsters like himself—except—haw—except De Ravenac."

"Hum!" quoth Jeremy. "De Ravenac?"

"Egad, yes! He 's their mentor, their—haw—model."

"And his club is Boodles, I think?"

"It is. Often there. High play—Boodles!"

"It is also one of your clubs, I believe, Major?"

"Correct, Veryan!"

"Will you introduce me there?"

"Pleasure, m' dear fellow."

"To-day? Now?"

"Haw—delighted?" said the Major, rising, but as he did so, Moxon knocked and opened the door to announce:

"The Honourable Robert Stukely."

"Haw!" exclaimed the Major. "M' dem'd nephew!"

"Good God—my uncle!" exclaimed the Honourable Bob, halting on the threshold; and meeting the Major's glare, his assurance wilted somewhat as he made his bows. And a very comely, dandified young gentleman he was, and sufficiently haggard to suggest himself modishly dissipated.

"Er—Mr. Veryan," said he, fumbling his hat a little awkwardly by reason of his uncle's stony glare, "may I have the favour of a word with you?"

"You have it!" answered Jeremy. "Pray be seated, sir." At this, the nephew sat down—lightly—and the uncle rose—heavily.

"Don't go, Major," said Jeremy. "I guess Mr. Stukely's business and shall despatch it immediately." Here the uncle sat down again and the nephew, having cleared his youthful throat, bowed.

"Mr. Veryan," said he, "I 'm here on behalf of my friend Mr. Armadale, who begs you will name some gentleman to act for you that the—the affair may be concluded as speedily as possible."

"There will be no affair!"

"Oh—reely, sir?" ejaculated the Honourable Bob, beginning to goggle.

"Where is Mr. Armadale lodging?"

"At his old rooms in Jermyn Street."

"Will you bear him a note?"

"With pleasure, sir."

So, while uncle glared at nephew and nephew looked anywhere but at uncle, Jeremy took pen and paper and wrote:

"DEAR DICK,

"See Ruth and don't be a fool.

"Your friend,

"JEREMY."

"And pray, sir," enquired the Honourable Bob, rising and taking the note Jeremy proffered, "when does the meeting take place?"

"It does n't!" answered Jeremy.

"Oh—reely?" exclaimed the Honourable Bob, staring. "Dick—I mean my principal, Mr. Armadale, is very determined on 't."

"But I 'm not!" answered Jeremy.

"Oh, reely? Then what do you propose, sir?"

"Nothing!"

The Honourable Bob nearly gaped, and stared from Jeremy's determined visage to the letter in his hand with eyes of horrified understanding:

"Perhaps, sir," he hazarded, "can this possibly be an apology, sir?"

"No!" answered Jeremy, smiling.

"Then b'ged, sir! I don't understand your attitude in the least. When a gentleman asks a gentleman to fight, that gentleman must fight—if he 's a gentleman—bound to!"

"Not always, sir!" answered Jeremy. "Pray give my note to your friend Mr. Armadale and say that ends the matter, so far as I am concerned—stay, though! Does Monsieur de Ravenac know of this foolish business?"

"To be sure he does, sir," answered the Honourable Bob a trifle haughtily. "De Ravenac will arrange the final details, and they could n't be in better or—more experienced hands."

"They won't!" nodded Jeremy.

"Sir," retorted the Honourable Bob, his pale cheek flushing, "one thing is positively certain—either Mr. Armadale receives your fullest apology or he—fights!"

"Then he 'll fight alone, sir!" answered Jeremy gravely. For a moment the Honourable Bob seemed about to retort, but checked himself, and bowing profoundly, hurried away.

"Haw!" said the Major as the door closed. "Doubtless, m' dear Veryan, your very extraordinary action is 'spired by the best motives but—haw!"

"Can you doubt it, Major?"

"Haw! Veryan, I don't. My hand, sir! Now, if y' are ready, we 'll step across t' Boodles."

They found the club rooms somewhat crowded; here were gentlemen who snuffed and talked, gentlemen who smoked and listened, gentlemen who read newspapers and gentlemen who did most of these together, in especial a bull-voiced, fiery-eyed, ancient gentleman in a blue spencer who loudly invoked eternal condemnation upon the government, individually and collectively.

"Haw!" exclaimed the Major suddenly. "De Ravenac yonder—surrounded by—haw—youngsters as usual and all looking this way—don't notice 'em——"

But Jeremy was already advancing towards these gentlemen who watched his approach with a lively interest.

"*Tiens!*" exclaimed the Chevalier. "Be'old Monsieur Veryan! Eet is, sir, that you come to find my dear friend Richard Armadale, p'raps?"

"No, sir—you!" answered Jeremy.

"*Eh bien*, monsieur; you see me! And how then? What is your pleasure with myself, sir?"

"To bet!"

"*Comment?* To bet—with me, sir? A wager, is it?"

"Yes," scowled Jeremy. "They tell me you have a fighting man, Ben Holt, the 'Hoxton Slasher,' and are eager to back him against any one, except Jessamy Todd, for any sum. Is this so?"

"*Par example*, monsieur, there is nothing more sure."

"Then I accept your challenge."

"Aha! Is it you 'ave discover a man to fight my 'Slasher,' sir?"

"Yes."

"Who is your man?"

"An unknown," answered Jeremy, "but I 'll back him for any sum you please."

"*Mon dieu!*" laughed the Chevalier, glancing round upon his three youthful companions. "We perceive that a sportsman the most determined is come to town at last! A gambler the most desperate! Monsieur Veryan, shall we say five 'undred guineas?"

"No!" growled Jeremy, and smiling contemptuously, turned away.

"A thousand guineas!" cried the Chevalier.

"Double it!" answered Jeremy, turning back again. At this the three young gentlemen glanced at each other and sat up; also the buzz of conversation in the room about them languished suddenly except for the old gentleman in the blue spencer who was fiercely anathematizing the government's foreign policy.

Then the Chevalier laughed lightly and shook his glossy curls.

"No, no, but certainly not, monsieur! Since you are the gambler so feroce, I say—five thousand guineas!"

"Treble it!" said Jeremy.

At this all voices were hushed; even the old gentleman in the blue spencer was mute at last, and all faces were turned in the one direction.

"Haw—Veryan!" whispered the Major in anxious warning. "M' dear fellow—haw—ye know——"

"Fifteen thousand guineas!" said Jeremy, his harsh voice very distinct in the pervading quiet, while the silent company stared from his grim visage to the Chevalier's handsome features.

"But no, monsieur!" he smiled with a graceful little bow. "No, no—let us make it—twenty thousand guineas!"

"Add another ten thousand!" said Jeremy.

And now was a stillness utter and absolute, a tense unearthly hush of breathless expectancy. Wild and desperate play was too frequently the rule, but here was more than mere gambling; thus every eye watched these two men who fronted each other in such unspoken yet deadly hostility. For a long moment it seemed none moved while the Chevalier glared up into Jeremy's square aggressive face.

"Well, sir, do you accept?" enquired Jeremy, at last. "Is it thirty thousand guineas?"

The Chevalier, staring up into his questioner's steady eyes, did not answer at once, and when at last he spoke, his voice and manner had altered strangely:

"You are—mad!"

"No!" answered Jeremy. "But I seldom gamble and when I do, well—I gamble. Do you accept?"

"But no, sir," answered De Ravenac in his ordinary tone. "*Vous êtes folle!* Yet even folly so great has the—how you say? limit, *hein?* I 'ave name twenty thousand guineas and this satisfies me—oh yes! You are prepared to place 'alf this money with the stakeholders—yes?"

"The whole sum if desired, sir."

The room was astir with movement and buzzed with eager talk; a gentleman who would have outfaced a national crisis and disaster itself with a stoical calm, waxed mightily excited over the prospect of two men pummelling each other. And so rose a clamour of talk; Jeremy became the centre of a ring of enthusiastic sportsmen, full of passionate enquiry, who questioned him vociferously.

"Who was 'the unknown'?"

"Where would it be fought?"

"When was it to be brought off?"

"Why not in town—say at Gentleman Jackson's?"

"But why not in the country remote from the dem'd law's interference?"

Jeremy was overwhelmed with earnest proffers of assistance, whereat he shook his head; with advice, to which he hearkened patiently; with good wishes, for which he was grateful. He was offered such private sites for the combat as:

Parks.
Meadows.
Barns.
Stables.
An oast-house.
A drawing-room.
A quarry.
A ruined castle.

But always the eager question was repeated:

"Who was this unknown champion upon whose fistic prowess was to depend a wager so immense?"

"Gentlemen," he answered, and instantly all was hushed attention, "forgive me, but I prefer to keep his name a secret for the present. All I can say is that he is young and willing, trained to an ounce and will fight to his last gasp."

At this was pandemonium:

"Bravo!"

"Good luck to 'the unknown'!"

"Demme, but I'll risk a hundred on him myself!"

"Not for me—none o' your 'unknowns' carries my rhino!"

And so forth; until this clamour was stilled by the clear, incisive voice of the Marquis of Jerningham, who spoke as one having authority:

"Veryan, will you leave the arrangements to me?"

"Gratefully!" said Jeremy.

"Then perhaps you'll be good enough to come with me—you too, Piper. This way!"

And so, following the Marquis and with the Major at his elbow, Jeremy threaded his way among gentlemen who shook his hand effusively or their own heads warningly, who wished him luck or stared mumchance, until he found himself in a small room where sat the Chevalier with divers of his youthful satellites. Here, forthwith the matter was solemnly and profoundly discussed in its every detail, and duly set down and recorded for the behoof of future ages and unborn generations, thus:

> That Jeremy Veryan, Esq., of Veryan, Sussex, does wager the Chevalier Gaston de Ravenac an even Twenty Thousand Guineas that his man (name undeclared) shall beat Ben Holt, known as the "Hoxton Slasher" with bare knuckles in a ring to be set up at Gentleman Jackson's Academy or such other place as may be selected. It is further agreed that if either gentleman, namely, Jeremy Veryan, Esq., or the Chev. de Ravenac fails to have his man in the ring at 3 o'clock sharp on the day, being the twentieth inst. of this month, he shall forfeit his entire stake.

"Agreed, gentlemen?"

"But certainly, sir!" answered the Chevalier, bowing.

"Yes!" nodded Jeremy. "With the proviso that if I should fall sick or receive such injury as may prevent my attending the fight, the wager be declared void."

"Sir," said the Marquis, "this is somewhat unusual."

"My lord," answered Jeremy, smiling a little grimly, "so is this wager."

"Haw!" quoth the Major, ponderously emphatic. "Y' are right there! B'ged, so it is! Dooced!"

"Do you consent to this, Monsieur de Ravenac?"

"*Parfaitement!* Oh yes. It gives Mr. Veryan a chance to withdraw from 'is adventure so rash—'e may grow seek with the anxiety——"

"Then, gentlemen, if all 's agreed, be good enough to sign your names," said the Marquis.

This done, Jeremy (with the Major beside him) made his way back through the crowded rooms (where his name sped before him) pausing now and then to bow or shake hands with some well-wisher, and had almost reached the door when it opened violently and Mr. Armadale entered hastily, accompanied by the Honourable Robert; beholding Jeremy, he halted and became at once haughtily scornful and a little theatrical:

"Mr. Veryan," said he, in voice loud enough to command attention near and far, "pray what is the meaning o' this note of yours?"

"What it says," answered Jeremy.

"Ha!" exclaimed Mr. Armadale, advancing one step in haughty but threatening fashion. "By heaven, sir, do you actually dare to mean you refuse me the satisfaction of a gentleman?"

Jeremy nodded.

"Why, then," said Mr. Armadale, flushing angrily, "here and now I denounce you publicly as a despicable craven! Sir, I name you coward!"

"Very well," answered Jeremy; "now get out o' my way!"

"What—what?" stammered Mr. Armadale, forgetting dignity in amazement. "Will you take the word 'coward'?"

"I have!" answered Jeremy.

"Then to 'contemptible coward' I add 'hypocrite' and 'liar'."

Jeremy smiled, and this, or something in his rugged features, seemed to goad Mr. Armadale to an ungovernable frenzy for, uttering an inarticulate, passionate cry, he sprang forward with clenched fist; but as he struck, his arm was seized and wrenched aside, and Jeremy spoke in voice a little harsher than usual:

"Armadale," said he, his painful grip tightening, "do what you will, say what you will, I shall never fight you!" Then, setting Mr. Armadale out of his path, he walked from the room, followed by a sudden clamour of voices and gusts of derisive laughter that rang in his ears with such cruel mockery as brought his teeth together in a vicious snap and thus, scowling and grim, he went his solitary way.

# CHAPTER XXXI

## WHICH FINDS JEREMY IN A VERY AWKWARD SITUATION

REACHING the street he trudged on, plunged in gloomy reverie, when a voice haw-ed close by and he turned to find Major Piper beside him; and Jeremy noticed that the Major was very red in the face, that his glance wandered, and that he was at his very heaviest.

"Haw!" quoth the Major, falling into step.

And after they had walked thus, shoulder to shoulder for perhaps two hundred yards, Major Piper cleared his throat, squared his shoulders, glanced at Jeremy and said:

"Haw!"

"An unfortunate incident!" said Jeremy.

"Dooced!" agreed the Major, and they tramped on in silence again.

"It is kind of you to—to stand by me," said Jeremy, a little awkwardly. "Very friendly!" The Major looked uncomfortable. "I suppose I am quite discredited—at least, in the clubs?"

"'Fraid so!" nodded the Major. "And that," said he, with portentous shake of the head, "is the—haw—the dooce, y' know."

"You think I ought to fight?"

"Veryan—I do!"

"Hum!" quoth Jeremy thoughtfully.

"No man of honour, m' dear Veryan, can possibly—haw—pass over such an affront—so public—such words——"

"Hum!" quoth Jeremy again. "The words were 'craven' 'coward' and 'liar'!"

"B'ged!" exclaimed the Major, with a flourish of his cane. "No man could swallow 'em! Impossible, quite!"

"I can," said Jeremy grimly.

"Haw!" gasped the Major, and fell out of step.

"And," continued Jeremy, smiling into his companion's shocked face, "having swallowed 'em, I find myself none the worse."

The Major goggled in horrified amaze.

"But—my dear Veryan," he murmured in gentle reproach. "Haw—ye know—a man who should fight and won't—is n't—can't be—haw—you understand, m' dear fellow?"

"Very well," said Jeremy. "I won't fight Armadale, but if you think I ought to fight somebody or other, fight I will!"

"Eh, what—eh, fight—fight whom?" stammered the Major.

"Well, London offers a wide selection, Major. Who is esteemed the best pistol shot in town?"

"Gronow," answered the Major. "Though, to be sure, there 's Jerningham and De Ravenac and Lord Alton and——"

"Enough, sir," said Jeremy gravely, "here 's a fine selection—one of these shall serve. So you see the man I fight will be a more formidable opponent than Richard Armadale."

"Veryan, are you—haw—serious?"

"As death!" answered Jeremy fiercely.

"Haw!" said the Major, and dropped his cane.

"When I fight it will be to kill!" said Jeremy, picking up and returning the Major's cane. "Perhaps, when the event takes place, I may count on you as my second?"

"Honoured!" said the Major and walked on a while, heavy with thought. "But m' dear Veryan," said he at last, "they are all crack shots—twelve paces—or twenty—haw—deadly, y' know——"

"So am I!" growled Jeremy.

"My lodgings!" said the Major, halting suddenly before a somewhat dingy door. "Will you—haw—step in?"

"Thank you, not now. I'm expecting an important letter."

"Then adieu, Veryan!" Now as they shook hands, Jeremy found the Major's grasp very warm and hearty. "You can depend on me m' dear fellow—haw—at any time."

"I' m grateful!" answered Jeremy and forthwith hasted away, spurred on by an eager anticipation for that letter which was already five days overdue. Reaching his abode, he found letters galore but not one in that writing his eyes yearned to see.

"Are these all?" he demanded.

"Indeed sir!" answered Moxon, whereupon he became lost in troubled thought: "Five days and not one line from Olivia! Was she ill—or—? To be sure, she would have received Richard's letter by this! Could it possibly be that she believed him the faithless trifler Richard had most probably described him? No—a thousand times—no! Then why—why, in mercy's name, had she written no word? Ha—She was ill perhaps— She must be!" And instantly he became a prey to harrowing anxiety and growing fear. So distracted was he by these dark forebodings that it became necessary for Moxon to emit four discreet coughs before Jeremy once more became aware of him.

"Well, Moxon?"

"I regret to inform you, sir—the boy has run off—levanted, sir."

"Since when, Moxon?"

"Last night, sir."

Jeremy passed a hand across his brow wearily.

"Poor child!" said he.

"Sir, there is a person—to see you."

"What kind—who?"

"With whiskers, sir! About a dog, sir. I assured him you were not in the habit of purchasing dogs——"

"You are sure there are no other letters?"

"Perfectly, sir."

"Who receives the letters?"

"It is James' duty, sir."

"Where is he?"

"Out at present, sir, overseeing the transportation of Mr. Armadale's effects."

"I 'll see him when he returns. And the little lad has left me! I wonder why?"

"He is probably happier in his native environment, sir."

"Hum!" quoth Jeremy, and sighed.

"About the—person, sir."

"Bring him up when I ring!"

Heavy-footed, Jeremy mounted the stairs and reaching his chamber, sank down upon the bed, elbows on knees and head in hands, bowed beneath an incubus—an ever-growing expectancy of approaching evil that troubled him greatly. And after some while as he sat thus, staring blindly at the carpet, his mind harassed and perplexed, he heard a faint sound, and looking up, beheld a small, meek-seeming man, whose face peered out between large drooping whiskers, and whose bright eyes having apparently noted Jeremy, the room, and its contents at a single glance, were now humbly abased.

"Who are you?" demanded Jeremy.

"Only Dan'l, sir. About the dog, that 's all."

"What dog?"

"Yourn, sir—name o' Bill. An' I vas to say 'e 's all right now, thanks t' Jarsper and Bryant and me—though I don't count, no'ow."

"What d' ye mean?"

"Pizen, sir! But we acted according and prompt, so Bill 's alive an' 'earty in consequence. Though I did n't do much."

"Ha—d' ye mean they tried to poison him again?"

"No—I means they did it, sir. But we took it in time—leastways, they did——"

"But how did it happen? Have you any suspicions?"

"Jarsper may 'ave, sir; I ain't—bein' only me."

"And Mrs. Revell—how is she?"

"So so, sir! Been a-weepin'!"

"Ha—weeping?"

"'Eavens 'ard, sir! I 'appened to twig 'er at it once or twice in the little arbour in the gardin."

"And why—why?"

"Becos' 't is ooman's natur to pipe their eye—leastways so they say—I don't know."

"Was it because o' the dog?"

"No, sir, I reckon 't was the letter——"

"Letter? What letter?"

"Well, signed Richard, it was——"

"How do you know?"

"Well, ye see, sir, my gammer kep' a dame school and taught me to read a bit—and I 'appened to get a peep at this here letter. 'Ows' ever, Jarsper says I 'm to tell ye 'e 'll be back to-night and will you meet 'im at the 'Gun,' seein' as 'e 's got summat——"

A sudden knocking on the street door; Moxon's smooth tones in the hall below; a woman's hysterical voice; swift, light feet upon the stair—and then Lucy Western was in the room, a beautiful, wild creature from little sandalled foot to the glossy tresses that had escaped her hood.

"Oh—oh, Mr. Jeremy, is it true—is it true? she panted. "Nay, surely—surely, ye won't be so cruel—so wicked?" And she thrust a crumpled letter into

Jeremy's fingers and all before he might utter one word. So, silent still, he smoothed out the paper and read this:

"To Mistress Lucy Western.

"If you would prevent a duel, avert bloodshed and save your friend Mr. Richard Armadale whose life is threatened by Mr. Veryan, go at once and intercede with Mr. Jeremy, plead with him on your knees, if necessary. You will find him at home this afternoon between the hours of three and four.

"A Friend."

"Oh, dear Mr. Jeremy," cried the distracted girl, "you won't kill him—will you?"

"Hum!" said Jeremy thoughtfully, and scowling at the letter. "Whoever wrote this knows your real name!"

"Dear sir, you winnot fight him!—You must n't! You shannot—— Oh, sir, I pray and beseech—don't go for to fight!"

"Eh?" said Jeremy, glancing into her tearful face. "Fight? No, no, child, of course not! But who wrote this letter, I wonder?"

"Indeed, but I dunnot know, sir—'t was pushed under the door. But, oh, Mr. Jeremy, please—please don't fight! Don't kill him, sir, or I think you 'll kill me, too——"

"Rest assured, I shall never fight Richard——"

"Take an oath, Mr. Jeremy. Oh, please swear on your word of honour."

"I swear, child! There, there—be comforted, sit down, girl." But instead of so doing, she slid to her knees and hid her face against the bed.

"Oh, Mr. Jeremy," she moaned, "how may I ever be comforted and my poor heart a-breaking for him?

And yet I do deserve to suffer—me as doubted his goodness and him such a grand, brave, noble gentleman!"

"My poor child," said Jeremy, looking down at her lovely stricken form, "don't grieve! If you truly love each other, as I believe you do, these troubles will pass. Have faith in your love—and the Future."

"But, oh, Mr. Jeremy—never to see him again—never to hear his dear voice! We 'm parted—for ever—he said so! Oh, sir, I wish God would be so kind to let me die!"

"Hush, girl! Only have faith and Love will find a way."

"Oh, Mr. Jeremy—dear sir—do 'ee think so indeed? Is there hope for me? Do 'ee think his love, maybe, is not dead?" Now in her eager questioning she set her two shapely hands on Jeremy's shoulders and lifting her face to his, back fell her hood, revealing the shining glory of her hair.

"Girl," he answered, smoothing her wayward tresses with gentle hand, "when man and woman truly love, nothing may kill that love—nothing, not even Death——!"

And then a third voice spoke (a voice of that soft, rich quality called contralto), though to be sure it quivered strangely and with a little gasp between the words:

"So then—Richard was right—after all—and my faith only—idlest folly. Oh—unworthy!"

And lifting his head, Jeremy looked into the eyes of Olivia. Fate (directed by a certain malignant agency) had chosen this of all moments to bring her to him.

Motionless she stood, eyes very bright beneath knit brows, delicate nostrils quivering, lips close-set, shapely body vibrant with a scornful disgust beyond any words. Jeremy stared, dumb and spell-bound, he did not even lift his hand from Lucy's head as she cowered against him, startled by this sudden apparition. And thus, before he could move, before his unready tongue could find speech, Olivia turned and was gone, fleeing swift-footed from the place as from abomination. Then he was up, had bounded to the stair, only to hear the street door slam; but down he leapt, nearly upsetting the astonished Moxon, and wrenched open the door only to see the fugitive aided to a closed carriage by Mr. Armadale.

"Olivia!" he cried hoarsely. Mr. Armadale merely glanced in his direction, sprang after his sister, and the vehicle was in motion before Jeremy could reach the pavement; so he stood where he was, to watch the carriage turn round, and thus, for one brief instant, caught a glimpse of the handsome, sardonic features of the Chevalier de Ravenac.

He was still frowning after the carriage when he was aware of the meek and mournful Daniel whose gaze was bent in the same direction.

"Where—how did you vanish!" demanded Jeremy bitterly.

"Only the clothes press, sir."

"What the devil for?"

"Becos' when a young gent and lady meets, they wants to be alone—leastways so I've 'eered—but I dunno!"

"Fool!" exclaimed Jeremy, scowling after the carriage again.

"Yessir!" answered Daniel meekly, touching the brim of his shabby hat! "And I'm to tell Jarsper as you'll be round at 'The Gun' to——"

"Tell him anything!" growled Jeremy.

"Werry good, sir! But that gent in the kerridge yonder—Mr. Ravvyneck?"

"Well?"

"If 'is 'air chanced to be—light now! And if 'is whiskers——"

"Pardon me, sir," said Moxon at this moment, 'but the young lady, sir—she is, I fear, on swooning's verge——"

"Ha—I was forgetting!" sighed Jeremy. "Order the closed carriage, Moxon."

Lucy was seated upon the lowest stair, her lovely face bowed in her hands.

"Come, child," said he, "I'll take you home."

"Oh, Mr. Jeremy," she whispered, lifting her head wearily. "Who was she—the lady? Ah, why do you look so—so terrible? What was it?"

"A nightmare!" he answered.

## CHAPTER XXXII

### WHICH IS A SHORT CHAPTER OF NO PARTICULAR INTEREST

LEARNING that Olivia was staying with her brother at his former lodging in Jermyn Street, Jeremy wrote to her there, a letter of explanation painfully explicit and, awaiting her answer, suffered hours of feverish impatience, only to receive his own letter at last, sent back to him unopened, its seals unbroken. Tearing up this futile missive, he set forth in person and haunted Jermyn Street and the neighbourhood for two days, with the utmost determination, in the desperate hope of meeting her.

It was then towards evening upon the second day as, heavy of step and weary of mind, he trudged this street of St. Jermyn, hating its every flagstone, tile and brick, jostling and jostled by the careless throng he scanned so earnestly, there loomed in his purview the square and very solid form of Mr. Shrig.

"Evenin', Mr. Wee, sir!" said he, touching the brim of his hat with the knob of his stick. "Sir, I 've got a bit o' noos for ye at last—fax, sir—F A C T S—fax!"

"Hum!" quoth Jeremy, his glance wandering.

"I 've been expectin' you round at 'The Gun' these two days, sir."

"I 've been busy!" answered Jeremy, his earnest gaze always upon the fashionable throng. "I am busy."

'And all in wain, sir!"

"What d' ye mean?"

"Mrs. R., sir, she 's back to Priory Dene."

"Ha!" growled Jeremy. "How d' ye know?"

"By means o' Dan'l, sir. She went last night along o' Mr. Armadale. And Mr. Ravvynack to see 'em off."

"Gone, eh?" said Jeremy dully and stood staring blankly down at the pavement.

"And you 'll foller her, I pre-soom, sir?"

"Follow her?" repeated Jeremy with the same blank stare. "Follow her?"

"Lord love ye, pal, don't take on so!" quoth Mr. Shrig, struck by the expression of his companion's rugged features. "Women be kittle cattle."

"Are they, Jasper?"

"So I 've heered, pal. And they only runs to be pursooed."

"D' ye think so, Jasper?"

"Ah!" nodded Mr. Shrig, as they passed on slowly side by side. "So why not pursoo?"

"Hum!" quoth Jeremy, pondering the question. "No, I think not!"

"But s'pose she expects pursoot?"

"She 'll be disappointed."

"But ecod, pal, if a lady vants pursoot and expects to be pursooed, vhere 's the 'arm in purscoin'? Mr. Wee, pal, the vord is pursoot—and wrote in capital letters!"

"I think not," said Jeremy and sighed. "I 'm sure not!" said he, and scowled.

"Might I ax your reason, sir—as a pal?"

Now reading the sincere friendship in Mr. Shrig's look and tone, and feeling himself suddenly destitute and more at a loss than ever before, Jeremy answered impulsively:

"Yes, Jasper. Because ever since I was struck down at Priory Dene I 've lived in a Fool's Paradise."

"Meanin' sir (speaking as a pal) you vas in love?"

"Meaning, Jasper, that I dreamed she loved me—but I 'm awake at last!"

"Are you, pal?"

"I am!" growled Jeremy bitterly. "I always knew no woman could truly love me. I 'm not the sort!"

"And is this here your reason for not pursooing?"

"It is."

"But then, pal (speaking as a pal, mind!), the lady also 'as a reason for cutting her stick—or, as you might say, hopping 'er perch and running off."

"True!" nodded Jeremy scornfully. "The letter written by her brother—and he mad with foolish jealousy."

"Lord, no, pal—that ain't said lady's reason."

"What, then?"

"Sir, I 'll tell you (speaking werry much as a pal, mind!). Did n't Mrs. R. ketch you a-cuddling of a werry lovely young fe-male—in your bedroom?"

"Eh!" exclaimed Jeremy, halting suddenly. "The devil——"

"No, the young fe-male, sir! Lucy Vestern, pal! And, though none o' your seekin'—in your bedroom, Mr. Wee! And 't is in ewidence, you ackerchally a-sitting on your bed wi' the lovely young fe-male a-veeping in your arms——"

"By heaven!" gasped Jeremy. "Did she think—could she possibly think—dared to suspect——"

"She did, pal! And werry nat'ral too! Anybody else vould ha' thought the identical same, and you can lay to that!"

"Poor Lucy! Thank Heaven your man Daniel was with us!"

"But in the clothes press, pal, and consequently out o' Mrs. R.'s sight!"

"Can she believe so vilely of me?" quoth Jeremy indignantly.

"She can, pal, seeing as you ain't one o' these here archangels with vings but only a huming man. To be sure, women is confidin' creeturs—up to a p'int, but reach that p'int and confidence flies up the chimbley."

Heedless of the curious glances of the passers-by, Jeremy stood scowling down at the pavement, again lost in his thoughts until aroused by his companion's touch.

"Vot are you a-going to do, Mr. Veryan, sir?"

"Nothing! Anything!"

"Werry good, sir! And where might you be a-going?"

"I don't know. Anywhere!"

"Werry good again, sir—step along o' me." So side by side they went on again, Jeremy with scowling gaze bent earthwards and careless of direction until, becoming aware they had left the stir of the busy street behind them, he glanced up to find himself in a small, quiet mews or stable yard.

"What place is this, Jasper?"

"Nowheers in partic'lar, pal—foller me, sir!"

So saying, Mr. Shrig led the way to an empty stable where was a ladder that rose to an open trapdoor above; up this ladder Mr. Shrig climbed, beckoning Jeremy to follow, who, mounting in turn, beheld a loft with a great pile of fragrant hay in one corner and another ladder that led up to yet another trapdoor, whence dangles a pair of legs that Jeremy thought vaguely familiar.

"'Ow goes it, Dan'l?" enquired Mr. Shrig.

"Fair to middlin', Jarsper," answered the legs.

"Are you takin' the night watch, Dan'l?"

"I be, Jarsper. Jarge relieves at ha'-past four."

"Anything to report?"

"Jarge see Number Two go in early 's morning about four o'clock——" Mr. Shrig gave a sort of leap.

"Eh—Number Two?" he repeated in tones of awed but rapturous surprise. "Number Two, Dan'l? Was Jarge sure, Dan'l, sure?"

"Sartin!" answered the legs.

"By Goles!" exclaimed Mr. Shrig and hugged himself in a strange kind of ecstasy. "By Goles, if my de-ductions is correct it 'll be domino me, arter all! Has Number Two come out again, Dan'l?"

"Not yet, Jarsper. Number Four come out 'arf an hour ago."

"And 'ow did 'e seem, Dan'l?"

"Wild-like, Jarsper."

"Good again! And Number Vun?"

"Ain't appeared."

"What are you watching?" enquired Jeremy, staring up at the legs that twitched now and then.

"Moosoo Ravvynack's ken, pal."

"And what are the numbers—or who, Jasper?"

"Dan'l shall tell you, sir. Number Vun, Dan'l?"

"Mr. Ravvynack," answered the legs, writhing.

"Number Two, Dan'l?"

"Mr. O'Leary."

"Number Three, Dan'l?"

"Sir James Trevor."

"Number Four?"

"Mr. Arthur Trevor."

"And Number Five, Dan'l?"

"Joseph Sims."

"And now, Mr. Wee, pal, if you 're wishful to hear and see summart as 'll sap-rise you, let 's be toddling, sir."

"Where?"

"To your house, sir."

"As you will," said Jeremy; whereupon Mr. Shrig turned and addressed the legs:

"At Mr. Wee's if I 'm wanted, Dan'l!"

"Ay, ay, Jarsper!"

## CHAPTER XXXIII

### WHEREIN MR. SHRIG NARRATES CERTAIN FACTS

"ANY letters, Moxon?"

"Merely bills, sir, I regret to say."

"Bring wine!" said Jeremy, ridding himself of hat and cane. "And see no one disturbs us." And upstairs forthwith he ushered Mr. Shrig; softly after them entered Moxon, bearing a tray with decanters and glasses which he set down tenderly, and departing softly, closed the door noiselessly.

"First, sir," said Mr. Shrig after some while, setting down his empty glass and leaning back in his chair. "I must ask for your solemn Bible oath and likewise vord of honour as you 'll not interfere in any o' my plans nowise and nohow! Agreed, sir?"

"Agreed!" nodded Jeremy.

"Werry good!" nodded Mr. Shrig. "I 'll begin wi' Ben Western, head gamekeeper at Weryan."

"Why him?"

"Because he 's got a sister, a vidder—maiden name Rose Western. You never heered sich a name to remember, p'raps?"

"Never."

"Hows'ever, Mr. Wee, this here Rose is your own mother's foster-sister and twenty-three years ago was her maid."

"Ah!" exclaimed Jeremy, suddenly intent.

"Sich is the fact, sir. Now the night arter your feyther gets killed and your poor mother is took ill, she comes stealing into Rose's bedroom, like any pore frightened ghost, and gives Rose a little reader—or, as you might say, book. 'Rose,' says your mother, a-vispering distracted-like, 'Rose,' says she, ''ide it. Oh, 'ide it!' So Rose takes the book, 'ides it werry careful and two days later your poor mother takes and dies. But just afore the end she begs everybody to leave her alone wi' Rose. So soon as the room is clear, your dying mother steals summat from under her pillow—frightened-like—and gives Rose a crumpled paper. 'My baby,' she vispers (meaning you, Mr. Weryan), 'my little 'elpless baby!' says she. And, sir, that 's the last word she ever speaks! And here pal, is that werry i-dentical letter!"

Very reverently Jeremy took that pitiful scrap of paper and bowing his head, saw thereon these words, feebly traced by the dying hand of the mother he had never known:

> Oh dear Rose, I am full of dread for my little baby—I cannot tell why. Should anything happen to me take him away—steal him away to Mr. Gillespie in London and implore him if ever he loved me to protect my helpless solitary child. Do this for me Rose, or

Speechless awhile sat Jeremy, staring at these faint characters, while Mr. Shrig, respecting this silence, held his peace.

"I 'll keep this!" said Jeremy at last.

"Werry good, sir! So there 's your mother and feyther dead and you an infant and, by the vill as your feyther meant to revoke but didn't, your mother's brother, Sir James Trevor, becomes executor an' trustee and your guardian—but, sir, when he comes to take over—there ain't nobody to guard, because Rose has wanished and you along of her— Such is the fax so far; do I make 'em plain, pal?"

"Yes. Go on!"

"Rose brings you to Mr. Gillespie, shows him your pore mother's letter (same bein' now in your fist)—but she don't say anything about the little reader—vich is a great pity! Then Mr. G., being a werry determinated man and famous lawyer, goes to your uncle, Sir James T., and his friend Mr. Openshaw, and being so werry extryordinary determinated, settles for you to be left in Rose's care. Later on, so soon as you 're old enough he contrives to have you sent to a school where he can keep his eye on you—continual——"

"Why Jasper?"

"Pal, I 'm a-comin' to that! In the meantime, Rose marries a man name o' Sims, as vas your uncle, Sir James' walet, and they come to London and there a son is born to 'em being Joseph Sims, as is to-day your cousin, Mr. Arthur Trevor's, groom—a peeping, prying sort o' chap."

"Very!" nodded Jeremy grimly.

"Now it ain't long afore Rose finds out as Sir James Trevor is a-paying her husband money—reg'lar, vich money don't do him no manner o' good, for 'e takes to drink and later on buys a riverside tavern called the 'Jolly Waterman,' and later still (though why I dunno) 'e changes 'is name from John Sims to—Jos. Shields——"

"Ha!" exclaimed Jeremy.

"Sich is the fact, sir!" nodded Mr. Shrig. "Now vun day, being drunker than common, 'e tells Rose summat (though vot, I dunno, she refusing to tell same to me), but it so upsets her that she leaves 'im and, 'iding 'erself in London, takes in lodgers and among 'em—Mr. Lockett. Am I clear, sir?"

"Quite!" said Jeremy, refilling Mr. Shrig's glass.

"Thank 'ee sir—'ealth and happiness, pal! Now all these years Rose has kept this here little reader safe and secret, but, about two months ago, she took ill and thinkin' o' death, this secret is too much for 'er, so she writes to her son, Joseph Sims, to wisit her, and vhen 'e comes she, bein' sick and solitary, con-fides to him all about the little reader, d 'ye see. Now son Joseph (being such a werry peepin', prying sort o' cove) ewidently knows summat, for 'e gets precious excited, asks for the little book, begs, pleads, threatens—and Rose, pore soul, being frightened, tells him she 's sent it to—you——"

"To—me!" exclaimed Jeremy in wide-eyed amazement.

"Your werry own self, sir—sich is the fact, pal! So back to Weryan goes Joseph Sims—and mark vot follers! The werry same night you are waylaid upon the road and all but killed!"

"Ah!" growled Jeremy. "Go on, Jasper."

"Now mark vot follers again! So soon as you are able to travel, I takes precious good care to let it be known as you and me are a-starting for London for to see your lawyer. And vot 's the consequence? Pal, the consequence is—my mare is hocussed!"

"I remember!" nodded Jeremy.

"Hows'ever, thanks to Dan'l and a ditch, us gets to London ahead o' the pursoot, though werry closely followed. And by 'oo? Pal, by Moosoo Black Viskers!"

"De Ravenac?" exclaimed Jeremy, starting. "But why by him? How is he concerned?"

"That, sir, is the question, pal! But mark vot follers again! We find Mr. G. that morning werry much alive and we see him that night—werry dead—and all by reason o' that little reader!"

"God in heaven!" cried Jeremy, leaping to his feet. "What can be the secret of this little book?"

"A pretty black un, sir."

"But what, Jasper, what? And where is the accursed thing?"

"Here, pal!" And from waistcoat pocket, Mr. Shrig drew a small, morocco-covered notebook. "Not much to look at, Mr. Wee, sir," sighed he, shaking his head at it, "yet there never vas a book as ever I see or heered on as caused more misery and bloodshed. For, sir, 't is in ewidence as Mr. G. was a-vaiting for Rose Sims to bring him this 'ere book the night as Murder took him so wiolent. 'T was to get back this 'ere book as his murderer killed him—and all in vain, because Rose Sims being ill that night, never brought it. 'T was by reason o' this book John Sims, alias Jos Shields, got drowned. 'T was——"

"But—but——" stammered Jeremy, "I thought Shields was the murderer—you said so—repeatedly——"

"And for a werry good reason, sir! But, Lord love you, pore Jos Shields 'ad n't no more to do wi' it than you or me."

"Then, in Heaven's name—who, Jasper, who?"

Mr. Shrig turned the little book over and over thoughtfully. "Mr. Wee, pal," said he at last. "I rayther fancy his name is wrote down 'ere! Have a peep!"

Taking the little book, open at the flyleaf, Jeremy sat rigid and staring, for he saw those two names:

JAMES TREVOR

(This written in delicate, cultured hand, but crossed out and beneath)

JULIUS OPENSHAW, May 2, 1795.

(This dashed off in bold, sprawling characters.)

"Which?" gasped Jeremy. "Which?"

"Pal, you may take your ch'ice!" answered Mr. Shrig. "Look it over, sir, and choose according."

Turning the pages with clumsy fingers, Jeremy saw it was a memorandum chiefly devoted to the record of betting transactions, with names, addresses and brief notes hastily jotted, being all in the same sprawling hand. But midway through the book were two pages that bore no writing whatsoever.

"Aha," quoth Mr. Shrig. "You 're wondering about them blank pages, sir? Puzzled me at first, they did. Give it here, pal, and I 'll show ye." Taking the little book, Mr. Shrig set it where the warmth of the fire might reach these blank pages. "Vatch now!" he murmured.

And slowly, little by little, upon these seemingly empty pages characters began to form, growing ever more distinct until, stooped above them, Jeremy could read these lines traced in the same bold caligraphy:

> In consideration of what happened on June 3, 1798, I promise to pay J. O. One Thousand Pounds per annum, in perpetuity.
>
> JAMES TREVOR.

(the name written in the same fine and delicate hand).

"Good God!" whispered Jeremy. "It was on June the third, seventeen hundred and ninety-eight, that my father was killed!"

"And you reckernize the signatoor, sir?"

"Yes!"

"Now peep on t' other page."

Almost unwillingly Jeremy obeyed and read the words:

> Upon the day I, or my son, shall inherit the Veryan estates I promise to pay J. O. the sum of Fifty Thousand Pounds.
>
> JAMES TREVOR.

Drawing a deep breath, Jeremy glanced up to find Mr. Shrig regarding him with expression of serene content.

"Sir," said he, tapping the book Jeremy had passed back to him, "here 's the reason o' your dying mother's fears! Here 's the reason Mr. Gillespie vatched over you so constant—from child'ood's hour!"

"But why—why dare to write such things, Jasper?"

"Why, d 'ye see, pal, 't is wrote secret, and then it puts vun on 'em in t' other un's power."

"Jasper, where is Openshaw?"

"Ah, pal, that 's the question again, sir! Likewise 'oo is 'e? Sir, there 's only two in this vicked vorld beside himself as knowed that—Mr. G. being vun."

"Gillespie?"

"Ah! You 'll mind the message as he left on the table wrote in his werry own gore: 'J BEWARE OPSH IS'—that 's vot 'e wrote. And vot should Opsh mean but Openshaw? Mr. G. vas trying to warn us who Openshaw vas, but died afore 'e could do so. Ay, Mr. G. knowed and t' other un as knows is your uncle, Sir James Trevor!"

"Then let us go to Veryan instantly and force the truth from him!"

"No, pal! Can't be done, sir, for though used to takin' risks now and then, I ain't wenturesome nor yet fool'ardy! They got Mr. G. and John Sims, alias Jos Shields and you almost, ditto me—shot clean through my dicer last time—you can spot the 'oles if you look! No, Mr. Wee, pal, I don't make no move till my proofs is all complete——"

"Then I will," said Jeremy grimly. "And at once!"

"I wenters to think not, sir."

"Nothing shall stay me, Shrig," quoth Jeremy, rising.

"Ex-cept your word-of-honour promise, Mr. Wee." Jeremy growled and sat down again.

"But, great heavens, man, what shall you do?"

"Sir, I 'm a-doing of it as I sit 'ere. My twig is limed, pal, my 'ook is baited, my net is spread——"

"Are you sure—certain of these hideous facts?"

"Sir, my fax is always sure."

"Lord!" groaned Jeremy. "What horror!"

"As ever vas, sir—a lovely case, and, mark me, it 's going to grow 'orribler or my name ain't——"

Mr. Shrig started and turned, as did Jeremy, to see a face peering in at them from the window, a small face apparently suspended high in air, with nose flattened against the pane and eyes rolling in hideous fashion. In an instant Jeremy had reached the window, opened the casement and hauled the intruder to safety.

"'Ullo, guv'nor!" quoth the urchin, wholly unabashed. His clothes were somewhat ragged and himself comfortably dirty, but his eyes were as mischievously bright, his face as full of elfish wisdom and his manner as indomitable as ever. "'Ow goes it, guv'nor?" he enquired cheerily.

"Lord!" exclaimed Jeremy, staring down at the impish face. "You might have fallen—broken your confounded young neck!"

"Not me, guv'nor, I ain't breakin' no necks—climb anythink, I can. An' I got a message for the Bashaw."

"Who?"

"Why, 'im!" answered the Imp, stabbing small, grimy finger at Mr. Shrig. "For 'im, guv'nor, th' Bashaw o' the Pigs."

"Meaning me, sir," explained Mr. Shrig.

"Jasper, in heaven's name—how old is he?"

"Pal," answered Mr. Shrig, beckoning the Imp, "in regard to smooth files, knowing cards and general vide-awake downiness, Methusalem was a cooing babby to this b'y. Now, vot 's the office, sonny?"

"Well, I was to whisper it, mister—so douse your napper and gimme your ear-'ole."

Now as he hearkened to the boy's sibilant whisper, Mr. Shrig nodded in placid satisfaction.

"Aha—Number Four, eh?" quoth he. "Well, trot off, sonny, trot and tell 'em as I 'll be along in a pig's visper—off with ye!"

"And not by the window!" warned Jeremy, whereupon the Imp grimaced and vanished by the door.

"A re-markable sharp b'y that, sir," said Mr. Shrig, rising, "as I 've took the liberty o' borrering for a day or so, promising to return same in good order. And now I 'll toddle, sir, only reminding you, pal, that according to your solemn promise you're bound not t' interfere by vord, look or deed—no matter vot may 'appen!"

Left alone, Jeremy sat bowed above the table, heeding no more the dangers that menaced him, his hopes and sorrows quite out of mind; even Olivia herself forgotten a while, as he stared down at the pitiful unfinished letter written in such fearful, desperate haste by his long-dead, youthful mother.

And it was for himself she had suffered, had feared, had pleaded with dying voice and hand—for him!

"Shall I bring lights, sir?"

Jeremy lifted heavy head and glanced where stood Moxon in the gloom.

"No!" he answered.

"Will you partake of supper, sir?"

"No. I 'm going away, Moxon. Look after things till I return. You may hear of me at the 'Gun' in Gray's Inn Lane."

## CHAPTER XXXIV

### CONCERNING ARTHUR TREVOR, HIS STRANGE METAMORPHOSIS

So to the "Gun" went Jeremy, there to be welcomed by the Corporal and Jessamy Todd with such a warmth of unaffected gladness as comforted him not a little.

And now, seated between them on the great oak settle before the banked fire where swung a big, black pot, he drooped weary head and sighed.

"Brother," enquired Jessamy, after some while, "what 's your trouble?"

"Life!" growled Jeremy.

"Then may be three or four fast rounds might 'elp ye to think better of it, brother? There 's nothin' like a good, stiff punch, now and then, to teach a man the j'y of living! What d' ye say, brother?"

"No!" growled Jeremy, and shaking his head at the great, black pot, he sighed again.

"Sir," said the Corporal, lifting the lid of the pot very dexterously with his shining hook, "are ye hungry?"

"Hungry——" began Jeremy, in bitter negation—but from the black pot there stole to him an aroma so coyly arresting, so subtly delectable that, though weary and sick at heart, his mouth watered. "Hum!" quoth he.

"Sheep's jimmies, sir—stooed!" explained the Corporal.

"With onions, brother!" added Jessamy.

"Also po-taters!" nodded the Corporal.

"And a turmut or so!" said Jessamy.

"With a handful o' yarbs!" quoth the Corporal.

Jeremy stared at the black pot and, remembering he had eaten nothing all day, was immediately ravenous.

"Jess was just about to lay the cloth, sir, while I dish up," said the Corporal, rising.

"Then I 'll help," said Jeremy, rising also.

Very speedily the cloth was laid and down they sat together, forthwith. And after a somewhat protracted silence Jeremy leaned back in his chair and glancing from the herculean, comely-faced Corporal to the clean-limbed, athletic Jessamy, found them regarding him with that look which only Friendship's eyes may hold, and knew within himself that the love and goodwill of true men is the best and greatest blessing in all this troublesome world. Therefore he extended a hand to each and drawing them near, told them a certain item of news which caused Corporal Dick to gasp and rub his clean-shaven chin, and Jessamy to view him over with eyes suddenly anxious.

"Twenty—thousand—guineas!" exclaimed the Corporal, at last. "Pro-digious!"

"And—in so short a time, brother!" sighed Jessamy.

"I wish 't was to-morrow!" growled Jeremy.

"And 'the Slasher' at the very top of his form, I hear, brother!"

"So much the better."

"Twenty—thousand—guineas!" repeated the Corporal. "Im-mense!"

"And 'the Slasher's' never been beat yet!" quoth Jessamy.

"Why, then," said the Corporal, "he must be!"

"He shall be!" exclaimed Jessamy.

"I think he will be!" nodded Jeremy.

"We 'll go into the country," cried Jessamy, fired with sudden joyous enthusiasm. "I know the very place—in a little wood—we 'll camp there. Ah, brother, there 's nothin' like fresh air, wind in the trees—birds a-carolling! Cool water to bathe in, lush grass to fall on and, at night, a fire to sit by and stars to look at till they wink ye to sleep!"

"And I 'm sick o' the town!" growled Jeremy. "We 'll start to-morrow, Jessamy."

"To-morrow it is, brother——"

"And there 's some one at the side door!" said the Corporal. "And it ain't Jarsper's knock."

"Then wait and let 'em knock again," quoth Jessamy.

But no need was there to wait, for the knocking continued with scarcely any intermission—a dull persistent rapping; so forth went the Corporal in response. Ensued a murmur of voices in question and answer, the tread of hasty feet and into the kitchen stepped Arthur Trevor. His handsome features were pale and careworn, his graceful figure had lost its easy swagger, his air of confident assurance was replaced by a furtive, hunted expression that bordered on abject fear.

"You!" exclaimed Jeremy, and rose, scowling.

"Jerry—Jerry—oh, for God's sake, give me five minutes alone!"

Jeremy stood mute and staring, for these wild eyes, these tremulous hands outstretched in passionate supplication, these pitiful, quavering accents, shocked and appalled him.

"Jerry—Jerry—let me speak to you alone—for God's sake!"

Jeremy glanced from his cousin's distorted face to the watchful Corporal and keen-eyed Jessamy, and nodded, whereupon they departed, closing the door behind them.

Then Arthur sank weakly into a chair and covered his face with shaking hands.

"What is it—this time?" enquired Jeremy.

"Death——" gasped Arthur, "death or disgrace, Jerry! I 'm caught—trapped—in the devil's clutches, and he 's hunting me to death and damnation! I must get away at once—now—overseas! I can do it if you 'll help. A couple o' hundred, Jerry—a hundred—I can reach Dover by dawn—I must!"

"What have you done, Arthur?"

"Only what he meant I should—what he planned for, schemed for like the devil he is! A trap baited by him for my ruin, Jerry—and now—he 's got me—grovelling under his heel—down in the slime!"

"And his name, Arthur?"

"De Ravenac—curse him! He 's turned on me, Jerry—to my damnation! I thought him my friend—till yesterday. It 's the woman; he means to have her, body and soul—in spite o' me, in spite of herself—ah, in spite of God and the devil—and have her he will—poor creature!"

"Who, Arthur?"

"Oh, egad—can you ask? Who but Olivia Revell? Is there any other woman may compare? I tell you, Jerry, he means to have her—fair ways or foul—damn him—and he will—he will!"

Jeremy crossed to the hearth and staring down blindly at the smouldering fire, shivered violently; while Arthur, crouched miserably at the table, alternately groaned and pleaded:

"I 'm lost, Jeremy, lost unless you help me. And what 's a hundred guineas, or a thousand, to you? You were always the lucky one——"

"Was I, Arthur?"

"Yes, by God! Were n't you the heir? Everything to be yours some day, while I— Oh, damnation! Help me, old fellow, help me."

"Do you—love Mrs. Revell? Does—he?"

"Damn him. I only know he wants her and means to have her—I 'd call him out—fight him, but he has only to whisper a word—and I 'm discredited—disgraced——"

"D' ye think—she—loves you, Arthur?"

"Sometimes I 've thought she did, but I was never quite sure; 't is what makes her so dev'lish alluring! And now—now I 'm ruined by my love for her!"

"How?"

"Because I refused to be warned off. He had the damned audacity to tell me he permitted no man to make love to her—forbade me to see her, and I told him to go to the devil. Then he laughed—told me he 'd schemed to remove me—trapped me through my own folly! And, by God, Jerry, he means to put me away. Transportation—prison—the chain gang; this or suicide unless you will save me! A hundred pounds, Jerry, a miserable hundred——"

"And—Lucy Western?"

"I 've forgotten the little fool."

"Why did you carry her off?"

"You 're mad!"

"No—you 're lying! Speak truth and I help you."

"I meant the girl no harm I swear——"

"The truth!"

"Well, some women need a strong hand—they like it—Oh, pummel me if you will only give me the money—save me from worse than death, Jerry—for your mother's sake——"

"My mother! You!" said Jeremy, and meeting his look, Arthur quailed.

"Jerry—oh, Jerry," he pleaded, "for heaven's sake, be human! After all, we 're akin——"

"In this purse are fifteen guineas; three hundred more shall be——"

A single loud rap on the door brought Arthur to his feet, staring aghast.

"Who is it?" he whispered. "Oh, damnation, who is it?" But even as he spoke, the door opened and a small, round head shot into view.

"Gent 'ere name o' Mister Trevor?" enquired the Imp.

"Why d' you ask, boy?" enquired Jeremy.

"Well, 'cos I got a writin' f' 'im, I 'ave."

"Who from?" demanded Arthur, eyeing the small figure very much askance.

"Well, I wos to say 'from a friend,' I was."

"Show me."

"Well, but is your name Mr. Trevor esk-wire?"

"Never mind—give me the letter or go!"

"Yah-boo!" cried the Imp, dodging this way and that the better to view Mr. Trevor's person. "Brown 'air, bloo ogles, a dandy rig an' jools—you 're 'im! So 'ere 's the writin'—cop 'old, guv'nor!" So saying, the boy thrust a grimy, folded paper into Mr. Trevor's reluctant hand, grimaced at Jeremy and darted away, slamming the door behind him.

Surveying this missive with a lively distaste, Arthur unfolded it, glanced at it, stared open-mouthed and uttering a stifled exclamation, sank into his chair to sit gazing at this dingy scrap of paper with its few, roughly printed words like one awed and spellbound.

"Impossible!" he muttered at last, oblivious now of Jeremy's very existence. "Impossible!— And yet——?"

Rigid and motionless he sat, seeming scarcely to breathe, his head bowed between fierce-clasping hands —his features twisted and convulsed in a very agony of thought, like one striving desperately to remember, searching his mind for past events, racking his brain for some vague clue.

"By God! Yes!"

The words were a mere whisper but, uttering them he raised his head, and Jeremy, beholding his contorted face, saw Suspicion grow to Belief, and Belief to a wildly triumphant Certainty; then he was on his feet and Jeremy recoiled in stupefaction, so vast, so altogether unbelievable was the change in him. The abject slave had become the gloating tyrant. Laughing suddenly, Arthur Trevor clapped on his hat, and folding his arms, fronted Jeremy with all his old assurance, cheeks flushed, eyes aglow, his whole being transfigured by a great and awful triumph.

"Ha, Jeremy—most virtuous cousin," he cried. "You may keep your money; the lion is tamed, the bull ringed, the devil's an ass! Oh, Jeremy, I've got him at last—here, under my foot, to the end of his days!"

And laughing again wildly, Arthur ground his heel viciously against the tiled floor. "Ha, by God, he shall kneel to me yet and kiss my boots! He shall fetch and carry and crawl to my whistle! I'm his master, his God Almighty to blast him when it pleases me. Tyburn, Jerry! Gallows and Hangman! Ah, curse him, he shall suffer a year for every pang he made me endure! Hell for him now, in this life and the next! Blind fool that I was not to have guessed—have known—have seen! And yet, egad—such cleverness, such devilish cunning! But I know at last, thanks to this scrap o' paper. Only seven words, Jerry—shall I show ye? No, my virtuous Sobersides, find it for yourself! Seven words, but here is Power, Wealth, Beauty—all the best o' life—and so——!" With a sudden extravagant gesture, Arthur raised the paper to his lips, kissed it fiercely, and setting it upon the fire, thrust it down into the glowing embers and watched until it had consumed; then he laughed again and nodded.

"Should you ever see that boy again, give him this from most grateful me." And Arthur tossed a guinea upon the table. "Good-bye, my old Jerry; when next we meet you shall behold my apotheosis!" Here, meeting Jeremy's wondering look, he laughed louder than ever and nodding, strode away, his face distorted by that same look of dreadful, gloating triumph.

Sinking wearily upon the settle, Jeremy became a prey to the blackest depression; but presently roused by a faint sound he glanced up to see Mr. Shrig staring pensively out of the window.

"Pal," said he, in strange, troubled voice, "come and look 'ere!" Crossing to the window, Jeremy beheld his cousin Arthur striding jauntily along the alley. "Look at 'im, pal, look at 'im!" sighed Mr. Shrig. "There 's a change for ye! See the cock of his head, twig the set o' them shoulders! And he 's so young, pal, so werry young for it. To be sure 'e ain't a good young gent—not by no manner o' means 'e ain't, and therefore no great loss to the community—and there 's a power o' comfort in that!"

"Why, Jasper?"

"Sir, if my concloosions is co-rect, pal, Mr. Arthur Trevor is a-going to bite off more than he can chew, and if 'e does, sir——" Mr. Shrig's look grew as troubled as his tone, "if 'e does 'e may—choke a bit, and if so be 'e chokes, my suspicions 'll be proved fax at last and my case done and ended."

"What d'ye mean, Jasper?"

But, instead of answering, Mr. Shrig sighed again, shook his head and walked heavily away, leaving Jeremy to his dark and most unhappy meditations.

## CHAPTER XXXV

### OF GABBING DICK, A PEDDLER, HIS NEWS

A YOUNG sun shone resplendent, his early beams chequered by leaves astir in the soft and fragrant wind; birds carolled in glad harmony, the brook bubbled merrily, dew sparkled, and all Nature seemed exultant, for it was early morning.

And forth from the pool sprang Jeremy, scattering the sun-kissed water in sparkling drops, his every nerve a-tingle with exuberant life, his eyes bright with the joy of it; and Jessamy Todd, hissing cheerfully as he towelled himself, turned to view his companion's naked might with expert eye—the depths of chest, sweep of shoulder, narrow flanks and powerful limbs of him; and noting the assured and buoyant ease of his every movement, Jessamy nodded with a dawning smile which came but to vanish, leaving his look as anxious as ever—for Jeremy had sighed.

"Brother—why?" demanded Jessamy as, side by side, they began to clothe themselves. "Wi' that chest an' shoulders, them arms an' legs as the good Lord's blessed ye with, wherefore sigh so constant?"

"Do I, Jessamy?"

"A bellers could n't compare, brother! Ah, and you groaned in the night—frequent! Why, brother, why? Look at the sunshine, hark at them blessed birds—ain't you happy?'

"No!" answered Jeremy, frowning down into the sparkling water.

"Brother, this ain't nat'ral, 'specially on such a j'yful morning. And, wot 's more, it ain't right in a fighting man, nor fair to his trainer!"

"Hum!" growled Jeremy.

"Also the good Lord meant all men to be happy."

"D' ye think so, Jessamy?"

"For sure! Brother, all men would be as 'appy as birds and as merry as grigs if 't was n't for themselves. What 's your trouble, brother?"

"A man."

"Good! I mean 't is better than if 't was a woman. And what manner o' man?"

"One somebody ought to make an end of—soon!"

"Nay, leave him to the Lord, brother."

"Ha!" exclaimed Jeremy. "He has been left to the Lord for forty-odd years, and to-day, flourishing in his vileness, arrogant in evil, he threatens to blast Innocence and befoul Purity."

"Brother, the Lord will protect His own!"

"Hum!" growled Jeremy. "Yet how often is Innocence the victim of brutish evil! And this matter being very urgent, the sooner I kill him the better."

"Eh— Eh?" gasped Jessamy. "Kill him!—You?—murder, is it?"

"A duel, Jessamy."

"Why, they 're much of a muchness. But, oh, brother, to think o' you standing up to shoot a man an' be shot at! It ain't nat'ral and therefore 't is all wrong. Pistols an' sich like devil's contraptions ain't in the good Lord's scheme o' things. The Lord o' Creation, knowing man's natur', give him two fists, good honest weapons, brother, and they should be enough! And—s'posing he kills ye?"

"He probably will!" growled Jeremy.

"Lord God!" quoth Jessamy, in groaning voice. "And you in sich tip-top form! S' nimble on your pins! Wi' sich an arm—and them shoulders! And sich foot work! And all no good agin a coward's bullet! And *if* he kills ye, how then?"

"What matter if I kill him? I 'm solitary and of no great importance, and——"

"Ay, but you are, brother! We be all important in the Lord's eyes. He gave us life to live for the good of our kind——"

"Or die for it, Jessamy. And there would be few to miss me—except my dog Bill, and he's probably forgotten me by now."

"Well, what about Corporal Dick an' me, not forgettin' Jarsper?" demanded Jessamy with some heat.

"Ay, to be sure, I was forgetting. Forgive me! God knows I should be solitary without ye—especially you, Jessamy Todd!" And, clasping sudden arm about the ex-champion, Jeremy squeezed him impulsively and mightily; whereupon Jessamy squeezed back and flushed immediately and stared up at the blue heaven, while Jeremy scowled down at the sparkling water again, and both awhile sat mumchance like the very Britons they were. Said Jeremy at last:

"I did n't black your eye last evening as I feared."

Answered Jessamy, "No matter, you knocked me down, brother."

"A lucky blow, Jessamy."

"Timed to a second, brother."

"To be sure, I'm pounds heavier than you, Jessamy."

"Brother, I 've beat coves stones heavier afore now. And none ever give me such a leveller, and nobody never struck a cleaner, truer, sweeter blow in this world—no, not even me."

"You 're mighty generous, Jessamy."

"And you 're a mighty hitter, brother, a born fighting man— And there 's the kettle a-biling at last! If you 'll brew the coffee, I 'll fry the bacon. Are ye hungry, brother?"

"Surprisingly."

"Then I 'll cut the bacon thick—nothin' like bacon consoomed in the open air and ate moderate, too much not being overgood for the bellers, the wind, brother, though to be——"

"Jessamy Todd, ain't it?" enquired a dismal voice, and out from adjacent thicket stepped a man with a great pack on his shoulders. "Jessamy Todd, ain't you?" he repeated. "If so, wot o', mate—if not, no matter!"

Bacon on knee and knife in hand, Jessamy surveyed the intruder, eyeing his squat person from dusty boots to the round, unlovely face beneath weather-beaten hat, with no great favour.

"Yes," he answered, "and your name 's Dick, I think. Gabbing Dick, ain't you?"

"That 's me, mate!" nodded the peddler.

"Friend o' Tinker Jarvis?"

"That ain't me, mate. I ain't friends wi' nobody. Dang the world, I says, and everybody in it—'specially furrineers and most 'specially French gents!"

"Have ye seen Tinker Jarvis o' late?"

"Ah! This here 's one o' his campin' places; when I see your smoke I thought you was 'im. 'E 'll be 'ere to-morrow, I expect, unless 'e 's cut 'is throat."

"What d' ye mean?"

"Mean?" repeated the peddler, spitting viciously at a butterfly hovering near. "All folks comes to a end some day, don't they? And most on 'em bad ends—'specially tinkers, and a good job too! Very well, then! Will ye be wantin' ever a broom, now?"

"No!" answered Jessamy, beginning to cut the bacon.

"Or a belt wi' a good steel buckle——"

"No!"

"Or a penknife wi' a edge like a razor——"

"No!"

"I thought not!" growled the peddler, staring at the bacon. "Then ye might ax me to sit down an' peck a bit."

"I might," said Jessamy.

"Then I will!" quoth the peddler, stumping forward and slipping off his pack as he came; whereat Jessamy stared quite at a loss.

"What about it, brother?" he enquired.

"Yes!" nodded Jeremy.

"Why, then, you 're welcome, Gabbing Dick."

"No, I ain't!" snarled the peddler. "I ain't never welcome nowhere, no time, by no one, but I don't mind—dang 'em all, I says. And I likes my bacon cut extry thin an' plenty on it, mate, and my coffee good an' sweet."

And presently, the coffee steaming fragrantly and the bacon hissing in the pan, they sat down to breakfast: then Jessamy, as was his wont, offered up a short grace though his reverent voice was well-nigh drowned by the peddler's snorts and voracious mastication.

"D' ye never ask a blessing, Gabbing Dick?" demanded Jessamy, frowning.

"Not me. I ain't got no cause for blessing nobody nor nothing' mate."

"D' ye never pray, Peddler?"

"Ah—frequent! I prays for vengeance on them as treats me bad—'God strike 'em dead,' I prays, 'or deaf, or dumb, or blast 'em!' Oh, a powerful pray-er, I be."

"Why not pray God bless 'em, instead?"

"Because I ain't no 'ipocrite. There ain't nobody I wants God to bless, 'specially furrineers—and dang all French gents!"

"Why French?" enquired Jeremy.

"Because I 'ates 'em. And if you 'll gimme some more coffee an' don't forget the sugar, I 'll tell ye why."

His mug refilled, the peddler tasted it, nodded, smacked his lips and continued:

"Well, yesterday 'ere 's me trampin' the road, thinkin' wot a lot o' dead folks there must be, seeing as folks has been a-dyin' ever since the world began—when I meets a Eve, a young 'ooman, a lady an' a reg'lar 'igh-stepper, an' I tries to sell 'er a brooch an' bracelets, or neck chain, d' ye see, failing o' which I tries 'er wi' a belt, also a penknife, likewise a razor, when a big dog comes a-runnin' at me. But I be used to dogs, so I waits wi' me stick ready to bodge it in 'is eye, but 'Come 'ere, Bill!' says she and——"

"Bill?" exclaimed Jeremy.

"Ah—Bill."

"And a big dog, you say?"

"Ah! 'Come 'ere, Bill!'" says she, when up steps a tall gent, a furrineer Frenchman by 'is lingo, and afore I knowed it, fetches me a clout acrost me back wi' his cane an' another on me nob—dang 'im! Then the dog Bill, being a English dog, takes me part an' makes to fly at the French gent—dang 'im again! Then the lady ketches 'old o' the dog an' screams because the French gent 'as pulled a dagger out o' his cane. Then along comes a manservant an' takes the dog away. Then the lady beckons me an' gives me—never you mind 'ow much—an' tells me to go. Which go I did, mighty quick. But arter a bit I looks back an' sees the gent 'as got 'old o' this 'ere Eve by the two wrists an' she a-trying to pull away. But 'e only laughs an' says summat an' makes to kiss 'er, but seein' me a-watchin' stops to threaten me wi' 'is cane."

"And this was—yesterday?" enquired Jeremy.

"Yesterday evenin'! An' the last I see of 'em, 'e 'as this lady in 'is arms, she a-strugglin' an' strivin' Eve-like, an' 'im a-kissing of 'er—face an' 'air an' neck—kisses, ah, love kisses! Adam an' Eve an' the Snake!"

The tin plate slipped from Jeremy's knee, spilling its contents on the grass; slowly he stooped and picked up the plate, then, very deliberately, set his foot upon the bacon rasher, crushing it deep into the turf as if it had been something loathsome and abhorrent, while the peddler stared at him open-mouthed and Jessamy watched his distorted face with eyes more anxious than ever.

At last, having eaten and drunk to repletion, the peddler grunted and rose.

"You won't be wantin' to buy nothin', I s'pose?" he enquired, picking up his pack. "Hankercher, say, or a pair o' garters for your gal——"

"No!" said Jessamy.

"Why, gals like fairings an' such, an' there 's nothing like a pair o' gart . . . Oh, all right!" he whined, for Jessamy had risen. "Tis an' ard, crool, world, so dang it, says I!" Therewith he shook his head dismally, spat dolefully, and stumped mournfully away.

Then Jessamy set himself to wash the breakfast things in his quick, deft fashion and to put the little camp in order, pausing now and then to glance anxiously where Jeremy sat all unheeding.

"Well, brother," said he at last, stepping forth of the small tent they had pitched in the shade of a tree, "we 'll fib four rounds, light sparring—if you 're ready?"

"I 'm not!" growled Jeremy.

"Not?" exclaimed Jessamy, staring in wonderment.

"I sha'n't spar, this morning."

"Oh! Then wot will ye do, brother?"

"Walk."

"Where to, brother?"

"A place called Priory Dene," answered Jeremy, and rising as he spoke, stepped into the little tent and presently came forth clad for the road.

"How far is it, brother?"

"Seven or eight miles, I judge."

"Brother, what 's to do?"

"Come and see!" growled Jeremy.

## CHAPTER XXXVI

### THE APOTHEOSIS OF ARTHUR TREVOR

HEEDLESS of dirt and heat and sun glare went Jeremy, his scowling gaze ever upon the distance ahead, grim purpose in every clean-cut line of him; in so much that Jessamy Todd glanced at his rugged features very often in patient yet ever-growing perturbation.

Thus tramped they mile after mile and with never a word until they came at last to a certain stile that gave upon a broad meadow with a coppice beyond. Here Jeremy paused and stood awhile leaning upon the stile, lost in the same gloomy abstraction until roused by his companion's voice:

"Where now, brother?"

"Yonder! The house stands away beyond the wood."

"And you are here—to kill?"

"Yes."

"And what then, brother?"

Jeremy turned to scowl, but seeing the profound trouble in the speaker's face, smiled instead.

"Why, Jessamy," said he in that so unexpectedly gentle voice of his, "never grieve, man."

"Oh, brother," groaned Jessamy. "God keep your soul clean o' bloodshed."

"Never trouble about me, Jessamy."

"How may I not, sir? Y' see I 've took the liberty o' regarding you as a friend and brother, Mr. Veryan, sir"

"I 'm proud of your friendship."

"Then sir——"

"Call me 'brother'."

"Thank'ee, sir—so be it, brother. And being so, I makes bold to ax you, brother, who is this man as you 'd kill? And why?"

"His name is De Ravenac——"

"Him!" exclaimed Jessamy, starting back. "Then —oh, brother—the Lord help us!"

"I think He will, Jessamy."

"Sir, I knew Mr. Raveynack—he was my patron once. I 've seen him shoot off a pistol many 's the time, and brother, he never misses—never!"

"Neither do I, Jessamy."

"But—if he kills ye—shoots ye dead——?"

"Death seems none so dreadful—nowadays."

"Ay, you be too young an' strong to fear it, brother. 'T is only the old an' ailing as dreads to die."

And presently Jeremy vaulted the stile and began to cross the meadow. Now as they went, side by side, Jessamy Todd took off his hat and lifting earnest face to the blue heaven, prayed very fervently, thus:

"Lord God, Father o' Life, let not this Thy son that is s' young an' strong know death yet awhile, and oh, Lord, I beseech Thee to stay him from killing of his enemy, so that when he comes to Thee at last, he may come clean an' sweet o' soul. And this I pray because he is my brother as I do love—and for the sake o' Thy blessed son Jesus. Amen, Lord."

And now as they walked, Jeremy went with head bowed, being full of awe, and a new humility; thus, side by side, they entered the little wood, neither looking at the other, nor speaking.

Suddenly was a rustle of leaves and out from the under-brush some distance before them stepped a large dog who halted to survey them, began to growl, but in that moment tried to change it to a joyous whine, a bark of ecstatic delight and, making a botch of all three, came bounding towards Jeremy, his sinuous body all writhing welcome from head to tail.

"Why, Bill!" exclaimed Jeremy; and then they had met, the man stooping with hand outstretched, the dog, whining rapturously, leaping to nuzzle that hand, to butt at it with great, square head and finally to crouch at the man's dusty feet and look up adoringly into the face bent above him.

"Lord, Bill, my lad," quoth Jeremy, pulling at stubby ear. "You 've grown almost handsome."

"Bill!" called a voice, whereat Jeremy started and glanced up to behold Olivia within a dozen yards of him. At first he thought her strangely pale, and then unduly flushed as, halting suddenly, she stared back at him. Then, and before he could find a word, she turned and would have left him; but quick-footed, Jeremy barred her way and taking off his hat, bowed.

"Madam," he began, but in this moment he thought to read in her eyes, in the quiver of sensitive lips and all the troubled beauty of her, a painful agitation beyond words, and reaching out his arms, "Olivia!" he murmured. And then he saw he had been mistaken, for now, in eyes and lips, in all her shapely figure from sandalled foot to dark braids of hair, was a serene and stately dignity, a cold aloofness that struck him dumb.

"Ah, Mr. Veryan," said she in her rich, soft tones. "You have come for your dog, of course?"

"Yes—no—no!" answered Jeremy, frowning. "Why—Olivia, why do you treat me so unjustly?"

"Oh, pray spare me your reproaches!" said she lightly. "I shall be sorry to part with Bill, but since you are here, pray take him and—go."

"Why do you give me no chance to explain?" demanded Jeremy.

"Explain?" she laughed, viewing him beneath raised brows. "Can you pretend to any explanation, sir? Can you explain away the evidence of my own eyes?"

"I did!" growled Jeremy. "But you sent back my letter unopened."

"Letter?" she repeated, with a little gasp. "Your—letter?"

"Addressed to you at your brother's lodging."

"Oh," said she, in the same breathless manner. "You—you addressed it there?"

"That letter explained everything, Olivia."

"There are some things, Mr. Veryan, can never be explained."

"Then Mrs. Revell, I 'll explain now——"

"Indeed, sir, there is no need!" she retorted. "The girl is sufficiently handsome!"

"She is also pure and good——" began Jeremy.

"Oh, to be sure, sir!" nodded Olivia. "A very angel of light and holiness, I grant you—though to be sure——" Olivia laughed, but her white hand clenched itself suddenly.

"Madam," growled Jeremy, "your levity is out o' place."

"Sir," she retorted. "So are you—the high road lies yonder!"

And turning she walked slowly on, humming a sprightly air softly to herself while Jeremy, his frowning gaze bent earthwards, trudged heavily beside her, very gloomy and immensely determined. Now glancing up, after some while, he saw they had reached the rose garden; afar off he could discern that shady corner where stood the rustic arbour. And beholding this fragrant bower he halted, being deeply stirred by all the bitter-sweet memories its mere sight awakened.

"Olivia," said he, his voice hushed and tender, "don't you remember——"

"Too well, sir!" she answered in tones that choked the words upon his lips. "Why have you followed me here, Mr. Veryan?"

"To vindicate a good, sweet maid—to explain——"

"I repeat, sir, there is no need; her surpassing beauty explains—everything!" Thus lightly speaking, Olivia plucked a red rose that bloomed near by and stood turning it in idle fingers.

"Mam," quoth Jeremy harshly. "Lucy Western is my head gamekeeper's daughter, as good as she is beautiful, and loves your brother——"

"But," said Olivia, smiling down at the rose, "she steals to you in the privacy of your chamber——"

"Damnation!" exclaimed Jeremy and, catching the slim hand that toyed with the rose, he swung Olivia to meet his scowling gaze. "D' you think—do you dare impute——" Olivia looked up into his fierce eyes and laughed.

"I think, Mr. Veryan, that you are merely a very ordinary human male who is bruising my poor wrist." Jeremy loosed her and stood fuming in speechless indignation, while Olivia, lifting the rose to delicate nostrils, inhaled its fragrance with little, dainty sniffs.

"Olivia," he began at length. "This poor child came to plead with me for your——"

"Mr. Veryan," she interrupted, "the matter ceases to interest me."

"Madam, the matter is vital to my happiness——"

"Which, sir, is no concern of mine."

"Ha!" exclaimed Jeremy, falling back a step. "You mean——?"

"That I have ears and eyes!" cried Olivia in sudden fury. "That I heard your words of love—saw her arms about you! Oh, for shame—for shame! Let this hateful mockery of protesting innocence end! Do not try to stultify my reason by such contemptible deceit. Go—go back to your pure angel—leave me before I despise you more than I do."

"Hum!" quoth Jeremy, marvelling at this sudden outburst.

"Go!" she repeated, viewing him like an offended goddess. "Go before you become utterly contemptible!"

"So you won't hear me, Olivia?"

"Not another word. Had you boldly confessed your fault—pleaded your man's weakness—asked my forgiveness, I would have listened and might even have forgiven you—in time, though never forgotten. But now—go, sir. Your attempted explanation insults my reason."

"Then," growled Jeremy, "if I may not explain to you, De Ravenac shall explain to me."

"De Ravenac?" she questioned in sudden apprehension. "Why him? What do you mean?"

"That when he has explained I 'll brand him for the scheming rogue and liar he is."

"But how—how is he concerned in your—unfaithfulness to me?"

"To death!" answered Jeremy, scowling towards the distant gables of the house that seemed to scowl back at him; but before he could make a step thitherwards, Olivia was before him, barring his advance.

"Ah!" she exclaimed, reading his purpose. "You mean to force a quarrel on him—a duel! No, no—you must not—shall not. I forbid it!" Jeremy smiled grimly. "Mr. Veryan, I say you shall not!"

"Mrs. Revell," he answered slowly, "nothing on earth shall stay me."

"He will—kill you!"

"However, I shall certainly kill him."

"Ah, God!" she whispered, clasping her hands with sudden, wild gesture. "Not this, Jeremy. Oh, not this! Anything but this. See now, I will listen to your explanation. Take me into the arbour. You shall explain away your Lucy Western—I will believe my eyes deceived me." Gone now was all her proud serenity, her cold aloofness; in place of offended goddess was a woman, very humble and tender, who pleaded gentle-voiced; beholding which sudden transformation, Jeremy stared amazed and faintly disgusted.

"Take me into the arbour," she whispered, "our arbour, Jeremy!"

"No!" he answered. "De Ravenac shall do the explaining." And turning, Jeremy strode towards the house; but before he had gone three yards she was beside him, a pale creature trembling and distraught.

"Where—where are you going?" she questioned breathlessly.

"To find him."

"But he is not here——"

"He was, last night."

"He left this morning, thank God!"

Jeremy strode on.

"I tell you he is gone!" said Olivia with the same breathless vehemence. Jeremy merely lengthened his stride.

"Do you doubt my words, sir?" she demanded angrily. Jeremy strode on unheeding, which roused her to sudden fury, for she grasped his arm and shook it in frenzied hands. "He is not here!" she panted, "I tell you he is not here!"

"Madam," said Jeremy. "Pray loose me."

"Will you go?" she cried. "Will you leave now—this instant?"

"No!" he answered, moving on in spite of her.

"Ah, don't you believe me? Do you think I would stoop to lie—to such as you? I say he is not here. I tell you he is gone——"

Then Jeremy halted, for—even as she spoke—the Chevalier de Ravenac appeared at the farther end of the rose garden and, unaware of their presence, paused to glance back whence he had come. And now Olivia was whispering in passionate entreaty:

"Jeremy—go! If ever you loved me—go. I beseech, I implore you—go before he sees us." But Jeremy stood motionless, staring at De Ravenac who, still wholly unaware of them, was glaring back at the house he had just left, his eyes fixed upon a certain window, his whole face convulsed with an expression that drew and held Jeremy's wondering gaze, for fear was there, and hate and baffled rage; it was indeed the face of a man in torment, yet in nervous hand that opened and clenched itself, in sombre eye and merciless line of mouth was an indomitable strength of purpose. For a long moment the Chevalier stood thus, staring back at the house as if it held some frightful thing that must be annihilated ere it rise and destroy him; then, hearing Bill growl, he turned sharply, and Jeremy marvelled anew, for as the Chevalier came sauntering towards them he was smiling, his sinister face as calm and assured as ever.

"*Ah, ma toute belle,*" said he, addressing Olivia with his stateliest bow. "I 'ave seek you all the morning. You promise las' night to talk this day the sad affairs of our poor Richard, *n'est-ce pas?* So p'raps Monsieur Veryan will excuse——"

"Willingly," answered Jeremy. "Madam, pray leave us."

"No!" said Olivia, pale but determined.

"Then stay!" growled Jeremy and turned upon the Chevalier; but now was a sound of voices and the Honourable Robert Stukely appeared, accompanied by two other gentlemen as youthful, as elegant and modishly dissipated-looking as himself. But all at once they forgot their affectations, forgot even themselves and stood rooted to the spot, all three, in staring amazement as Jeremy's harsh voice reached them.

"Mr. de Ravenac," said he, "I salute you for the rogue and liar you are!" And taking off his hat, he struck it into the Chevalier's face.

The three young gentlemen gasped. Olivia cried out and, sinking to her knees, hid her face against Bill's quivering body. The Chevalier bowed.

"Monsieur Veryan," said he, between pallid, smiling lips, "I shall now kill you with a pleasure the most extreme!"

"At your service, sir!" answered Jeremy.

"My pistols," smiled the Chevalier, beckoning airily to the three gaping gentlemen.

"What—what—here?" quavered the Honourable Robert.

"But certainly. If madame will be so good to leave us and you, *mon cher* Denby, will bring my duelling pistols, we can finish our affair in the—'ow you say?—wink of the eye."

With a swift, supple gesture Olivia rose and sped away, the great dog trotting beside her; then, while one young gentleman hurried off for the instruments of destruction the other two hastened to make the necessary arrangements, pacing off a strip of green-sward with the utmost care and precision, talking anxiously together the while in subdued voices.

"Twenty-four paces, De Ravenac?" enquired the Honourable Robert a little nervously.

"Twelve!" answered the Chevalier.

"Six!" said Jeremy.

"And *mon cher* Robert, p'raps you will oblige by acting for Monsieur Veryan?"

"Honoured!" answered the Honourable Robert, as back hurried Mr. Denby, somewhat out of breath, bearing a flat mahogany box. And now, under Jeremy's watchful eye, the deadly weapons were loaded and primed with all due care, and rising from his knees, a pistol in either hand, the Honourable

Robert glanced from scowling Jeremy to the smiling Chevalier.

"Twelve paces, I think?" he enquired.

"Ten!" said the Chevalier.

"Five!" growled Jeremy.

"Oh, God!" gasped Mr. Denby, mopping youthful brow. "Oh, God, 't will be murder!"

"Tush!" growled Jeremy. "Five paces or fifty, we shall not miss, so what matter? Give us the pistols."

But even as he spoke, Olivia appeared.

"Quick!" she cried to some one behind her. "Stop them if you can. Oh, for God's sake—stop them!"

"With pleasure!" answered a cheery voice and out from behind the tall yew hedge stepped Arthur Trevor. For a moment he stood surveying the company with a certain assured and complacent satisfaction, then laughed suddenly as at some rare and secret jest.

"Give us the pistols!" repeated Jeremy.

"No, no!" said Arthur lightly. "Indeed, gentlemen, I grieve to say your lust for blood must be disappointed; my lady commands and I obey——"

"You?" exclaimed Jeremy contemptuously.

"I!" nodded Arthur. "Restrain your natural ferocity, cousin Gruff and Glum, Monsieur de Ravenac will not fight."

"Ged—won't he, though!" cried Mr. Denby.

"Eh—not fight?" exclaimed the Honourable Robert. "Oh, reely, my dear Trevor, he must and he will, of course; the affront was too outrageous—reely!"

"Ged—I should think so!" nodded Mr. Denby. "Fellow actually struck him—hat, y' know!"

"Nevertheless," said Arthur, smiling round upon the astonished group. "I can assure you the Chavalier will not fight—faith, I'm willing to bet any man any money———"

"Ged, Trevor, I 'll take you—a pony!"

"No, no," chuckled Arthur. "I don't bet on certainties."

"But what—what does De Ravenac say?" stammered the Honourable Robert, whereupon Arthur Trevor laughed more joyously than ever, while the Chevalier, his gaze always upon the grass at his feet, smiled also.

"Tell them," chuckled Arthur, "tell 'em, De Ravenac, that you positively refuse to fight."

"But certainly!" said the Chevalier, his gaze still abased, his mouth still twisted in sardonic smile. "My dear friend Arthur, 'e is right—*Oh, parfaitement!* I do not shoot Monsieur Veryan to-day—no. I am a man of the reputation proved with the pistol or *epée* so often that I can pass over the affront and permit Mr. Veryan to live—Oh yes."

"Must I strike you again?" growled Jeremy.

"*N'importe, monsieur!*" smiled the Chevalier. "I 'ave say I do not fight—*voilà*, it is enough!"

"Moreover," said Arthur, struggling against his unaccountable mirth, "the Chevalier is about to deprive us of his company; important business calls him away—eh, De Ravenac?"

"But, yes, *hélas!*" sighed the Chevalier. "Business of the most important—of life and death."

"And," continued Arthur, "you are forced, much against your will, to tear yourself from us at once—now—this instant?"

"But yes, my dear friend."

"B'gad," tittered Arthur, "d 'ye know, I guessed as much and ordered your carriage accordingly; you 'll find it ready and waiting."

"*Ah, mon cher,*" exclaimed the Chevalier, patting Arthur affectionately, "what prevoyance, what forethought! And yet, *cher ami,* even you do not dream 'ow *très, très* important, 'ow extreme—'ow you say—urgent—is this business. But p'raps you know some day, *mon vieux*, but then—p'raps not. Adieu, my friend Arthur, to-day you laugh, so I laugh too—ha, ha! Gentlemen, your servant most devote. Madame Olivia, I kiss your so pretty feet and carry your beauty in my 'eart—adieu!"

So saying, the Chevalier bowed and went his leisured way, nor did any speak until his stately form had disappeared.

Then Olivia sighed and looked up wistfully to meet Jeremy's scowling gaze; from him she turned to his smiling, debonair cousin.

"Pray take me to the house!" said she. Arthur bowed, offering his arm with a flourish, and on his smiling face, in his whole masterful bearing, Jeremy read again that self-same dreadful exultation.

And thus, upon his triumphant cousin's arm, Olivia went her way with never a backward glance, and after them the three young gentlemen who muttered together.

Now presently, as Jeremy stood there very full of black and bitter thoughts, he heard a light step and glanced up to find Jessamy beside him.

"Ha, Jessamy," said he in fierce self-scorn, "here stand I a very fool—a failure as ever and—even my dog deserts me."

"Nay, brother," answered Jessamy, shaking his head; "here stands you safe and sound—which is good! But clear o' your enemy's blood—which is better. For here was a miracle o' God, brother; the Lord's hand was over you. Ay, the Lord hath surely answered my prayer. So now, brother, let 's give thanks unto the Lord, for He is good, for His mercy endureth for ever. And as for failure, brother, you ain't got the look of it—not you! And as for your dog—well, there's a creatur' as won't desert you rain or shine, come fair or foul, and that 's me, brother, so long as you needs me."

Now looking into the speaker's honest eyes, Jeremy bowed his head and was mute awhile; when at last he spoke his voice was strangely humble:

"Rain or shine, fair or foul—I'll need you, Jessamy, for you are a better man than I. Come, let us go, my brother."

## CHAPTER XXXVII

### GIVES SOME DESCRIPTION OF A FIGHT

UPON the famous Brighton turnpike where the road turns west towards Henfield, in a great, green hollow hard beside the way, a vast company was gathered; a pushing, jostling, jovial multitude, whose increasing clamour woke a thousand echoes, breaking the solemn hush of swelling hill and down.

Here were noble lords and honest tradesmen, sturdy farmers and lusty, smock-frocked hinds; since early dawn had they been gathering in gigs, curricles and carts, in stately coach and lumbering waggon, on horseback and afoot; from village, town and hamlet had they come, careless of dust and fatigue, and all hither drawn to this remote and greeny solitude by love of that game which consists in two men pummelling each other so long as flesh and spirit may endure.

And still they came; the long road roared to the tread of countless feet, the ring of hoofs and grind of wheels, while dust rose in billowing clouds, far as the eye could see. And, being hale and merry, this motley concourse laughed and sang, pushed and jostled good-humouredly enough, about a roped-in square of velvet turf wherein two mighty men were to strive together for their own glory and the profit of their patrons and backers, bruising and battering each other to decide which of two gentlemen should win the tremendous sum of twenty thousand guineas.

"Twenty—thousand—guineas."

It sped from lip to lip, it was whispered, it was

shouted; the words buzzed beneath the ceaseless hum, the cheers and strident laughter.

"Twenty—thousand—guineas."

A certain tall, dark, foreign-looking gentleman, a veritable Grand Seigneur, hears it as he makes his stately way to the ring-side, bowing to right and left and exchanging salutations with his numerous acquaintances, yet wholly unaware of the small, meek-seeming man in drooping whiskers, who edges his shabby person through the crowd with such unobtrusive dexterity, following—following with his sharp eyes ever in the one direction, quite unregarded by this stately gentleman, or any one else for that matter, as he slips, humbly apologetic, through the press, following—following, silent, unheeded, unfaltering.

And yet this grand gentleman might seem a little anxious, for despite his stately bearing and courtly salutes, though his lips smile, his brow is sombre and his keen glance roves constantly here and there as if in quest of some expected yet dreaded object. And presently he halts suddenly, his gaze upon a laughing group of buckish sportsmen among whom is Arthur Trevor, and once again his face is convulsed with that same expression wherein is hate, stark fear, and dark indomitable purpose. Then he moves on, nor does he pause until he reaches a man who stands close beside the ring, a burly fellow conspicuous by reason of his white hat and vivid neckerchief, a loud-voiced, bullying fellow who, feeling himself touched, turns with a snarling oath, but meeting the gentleman's eye recoils and, cringing abjectly, touches the brim of his white hat again and yet again.

"Did n't know 't was you, me lord!" he whines.

"Is everything prepared?"

"Yes, me lord—I 've only got to wave me 'at and the lads——"

"Silence! And no bungling!" And turning stately back, the grand gentleman saunters away to mingle with other great ones, whose noble persons are roped off, exempt from the vulgar herd.

Up climbs the sun high and higher above the surging crowd that shouts and sings, cheers and laughs, finding within itself a thousand matters for mirth and jollity. Two o'clock and an hour to wait! Yet who cares—the sun shines, life is good, and three o'clock must come. So hurrah, lads, for Old England and the Fancy.

At half-past two some one shouts a name and a sudden hush ensues as through the crowd strides a powerful fellow, his face and hands wellnigh black with pickling to harden them against lusty blows, his stalwart form swathed in shawls and overcoat, his seconds and bottle holder at his heels.

"It 's Holt!" shout those adjacent. "'T is Tom Holt—here 's Tom the Hoxton lad—three cheers for the 'Slasher'!"

Forthwith the crowd takes up the name and roars it to the welkin until the fighting man grins and waves his acknowledgment, then turns deferentially to listen to his patron's admonitions, this tall, stately gentleman whom the "knowing ones" recognize as the Chevalier de Ravenac who, though a Frenchman, has the good sense to live in England and is consequently a hearty fellow, a true-blue sportsman, and is cheered accordingly while he confers with his gladiator; and though his words are few he says them with a flash of white teeth and glare of the eyes that render his handsome face more sinister than usual. At a quarter to three the crowd grows restless and loud demands are heard for "the Unknown."

"The Unknown"—where 's "the Unknown?"

At ten minutes to three Major Piper, arm-in-arm with the Marquis of Jerningham, consults his watch three times in the same minute, shakes his head, sighs and ejaculates:

"Haw!"

"B'gad!" exclaims the Marquis, glancing at his own watch. "Looks as though Veryan must forfeit!"

At five minutes to three a fast-driven gig is seen approaching and the crowd roars in vehement welcome as, before it has reached a standstill, forth springs a slender, shapely man of no great size, and down jumps a tallish gentleman in modish hat and long be-frogged surtout, and together they make their way through the cheering throng that opens to give them passage.

"A near thing, brother!" pants Jessamy. "They nigh managed to delay us!"

"But not quite!" answers Jeremy.

"Mr. Veryan," cries a loud clear voice, "are you present, sir?"

"Yes!"

"It lacks but two minutes to the hour; is your man ready?"

"Yes!" answers Jeremy again, and taking off his hat sends it spinning aloft to fall into the ring and, climbing in after it, stands still wrapped in his long surtout, looking round upon the sea of eager faces rising row upon row within this great, green hollow, an amphitheatre designed by Nature, it would seem, for just such an occasion.

"Mr. Veryan," cries the clear voice, "where is your man?"

For answer Jeremy strips off his long coat and stands before the staring multitude, stripped for the fray.

A moment's silence and then there is a hoarse murmur, rising and swelling to deafening cheer on cheer:

"Hurrah for the 'Fighting Corinthian!'"

But Jeremy, all unheeding, is regarding his antagonist, this stalwart fellow, his eyes (set too close together beneath jutting brow), his bull neck, deep chest, knotted arms and powerful legs; and as Jeremy surveys him, so the "Slasher" surveys Jeremy, then turning towards a certain quarter of the crowd, grins and nods confidently. Now, glancing thitherward also, Jeremy beholds the man in a white hat.

"Look, Jessamy," says he; "'t is the fellow Ben."

"Ay," nods Jessamy, "and a precious ugly gang astarn of him, brother! I 'm pretty sure there 's——"

"Time!" cries the loud, imperious voice, and Jeremy steps to the middle of the ring where stands his opponent who, grinning still, holds out his right hand, whereupon Jeremy reaches forth his, but scarcely have their fingers touched than the "Slasher" leaps to vicious action; up swings his left fist and as Jeremy staggers back, the "Slasher" bores in with thudding right, then, closing, grapples him in mighty arms and for a moment they sway together close-locked, and a myriad voices scream and shout, hoot and cheer, as down goes Jeremy beneath his powerful assailant.

And now is hoarse laughter and jeers, for as Jeremy rises, his face and chest are spattered with blood, and from that quarter where stands the man Ben rises a screech of fierce jubilation.

"First blood to the 'Slasher!' Hurrah for the Hoxton Lad!"

"I lay ten to one against the Corinthian!" cries a man hard beside Jeremy's corner of the ring, a large, flabby-faced person with ferocious whiskers. "Ten to one!"

"A tricky customer, brother, and game by his looks!" says Jessamy, busied with water and sponge.

"So much the better!" growls Jeremy.

"And means to rough it, brother."

"Then so do I!" nods Jeremy.

"Well, remember your feet, brother——"

"Ten to one!" bellows the flabby-faced man in the voice of a Stentor.

"Think I 'll lay a monkey," says the Marquis, fingering his cravat. "Are ye betting, Piper—against Veryan, of course?"

"Haw!" says the Marquis ponderously. "No, m' dear f'low—not a—haw—dem'd groat!"

"Twelve to one!" bellows Flabby Face. "Twelve to one I offer—who takes me?"

"I do!" growls Jeremy, catching his eye.

"Eh—eh? Very good, sir—what 's your figure?"

"A hundred!"

"Done with you for a hundred!" and Flabby Face nods so vigorously that his whiskers appear fiercer than ever.

"Time!" cries the fateful voice and rising, Jeremy walks towards his grinning adversary who hastens to meet him, eager to renew the fray, while the air rings with such comments as:

"Don't hurt him, Tom! 'E wants to kiss and be friends, lad! Finish him, Tom, polish him off quick! At him, lad, tap his claret again!"

Calm-eyed stands Jeremy, albeit watchful and poised for swift action while the "Slasher," thus encouraged and flushed by his initial success, feints with right and left, ducks here, ducks there and finally, like the bold and dashing fighter he is, rushes in—to be met by a jarring left, staggered by hard-driven right, two resounding blows; whereat is a cheer that swells to a roar as, gasping, the "Slasher" dances out of danger, grinning still but cautious now, while Jeremy, grim-lipped and steady-eyed, follows him; thus for a while they feint and spar for an opening, they duck and dodge until the ever-impatient crowd roars at them to fight. But Jeremy, all unheeding, watches and waits the chance which he knows must come.

Suddenly the hoarse clamour subsides for, spying his opportunity, Jeremy is upon his man and begins to fight in veriest earnest—in and out and in again, swift and light-footed, hitting, parrying, stopping, ducking and doubling now here, now there, but smiting with stinging left and bone-jarring right until the

"Slasher," dazed and breathless, reels backwards across the trampled ring while the crowd rocks and sways and roars ecstatic. But if Jeremy is swift and strong the "Slasher" is mightily framed and built for punishment and now, remembering his superior weight, he means to use it; therefore he stoops battered head and hurls himself against his elusive foe, is checked by a lightning uppercut and, as he straightens—out shoots Jeremy's powerful right, timed to the second, and twisting upon his heels the "Slasher" goes down heavily, full length.

"Oho, brother," yells Jessamy, above the raving clamour, "no man ever struck a sweeter blow—no, not even the Archangel Michael!"

"Five!" wails Flabby Face, "I offer five to one against the Corinthian—five——"

"Done!" nods Jeremy.

"And scarce a mark on you, brother!"

"Fancy I 'd better hedge," murmurs the Marquis, resettling his cravat. "Veryan 's better than I thought, y' know."

"Haw!" nods the Major. "I 'll lay ten on him myself, m' dear f'low."

"Brother," says Jessamy, glancing towards the busy seconds in the "Slasher's" corner, "you 've got his measure, but he 's full o' devil's tricks, and seein' who 's backing him, be cautious, finish him as soon as you can and——"

"Time!" cries the voice of authority, and immediately all is hushed as the two adversaries face each other, the "Slasher" eager and willing as ever, his swollen features twisted in their habitual grin, Jeremy sombre-eyed, his head bowed a little, fists well up and elbows in. Scarcely are they in distance than the "Slasher" is upon him, and foot to foot, blow for blow, Jeremy meets him, and the watching multitude, silent and entranced, watches the quick, lithe play of these supple bodies, the flash of powerful arms, the dexterous shifts of ever-moving feet, to the accompaniment of hissing breaths, gasps, the smack and thud of sledge-hammer blows; once Jeremy is beaten to the ropes and once he slips to his knee, but is up before the "Slasher" can reach him and fighting fiercely as ever, though scathless no longer, for there is an ugly contusion above one eye, there are livid marks upon his white skin—but the "Slasher" is all blood from hair to belt, his nose and mouth are a red smear, his eyes glare wildly, for his strength is going; and thus, being desperate, he fights the more wildly and is but a surer mark for Jeremy's unerring blows until, gasping, sobbing, he sways forward and goes down, his scarred face upon the trampled grass.

"Brother, how 's the bellers?"

"Well enough!" gasps Jeremy.

"Two to one on the Corinthian!" bellows Flabby Face hoarsely, his whiskers seeming to languish a trifle.

"Another round and you have him, brother!" says Jessamy, setting the water bottle to Jeremy's parched lips.

"Time!" cries the fateful voice.

The "Slasher's" battered visage has lost its grin at last; his mighty chest heaves distressfully and his one eye (the other is fast closed) watches Jeremy's terrible right fist apprehensively.

Flabby Face bellows as loudly as ever, though his whiskers have about them a wistful appearance approaching meekness, as the combatants wheel and circle or close in desperate strife to and fro upon the trampled sward; but the "Slasher," though game as ever, fights now on the retreat, yet time and again Jeremy's blows draw blood, weakening him visibly, whereupon, above the frantic cheering, rises a fierce howl from that part of the crowd where stands the man in the white hat, at which threatening sound the "Slasher," as if it were a signal, stumbles and falls.

And thus as round succeeds round, Jeremy begins to sicken at the ghastly punishment his blows inflict and to pity his antagonist who, bespattered with blood and features swollen out of all recognition, yet fights on desperately until he drops.

It is as they meet for the twentieth round that the "Slasher" seems suddenly endued with fresh strength for, ducking Jeremy's left, he comes to a grapple and down they go together, but, even as they fall, up comes the "Slasher's" murderous knee, unseen by any eye and Jeremy sinks upon the grass and lies helpless, groaning and gasping horribly.

Thereafter he is dimly conscious of water dashed in his face and of pain that numbs his every faculty.

"Brother, how are ye?"

Half a minute's respite and his strength gone, his breathing an agony—a rib stove, perhaps—and only thirty seconds—thinks Jeremy.

"Brother—oh, brother, how are ye now?"

"Better than—I—seem," gasps Jeremy.

More water that deluges him, cool and beneficent, making his breathing less of pain. "Perhaps the rib is sound, after all?" thinks Jeremy.

"Brother, can ye go another round?"

"I 've hardly begun to fight—yet," gasps Jeremy.

"Time!" cries a merciless voice that is the voice of Fate, of Destiny, or remorseless Duty, and therefore must be obeyed, so up to reeling feet gets Jeremy and staggers forth, dazed, breathless, half-blind, fighting mechanically, his swooning flesh upborne by indomitable spirit, the unquenchable determination to endure to the last extremity.

Blows shake him from head to foot, blood chokes him, breathing is an agony, but he fights on, expecting no mercy and finding none until he lies, his throbbing brow pillowed on cool grass.

And then Jessamy's friendly voice is in his ears, Jessamy's ministering hands are about him.

"Water!" he gasps.

"Must I throw up the sponge, brother?"

"No! Damme—the fellow can't—fight all day, Jessamy."

"B'ged!" sighs the Marquis. "Here 's the end o' poor Veryan, Piper——"

"Haw!" says the Major. "Wait a bit."

"Twenty to one against the Corinthian!" bellows Flabby Face, his voice as loud, his whiskers as bellicose as ever.

"Are ye quite blind, brother?"

"Not—not quite—Jessamy——"

"And you 'll fight on?"

"Of course!"

"Then fall wherever he hits ye——"

"My strength is coming back—and my wind——"

"Hush, brother—not so loud. Let 'em think you 're done."

"Twenty-five to one against the Corinthian!" roars Flabby Face. "Don't any one take me at——"

"Yes!" gasps Jeremy. "A hundred!"

"Oh, brother—Lord love ye!" cries Jessamy, folding an arm about Jeremy's drooping shoulders. "You 're game to the——"

"Time!" calls the inexorable voice.

So up rises Jeremy and, faltering a little in his stride, crosses to where the "Slasher" waits to finish him, a tigerish gleam in his solitary eye; beholding which look, Jeremy clenches his fists and draws a deep breath that is a prayer of thankfulness for the strength waxing within him with every throb of his heart.

"Wot, ain't y' 'ad enough?" grins the "Slasher." Jeremy shakes his head. "Lord, but you 're a mess!" laughs his opponent tauntingly. "Stand still and lemme finish ye!"

"Come on!" croaks Jeremy, while the onlookers stand hushed and mute in anticipation of the expected end. The "Slasher" laughs, hoarsely triumphant, and feints with his left, whereupon Jeremy flinches, drops his guard and in leaps the "Slasher"—but as he comes, Jeremy leaps also, out shoots his right fist, with all the strength and weight of arm and body behind it, a terrible blow, clean and true upon the angle of the jaw and the Hoxton Slasher is hurled backwards to fall headlong and lie with limbs wide-tossed, very silent and still.

For a moment there is a deathly hush, then from earth to heaven goes up a cheer, a roar, a frantic riot of sound, what time Flabby Face melts unostentatiously into the crowd and is gone; the Chevalier standing beside the white-hatted Ben utters a fierce, low word of command, whereupon the fellow takes off his white hat and waves it above his head.

"Egad!" exclaims the Marquis, gripping his cane in ready hand. "I almost fancy those rough customers mean to break the ring."

"Haw!" says the Major. "They are! Expected it, m' dear f'low, so came—haw—prepared," and from capacious pockets he draws two small but eminently serviceable pistols.

Thus Jeremy, staring down out of fast-closing eyes where sprawls his unconscious antagonist, unresponsive to the desperate ministrations of his seconds, becomes aware of a fierce clamour, yells and cries with a sound of desperate conflict, and turns to find Jessamy beside him.

"Brother—lie down!" shouts Jessamy, clasping him in protecting arms. "Down wi' ye, afore the mob gets ye——"

"Not I!" mumbles Jeremy between swollen lips. Hereupon Jessamy catches him, throws him, and as he lies, covers him with his body. The clamour sweeps nearer, a rush of countless feet, and spurned by these trampling feet Jeremy knows no more.

## CHAPTER XXXVIII

### HOW JESSAMY PRAYED AND JEREMY DREAMED

DOWN beside the willow-shaded pool Jessamy was whistling merrily and making a cheery clatter of plates and dishes as he washed the breakfast things, while Jeremy, outstretched upon his pallet before the little tent, blinked drowsily in the sunshine and hearkened to the blithe morning carol of the birds; and yet despite this glad chorus, despite Jessamy's joyous whistling and the kindly sun whose beams comforted his bruised body and touched his disfigured face like a caress, he turned and tossed, grumbled and groaned, and finally shouted for Jessamy who hurried to him forthwith, a dishclout in one hand, frying pan in the other.

"What o'clock is it?"

"Nigh ten, brother—and what then?"

Jeremy merely growled.

"Ain't you dooly grateful, brother?"

"For what?"

"Benefits received——"

"Benefits?" snarled Jeremy. "I ache all over."

"Which ain't to be wondered at, brother."

"Look at my face!"

"Which I 've seen worse—and, moreover, you won a great fight——"

"But—lost all else!" sighed Jeremy.

"Meaning—the lady, brother? Why, she seemed a bit off-hand like, I 'll allow. But while there 's life there 's hope, and you 're alive enough—though you might be dead, ah—an' would be, if 't was n't for Major Piper's pistols, and the Marquis and t' others o' they Corinthians——"

"And you, Jessamy, and you! I'm a thankless dog."

"No. You're only in love, brother—which is apt to ketch a man in the temper—shake his liver and such, making him mopish, so I 've heered, 'specially if matters goes a bit rough."

"Rough?" growled Jeremy. "Everything has always gone rough with me—and always will! Life is a barren, dismal waste! And she believes me a faithless liar, Jessamy!"

"But then, brother, seein' as you ain't, 't is no matter. So leave it to the Lord an' go to sleep."

"And how may I sleep?" demanded Jeremy pettishly.

"By closin' your peepers and breathin' deep an' regular."

"Tush!" exclaimed Jeremy, clenching bruised hand and wincing with the pain of it.

"Tush it is, brother! But try to sleep whiles I enquire o' the Lord in regard to your lady."

"She's not mine—never will be!" groaned Jeremy.

"This is as the Lord wills! If He's minded you wed 'er—why, wed her it is, brother. So leave it to the Lord—and me as be His humble servant—amen!"

"You've wonderful faith, Jessamy."

"Ay, the Lord is my Shepherd, brother. Now close them peepers o' yourn—come!"

And so, because the sun was very bright and his eyes somewhat dazzled and smarting, Jeremy obeyed and, despite his troubles of body and mind, was presently fast asleep. As for Jessamy, having cleaned the frying pan and set everything orderly about the little camp as was his custom, he came to survey the sleeper, whose grim face was grimmer than ever now, by reason of the disfiguring scars and bruises; and bowing reverent head, Jessamy prayed silently yet fervently awhile; thereafter he stepped softly into the glade behind the little tent, loosed the sleek horse that browsed there and staying not for saddle or bridle, mounted and rode away.

And Jeremy, deep plunged in refreshing slumber, dreamed wonderfully: for in this dream he became all that he was not in reality—a slender youth, splendidly handsome, his rugged features magically transformed, his knotted hands slim and elegant; and this glorious self adored by a peerless creature, a woman of transcendant beauty utterly unlike Olivia in every particular, and yet Olivia's very self. And she—that was and yet was not Olivia—loved him undoubting, worshipped him for the triumphant demigod he was. Humbly she knelt, reverent with love of him and his achievements, to smooth his raven, silky locks—stooping—stooping lovely head slowly, shyly, to kiss his marble brow, his roseate lips. Jeremy awoke and, knowing all this only the folly of a futile dream, groaned—then held his breath, for something had splashed upon his cheek, and opening his eyes he beheld other eyes dimmed by tears, rosy lips that quivered with tenderness ineffable, a shapely head bent over him.

"Olivia?" he exclaimed, wondering.

"Oh, my poor child!" she murmured; and now her soft arm enfolded him. "How they have hurt you!"

"Why—why, Olivia!" he stammered.

"Your dear face——"

"Made for hard knocks, Olivia—and I 've no looks to spoil, so what matter?"

"How you must have suffered!"

"No—indeed—no——"

"I heard you were hurt," sighed she, tenderly stroking his towlike hair.

"Oh—indeed?" he muttered, shrinking a little beneath the caress. "I—you surprised me, I was asleep——"

"And groaning, dear Jeremy."

"I was—only dreaming."

"An evil dream, Jeremy!"

"No—merely foolish."

"And hearing you were hurt, I came, of course, to take care of you."

"But I 'm well enough, Olivia—besides, I have Jessamy Todd——"

"And so I shall stay," she continued placidly, "and nurse you till you are strong again."

Now at this he was minded to laugh and then to weep, and so turned to hide his battered face upon his arm.

"Why," he demanded harshly, "why are you so changed?"

"Because you need me, Jeremy, as much as I need you—almost."

Here he turned to look at her and beheld in her deep eyes, in tender lips, in her very attitude as she knelt beside him, that same adoring look he had visioned in his dream; it was in every supple curve of her beautiful body, insomuch that his breath caught and he averted his eyes awhile.

"Then you—know the truth—at last?" he questioned.

"Only that you are Jeremy—the only one!"

"You have learned the truth about Lucy Western?"

"No," she murmured gently, "I have only learned the truth about—myself."

"What truth?"

"That I love you, Jeremy, and always shall."

"Even though you believed I deceived you?"

"Why, of course!" she answered with a tearful little laugh. "When a woman truly loves she must needs forgive. And so, whatever you have done, whatever you may do, always—always I shall love you—here, deep down in my heart, just because you are—Jeremy."

Then, clean forgetting bruises, sorrow and pain-racked body, he clasped and drew her close and closer until there stole to him that elusive fragrance which seemed part of her and the which had haunted him so persistently.

"Will you marry me—soon?" he asked suddenly.

"Whenever you will, Jeremy."

"Oh, wonderful!"

"Why, pray?"

"I 'm such an unlovely fellow——" Here she raised her head to kiss his unshaven chin. "Such an awkward clod, Olivia."

Here she stooped to press her soft lips to his bruised right hand, whereat Jeremy, being greatly moved and finding no adequate word, was silent, but folded her the tighter and she, nestling in his embrace, sighed, yet spoke a little plaintively:

"You are very strong—for an invalid, sir!" Instantly his hold relaxed. "But I love your strength, Jeremy. And I 'm proud of you, not only because you can endure pain and overcome other strong men—oh, I heard all about your hateful fighting—but because you can overcome yourself—because you could endure the word 'coward' and men's scorn. How can you wonder I love you? And because of this—look into my eyes—you will promise me never, under any provocation, to fight Gaston de Ravenac——"

"But," began Jeremy——

"Promise! Ah, Jeremy, he would kill you—I know it! And your life is too precious. You are mine. It was for this I lied to you in the rose garden, told you he 'd gone. Oh, I would tell a million lies to save your dear body from harm! So promise me, Jeremy. promise!"

"Have you seen De Ravenac lately?"

"Not since that day in the rose garden when Arthur stopped the duel and persuaded him to go away."

"Hum!" quoth Jeremy thoughtfully "I still marvel how Arthur did it."

"He seems changed of late. Richard and he are always together."

"Is he still at Priory Dene?"

"He left this morning, suddenly, to meet Mr. Shrig, the law officer."

"Ha—Jasper Shrig! I wonder why?"

"Richard went with him."

"How is Richard?"

"A little wild——" Here Olivia sighed, wherefore Jeremy kissed her and for a while they forgot all else save their present joy. Now as they sat thus, silent for the most part, since great happiness is beyond speech, they beheld Mr. Shrig at no great distance hurrying towards them.

"Sir an' mam," said he, taking off his hat to wipe moist brow, "axing your pardin's both—but regarding Mr. Arthur Trevor, mam, left for London two hours ago, they tell me—might you know why, mam, if you please?"

"He said because of the letter you wrote him."

"The letter? As I wrote him. Oh?" repeated Mr. Shrig, pinching thoughtfully at his chin.

"So he told me," answered Olivia.

"The letter as I wrote him—ah!" echoed Mr. Shrig. "Pre-cisely, mam. Did you 'appen to see this letter, mam?"

"Yes, he read me the passage where you directed him to go straight to the—the inn and avoid any chance of meeting Monsieur de Ravenac!"

"Ay, to be sure!" nodded Mr. Shrig. "To be sure—straight to the—the 'Jolly Vaterman'—'t was the 'Vaterman,' eh, mam?"

"Yes, that was the name."

"Aha!" murmured Mr. Shrig and stood staring into the interior of his hat as if he had discovered there something rather horrible.

"What, now?" enquired Jeremy. "What is it, Jasper?"

"Sir, my gig 's a-vaiting close by; p'raps you 'll step so fur."

So, with a murmured word to Olivia, Jeremy rose.

"Sir," said Mr. Shrig, so soon as they were out of earshot, "I never writ that letter to your cousin Mr. A.!"

"Then who did?"

"A creetur' as I 've drove frantic and desprit' and conseqvently a dangerous creetur'!"

"How does this affect Arthur?"

"Why, y' see, pal, I used Mr. Arthur to do the driving."

"How, man, how?"

"By means o' seven words printed on a scrap o' paper——"

"Ay, I remember now. I remember Arthur's strange triumph! What were those words——"

"And if," continued Mr. Shrig, shaking his head, "if you should ask me the name o' this here creetur', as if formed like a man, I answer you—Openshaw—Julius Openshaw!"

"Ha!" exclaimed Jeremy, grasping the speaker's arm. "So then you 've found him—at last!"

"Sure enough, pal!"

"How? Where? Tell me, Jasper."

"No, no. I must be off, Mr. Veryan, sir—'t is life an' death."

"What do you mean?"

"Your cousin Mr. A.!"

"What, is he in such danger?"

"Up to his werry ears, pal! Ay, by Goles—he is so—every minute counts——"

"Wait!" cried Jeremy and hurried back to Olivia. "Dear," said he, "I must go to London—now, at once!"

"London?" she repeated. "Oh, Jeremy, are you strong enough?"

"Quite! I 'd go if I had to crawl!"

"Is Arthur in trouble again?"

"I don't know."

"And must you go, Jeremy—leave me so—very soon?"

"Yes," he answered, clasping her in yearning arms, "a few short hours, beloved."

And presently, finding him thus determined she sighed and brought his hat and surtout, helped him on and buttoned him into the heavy garment with reluctant fingers.

"You 'll take care," she whispered, clinging to him, "for, oh, Jeremy, you are taking all my happiness with you and if—if any harm befalls you—it will harm me too. Oh, Jeremy——"

Reaching the highway, they beheld Mr. Shrig in his high-wheeled gig talking to Jessamy Todd.

Seated beside Mr. Shrig, after painful scramble to this lofty perch, Jeremy reached down and despite bruised fingers, grasped Jessamy's hand, wringing it hard.

"Jessamy," said he, "your praying is as wonderful as your faith—take care of her!"

"Never fear, brother!"

Then Mr. Shrig flicked his powerful roan mare and they bowled smoothly away. And Jeremy, glancing back, thought he read again in Olivia's eyes that same look of deep and reverent worship.

## CHAPTER XXXIX

### TELLS WHAT HAPPENED AT THE "JOLLY WATERMAN"

THE big roan mare proved a fast goer, and yet a long and wearisome journey they made of it, for Mr. Shrig seemed lost in thought, and Jeremy, what with his bruises, the jolting wheels and his general discomfort, had small desire for conversation.

Evening had fallen when at last they reached the outskirts of the great city and, turning from the main thoroughfare, drove through a maze of narrow streets which seemed to grow ever the grimier and more sordid, until eventually Mr. Shrig pulled up in the small, dingy yard of a small and dingier tavern and throwing the reins to a dingy man who had appeared from dingy stables, clambered down to earth and aided Jeremy to do the same.

"Where are we, Jasper?"

"Follow me, pal," answered Mr. Shrig and, with a muttered word to the dingy man, he strode off with Jeremy limping stiffly beside him.

"What do you expect, Jasper?"

"Anything, Mr. Wee, sir."

"Well, where are we going?"

"It ain't fur, pal."

Presently upon the air was a smell Jeremy remembered and, turning a corner, the river lay before them, sullen and mysterious in the failing light. Mr. Shrig walked like a man in haste, albeit a cautious man, for he avoided open spaces as much as possible and his keen gaze roved continually. Soon, to Jeremy's relief, the pace slackened, though Mr. Shrig's caution seemed to increase, for he crept forward, peering, and finally halted; and Jeremy, looking whither he looked, saw again that lonely and most dismal of taverns that went by the name of "The Jolly Waterman."

Going on again, Mr. Shrig led the way to a row of tumbledown outbuildings in the rear and halting at a certain door, tried it cautiously, but finding it fast drew from an inner pocket a small implement, thrust it into the lock and after a moment's fumbling, the door swung open upon a black interior.

"Ketch 'old o' my coat, pal," he whispered, "tread soft an' mum's the word!"

Across an uneven floor that creaked to their stealthy tread, down a flight of precipitous stairs, along a narrow, stone-flagged passage, through another door and into an unseen apartment that felt unwholesomely warm and close.

"Pal," whispered Mr. Shrig in the pitchy darkness, "here 's a chair, d' ye feel it?"

"Yes."

"Then sit in it and don't move till I come back!" and Mr. Shrig was gone so softly that Jeremy marvelled. For maybe ten minutes he sat there, waiting and blinking upon the dark; at length, somewhere beside him in the blackness something stirred.

"Pal!" The whisper was in Mr. Shrig's voice beyond doubt, and yet Jeremy sensed in it some subtle, some indefinable change. "Pal, are ye there?"

"Here, Jasper!" A hand touched his shoulder, crept to his arm and clenched there, fingers that twitched and quivered oddly.

"This vay, pal, and easy!" On again, up more steps and so to a chamber aglow with a soft light that beamed in through a small vent in one wall, and before this vent a wooden stool.

"Pal," whispered Mr. Shrig, his face strangely pale, "bide ye here till I come back, and votever may 'appen —mum 's the vord! Agreed?"

"Yes, but . . ."

"Remember, *votever* you may see, no matter what you see, you sits here and keeps mum! Agreed?"

"Yes, Jasper; but what are you expecting?"

"The end o' this here case—one way or t' other, pal. But mark this, if so be I should n't come back in—say 'alf an hour—you go and—go precious silent, and precious quick!"

"But, Jasper——"

"Werry good!" said Mr. Shrig and vanished.

Now, sitting on the stool, Jeremy found his eyes came immediately opposite the vent in the panelling and thus found himself looking down into a long, low chamber, a strange place, half kitchen, half cellar, lighted by a battered ship's lantern that hung from one of the massive rafters, each of which supported many and divers articles as: coils of rope, an old musket, strings of onions, an ancient fur cap, an oilskin coat with a hundred other oddments; while in shadowy corners and against dingy walls stood oars, spars, barrels, boxes and strange-shaped bundles. With his first glance, Jeremy recognised the place, and remembering his last visit, glanced instinctively towards that corner where had lain a murdered man, the draped body of Jos Shields; and even as Jeremy looked, his flesh crept with sudden deathly cold—for that ghastly, shrouded thing was there yet—or one very like it. Surely—surely yon was the same old piece of sail-cloth even now falling in such hideously revealing folds about the thing below, this shape it covered—from the round curve of head and face, to the sharp outlines of upturned toes? Jeremy shivered violently and averted his eyes, telling himself this was some trick of light and shadow; yet when he looked again, the thing seemed as horribly suggestive as ever; therefore he turned away altogether and bowing head in hands, strove vainly to think of Olivia.

Thus sat he, motionless and expectant of—he knew not what—hearing no sound but the heavy throbbing of his own pulses, 'whelmed in a dreadful stillness, a deathly silence which, as the moments dragged by, became more ominous, pregnant of evil, of danger. And then, hoarse and loud rose a sudden cry—a vague scuffling—the short, sharp report of a shot, and thereafter a silence more profound and more horrible than ever. Up started Jeremy and turned to the door, but mindful of his promise, halted and constrained himself to sit down again; and thus, having nothing better to do, he stared once more at the room that was half cellar, half kitchen, viewing the very many objects stored there until his gaze rested again upon that draped thing in the corner; and the longer he looked, the more anxious he became to see and know what manner of thing this was.

All at once some one whistled softly, a clear, imperious summons. Footsteps at last—the slow, deliberate tread of one who strode masterfully, and hearkening to them, it seemed to Jeremy that, somewhere, at some time, he had heard such a tread before. On came these unhurried feet, nearer and nearer, while Jeremy, crouched in the shadows, stared down into the room, watching the door and scarcely daring to breathe.

Smoothly, deliberately, the door opened and a strange figure entered, a tall form enveloped from head to foot in an old, hooded boat cloak. Closing the door, this figure advanced into the room, and with the same unhurried step, crossed the floor and halting suddenly, hooded face bent, stood looking down at that which had so often attracted Jeremy's gaze, that thing beneath the sailcloth whose dingy folds seemed to reveal so much.

Some one laughed softly; from beneath the boat cloak came a white and shapely hand which, with sudden, vicious gesture of the elegant cane it grasped, lifted and tossed back the sailcloth. Thus Jeremy saw at last that which it had covered, and caught his breath numb with sick horror, glaring down at the pale, dead face of his cousin, Arthur Trevor. Even as he gazed the white hand raised the cane as if to smite it down across this dead face but in that moment was a hoarse challenge:

"In the King's name!"

For a moment the cane hung suspended above the dead; then was a leap, a fierce cry, a stamp of feet, and Jeremy beheld two forms close-grappled in mortal strife, writhing shapes that bent and swayed together, half hidden in the heavy folds of the boat cloak; a streak of red flame, a deafening explosion.

Somehow, anyhow, Jeremy stumbled down steps and along a crooked passage to light—an open door.

Mr. Shrig leant against the wall, panting and staring down at that which lay shrouded in the tumbled folds of the boat cloak:

"Diddled again!" he gasped. "The law—and self is—cheated again, pal——"

"Dead, Jasper?"

"As my—great-grandmother!" gasped Mr. Shrig. "Here 's fruit ripe for the gallows as ain't never a-going to blossom, more 's the pity!" So saying, Mr. Shrig sighed, stooped and, jerking away the folds of the cloak, revealed what they had hidden. "You know 'im, pal?"

"The Chevalier de Ravenac."

"Werry true, pal, and the murderer o' your cousin, Mr. A. But 'oo else lays afore you—look at 'im! Eh, ye don't know, says you? Then I 'll tell ye, says I—here 's Julius Openshaw, as murdered Mr. G. But 'oo else is he? Eh, ye don't know, says you? Then I 'll show ye, says I. Vatch now!"

Mr. Shrig nodded grimly and, stooping above the dead, reached out his hand, making therewith a sudden motion, whereupon Jeremy recoiled, uttering a cry of horror and amazement, for in place of black whiskers and glossy raven locks was a smoothly handsome visage crowned by golden curls.

"God in Heaven!" gasped Jeremy, for he was looking down into the dead face of Mr. Terence O'Leary.

# CHAPTER XL

## WHICH, BEING THE LAST, IS MERCIFULLY SHORT

"A BAD business!" sighed Mr. Shrig.

"Horrible!" said Jeremy, shivering in the night air as he turned to look his last upon the "Jolly Waterman."

"Life," continued Mr. Shrig plaintively, "life is full o' disapp'intments to a man as takes a pride in his perfession. Here 's my two birds caught, pal, two extry special Capital Coves, as ought to swing—but won't swing and can't swing, being no better than corpses! And arter all my trouble! Sich disapp'intments is enough to sour a man. One o' 'em dead I could ha' took kinder, but . . . both!"

"Both?" repeated Jeremy, starting. "I saw but one——"

"You must ha' heered t' other, pal."

"Ah—the shot! Who was it, Jasper—in Heaven's name—who?"

"The blackymoor, pal, the big mulatter——"

"What . . . Pompey?"

"Ah," I took 'im red-'anded, as ye might say. And 't was him or me, so I made it—him!"

"Was it he who—actually——?"

"Killed Mr. A., according to orders. Same as 'e tried to kill you on the road—throwed you into the ruined priory an' left ye for dead. So there 's both on 'em gone, leaving us only your uncle Sir James . . ."

"Forget him!" said Jeremy sharply.

"Eh? But Lord, Mr. Wee, sir, vot are you a-going to do?"

"Nothing! The death of his son is his punishment."

"Blow my dickey!" ejaculated Mr. Shrig. "D' ye mean to say . . ."

"Nothing!" repeated Jeremy.

"Life," sighed Mr. Shrig, mournfully, "life grows 'arder and 'arder!"

Silently they walked back to the dingy tavern and silently drove westwards, until Mr. Shrig pulled up before Jeremy's lodging.

"Will you come in and take a glass, Jasper?"

"No, Mr. Wee, sir. There 's disapp'intment as can only be met dooly by a jorum o' Corporal Dick's Vun-and-only, and this here is one on 'em. But regarding that b'ye as you lent me, he 's a precious sharp lad vith a nat'ral gift, or, as you might say, leaning, towards my perfesssion. So if you can spare 'im, I 'd be glad to take same over for good."

"D' ye think he 'd be happy?"

"As a bird, sir . . . me and the Corporal 'll see to that."

"Very well, Jasper. And you won't come in?"

"Thank 'ee, no."

"Then we part here."

"Yessir. Though you 'll drop into the 'Gun' now and then, p'raps?"

"Surely!"

"Then good-bye, Mr. Weryan, sir! And," added Mr. Shrig as, having shaken hands, he gathered up the reins, "when you 're safe vedded to Mrs. R.—if the first should 'appen to be a b'ye, I 'd 'umbly suggest as Jarsper ain't a bad name——"

. . . . .

"Anything to report, Moxon?"

"Nothing of any moment, sir. And may I venture to tender you my most respectful congratulations upon your fistic victory, sir?"

"You heard of it, then?"

"I saw it, sir."

"Hum!" quoth Jeremy.

"Will you partake of supper, sir?"

"No—yes, anything will do."

But, having eaten his solitary meal, Jeremy became a prey to evil thoughts, haunted by gloomy horrors, until the memory of Olivia came like some sweet, fresh wind to sweep them clean away; and stretching weary limbs, he breathed a sigh that was a prayer of thankfulness for her and for to-morrow. A few short hours and he would see her again. A few short weeks and she——

Here a knock at the door interrupted him.

"Come in!" said he drowsily. "And you may go to bed, Moxon."

"It is n't Moxon!" said a voice, and Olivia herself was in his arms—had slipped thence to her knees, her eyes more adoring than ever, her voice a caress.

"I could n't wait. Lucy Western has been with me; she came to-day just after you left. Oh, Jeremy, how I have wronged you—but, oh, my dear, how I do love you. Ah, no—don't kiss me any more—yet! Richard is here."

"Where?" enquired Jeremy, rising and opening the door, whereupon Mr. Armadale, unwontedly humble and diffident, enters.

"Veryan," said he, viewing Jeremy's battered countenance somewhat askance, "I was a—a most prodigious, blind fool."

"Were you, Armadale?"

"Jeremy, I desire to—ask your pardon."

"Do you, Richard?"

"Jerry—dear old Jay, can you—will you forgive?"

"Surely, Dick."

"Then," cried Mr. Armadale, clasping and wringing his hand, "you 'll come back with us to Priory Dene—to-morrow, of course?"

"To-morrow!" said Jeremy, turning to look at Olivia.

"Ah," sighed Olivia, looking at Jeremy, "thank God for—to-morrow!"

THE END